A MODEL MURDER

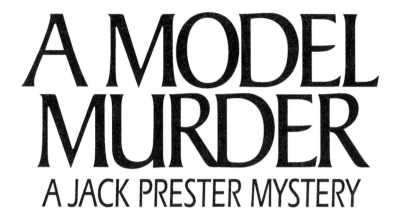

A MODEL MURDER

A JACK PRESTER MYSTERY

SANDY DENGLER

MOODY PRESS
CHICAGO

ISBN: 0-8024-2177-6

1 3 5 7 9 10 8 6 4 2

Printed in the United States of America

Contents

1
Jack of Hearts

B y cracky, it was. A human body.

Winthrop Spalding froze in midstep. It couldn't be. Sure looked like it, though. He set aside his rollers filled with clams and his clam shovel and cautiously climbed down closer to the surging sea for a better look.

Here the ocean pounded directly against the rocks of the shore, against endless piles of black, slippery boulders festooned with barnacles, periwinkles, blue mussels, a dozen kinds of slimes and algae. Relentless sea against unyielding Maine granite, forever and ever. The clam flats, oozy skirts of mud that formed a buffer between sea and land, lay behind him nearly a quarter of a mile.

Winthrop had been doggedly slogging back to his car after an afternoon's work digging. An honest day's work for an honest buck. And now this.

Looked like a woman, face down, sloshing in and out with the shifting surf. Her long black hair floated, tangled in the rocks, and washed free again. He knew that hair. This was one of those fancy models from New York or someplace, who were up taking pictures for some magazine. He'd seen them a couple times, working here and there on the island. In that photo party there was a black girl (not real black, but you could tell she was colored), two blondes, and this brunette.

Now what? He knew from TV that you shouldn't ever disturb the scene of the crime. On the other hand, this probably wasn't the scene of the crime. This was probably just the scene where the body happened to float to.

Winthrop sat down on a big boulder and considered this a minute. He was short and slim and wiry, particularly as today's football-player-sized kids went. His sixty years had put a lot of gray in his hair and taken a little of the spring out of his step. Not much. A little. He probably wasn't up to carrying this tall girl the additional half mile to the road. Besides, he had on his knee-high rubber boots today, not the best things to wear if you want sure-footed-ness.

He ought go tell someone, of course. But if he walked clear to his car and drove to a phone, the body'd likely float away, with the tide coming in already. On the other hand, he wasn't supposed to touch anything. He knew that much.

Knowledge of the tides and currents triumphed over knowledge gained off the TV. If he didn't touch it, there'd be nothing here when he got back with the authorities— Hancock County sheriff, probably, this far from town, or maybe the Acadia Park rangers. Then the county or the rangers would waste a whole lot of his tax dollars having to go look for it.

He stepped carefully, balancing and holding on all the way, down to the body. He leaned, stretching, and grasped a clammy, cold ankle. He sat back and drew the woman up across the rocks, inches at a time, to high-tide line.

Then Winthrop Spalding picked up his rollers and his clam shovel and continued on to his car.

* * *

Boy, was Jack pooped. Body parts he didn't know

8

could talk were telling him things he didn't want to hear. He was stiff as a crutch and half as lively.

When stupider ideas were coined, this was the one they'd have to beat. How could he be so dumb? When he got this job of National Park Service investigator-at-large, so to speak, Jack Prester had settled in Hutchinson, Kansas, a central location within two days' drive of any national park in the contiguous United States. Naively, he had believed the highway map that promised him any venue in forty-eight hours. As so many promises do, this one extracted an arduous and painful toll.

The road from Kansas to Maine had turned into a long, long, hard, two-day drive, and he wasn't there yet. At least this was, according to the map, the last short leg— not that he believed maps anymore.

He had driven through Ellsworth and past the Stanwood Wildlife Sanctuary, a place he wanted to come back and look at when he had some time. He had gone through a cluster of buildings that called itself Trenton. He had passed two lobster pounds, both closed. Were they closed for the year, it being the middle of October, or were they open weekends, it being the autumn color season? Now he drove across a smooth, low, cement bridge, from mainland America onto Mt. Desert Island, Maine.

Beside him, Maxx snarfed and noisily licked his chops. The big black Lab lay curled up on the passenger seat, snoring. In warmer weather, Maxx usually rode in back. Jack had installed a jump box in the front of his pickup's long bed, and a three-feet-high-by-three-feet-deep steel cage in lieu of a tailgate. The cage doubled as a dog kennel and holding tank for suspects, should Jack ever be clever enough to catch a suspect. Today in the autumn chill, whipping along freeways at sixty-five or so, Maxx rode in the cab.

The mutt had spent half the morning slurping on various parts of his anatomy. He had spent the next hour just being obnoxious, licking Jack's arm, drooling on the rolled-up sleeve of his chambray shirt, slobbering on his jeans' leg, putting noseprints on the windshield, and shoving his head up under Jack's elbow—his *Pat me!* gesture.

Now, worn out from the taxing rigors of being a total jerk, he snoozed, with his broad, boxy head shoved up against Jack's hip. If there were a doggy version of the odd couple, Maxx was the quintessential Oscar Madison.

The timing for this trip couldn't be better, Jack mused. New England was known worldwide for its spectacular fall color, and he was driving through the best of it. Maples splayed vivid reds, oranges, and salmon pinks across the landscape. Yellow alders, horse chestnuts, and brown oaks struck fetching poses in front of dark and frowning evergreens. Gorgeous. Truly gorgeous.

Jack hit the brakes and pulled over just beyond the bridge. Maxx slid unceremoniously off onto the floor.

"Next time, wear your seatbelt." Jack scooped up the leash as Maxx scrambled back up onto the seat. "Come on. And behave yourself. If these people are who I think they are, they're sophisticated, high-class city folks."

He slipped into his sheepskin-lined denim jacket and pulled his Stetson out of the wire hat rack on the back window. He got out and essentially ground to a halt. He felt incredibly wooden from sitting so long. He appreciated the lining in his jacket. The clammy chill of this marine air went right through him. He stood on the road shoulder a moment, looking around.

The bridge crossed a narrow strait between the mainland and the island, with a tiny stepping-stone island in between. Rocky, boulder-studded ground lined the shore of Mt. Desert Island here as it lined the shore of the mainland over there. Fallen trees and various jetsam drew dashlines among the rocks. Two vans, their back doors gaping open, were parked along the shoulder immediately behind Jack's pickup.

Two hundred yards away on the cluttered rocks of the island shore, half a dozen people milled about. A big tin reflector screen and what looked like a folding table with equipment on it stood near them. This ought to be the fashion photography crew for whom the murdered girl had worked.

As Jack approached them, he could make out the activity on the rocky shore. A girl was posing out by the water, as a photographer and the other ancillary folk gathered around.

A bulky fellow the size of a bull buffalo suddenly charged away from the others. At a trundling lope, he ran down along the shore. The bruiser seemed headed for a man stooping and digging in a distant mud flat. Jack walked on past the party at the water's edge to his right and paused to watch the Incredible Hulk go after the digger.

The digger, a wiry, spry little guy half his accoster's weight, stood erect as the buffalo charged up to him. The buffalo waved his arms. From the gestures it was obvious he was telling the slim little guy to go dig somewhere else. The slim little guy stood his ground. The buffalo grabbed him, shoved him down into the mud, and was hauling him back to his feet by the time Jack could yank Maxx's collar off and yell, "Maxx! Go hold him!"

Maxx, bless his doggy heart, was one of those mutts that just loved to play police dog. He didn't often get the chance, so he made the most of any chance he got, grandstanding, acting gruff, laying it on thick. It wasn't a real good attitude for a dog to have, but Jack forgave it, probably because he shared it.

Maxx boiled forward now from 0 to 60, accelerating so impressively he tore up grass.

Jack broke into a run. He could hear Maxx snarf and growl in basso profundo. The digger and his adversary both turned and froze in place as a hundred fifteen pounds of coal black Lab came hurtling toward them. Maxx's ponderous charge lost a little of its impressiveness when he left the grassy bank and floundered out into the tideflat

11

mud. Slurping and galumphing, he porpoised his way toward the buffalo.

Son of a gun if the buffalo didn't reach for a weapon in an underarm holster!

Jack yelled, "Freeze! Police!"—a superfluous order if ever there was one, since both men were standing there with roots that sank to bedrock.

"Maxx. On guard." Jack slowed up as he left terra firma and sloshed out into terra mudda. The greasy slop sucked at his running shoes. His shoes and socks both would never come clean again. Probably not his jeans, either.

He was breathing heavily as he approached the two, as if he'd been sitting still in a truck seat for thirty-two hours. He pointed a finger at the buffalo, since his revolver was holstered at the small of his back and he didn't feel compelled to go for it just yet. "Just keep it tucked away, or we put you away."

Cautiously, reluctantly, the buffalo raised his hands wide. The scowl on his face would have fried an egg. He wore a dark green nylon parka emblazoned in pink with "Sitting Pretty." He didn't look the least bit pretty, with crooked teeth, a burr haircut, and a white scar down his cheek. But then he wasn't sitting. Maybe sitting, he was prettier. "Who're you?"

Jack dug out his badge case. He wasn't expecting to need it so soon. He held it up at an angle conducive to clear viewing. "National Park Service out of the Washington office, investigating the death of Veronica Wayne."

The fellow growled, "I don't know you." His deep, gravelly voice sounded like a cassette player when the batteries are running low.

"And at this rate you never will. I assume you're security for the company doing the fashion magazine layout. I recall Sitting Pretty is the company name. John Prester."

The goon looked down at Maxx. "I suppose he's outa the Washington office too."

"You bet! Expertly trained and sharp as a banana."

Maxx was pouting. Whether the buffalo could tell or not, Jack knew. Maxx was grasping the fact that there would probably be no action, and he was a sore loser. He looked pretty ferocious, though, for a banana.

The bruiser studied Jack a good five seconds. The tree-thick arms drooped. "Clyde Wilkins. What do you want?"

"It appeared from the road there that you two have a difference of opinion. I figure this gentleman and I put together probably equal your weight, especially if we throw the dog in too. Just keeping things even."

The spry little digger chuckled. "He thinks I oughta move somewhere else. As if I could dig clams ashore." Why was the man chuckling? His seat and legs were wet as an eel from getting pushed into the slop.

Jack realized, now that he got a better look at him, that the fellow had to be at least sixty years old.

"He's in the way of the shoot," Wilkins snarled. Barely masked rage clouded his face.

The clam digger appeared bemused and not the least bit worried that he might get his head knocked off in any ensuing fight.

Jack weighed the situation a moment—and what cooperation he might need from Clyde Wilkins during the investigation. "Tell you what. Let him dig clams. He'll add local color to your backgrounds, and since he's so far away, you won't need a model release." He paused for effect. "And I'll forget you went for that gun."

"I got a permit."

"Not to intimidate."

"I was protecting myself from that cur."

"Then call it a draw." Jack took a giant step aside. The mud slurped like a calf getting dinner. The guy had a good five miles of America left to walk past Jack in, before the Atlantic Ocean began in earnest. The side step was a suggestion.

The buffalo took the suggestion. Still snarling, he slogged to high ground and headed back toward his party.

"Shot tide today," the digger announced. "Better get back to it, if I'm gonna fill the rolluh yet."

"Shot tide?"

"Shot tide. Not as low as usual."

"Shot. You mean like a giant is tall but a dwarf is shot."

"Ayuh. That's what I said."

"Jack Prester." Jack reached out for a handshake. And got one. "Winthrop Spalding."

The name rang a bell. "You found the girl's body two days ago."

"Ayuh. How'd you know that?"

"My boss mentioned your name when he was briefing me about this case. You're famous all the way down in Washington, D.C., where my boss is, and Kansas, where I came from."

"Clear from Kansas!?"

"Crazy, isn't it? Good luck clamming."

The wizened man nodded. "Good luck with that outfit." He turned aside, prowled all of two steps and stuffed his tool, a low shovel sort of thing, into the mud. He dug and prized a bit and brought up a scoop of dripping mud. Deftly he extracted a clam Jack wouldn't have found in a year in that slime and dropped it in a slatted carrier made of wooden lath.

"Maxx. Come." Jack waded back to high ground, his every step sounding like a kid who had just eaten chocolate licking his fingers. His toes, soaking wet, ached with cold.

He put Maxx's collar back on and brought him under tow. Maxx was even muddier than Jack. The dog's feet sank in up to his belly. They walked the two hundred yards through dying autumn grass to the cluster of people.

A tall, lovely, honey-blonde girl with waist-length hair stood picturesquely, holding a wide-brimmed hat on her head as her yellow, spring-looking dress swirled in the breeze. The dress was sleeveless, the temperature at the moment maybe forty-eight. At most.

A photographer was shooting at twelve frames a minute as he crouched in front of her. He twisted and turned, aimed from this angle and that. An assistant held a three-foot wide square reflector, trying to make the murky, overcast afternoon into a bright spring day.

In a ripstop nylon parka like Wilkins's, a tall, thin, scrawny woman a decade older than anyone else here stood off to the side frowning. In fact, her frown looked engraved into her face, as if she perpetually grumped. Her short-cropped dark hair was graying.

In canvas directors' chairs nearby sat two pretty girls, wrapped in blankets. One was a platinum blonde with straight, shoulder length hair, and the other a black girl. Nobody looked happy except the girl being photographed, who was no doubt being paid handsomely to smile, and the vast majority here appeared downright miserable.

Clyde had continued out toward the road. He stopped, keeping a wary eye on Jack. He wasn't happy either. This fashion modeling business must be a real drag.

The thin woman in the parka was probably Edith Cray, the manager of this modeling agency. The photographer would be either Mike Kovik or Arturo Fracci. Jack had no idea what the assistant's name was. He didn't remember an assistant mentioned in any of the material Hal had faxed him. There had been a wardrobe mistress who doubled as make-up artist, but he didn't see anyone around like that.

The only one of the three models Jack could identify for certain was Athalia Adams, because she was the token black in this outfit. Coffee with cream, as all black models are. The two blondes looked too much alike to call.

Jack stepped up beside the shivering girls in the chairs and smiled. "Afternoon."

"Nothin' good about it," Athalia Adams grumped.

15

She drawled her words out in a Southern accent—Georgia or possibly South Carolina.

"Didn't say there was. Jack Prester, Miss Adams."

Her eyes went wide. "Do I know you?"

"Sure. Athalia Adams. We just now met."

The blonde beside her laughed, a tinkling giggle that didn't sound the least bit airhead. "Are you straight?"

"You need work developing better pick-up lines, Miss Laren. As opening remarks go, that's pretty much a bummer."

She shrugged fetchingly. "It can save a lot of time. How do you know who we are?"

"I'm only guessing that you're Lauren Laren. Shot in the dark. Fifty percent chance since you're one of two blondes. So I take it that's Marlette freezing down there in the yellow dress." He nodded toward the water's edge. "Does Marlette have a last name?"

"Not that she'll admit to." The blonde giggled again. "And you got the freezing right. Too bad goose bumps don't show in the photographs."

"Too bad they don't pay extra for them, so much per bump."

Miss Adams cooed, "I luuuhhhv the way you think. What you say your name was?"

"John Prester. Jack." Jack dropped down to a squat, the better to converse at eye level. "Maxx, sit."

"And who's this? Max?" Miss Adams nodded toward Maxx as the mutt plopped his bottom down in the grass. "He's so shiny black. Glossy. Not counting the mud, of course. And fat. No, not fat. I guess bulky's the word. Beautiful."

"Officially, he's Hall's Maximian Luxembourg. Maximum Licks and Burps."

The huge eyes got huger. "You wouldn' call that poor dog something so crude. He's so cute."

"Cute is as cute does. When he belches, dishes rattle."

The girls laughed aloud. Swathed in blankets, these professional glamour-pusses seemed unpretentious and relaxed.

Not the least relaxed was their fellow model, Marlette, in front of the camera. Jack could see her mouth quivering in the cold. Her lips were blue, her fingers white. The kid was suffering, earning every dime, no matter how many dimes she got for this job.

As he watched glamour in action, Jack tried to imagine any of these people murdering a pretty young girl. He couldn't.

And yet, quite probably one of the persons here had reduced Veronica Wayne's face to a broken and bloody pulp and cracked her skull. A crime of extreme violence. Extreme passion. And as he watched, he changed his mind. Any of the three young ladies here could have done it in a second, but not to a fellow model. To the person who arranged this miserable gig.

The photographer stood erect, and Marlette instantly lost her brilliant smile. Utterly smile-less, she came walking rapidly up the slope from water's edge.

Edith Cray called, "The white number, Lauren. Come on, come on, while we have the light."

"Lambs to the slaughter," the platinum blonde muttered. She stood up, tall and graceful, like a willow withe in the breeze. She started down toward the water in a lovely white summer dress as Marlette came up.

Jack pulled off his jacket. "Miss Marlette? Here. It's warm."

She didn't hesitate, didn't ask his identity, made no double take or doubtful glance. Like a rabbit ducking into its warren, she dived for the coat and did a half turn, sliding her arms into the sleeves as he held it for her. She clasped it around her front. She stood motionless for a count of ten, her eyes closed, as she apparently did nothing but blot up the body warmth in the sheepskin Jack had just been wearing.

17

She opened her eyes to him like the curtain rising on a ballet performance. They were wonderful deep eyes you dived into, like blue pools in Hawaii. Her five-nine almost matched his five-eleven, making the eye-to-eye nearly literal. His eyes were brown, as was his hair—no match there. Jack wouldn't necessarily bet the ranch on it, but she seemed to be a natural blonde. Her honey-gold hair tumbled in loose waves and disappeared inside his sheepskin collar.

"Jack Prester. How do you do. And Maxx."

"I'm pleased to make your acquaintance." She pronounced it *Oy'm playzed to mike your aquine-tance.* Her voice flowed smooth as syrup onto pancakes. "This feels so good I can't manage to feel guilty for taking your coat." *This fails sow good Oy cahn't mahnage to fail guilty for tyking your cowt.*

Jack fully intended to say, "Hey, it's my fault if I'm cold. I took it off." But he couldn't. He couldn't think. He couldn't react, as memories came flooding in. His heart was jammed up in his throat too tightly.

The only woman he ever really loved, the woman he wooed and won eleven years ago, spoke in silken tones just like Marlette—with a strong Australian accent.

Just like Marlette . . . except that his Marcia had been born and raised in northern Queensland, near Cairns. Her accent and Marlette's were different in subtle ways.

He said aloud, "You're from somewhere down around the Melbourne area. Victoria."

The blue eyes brightened. "That's right. Bendigo."

"Sure. North of Melbourne. Ever go on holiday up to Echuca? Ride the riverboats?"

"You've been there!" She pronounced been *bean.*

"Love the area."

Marlette looked past Jack toward his rig. She turned to the scrawny woman. "Edith," she called, "I'm going back to the motel."

The woman called back as her engraved frown deepened, "We'll need you at seven for the night shots at the dock."

"Come get me then." Marlette looked at Jack. "Will you take me back to my motel in Bar Harbor, please?"

"You don't know me."

She dipped her head toward his truck. Wisps of blonde hair followed belatedly. "Does your ute have a heater?"

"Yes, ma'am . . ."

"That's all I have to know." She started for the truck.

"Maxx, heel." Jack fell in beside her. "You're desperate."

"I'm not really made out of blue glass." *Oy'm nawt rail-ly mide out of blue glahss.* "I just appear that way." *Oy just ap-pair thaht why.*

Jack basked in the accent. Wallowed in it. So many memories.

From behind them Lauren shouted, "I'll be done in fifteen minutes, Jack. Can I get a ride in too?"

Jack wheeled and called to her, "I'll be right back."

Marlette handed the floppy hat to Clyde without slowing.

Jack jogged ahead in his soaked and muddy running shoes and had the passenger door open when she got there. He motioned Maxx up into his cage in back and slid behind the wheel. He glanced toward the photo party. Clyde, the security man, stood there scowling, as black as a Kansas thunderstorm.

Jack torched it off. One nice thing about Dodge Ram pickups—their super-sized heater really warmed the cab up in a hurry. He flicked the lever to the extreme red end of the spectrum and ran the fan lever up to high. He checked the mirror and pulled out onto the highway.

"Where's Kansas?" she shouted over the roar of the heater fan.

He looked at her.

19

"Your license plate." Not only was she beautiful, she was observant.

"Middle of the country. If Bar Harbor is Cairns, Kansas is Ayers Rock. I just arrived from there."

"Clear from Kansas?!" She lapsed into silence and stared ahead.

"Are you also going to ask me about my preferences?"

"That would be Lauren. She fancies herself efficient." The blue eyes flicked his way. "Right now I couldn't care less, and you told me your name, but I've forgotten. I only want to stand in a hot shower until I shrivel up."

"Has the whole shoot been like this? Freezing your socks off?"

"Horrid! Just horrid."

"When you get around to caring, it's Jack Prester."

"Jack. Jack of hearts." She laughed melodiously. "Fair go, mate!"

And Jack Prester was in love.

2
He Stole Some Tarts

In New Mexico where Jack grew up, the mountains jutted up out of broad desert basins, islands in an ocean of high, dry sagebrush. Scrub trees and chaparral covered their lower flanks, and ponderosa pines grew at their tops. But those dry forests were nothing at all like the forests he drove through now. In this woodland thick with undergrowth, saplings and low trees shouldered each other for living space.

The trees in New Mexico's ponderosa parklands were spaced out. You could ride a horse through them without getting your kneecaps dislocated. Not so here amid these puny, short, close-set trees. The woods crowded in, a tangled, floor-to-ceiling mat of deciduous trees and bushes. In New Mexico, graceful, wispy grass grew among the trees in places, and open soil—even loose gravel—softened your every step. Here there was not an inch of bare soil, not a blade of grass. A thick blanket of leaves and forest duff and creeping green plants covered the ground. The dense closeness made Jack vaguely uncomfortable, as if a million knotty eyes were watching and a million branches poised ready to reach out and grab.

Nestled within these rank, confining woods at Acadia National Park's north end, the visitor center perched on a ridge above the parking lot, looking down on the world like a castle keep.

Jack parked in the lower lot and walked up the broad outside stairs. Remarkable stairs they were, framed by low walls of well-cut and laid granite block. The chill air tasted moldy, filled with the lingering acerbic smell of tannin and limp, wet leaves. The trees all around him rustled in the breeze. Juncos flitted through the rhododendrons, clicking as if they had teeth, and flicking their white tail feathers. Jack had never been to Acadia before. The only Eastern woodlands he ever experienced had been Ozark Riverway and Buffalo River. He felt pent in then. He felt caged now.

Inside, the visitor center, like all visitor centers, promised ranger assistance, answers to questions, restrooms, and a book shop. A room to the side provided artful displays explaining the complex interactions of sea and land, ice and rock, time and man.

A blocky, matronly lady with short white hair perched on a stool behind the visitor center counter. She amply filled her gray uniform shirt and green uniform trousers, and yet she did not in the least look fat. The desk attendant smiled at him. Her name plate above the right pocket of her shirt introduced her as *Stella Smith*.

The government-issue clock behind her said 4:29. Jack had wanted to get here before 4:30. How was that for timing?

He bellied up to the counter and leaned on it, both elbows. He felt stiff and very, very weary. "Ms. Smith. The two questions you are asked most frequently are, 'Where is a restroom?' and, 'Where is a drinking fountain?' Is the third, 'Does the sun ever shine here?'"

She laughed. "I'm going to guess that your name is Jack Prester. Am I right?" She spoke with a charming and gentle Down East accent.

"Mr. Sarnoff is expecting me, I take it."

"Since nine this morning. He's some upset that you're late."

"Late is relative. I just completed a thirty-two-hour drive."

Her eyes grew wide behind her silver-wire glasses. "It took you thirty-two hours to drive up from Washington?"

"In from Kansas. My boss, Hal Edmond, lives in D.C. I don't."

The eyes assumed hubcap proportions. "Clear from Kansas?! You didn't fly?"

"Then I wouldn't have my truck here. My rig is sort of self-contained. I like it with me when I'm working." He didn't mention that he also liked his old familiar weapons with him, his sidearm and his shotgun both, and horsing guns through airports is a royal pain.

"I can't imagine liking a truck *that* much. I'll tell him you're here." She slid off her stool and reached for a phone set on the desk. "I guess I won't, either. There he is."

Jack launched himself erect and turned. A stocky, balding man was coming out of the "Employees Only" door. You couldn't call Warren Sarnoff fat, exactly, but he was built wide. His forehead extended so far back that he could lie on it and still gaze at the ceiling. He parted his hair in a straight horizontal line three-quarters of an inch above his left ear and combed the few remaining strands up over the top of his shiny pate and down the other side, as if he could make up in length of hair what he lacked in numbers.

"Mr. Sarnoff?" Ms. Smith called. "Mr. Prester."

The man came waddling over—no other word as clearly described his rolling, toed-out gait—and graced Jack with a grimace cleverly disguised as a grin. He looked at Jack's muddy shoes and jeans, obviously less than impressed.

They shook hands, but it still didn't feel friendly in here. "Glad you got here." Sarnoff didn't sound glad at all.

"So am I. I look forward to working with you." Pleasant words. No basis in fact. But then, that's what great men call *diplomacy.*

"Come back to my office. I'll give you what we have so far." Sarnoff turned on his heel and waddled back through the door.

Jack followed. He did all right on marathon drives, staying alert and keyed up for the endless hours. But when the marathon drives ended, he unkeyed for a day or two. His brain was fast turning into a glob of biscuit dough. He needed a ten-hour sleep to make up for the less-than-five-hours he'd gotten on the road.

Sarnoff led the way down the hall to his office. He by-passed the expected way in, through his secretary's office, and continued down the hall, to push in through his back door. He crossed to his desk and scooped up a wad of file folders tall enough to jack up a truck and change a tire. He plopped untold hours of reading into Jack's hands.

"Here are the reports and supplementals my rangers filed, and transcripts of interrogations and statements. I believe the Hancock County Sheriff's Department has information they haven't forwarded to me yet."

"My supervisor, Hal Edmond, intimated there were jurisdictional differences."

"Your supervisor say anything specific?"

"Not really," Jack fibbed. The other facet of diplomacy —bald-faced lies.

Actually Hal had said both Sarnoff and the sheriff were acting like two little boys in a sandbox with one Tonka truck. He warned Jack, too, that Sarnoff was not the least pleased with some Washington bozo stepping into his case. After all, the girl's murder was the only exciting thing to happen in the park since the fire of '47. Now it was being ripped from the poor man's grasp. The murder itself was a side issue compared to the ruffled-feather-smoothing this case would require.

Sarnoff headed for his back door, again by-passing

his secretary. "My maintenance staff is cut back for the winter, and they're stretched pretty thin just now. We won't have quarters ready for you until next Monday at the earliest."

"That's fine. I reserved a room at the Seaview."

"Seaview. That's where the models and all are staying. So you've begun your investigation already. I assumed you'd stop by here first." He sounded absolutely jilted, an angry and forlorn bridegroom left at the altar. He marched down the hall and out into the lobby toward the glass front doors.

"Investigation, no. Ferry service, yes. I arrived on the island an hour ago. On my way here I came upon them by the bridge. What they call a shoot, I believe. They drafted me to take a couple of the colder ones back to the motel."

"They never met you before, but they let you drive their people around."

"Desperate times call for desperate measures. The girls seem extremely disgruntled with their working conditions—standing out in the cold in summer frocks. Have they filed any formal complaints? Union, labor relations board, anything like that?"

"I wouldn't know. The sheriff's office might." There was that petulance again. Sarnoff stood in the door, holding it for Jack—an invitation to leave if ever there was one. "Anything else?"

"I'll check in tomorrow morning. Better to talk then than now, at quitting time. About nine?"

Jack walked out into a blustery wind. The weather was deteriorating. If the girls had to look summery on an exposed wharf tonight, they'd freeze solid. He was back in his jacket again, and still the wind made his muscles tighten up. Marlette was probably turning into one huge pink wrinkle in her shower yet.

"Nine's fine."

They walked down the stairs to the lower lot in silence. The juncos had apparently gone home. From his

25

vantage point on top of his cage, Maxx barked a greeting.

Sarnoff stopped dead and scowled at the dog. "You're aware of our leash laws. And dogs aren't permitted on the trails or up on Cadillac. Maintenance was picking up too much doo."

"We'll keep the area doo-less, yes, sir." More diplomacy.

Sarnoff mumbled some parting words and crossed the lot to a little red Honda.

The mud on Maxx had pretty well dried by now. Jack brushed him off with his hands. Then he opened the truck door. "Saddle up!"

Maxx bounded up into the passenger seat. Jack crawled in behind the wheel, bone weary. And his day wasn't over yet.

Bar Harbor Airport was nowhere near Bar Harbor—it was not even on Mt. Desert Island—but it was nowhere near anywhere else, either. So "Bar Harbor" was as good a name for it as any. Fifteen minutes got Jack from the Acadia Park VC to the inside of the terminal. A single room served as front desk, concourse, gate desk, waiting room, and baggage claim. A lighted Pepsi dispenser stood in the far corner and, beside it, one of those machines that you stick a bunch of quarters in and it may or may not decide to give you a little bag of stale pretzels or granola bars.

A smiling girl at the single short counter, the only person around, informed him all flights were on time.

Jack happened to know there were only two flights this evening, this one and one at ten-thirty. The ten-thirty one wouldn't leave Boston for another four hours. How did she know if it was on time?

Five minutes later a small commuter plane came doddering in and pulled to the door. Jack watched four passengers deplane down a little ladder and out onto the tarmac. As they headed this way, the pilot, no less, began unloading baggage. Why not ask Rembrandt to paint *Mail Pouch* on a barn?

26

The girl who manned the desk walked out with a hand cart. She helped fill it with the bags and came trundling back to the building with all the luggage—seven pieces—in tow.

Leading the pack of passengers, here came a leggy, pretty young woman with huge brown eyes and flyaway black hair trimmed in a short shag. She toted a bulging carry-on and a roomy, equally bulging shoulder bag. In a razzmatazz white angora sweater and designer blue jeans, she looked like a model.

And that was the whole idea.

Jack held the door for her, grinning. "Ev!"

She had a curious, grateful look on her face. She smiled. "Hello, Jack. Good to see you again so soon."

The other passengers, all looking equally grateful, came filing in.

"I didn't check anything through." She sounded almost as tired as Jack felt.

He took her bags and started out toward the parking lot. "So. Have a good flight?"

"How do you define 'good'?"

"Any flight that reaches its intended destination without deployment of emergency vehicles." He shoved past the glass doors into a stiff, cold wind.

She smiled again. That was twice in a row. Evelyn Brant, Miss Sober Accounting Wizard Out of the Washington Office, was loosening up. "Then I guess it was a good flight." Her voice paused. "Small planes bounce around a lot when it's windy."

"The other reason I drove in. I get seasick easily."

She stared at him with those huge, brown doe eyes. "Clear from Kansas?!"

"Everybody keeps saying that." Jack motioned Maxx to the ground and humped Ev's carry-on into the cage. "You still working out with lead barbells?"

"What? Oh. The bag. Maxx, that's enough now. No more licking. Hal suggested I should travel light—that I

27

wouldn't need much in the way of clothes. So I stuffed everything in that bag. Maxx, cut it out."

Jack clapped his hands and motioned Maxx into his cage in the truck bed. He closed the cage door and latched it.

"The girls are modeling some gorgeous clothes. You're going to have fun with this gig." Should he mention freezing to death? Nah. He opened the passenger door for her and walked around to the driver side.

He climbed in and kicked the engine to life. A little over two weeks ago, he and Ev had wrapped up a highly successful assignment at Death Valley National Monument. The attorney's office had all the prelims and raw data, but they'd need a lot more from him. He'd thought he'd be assigned to that. Now here he was, assigned to this. And Ev, whom he'd last seen a week ago, was going to be working with him again. Weird, the way life's pathway takes such unexpected twists and turns.

He wished he were more alert. He was stiff as a frozen carrot. "How much did Hal tell you?"

"He worked a deal with the owner of the modeling agency, some man named Harry in California." She hauled her seatbelt down. "I'm to step in and take over the dead girl's position as the fourth model. Hal says I'm to observe from the inside and tell you what I see and hear. I've never had any training as a model, Jack. I don't think I can do it."

"Sure you can." Jack pulled out onto the main road and headed toward the bridge. This would be his third time today across that bridge. The shoot had left their location, and the tide was in. The sea lapped up over rocks where Marlette had been standing an hour ago. "Watch what the girls are doing and do likewise. You're young and pretty. You'll fit right in."

"Where do you fit?"

"They know I'm investigating for the Park Service, and they know I'm new here. They think you and I were strangers until five minutes ago—never heard of each other."

"Then how can I report to you?"

"Because of the loss of Veronica Wayne, plus all the time the investigation consumed, plus some lousy weather, they're short-handed and way behind schedule. I took Marlette back to the motel. When I returned for Lauren, Edith—the manager—asked me if I would please drive out to the airport at five and bring in the new girl. That's you. Her boss—that's Harry—had called and told her you'd be coming. Perfect way for me to ostensibly meet you. So I'll just start dating you, so to speak, and we can compare notes and info. It's a lousy reason to date, I suppose, but I've heard lousier."

He expected a reply of some sort. Nothing. He glanced at her.

She was staring at him. Staring? Make that scowling. "When did you arrive here?"

"About two hours ago, give or take."

"And you're on a first-name basis with these girls already."

"Awash in lovely lasses, yes, indeed. Any man's dream assignment." He dropped his voice a little. "Never forget the reason we're here, Ev—that one of those lovely lasses was bludgeoned to death."

She suddenly waved a finger at the windshield. "It says Bar Harbor that way!"

"We're going to Northeast Harbor. They have a shoot down at the dock at seven. I'm to take you directly there. To work, to work."

"Shouldn't I check into a hotel first?"

"Edith already has your room lined up at the Seaview. She says you'll be modeling two outfits tonight."

"These lovely lasses are certainly efficient, aren't they?" Her voice sounded flat, even sarcastic, but she was probably just tired from the difficult trip in from Washington. She must have flown Dulles to Boston and then sat around waiting for this Bar Harbor flight. Bumpy flight at that.

29

"Edith is. She manages the agency's East Coast operation and nearly all magazine assignments. This particular assignment, apparently, is an umpty-ump-page layout for a major fashion magazine. Top drawer all the way. Nice break-in for a modeling unknown like yourself."

Her voice could have chilled down a blast furnace. "I did not earn a master's degree in accounting and budget analysis in order to preen and strut in some fluff magazine. I told Hal that."

"And he brushed it off."

"He certainly did. Says I'm the best person for the job and that's that." She pointed out the window to their right. "What body of water is that?"

"Somes Sound, according to the map. The only natural fjord in this part of the world. The whole island was under ice ten thousand years ago. Glaciated. The ice melted, and the land is still rising from losing all that weight. The hills, the shore, everything was shaped by ice. Lot of glacial oddities around."

"The land is *rising?*"

"An inch a century, according to the sources I read. If you feel butterflies in your tummy, like riding up in a fast elevator, that's why."

They drove up over a saddle beside a dark and looming hill and down past a quiet lake labeled Hadlock Pond. Down another grade, and they wound into a charming, tree-shaded village. "Northeast Harbor" said the sign.

Jack angled left at a Y, not for any particular reason. Good guess. The street left trees behind and curved down to the shorefront of the actual harbor. Jack saw no vans in the parking area. Sitting Pretty wasn't here yet.

There was what he wanted. Like a flame beckoning the moth, a restaurant's glowing plastic sign called him. He pulled into the parking lot. "I'm so hungry the dog's in danger."

"Do we have time?"

"It's an hour before you have to go to work."

"My stomach is still too upset to eat, but I'll sit and watch you."

"That bumpy, huh?" He left his hat in its rack. A Stetson on the Maine coast is like a yellow slicker in the Sahara, a bikini in Lapland. He wondered if Marlette had done much traveling in her line of work before she came to America.

He dug dog food out of the ammo box for Maxx, stuck it in his cage, and ushered Ev inside.

The hostess was going to seat them in a corner, but Jack offered to stand by five minutes until a table at the windows cleared.

They got a window table in two. Finally they got settled, and a waitress took their order. Ev stuck to tea and a side of toast. Jack ordered the scallops. When in Rome . . .

The view was worth the wait. Through giant picture windows they watched the rippling water of the harbor multiply the shore lights winking on here and there, some white, some amber, some ghastly blue-green. Small boats with their technicolor running lights entered and left the harbor. The overcast prevented any vivid sunset splashes. The misty gray simply deepened and darkened, silently swallowing details and muting color.

The waitress delivered Jack's clam chowder. He closed his eyes briefly to ask a blessing on their food— Ev's as well as his, since Ev didn't say grace.

Ev was watching the panorama of Northeast Harbor, rapt. "I suppose you remember my father is career navy. I'm thinking of all the seaports I've been in—and restaurants on the water like this. You'd think they'd be pretty much alike, but they aren't."

"This is nothing like Annapolis, huh?" Great clam chowder. Jack paused, wormed out of his jacket and hung it on the chairback.

"Or Boston, or Newport News, or Miami. Not the least." Ev was the last person in the world Jack would guess was an accountant, except maybe Clyde, the Sitting

Pretty bouncer. She was very pretty, not much older than the models, and her brusque, nervous ways seemed to be softening somewhat. He thought about the Death Valley job, how much she had changed in that brief week in California, and how she seemed so much warmer at this meeting than at their first encounter.

A silky-soft voice behind Jack cooed, "There you are!"

He stood and turned.

Marlette, her long honey-colored hair flowing free, floated down the aisle and alighted beside him as every eye in the restaurant followed her. "Clyde and Arturo came down early to set up, so I came along. I thought I might see you here." *Oy thot oy mought say you hare.* "If you were picking her up around five you'd likely come straight on down here, eh?"

"Good evening, Miss Marlette." Jack waved an arm toward Ev. "Evelyn Brant, your new colleague. Is 'colleague' the word? Miss Brant, this is Marlette." He drew a chair out for her. "Please join us."

"Ta." She sat. Her half-hour shower must have thawed her out completely. When frozen she had behaved frozen. Now she looked warm and pink and acted warm and lively.

And Ev, so friendly and open moments ago, now made Antarctic pack ice seem warm enough to grow pineapples.

Marlette's eyes flowed over him. "I was so cold this arvo I never did thank you properly. I apologize for being so rude. You were a fair dinkum gentleman—a lifesaver—and I appreciate you so much. I'm grateful!" *Oy'm grite-ful.*

"Happy to do it. You girls were really suffering. Why don't you wait in the van?"

"It's just as cold there, and Edith gets cranky if we're not instantly available."

"Easy for Edith—she was wearing a parka." Jack pondered the situation a minute and decided to stretch the truth a bit. To work, to work. "I explained to Miss Brant

32

here that I'm an investigator, which led to what I'm investigating. She has expressed some misgivings about filling in for a murdered woman. Was the girl—Veronica Wayne— openly fighting with anyone or seriously at odds with anyone?"

That musical laugh hung on the air. "Ronnie gave everyone on this crew the sterks. A fair cow, that. Constantly bunging on an act."

Jack translated for Ev into English. "The victim, Miss Wayne, infuriated everyone she worked with. Constantly fighting and arguing."

"Too right!" Those liquid blue eyes swarmed all over his face.

"Did she have a snout on anyone in particular?"

"Her boyfriend stoushed her last week. Big punch up."

"But he's down in New York."

"No. He's a photographer here. Mike Kovik. That's why Edith hired him. Ronnie insisted."

"Stoushed?" Ev asked icily.

"Knocked her around," Jack explained. "So theirs was one of those relationships where they loved and hated with equal passion."

Marlette's eyes were very, very blue. "Strange, isn't it, how people do? Now he's all broken up. In his room, drunk as a wombat. That was Arturo out there this arvo." Marlette's knee bumped against Jack's, and it didn't feel accidental.

"Arturo Fracci." Jack hadn't heard or used Australian slang in years. He reveled in the music on his ear. "Is he dating any of the girls?"

"All of them, sooner or later. He gets about." Her soft voice softened further. "Clyde says you claim to be a ranger, but I don't think he believes you. He doesn't think you look like a ranger. Especially with that cowboy hat you were wearing. Are you a cowboy?" The knee rubbed against his.

33

Here came Ev's toast and Jack's scallops.

"Is everyone who wears an Akubra a ringer? What can I order for you?"

"I've eaten, ta. I'd better go tell Clyde where I am. He worries more, now that—you understand. Excuse me, please. I'll see you shortly, eh?"

Jack started to stand as she left, but she swooped off too quickly. He settled into his chair. "That was a rapid exit."

"A big burly man with a white scar was shaking his fist at her out on the roadside there." Ev nodded toward the window.

Outside, his back to the restaurant, Clyde was gripping Marlette's arm, hustling her along. They crossed the street, headed toward the docks.

Jack watched until they disappeared beyond parked cars, musing about Clyde Wilkins's possessiveness. He wondered if it was directed specifically at Marlette or if it embraced all the crew. He looked at Ev.

Ev could have simply ordered bread. She could glare at it as she glared at Jack now, and it would have quickly toasted under the heat.

"What's wrong?" Jack liked the french fries.

"Don't you see through that? She was buttering you up. Acting cute. Flirting like mad."

"There's a law against flirting?" And these scallops were superb.

"And playing footsie." She snorted.

"That was under the table. You have X-ray eyes."

"I didn't need X-ray eyes to see that blatant display! I'll bet they're all tarts." Ev's glare escalated to just plain flame-throwing. "And you love every drippy minute of it. You're eating it up, aren't you!"

Why did her harmless pique irritate him? "I sense you don't like Marlette. You probably won't like Athalia or Lauren either. But your job, I remind you, is to become best friends with these girls and find out all you can about who might hate whom enough to bump whom off."

"I suppose next you're going to tell me that you're schmoozing up to that little tart because of the case. That you're investigating. Getting information."

"OK, so I won't tell you, but that's what I'm doing, yes. And I suggest you use Americanisms with discretion around Marlette. Some of them carry a different meaning in Australia."

On the Death Valley case, Ev had constantly expressed that she felt left out for one reason or another. Probably part of her ire now was that she felt left out of the exchange of slang. Oh, well. Jack was not getting paid to straighten Ev's nose if it got out of shape. Her nose was her own business.

He thought of the Aussie accent and blue eyes, the long hair, the silky voice, the knee touching his leg. Lousy job, this investigation business, but somebody had to do it.

3

Meeting of the Minds

11:59 A.M.

Jack thought briefly of what he had been doing exactly sixty-seven hours ago. He had been pasting his cordless phone to his ear with his hunched left shoulder as he moved around his apartment in Hutchinson, stuffing shirts and underwear into his duffle. He had tripped over the recumbent Maxx two or three times.

He had listened to Hal Edmond explain in excruciating detail the extreme tact this job would require. Jack would be having to mollify a lot of crumpled egos, said Hal. The news media would be pouncing on any little slip-up like a coyote on a field mouse, so Jack would have to proceed with caution, he said. That Death Valley case was cream compared to this one.

"Oh, yeah?" had been Jack's response. "You weren't the sucker who got shoved off the cliff or trapped in the burning trailer. Cream! Easy for you to say."

"Piffle," said Hal.

Piffle indeed.

Jack had gone to bed at 8:00 that night, arisen at 3:00 A.M., and was well beyond Kansas by sun-up. By 10:00 P.M. that first night on the road, he had driven a thousand miles.

Now, less than three days after that call, here he sat in a room full of the crumpled egos Hal had warned him about, applying tact for who-tied-the-dog. They sprawled at various degrees of ease around the big conference table in the basement of the visitor center. It was a motley crew.

The superintendent, Warren Sarnoff, acted every bit as disgruntled as when Jack first met him, despite that they had spent nearly three hours in this conference this morning. Jack liked to think he could charm a gopher right out of its hole, but he wasn't getting to first base with Sarnoff.

John Grayson was in charge of law enforcement in Acadia. A slim, small, quiet, sandy-haired man in gold-rimmed glasses, he tipped his chair back to two legs, crossed his arms, and simply listened for the most part.

Beside him squirmed a man who obviously had to be constantly doing something or he wasn't happy. This was Vernon Bondi, the park's maintenance supervisor. He came across as either a fifty-year-old kid who never quite got over his love of Tonka toys, or the one man you wanted on your side when the washing machine, shower, 220-outlet, automobile engine, sagging porch timbers, and the weather all turned on you simultaneously. He was one of those Columbo types whose hair never stayed combed and whose pants always had a grease spot near the knee.

Sumner Philips, with the Hancock County Sheriff's Office, must have been born with that white hair. It glowed like snow in moonlight, and Jack couldn't imagine the well-built man in any other color. Philips wore a suit and tie today, being in the privileged ranks of investigator as opposed to the unprivileged ranks that had to doll up in a uniform every working day. With dark blue pants and a light blue tweed jacket, he looked like something the Sitting Pretty photographers ought to be shooting for GQ.

And then there was the Hancock County assistant prosecutor, a woman with eagle eyes and condor talons and a lean and hungry build. She pulled her thick brown hair back in what is called a business do, plain and no-

nonsense. Sarnoff was grumpy and Edith Cray cranky, but Marian Hastings was just plain hostile.

In a wild stroke of diplomacy, Jack wore unprepossessing old clothes—a chambray shirt and jeans, and running shoes he couldn't get all the mud out of. He made certain Sarnoff had the head of the table and that he himself was seated halfway down one side of it. He emphasized thereby that he was just one of the guys. Except that he would be the one standing closest should anything unseemly hit the fan with this case.

Jack spread his hands. "We've all discussed what everyone else has found, at least in summary. Anyone think of anything they'd like to add that hasn't been mentioned?"

They muttered unintelligible nothings. Vern Bondi bounced up for the fourteenth time and refilled his coffee mug. He related to the coffee pot in the way a hyperactive second-grader related to pencil sharpeners.

Jack nodded. "I want to reemphasize what my role is —and is not. I am not the white knight that comes galloping in to put everything to rights. I am not a case coordinator or law enforcement manager inflicted from above. Acadia and the area in general are getting some bad press —Miss Wayne was apparently a major figure in her profession. Hal sent me in for two reasons. One was to show the media that the Park Service is not simply standing around yawning in the wake of this crime—we're doing something aggressive and definite. That's cosmetic, for the outside to see. For the inside . . ."

He thought a moment. "If you mail a letter in Bar Harbor and another letter in Northeast Harbor, they'll both get tossed in the same mailbag. They'll get sorted at a central station and sent off to their respective destinations." He paused. "Lord willing, I'm the sorting station. You dump all your data, observations, hunches, everything on me, and I try to sort it out. The difference between me and the postal service is that, when you dump your letter on me, you still keep your letter. You're still working with it, doing your job. I'm not here to take over anyone's job. I'm an additional resource. That's all."

And he remembered a third point. Might as well mention it. "Mr. Sarnoff and the regional director both have received flak already from the Maine tourist bureau. The tourism types are afraid of the adverse publicity and want a lid on this quick." He paused a moment for effect. "Frankly, I don't give a hang what the Maine tourist bureau wants."

He got two smiles and a grin. Sarnoff's puss and Ms. Hastings's remained sour. Jack laced his hands across his middle. "That's all I have."

That was apparently all anyone else had too. The group rose, rattling the plastic molded chairs against the plastic table, milling aimlessly, not sure it was OK to leave but eager to hit the old lunch box.

Jack motioned "Hold on a moment" to the law enforcement specialist.

Grayson paused and hovered by the window.

Hastings pursed her lips a moment. Did she automatically put the scowl on her face each morning when she put on her make-up? It would save time. "I'm still not certain what you expect to do here. I'm fairly familiar with the Park Service hierarchy, and I don't see where you fit in."

"You may remember in the papers an international incident at Yellowstone when a foreign envoy was killed. The rangers there got a lot of dirty looks they didn't deserve —they handled it the best they could. So an experienced ranger in the national office, Hal Edmond, was authorized to put together a unit that can step into sticky situations and unresolved murders—that sort of thing—anywhere in the Park system. Contiguous U.S., Alaska, Hawaii, Virgin Islands. Not to take over but to help out. Hal's Pals, if you will."

"SETs."

"Special Events Teams are another thing. This is new."

"How many hotshots in this unit?"

"So far, just myself and an accountant or two. It's experimental." Ev wasn't in it exactly, but Hal was using her. Since she was undercover, Jack didn't mention her. He didn't trust anyone here completely.

"Must be." She looked singularly unimpressed. "You said earlier we should all speak frankly. Very well. Frankly, I don't consider this case an appropriate opportunity for your agency to be conducting experiments. I've dealt with the FBI a time or two, and I have absolutely no confidence in the ability of federal investigators to get the job done."

Jack smiled amiably. "And some of the guys in the Washington office say the same thing about local law enforcement. Fortunately, most of the time we're all wrong about each other."

"All the same, I'll be keeping very close to this case. I don't want it messed up by incompetence."

Jack scratched his cheek, a slow and deliberate gesture. "I perceive, Ms. Hastings, that you will not be content forever with the title 'assistant.' Solving this case, or salvaging it from the blunderers, would open doors for you— at the very least improve your position when promotion time rolls around." He straightened. "More power to you. I admire ambition. I look forward to working with you."

She probably had her raptor eyes on the prosecutor's office itself—or maybe that of attorney general of the United States or prosecutor of the world. That was not his concern. Cooperating with her without letting her take over the case was his concern. She would be working not for justice but for Marian Hastings.

She studied him a moment. "You're not quite the country bumpkin you try to resemble. Call me whenever you turn anything up." With a few more words, she wandered off searching, ostensibly, for lunch.

Jack looked at the law enforcement specialist. "Mr.

40

Grayson? Hal said something about the use of a boat to get around with."

Grayson nodded. "We have two, a police patrol boat and a little runabout. The patrol boat is under repair. Sorry. The runabout's at Northeast Harbor, isn't it, Vern?"

Over by the coffee pot, sifting through the doughnuts that were left, Vern Bondi nodded. "Used to tie it up at Southwest Harbor, but there's less protected. We lost one in a winter storm a couple years ago. Broke its mooring, and there it was up on the rocks across the harbor, with holes in its belly. Now we keep it at Northeast. Want it now?"

Jack shook his head. "When you decide to pull the ultimate college prank and fill the Statue of Liberty up with crumpled paper, the pile of files in my motel room will get you at least to her belly button. I'd like to do some homework before I start talking to people. Three o'clock? Three thirty?"

"Three's good. I'll be at the maintenance yard. Know where it is?"

"I'll find it."

Vern picked out a chocolate-and-sprinkles doughnut and left.

Grayson was still standing there. "Anything else?"

"If you don't mind hearing my confession."

He smirked. "My mother always wanted me to be a priest."

"Forgive me for I have fallen asleep. I was going to tackle the pile you and Mr. Sarnoff gave me when I got to my room about a quarter to eight last night, but I was sound asleep by eight. So I didn't get down through very much of it. I did read your statement and Alan Messier's. I'd like to talk to Mr. Messier at length."

"He's pretty devastated. I put him on administrative leave."

"He feels responsible, your statement says."

Grayson strolled in closer and perched on the edge

of the table. The table creaked, an audible complaint. "His role on the Sitting Pretty job was to do what baby-sitters always do."

"Tag along with the photography crew and make sure they don't damage the resource? Keep them from trampling the vegetation, cutting down the trees, scaring the squirrels, whatever?"

"Right. Especially, help them avoid inadvertently shooting pictures of their models doing no-no things."

"Like walking off the established trails, picking flowers—if there were any to pick."

Grayson nodded. "There's holly and mistletoe around. Gathering cones. Also, the safety factor. These people have no idea that the rocky shore is slippery or that the water is so cold it will kill you in a couple minutes. That manager was going to have the girls playing in the water at Sand Beach—showing off swim suits, I suppose. Alan gave them a fast lesson about hypothermia. Got them to play on the beach instead. That was bad enough."

"So the water's cooled off already from summer."

"It never warms up in summer. If you see a photograph of an unidentified beach, and all the beach baskers are standing around on shore, you can tell it's Sand Beach. None of the swimmers will be in past their knees. The lakes warm up by late July or August, but the Gulf Stream bends east at Massachusetts and goes to Europe. The Gulf of Maine here is water straight down from the Arctic, all year."

"And this Alan took a paternal interest in the girls."

"In everybody associated with the job. Except that bouncer type. He and Clyde What's-His-Name didn't hit it off well."

"Alan felt he could have prevented the girl's death?"

"He's kicking himself because he left the scene early. Left them to themselves with promises of good behavior, you might say. He thinks if he'd stayed around, she'd still be alive."

"What do you think?"

"You read my statement."

"You very artfully skirted the issue."

Grayson smirked again. He was a master smirker. "He was supposed to be riding herd on them. He wasn't where he was supposed to be."

"And according to all the material I read so far, the interviews and supplementals, neither was anyone else. Every member of the party was off doing something else. Edith dropped Miss Wayne off at the motel and took the wardrobe mistress to the airport—"

"Ex-mistress."

"Right. She'd just fired her. Or the lady quit."

"Quit. Got in an argument with Cray."

"The other three models had picked up dates and wanted to go clamming, since Edith wouldn't be there. The photographers claimed they were out taking pictures for their own portfolios—separately, not together—and that left Clyde and two others with nothing to do, so Clyde sampled some local taverns."

"Not too local. Went into Ellsworth."

"Witnesses?"

"A guy says he was there at two. Nothing before then."

"And the girl died around noon."

Grayson shrugged and lurched erect. The table murmured appreciatively. Vern Bondi ought to oil something underneath there. "We think. The very cold water may have cooled her body temp quicker than normal. The medical examiner tried to sound definite, but he didn't fool me. She was tossed in immediately. But it could have been one or so."

"She cooled so rapidly her body temperature approximated that of a person whose metabolism might have quit an hour later. I see." Actually, Jack didn't see. Despite the good sleep last night he felt groggy and only half with it. His mind wasn't sorting and analyzing at all. He only

43

hoped it was storing. Now and then, his brain treated the data Jack fed it not like the valuable special-handling info it was, but like junk mail.

Grayson didn't ask if Jack wanted to know anything else. He said a few words of good-bye and left. No invitation to lunch.

Come to think of it, nobody here had invited Jack to lunch. Bunch of social poops. He shoved his chair back, kicked his sleeping dog, and reached for his hat. Maxx rolled to his belly and yawned.

"Mr. Prester? Telephone." Stella Smith stuck her head in the conference room door. She pointed to an AT&T Merlin on a sideboard.

"Thank you." He picked it up, punched the lighted line, and spoke his name.

"Jack?" Silky voice. "We're breaking for lunch at a rather nondescript looking cafe in Southwest Harbor. Might you join us?"

"Miss Marlette, I'm delighted the world is not full of social poops after all. I'd love to join you."

"Social what? Please don't call me 'Miss,' eh? It sounds so formal."

He turned on his fake Crocodile Dundee accent. "As you wish, luv. No worries, eh?"

"That's far better." Laughter tinkled. "'Spindrift' is the name of it, I believe. Something of the sort. Near the aquarium."

"I'll find it." That pile of reading could wait.

4
Spindrift

The modeling crew had been seated and served by the time Jack found the Spindrift Cafe next to the Mt. Desert Oceanarium in Southwest Harbor. No matter. A blackboard by the hostess's station announced the special of the day: crab salad sandwich with split pea soup. Jack ordered it menu unseen, with a large cola no ice, as the waitress seated him.

Marlette had saved him a seat beside her in a curved corner booth. Everyone in the booth greeted him, some more warmly than others—Marlette and Lauren on the hot side, Ev and Edith on the cold.

Beyond Marlette on her left sat Athalia. Then came Ev, then Lauren, and across from Marlette, Edith. The men sat by themselves at the table-for-four beside this booth, and Jack had his first look at Mike Kovik.

Kovik was a huge blond bear of a man, one of those people with fair hair and black eyebrows, and he was built like a weight lifter. Jack couldn't imagine him succeeding at something as artistic and delicate as photography any more than he could picture Clyde Wilkins in accounting.

He stood beside Kovik and extended a hand. "Mike Kovik. I believe we haven't met yet. John Prester, with the Park Service."

Kovik did not rise to shake. He didn't bother to shake at all. He looked at Jack the way Henry VIII would look at a stable boy, the way Maxx regarded lima beans. "So you're the hero who rescues the damsels in distress. The way the girls were going on about you, I thought you'd be tall, dark, and handsome."

"The world is full of disappointments. Pleased to meet you." Jack smiled and nodded to him and settled into the booth at Marlette's right.

Jack tried in vain to picture an evenly matched love-hate relationship such as Marlette described between Kovik and the murdered Veronica Wayne. Wayne was apparently about the same size and weight as Marlette. Pit this hulking Kovik against a wisp of a girl? Might as well drop a bale of straw on a Hostess Twinkie.

Clyde shot Jack a dirty scowl, an expression that seemed to pop onto his face automatically whenever Jack came near.

Arturo Fracci explained in an overwrought Italian accent how Europe's *langoste* is actually superior to Maine lobster. No one seemed to be listening to him.

The bland, callow photographer's assistant ate absently, staring at nothing. On second thought, he was staring at Ev and carefully pretending not to, his eyes boring holes in the wall within a few feet of her head.

Edith was doing the talking at this table, by turns ranking on the girls for petty offenses and describing what she needed next this afternoon. She glared at Ev. "Evelyn. Do you understand what I mean by that?"

"I'll walk her through it," Athalia interrupted. "Ain' no big thing."

"'Ain't no big thing.' Your theme in life." Edith's voice didn't sound as if she thought much of Athalia's philosophy.

"You really from Kansas?" Athalia looked at Jack and bit into her corned beef sandwich.

"Grew up in New Mexico. Country boy."

46

Lauren giggled and picked at some sort of white fillet on her plate. "That explains the hat. There aren't many fish in New Mexico, are there? It isn't anything like here."

"Not at all like here. I did a season in the Ozarks, though—Ozark Scenic Riverway and Buffalo River. They have catfish and carp you wouldn't believe."

"Catfish." Athalia nodded. "Beats this haddock any ol' day."

"Used properly." Jack grinned. "Only if used properly. While I was a seasonal ranger there, I lived in a trailer park with other seasonals. Two of them were courting. Frank and Karen. He'd pull some dastardly practical joke on her, and she'd do something back. Kept us all entertained."

Ev was developing a smirk. She'd heard his tales before. "This has something to do with catfish?"

"Madderafact. About the end of July, Frank's trailer started smelling like something died. Stank so bad he slept outside. He figured Karen was at the bottom of it, that she'd slipped something in, but hanged if he could find it. He searched the whole place a dozen times. He ended up marrying Karen a month early just so he could live in her trailer. Months afterward, the maintenance crew went up on the roof to drain the air conditioner and found the remains of this big catfish Karen had thrown up there, right next to the intake."

Lauren didn't join in the general giggles. She was looking at him oddly, even say affectionately.

Edith finished off her coffee and stood up, her food only half eaten.

Jack barely got himself risen in time.

She frowned at the tableful collectively. "You girls be changed and out there in five minutes. Do your make-up but don't fuss with the clothes. A local personnel agency claims they have the perfect wardrobe mistress for us. We'll see." She left without so much as a by-your-leave.

Clyde, Kovik, Arturo, and the assistant got up and

left with her. Clyde graced Jack with a "Watch yourself, pal!" look on the way out.

"Local woman." Jack sat down again. "To replace the wardrobe mistress who left?"

Athalia nodded. "Hair sometimes, make-up sometimes, costume coordination, detailing. That sort of thing." She jabbed Ev's arm. "C'mon, Evvie. I'll show you what she's talking about."

Lauren scooted out too. "Jack, are you coming along to watch?"

"Sure. It's either that or work for a living."

Marlette grinned, and the room filled with sunshine. "Heaven forbid you'd have to work."

"Sit inside a warm office when it's cold as a fish outside and twice as wet? I'd be terribly disappointed." Jack rose as the girls left. Marlette stayed sitting, so he sat down and tackled his crab salad sandwich. He wasn't into seafood normally, being a beef-eating country boy, but if you ate seafood anywhere in the world, the Maine coast was it. "You're not going?"

"I'll be there." She lowered her voice to a purr. "What do you do in evenings when you're not working?"

"Depends on the evening. Last evening I fell asleep before the birds quit chirping. Long drives turn me into a wet dishrag for a couple days."

She ran a finger up his arm. "Couple days? If you're up to putty now, you should be really interesting in a day or two."

"Oh, I do recover."

"The thing that I notice most about American girls, I think, is how bold they are. I envy that. If an American girl wants to date a man, she simply asks him."

"In Australia she'd rather die than ask first."

"Too right!" The liquid blue eyes were watching him, which would be a whole lot more romantic if they were watching him do something besides chew crab.

"So you want me to ask you out tonight because

you're too uncomfortable to do it yourself."

That laughter again.

Jack held her eye. "I'd love to, but I'm otherwise committed. I do want to get to know you better, though. Don't fill your dance card without me, all right?"

She smiled gloriously.

He stood up and let her out of the booth.

She paused and washed those blue eyes across his face. She left.

Diplomacy? He had just lied again, this time to a gorgeous woman. He was not, strictly speaking, committed tonight, except to a pile of reading material. But dating a murder suspect before the case cleared was highly questionable.

It took him maybe ten minutes to finish his lunch, get the check, help the waitress figure out who paid for what, learn that model agencies are lousy tippers, pay up, and head for the door.

Lauren Laren came in the door as he was going out. Her fine blonde hair brushed her shoulders softly, a very feminine effect.

He frowned. "Leave something behind in the booth?" He had checked, as he always did when leaving an area, and had seen nothing.

"No. Edith just changed our site. We're down behind a little shed on the wharf now, and I wanted to make sure you found out. Besides, I wanted to talk to you, if you don't mind."

"Mind? Does Ebenezer Scrooge mind discovering a shoebox full of twenty-pound notes in the bottom of his wardrobe? Does a chocoholic mind a stocking filled with Hershey Kisses on Christmas morning?"

She smiled, but it wasn't a happy smile. In fact, it was forced. He searched her face for contentment and could see none.

He was parked at the curb out front. He let Maxx out of his cage and snapped the leash on. He said a casual

"Heel," and Maxx took the order casually. Very casually. The mutt would range out, sniff at grass clumps and bushes, come wandering back. Old Maxx enjoyed a walk as much as anybody. He hated heeling.

They ambled along the street past the Oceanarium, Jack in his scruffy jeans and sheepskin-lined denim jacket, Lauren togged out in a lovely summer frock and that same old blanket.

How should he break the ice? "Most American citizens, when faced with cold, overcast weather like this, wear coats. How come you girls wear blankets instead?"

"So you don't mess up the clothes. You can lay the blanket over you. When you slip your arms into coat sleeves, you can wrinkle the clothes. One of Edith's edicts."

"Edith issues lots of edicts?"

"Yeah." Her voice wavered, dropped thirty decibels. "It's getting so heavy, Jack. I don't know what to do."

"Talk to me." He slowed the pace still further. They were approaching the wharf too quickly.

She stopped and stared at infinity at their feet. "When you took off your coat for Marlette yesterday . . ." She snickered. "And here I thought there weren't any gentlemen left in the world anymore." Her eyes rose to meet his. They weren't as blue as Marlette's. They were just ordinary blue. "And you're moral. At lunch you were talking about those two—Karen?"

"And Frank. Yeah. Neat couple. Really great."

"And moral. You too. You sort of took it for granted they wouldn't just live together—they'd get married."

"That's the God-given program, yeah."

She nodded. "And yesterday when you drove me back to the motel, you didn't ask for any favors or anything. Or Marlette either. I asked her if you did. Not that she'd tell the truth. The word is that you're a Park Service policeman investigating the murder, but I don't care about that. Besides, it sounds weird. Far-fetched. But you act like a gentleman, and you pay attention when people are talking."

"You're very troubled. It doesn't take an attentive listener to see that."

"Troubled, yeah. Like you wouldn't believe. I have a baby, Jack, did you know that?"

"No. How old?"

"Six months. He's with me. I had to bring him along because . . . well, this gig is ten days, and I just finished one for Avon's fashion catalogue, and I'm doing a Sears flyer next week. You see? If I didn't take him along I would never see him. And it's cheaper to find some retired lady to take care of him on the road than to hire a full-time nurse at home."

"I thought you girls made big bucks."

She blew a raspberry. "The established ones do. I'm just getting started. This is a wonderful opportunity for me. This is one of the biggest. Maybe even *the* biggest. But I don't get paid much, not yet. I'm not established, you know?"

"How long does it take?"

"If lightning strikes, a couple months. That's rare. Usually several years." Her whole demeanor brightened. She was describing dreams now, so much shinier than sodden reality. "I want to be famous. I mean, *really* famous! Known throughout the land, you know? And then I'll retire wealthy and spend my time and money helping other people."

"How old are you, really?" He tried to make his voice sound paternal and not the least accusatory.

She hesitated. Then, "Seventeen."

"You look in your twenties."

"People constantly guess my age wrong. I count on it. I've been modeling since I was fourteen, when I looked eighteen."

"Phony ID."

"Sure." She glanced up guiltily. "Why am I telling a cop this?"

"Because the cop's not going to dump on you, and you know it. You're making it in a tough world, and I admire that."

"But I'm learning a lot."

"I bet."

"I don't mean sex." She grimaced. "Oh, I learned all that since I was twelve, starting with my stepdad. The creep. I mean, learning about the other things of life. Like morality. I thought there wasn't any, but then I've been meeting people who are moral and honest—not like my mom and stepdad—and I'm thinking, this is how I want my little boy to see me. As a moral, honest person. Famous, but moral. Upstanding."

"Your parents didn't give you that? Then your world was even tougher than I guessed."

"It was a nightmare, and I was too dumb to know it. I know now. But the nightmare's still real. Except my little boy. He's the only sunshine I have right now."

Jack made his voice sound curious, not official. "Who's the father?"

She shrugged.

"Lauren?" He waited until her eyes were back on his. "Who's the father?"

Her eyes flicked away. "I don't know. Either Arturo or Mike. Probably Mike. My baby's first hair was black and coarse, and I thought Arturo for sure, but now it's getting very fair. Blond."

"Neonatal hair is usually dark. Is intimacy with the photographers a job requirement?"

"No. Well, sorta. Edith signed me about a year ago. I was thrilled! Edith is the tops. She always uses Arturo, and I think she might have just broken up with Mike when I came on. Anyway, she made it clear I had to be a company person. You know, cooperate. The agency is one big happy business family."

"Except no one is happy."

"No one. Not even her. It took me this long to realize she's a conniving witch. I want out, but she's my meal ticket. I don't dare quit Edith Cray. Her reputation in the business, you know? If I quit on her, I won't work anywhere ever again. And she's giving me a hard time about the baby. She says I should have got an abortion, and now she says she doesn't want the baby with me on the road. And she doesn't want me near Arturo."

"You didn't tell her your guesses on the baby's parentage?"

"She knew. She knows everything. And this gig—this is the last straw. I can't get a good sitter for the baby, and we're so cold, and working . . . here, I'll show you."

She hiked her skirt unabashedly, as if all Main Street were not watching, to reveal a big black bruise high on her leg. She dropped the skirt back into place unceremoniously. "That's from falling on those slippery rocks. I have another like it, further up. And do you know how cold this water is?"

"I've heard stories."

"We had to wade around in it. It's only Alan that kept us from having to get into it for real."

"Alan. The ranger who supervised the shoots made inside the park."

"He's so nice. He really cares. I think he had a thing going with Ronnie. She was such a spoiled brat. She didn't deserve him."

"I understand he's extremely upset about her death."

"I heard. That's another thing. Ronnie was a real witch, but not enough to die. I've known witchier. Edith, for starters. What if it's some nut? What if he has me in mind for next?" Her eyes locked onto his, and he could see the terror in them.

He stopped and raised his arms, and she stepped inside them. He drew her close, an avuncular bear hug, and held on. Her body was so tense it vibrated. He felt very fatherly, especially considering her true age. He was actually old enough to be her father, barely. "So other than being a good mother, and keeping your child, and working with a false ID that they might find out about, and getting your career established, and becoming famous throughout the land, and not having enough money, and putting up with all the stuff going on at Sitting Pretty, and worrying about being a murderer's next victim, what's the problem?"

She sucked in air and then giggled. "I can't imagine. Did I say there's a problem?"

Her head pressed against his shoulder, so he continued to hold her close.

Presently she continued. "Anyway. I think if I'm going to be an honest, moral person, the first thing is to confront Edith. Tell her I'm not going to be immoral anymore and ask her to stand up for me. Do you think she will?"

"If it profits the agency. So I'd approach it from that angle."

The head nodded against his shoulder. "And I'm going to get firm with her about other things too."

"Like having the baby with you."

"Yeah, like that. I guess . . ." She took a deep breath and started over. "I guess what I needed was someone to say I'm OK. And you're doing that. In fact, you're doing that without any empty words. And also you're not telling me what to do or saying I'm no good or anything. I think that's what I missed most growing up—someone to just approve. You know?"

"No. Not really. I got plenty of support when I was growing up, and it still didn't seem like enough. I can't imagine what it would have been like with none at all."

"There. That's what I mean about being honest. You didn't just say, 'Yeah, I know,' because it's what you wanted me to hear. You told me the truth. Real feelings. I have to learn how to do that."

"It's not easy. Must be really scary if you're not used to doing it."

"It is. It really is. Anyway, I'm going to talk to Edith." She clung.

He held.

She started to loosen eventually.

To work, to work.

Suddenly the world exploded. Jack was flying. Lauren was screaming. A man was yelling. Maxx was snarling. Ev was shouting, "Jack!" And all that happened before Jack hit the ground.

He landed on his shoulder, and if he didn't break something he nearly did. It knocked his breath out. He raised his head the moment it let him.

Lauren had fallen into a bush beside the sidewalk. She was squirming to get herself back on her feet.

And Maxx had huge, bruising Clyde Wilkins lying flat out on the ground. The dog's teeth were literally on the man's throat.

Jack lurched to his knees without benefit of his diaphragm or any other breathing mechanisms, for that matter. Another second or two and he made it to his feet.

Edith's voice screamed something angry. There she stood a hundred feet away, she and the whole Sitting Pretty crew, models and all. The photographers had their camera bags, and the assistant was toting the reflector on his shoulder.

Jack didn't call Maxx off just yet. First he retrieved that pistol from under the buffalo's arm. Only when Clyde's teeth were pulled did Jack order Maxx back. The mutt took his sweet time obeying. Old Maxx was so good at this—he didn't even leave any dents in the guy's throat. Jack picked up the leash with his free hand, just to make sure Maxx didn't get carried away with desire for a little action.

"Unprovoked assault on a law officer is good for a couple months in the pokey, Clyde." Jack had to take a breath before continuing. His shoulder and ribs really ached. "Why in the world would you think you're exempt?" He tucked the gun in his belt at the small of his back. He realized just now that he had no cuffs with him. His emergency restraint, the plastic zip-string that looked like the first part to get lost off some kid's toy, was wound inside the sweatband of his Stetson, which was locked up back in his truck.

Clyde stared at Maxx. In basso profundo, his gravel voice snarled, "You're taking advantage of her. It makes me mad. You stay away from the girls."

Now what? He wanted to think this through, and quickly, but his addled brain wouldn't cooperate. Maxx tugged at the leash, eager to flatten old Clyde again. Jack tugged back.

Jack pointed at the bouncer. "Stay right there, down on the ground. Move and I turn Maxx loose. Hear?" He snapped, "Heel," and headed for Edith. His gut hurt too.

With grumpy Maxx at heel, he parked in front of grumpy Edith, and he felt pretty grumpy himself. "He's your goon. I keep mine on a leash, and you're going to have to keep yours under control."

Edith's face was tight with fury. "I must ask you to stay away from the girls. You're disruptive."

"*I'm* disruptive! I'm the one with the sore shoulder and ribs and lungs. You seem to—" He stopped. "Come with me, please." He led Edith—a reluctant, hostile Edith —off down the street, out of earshot of the others.

He turned to face her and lowered his voice anyway, despite the fact that no one else would hear. "Your bouncer just gave me grounds for arrest. No ifs or buts. Witnesses and all. I'm going to write up the incident. It stays in the drawer for the moment. Any more trouble and out it comes, and down he goes. Are we clear on that?"

"He sometimes acts before he thinks. He—"

"Teach him logic, then. Do something. But he stays out of my face. Everyone's face. One more thing." He

56

lowered his voice still further. "There is a line between pampering and abusing. I don't recommend pampering, but I won't let you continue abusing. You'll improve the girls' conditions—there's no reason for them to sit in the cold when you're not using them, for instance—and you'll pay better attention to basic amenities, for them and for the others too. Or I go to my boss in Washington. He didn't get where he is by being a hermit. He knows the right people in the right places, including but not limited to OSHA and a few key unions. Are we understood?"

"You're playing at blackmail. It's unbecoming."

"Blackmail you to do what you're already supposed to be doing according to law and union regs? I shouldn't have to."

"You're meddling in something that's none of your affair. Your business is Ronnie's murder. It has nothing to do with—"

"And when the girls are miserable and distracted it hampers my interviews and interrogation efforts. So I have a vested interest. At least enough legal interest to make waves. Also, how do I know your labor and safety violations, not to mention your bouncer, were not involved in the murder itself? Heaven knows, if old Clyde can floor me for platonically hugging a woman on a busy street, he could do just about anything."

Her eyes crackled. "Do you care to prefer murder charges?"

"I'm working on it."

She studied him several minutes. "So you have a vendetta. Against me personally? Or against Sitting Pretty?"

"No vendetta. I just want to see you clean up your act, for your employees' sake."

She stared at him some more.

He wanted to rub his middle where his diaphragm had gotten all shook up, but it would have reduced his authority facade. He was bluffing now, purely and dishonestly bluffing. He was making threats he could not in a million years come good on, and he probably couldn't even get Clyde jailed for shoving him down.

But what could he lose? He already had lost any willing cooperation Edith might have offered. If she made the girls' stint a little easier, everyone came out ahead. Maybe Marlette wouldn't have to turn into a prune in the shower after coming in from work. Maybe Lauren could have an easier time juggling baby and career together. Maybe.

So he looked stern and unbending and, he hoped, possessed of power he certainly did not have in fact.

She turned away. "We're behind, and I'm losing daylight. We'll talk about it later."

"When later?"

"Tonight." She stomped off toward Clyde, and every word her body language spoke was "Fury."

5

JackPotLuck

Hostility itches.

Boy, does it itch. And Jack felt for all the world like scratching.

Superintendent Warren Sarnoff thrust another three inches of reading material into Jack's hands. The scowl on his face and his brusque manner told Jack exactly what he thought of this whole affair. He took Jack by an elbow and ushered him toward the glass doors and the muted late-afternoon light.

"Region said to cooperate," he droned, "and of course I'm happy to. If you have any questions, call me. I'm not available this afternoon, but tomorrow you can probably find me."

"Mr. Sarnoff," Stella Smith called from over at the desk, "did you tell him about the potluck?"

"Oh, yes. Park potluck tonight. Since you're not on the staff, you wouldn't really be expected to bring anything. There's a dance afterwards—Vern and his wife are avid social dancers." He paused, then chuckled mirthlessly. "And of course, we wouldn't expect you to find anyone to bring on this short notice. A date, so to speak. So don't worry about it. Stella can give you details." He turned and headed back for his office.

Jack might have been escorted to the door, but you don't dump Jack Prester that easily. As soon as Sarnoff turned, Jack reversed and sauntered to the desk. "What would the Park Service do without potlucks?"

"Starve, probably." She smiled. "It's a going-away for Vern Bondi. He's transferring to Saguaro National Monument in two weeks. Six o'clock out at the community building on Great Cranberry. He has a summer camp out there."

"A summer camp. You mean, like where city children are shipped out for a week apiece to feed the local mosquitoes?"

"No." She chuckled. "In its heyday, Mt. Desert Island here was where the very wealthy spent their summers. The *very* wealthy. When they talk about summer places around here, anything over forty rooms is a cottage. Anything under forty rooms is a camp."

Jack whistled.

Stella perched on her stool. "Vern has a lovely little three-bedroom bungalow out on Great Cranberry. They already have a renter for it."

"I see. He's not wealthy, so he lives in it all year."

"That's right. His father inherited it and gave it to him. As costly as homes are up here now, he'd never afford to buy something like that. None of us can."

Jack nodded. "Will the boat be available? John mentioned a boat."

"Whenever you want it." She fished around in a cabinet under the desk and brought up a key ring with a three-inch-long tag dangling from it. "The boat registration number's on the tag. Walk down the ramp and turn right immediately. It'll be tied up there somewhere."

With thanks and other pleasantries, Jack headed out the door, the keys in hand. He took his time strolling down that amazing dressed-stone staircase, trying to identify his own feelings.

Anger. That's what it was. Warren Sarnoff's hostility

and smug, snide attitude really angered him. "Happy to cooperate." And in the same breath, "Not available today." What bugged Jack worst of all was Sarnoff's condescending "I'll invite you, but you won't fit in." Maddening.

Jack was third-generation Park Service. No way he could fail to fit into a potluck. Potluck suppers were the be-all and end-all of park social occasions. They celebrated retirements, transfers, promotions, weddings, births, and other comings and goings. One, a Potty Luck at Big Bend National Park, marked the dedication of the new rest rooms down at Castolon.

He glanced at his watch. To arrive on time at the potluck out on that island, he would have to leave the dock in less than an hour. So Sarnoff didn't think he could contribute anything, huh? He broke into a run, galloping down the stairs three at a stride.

He yelled, "Stay!" at Maxx before the dog could hop out of his cage, flopped into the front seat, and practically burned rubber leaving the parking lot.

He stopped at the first little grocery he came to in Northeast Harbor. In the housewares aisle he quickly chose two plastic bowls, one big and one little. Picnic department: pack of paper plates and those mutant plastic spoon-fork gizmos. He grabbed a couple bags of chips on the way to the cooler. A pint of sour cream. A six-pack of Pepsi. A package of dry onion soup. Nine items. He was eligible for the express lane, but there wasn't any. The little market had but one cash register. But then, he was the only customer. He wished the cashier a hasty good day and hit the road again.

And Sarnoff didn't think he could round up a date that quick, huh? Fortuitously, Sitting Pretty had moved from Southwest Harbor to the Northeast Harbor wharf. He drove there and parked by the ramp connecting the wharfside with the T-shaped floating yacht slips.

Apparently Northeast Harbor offered three kinds of tie-ups. Fancy rigs worth more than Jack's apartment house

61

nestled in finger slips. Lobster boats and other obviously local craft tied at mooring buoys out in the harbor. And here between the slips and the shore, a jumble of little runabouts and outboards were tied in willy-nilly profusion to a rail strung along the floating walkway. The park's boat would be among them.

There they were. Jack spied the crew halfway out the finger slips, working beside a sleek-looking Boston Whaler. He grabbed his bag of groceries and jogged down the ramp and out onto the slips. He only belatedly noticed that Maxx had hopped out of his cage and joined him.

"Maxx, you dork!" But he didn't have time to put the dog back. "Heel and stay heeled, hear?"

Kovik was doing the photographic honors this afternoon, shooting Lauren in a shorts-and-tank-top set. With the overcast and threat of rain, the kid with the reflector really had his work cut out for him.

Clyde saw Jack coming and actually started to move toward him, but he stopped with a jerk and stood by Edith, watching. Who knows. Maybe she took Jack's suggestion about a leash literally.

Only a few hours ago Jack had threatened Edith with his powerless pitch for more humane treatment. He saw no discernible change in things. If anything, she pouted darker than ever. He was itching again.

Athalia appeared to be waiting in the wings, so bundled in her blanket you couldn't see her costume. An older woman Jack had never seen before was fussing with the bodice of Ev's dress, her mouth bristling with safety pins. That must be the new wardrobe mistress Edith had brought in. Ev stood there looking miserable, and Marlette didn't look any happier.

Jack took a moment to introduce himself to the wardrobe mistress. Her name was Thelma Hyde, and she lived in Seal Harbor. Ev would not be in front of a camera for perhaps five minutes yet.

Good. Jack could "date" Ev by taking her out to the

potluck, the perfect excuse, and find out what she had learned so far. His mind had it all worked out, but his head nodded to Mrs. Hyde ("Oh, call me Thelma, please!"), and his feet marched directly over to Marlette. His mind insisted this was not a good idea. His feet paid no attention.

Neither did his mouth. He grinned at the Aussie lass, and her grump dissolved into a bright smile. "Miss Marlette, the time-honored traditional way people in the Park Service celebrate any event is a potluck supper. I realize this is very short notice, and I apologize, but if you can knock off right now, I'd love to take you along out to just such a traditional social event. To get there in time, we have to leave now."

The luminous blue eyes studied his face for only a moment. "Edith? I'll be back at the motel . . ." She dropped her voice to its usual sultry, silky softness. "When?"

"Ten thirty, eleven."

The silken voice rose twenty decibels. "Late tonight."

Edith's voice behind Jack called, "I might need you!"

In fact, Jack was starting to feel really itchy again.

Marlette bubbled, "But then, Edith, you might not." She shrugged her blanket off her shoulders and left it where it dropped on the walkway.

Jack didn't bother to pick it up either. "Maxx, come on."

As he fell in behind Marlette, he happened to glance back at Ev. Her furious glare turned his itch into a torrid rash. OK, so technically he ought to take her. To work, to work. But you can't work all twenty-four hours of the day, so why should she act so angry? Women. Honestly.

"Whoa." At the shore end of the walkway he grabbed Marlette's elbow and drew her to a halt. "One of these lovely yachts is ours."

"We're going out in a boat?"

"To an island called Great Cranberry." His voice faltered as he read numbers, trying to match the tag on the key ring. *Aha.* "This green and white runabout right here."

63

He strode out across her foredeck and hopped down into the cockpit. "Welcome aboard the *Queen Mary.*"

Marlette giggled. "So long as it isn't the *Titanic.* If we must leave now, I'll not bother going back to the motel to change. It's too far. This that I'm wearing will just have to do." She gestured at her flimsy, off-white cotton jumpsuit, tied with a brilliant pink sash.

Maxx shoved past her and bounded eagerly onto the boat—and froze. His black puss assumed a shocked "What am I doing here?" look. The boat bobbed a couple times from the weight of his arrival. He weighed about as much as Marlette.

"Come on, Maxx. Come."

Against his better judgment, the dog stepped forward, his claws slipping and sliding on the fiberglass. He jumped down into the cockpit, but he didn't look at all as if he wanted to be here.

A plywood chest built in near the stern held flotation devices, flares, and that kind of thing. The vessel bobbed as Marlette came aboard. Jack handed her a life vest and donned one himself.

"Put this on, and then you can wear my coat over it. It'll get pretty breezy out there." He dropped his jacket at her feet.

"I'm beginning to feel guilty, always taking your coat."

"Don't think a thing about it." He got the big, heavy Johnson going on the third try and cast off the line. Cautiously he backed it out, but he still clunked into two other boats. He was probably going to make a royal fool of himself. He hadn't handled a boat in years, ever since Buffalo National River. And those were jonboats, not these sea-going vessels.

Edith came barreling up the catwalk with scowling Clyde at her heels. She skidded to a halt where they had been tied up moments before. "Marlette! Go change out of that! You know the rules!" She punctuated her frustration

64

with some choice words you just don't often hear at family picnics.

Airily, Marlette waved a hand. "Too little time, Edith. I'll try not to stain it with tomato sauce." *Oyl troy nawt to styne it with tu-mahto sawrss.*

Should he return to shore? Jack slowly and dramatically looked at his watch, smiled and waved to Clyde, and gunned it. "Will you pull in the bumpers, please?" Once past Edith, he eased the boat along the waterway and out into the harbor.

Marlette cackled gleefully as she hauled the last of the bumpers inboard. She glowed. "This is ripping good fun!"

And ripping good fun it was indeed. As they droned out into channel, a heady exhilaration washed through Jack. Part of it was the pure pleasure of cruising around the quiet waters in this little boat. Another part, possibly the larger part, was this lady perching herself on the vinyl seat beside his.

Jack managed to make it out to Great Cranberry without running aground on Sutton Island or little Bear Island, which were somewhat in the way. Neither did he bump into any nun buoys or get run over by some lobster boat, though the opportunities presented themselves.

He tied up close beside two other boats at the municipal dock and ordered Maxx to stay. The mutt didn't take at all well to being left behind.

Jack didn't have to ask where the potluck was. The interisland ferry had just arrived, spilling passengers with covered dishes and canvas tote bags onto the wharf. He simply scooped up his groceries and fell in with the crowd.

Marlette walked so close to his side that she brushed his arm with every step. "I didn't see a single water-skier as we came over. Don't Americans water-ski?"

"I doubt it, here. Water's too cold." They were walking upslope into a village tucked among a multitude of trees.

"Do you?"

"I did a little, at Buffalo. Buffalo National River. Mostly, though, we policed all the other skiers." He grinned at the memory. "There were these two guys, very obviously from the big city, with a rental boat and skis. One of them is standing on the end of the float pier with his feet in the skis. He's holding the towrope. And out in the boat, his buddy is revving the motor, ready to peel out.

"The guy on the boat yells, 'Is you ready, Ski King?'

"And the guy ashore yells, 'I is ready, Boat King!' And I'm running down the length of the pier waving my arms and hollering, 'Don't do it! Don't do it!'"

Her celestial blue eyes went wide. "Did they do it?"

"They did it. Fortunately, Ski King had a lousy grip. It jerked him off balance, and he sort of belly-flopped."

Her laughter made the darkening evening shine.

Just ahead of them, a family's evening shone not so bright. The wife, with a frown on her face, was chewing on her husband in angry undertones. Superthin, in tight blue jeans and a scoop-neck top, she looked like someone on network TV.

The husband wore more casual clothes, paint-spattered jeans, a plaid flannel shirt, and a green felt crusher hat. He looked very Maine woodsy, except for a can of beer stuffed in each hip pocket. He would shake his head and snap back just as belligerently. If those three grade-school-aged kids, two boys and a hyperactive girl, were theirs, no wonder they were cranky. Noisy, nasty, and undisciplined, all three were little Darth Vaders.

When the woman crabbed, "Alan, cut it out. You're making a fool of yourself again," Jack's ears pricked up. So this was probably Alan Messier, the ranger who had been overseeing Sitting Pretty in the park and who might possibly have been engaged in an illicit affair with the murdered girl.

He glanced at Marlette and knew his guess was right. She quite obviously recognized the man. You could tell by the way her eyes went everywhere else, the way she noticed everything except him. Did she, in fact, realize he was there? Of course. She was observant enough to read the "Kansas" on Jack's license plate. She had surely seen Messier, a known face among a slew of strangers.

What would a girl normally do in this situation—assiduously ignore the only other person she knew here or yoo hoo at him? *Hi, Alan! It's me.* She did not acknowledge that he existed anywhere on the face of this planet. The puzzle and its ramifications kept Jack's mind preoccupied for two blocks.

They arrived at a grange hall sheathed in dark-stained wood shingles, a homey place despite its barn size. Inside, it contained a single huge room with a little kitchen at one end and a low stage at the other. Jack headed straight to the food tables forming a solid line along the far wall. Already they were laden with casseroles both hot and cold, bowls of salad, a twenty-cup coffeemaker, and a dozen intriguing desserts.

With lovely Marlette at his side, he broke into his package of sporks for something to stir with. He mixed the onion soup and sour cream in his smaller bowl for the dip. Caught up instantly in the spirit of the moment, Marlette opened the chip bags and filled the larger bowl.

He scanned the sea of institutional dining tables and pointed. "That table over there with the vase of flowers is where Vern will sit. How about these two places here for us? You'll be able to see and hear everything going on."

"That's fine," she said, with an air that suggested any seat in the hall would do. He set out two paper plates and two sporks, to claim these two places and these uncomfortable steel folding chairs as theirs. In his haste he had neglected to buy napkins. Phooie. Lack of napkins damaged his air of false elegance. He stashed the grocery bag under the table, and they were ready to meet the world.

They just about did too. Over the next five minutes

Jack introduced Marlette to John Grayson, Stella Smith, and the guests of honor, Vern Bondi and his round, jolly wife. With perverse satisfaction he introduced the golden Marlette to the leaden Warren Sarnoff. In turn, he was introduced to about seventy-five people more than he could possibly remember. As always, Jack had familiarized himself beforehand with the names that went to the various park positions, but this was too big an ocean of faces to connect successfully to all of them.

Marlette didn't bother with names. But then, she didn't have to. A simple, eloquent, one-size-fits-all "Fair go, luv!" did anything she wanted it to. Anything at all.

In fact, Marlette was fitting in splendidly. She would be off on her own, talking energetically with some man, and then she would be hard by Jack's elbow. Then she'd be off somewhere else and suddenly back beside him again. At first her manner, while not reserved, seemed put on. An artifice. Then she loosened up and became the Melbourne city girl cosmopolitan enough to fit naturally into as rural a setting as you can get, a remote isle off the rugged Maine coast. She'd be a perfect Park Service partner, ready for anything.

Now what was he feeling? Unabashed pride. He had the loveliest woman in the county right here at his side, hanging on his arm, looking gorgeous, and she was his date. Nothing makes a man feel better than to cop the best, flashiest, most appealing woman in the place.

A loud child's voice by the door yelled something about a dog. *We all know what dog he's talking about, don't we?* Jack grimaced and headed for the door. He had told the stupid mutt to stay in the boat and now . . .

A hand gripped his arm and dragged him to a halt.

Jack wheeled.

Alan Messier. Maybe thirty, the guy loomed about as tall as Jack and a lot heftier. His speech didn't slur, but neither was it crisp. His blood alcohol level had to be topping point-oh-five. At the moment, Marlette was in her away mode.

Messier waved a hand in her general direction. "No. Believe me. No. You don't want to get messed up with that."

Jack extended his paw for a handshake. "Jack Prester, out of the Washington office."

The fellow stared at him a long, bleary moment. "I know. I heard you want to talk to me. John called this afternoon, said you wanted to talk to me. Don't get mixed up in that outfit, hear? That's all I got to say. Don't. Bad mistake."

"In what way?"

"Just listen to me. Don't."

"Be more specific. Why not?" Jack glanced over toward the door. Those two obnoxious little boys, ostensibly Messier's kids, had literally ushered old Maxx inside. One of them had Maxx's neck in a hammerlock Hulk Hogan would use on the Mad Mountain. The other was patting him with a couple G's of force.

Maxx was very good with good kids, infinitely patient and paternal. But his tolerance for bozos ran out in a hurry. He ducked and shook his massive head loose from the wrestler. Here he came, jogging across the room pretending he'd been called. You had to hand it to him—he was pretty good at picking Jack out of a crowd.

"Listen, Alan. I want to talk to you, yes. But first I'm going to have to bounce Maxx there, the jerk. I'll be back shortly."

Marlette had wandered over to the chips and dip. Someone near the food table laughed. Others joined. The modest laughter turned into gales of laughter. Marlette screamed. Instantly she disappeared, buried in a huge clump of protective macho types.

Jack shoved his way through the milling potluckers toward Marlette and discovered the source of the laughter.

A raccoon came waddling straight down the length of the food table, rolling along at that surprisingly swift raccoon gait that looks as if it's too slow to catch slugs. Jack headed for Marlette—after all, she was his date—as she broke out of the clump.

She latched onto Jack's arm in a death grip. "What is it?" Her blue eyes were big and bright enough to attract night-flying insects.

"Just a raccoon. Picture a brushtail possum with an attitude."

"What is it doing here?"

"Probably just trying to sample the abundant life. The spread of food here is a raccoon's idea of seventh heaven."

"How did it get here?"

"Any number of ways—a broken window, a door, the service entrance, an attic vent. Not to worry. Raccoons are a normal and necessary part of your national park experience." He would not mention that, lovable as they might look, they were absolutely vicious when cornered.

The two swarthy maintenance types who had hovered closest to Marlette said something about getting a rope to catch it. Just about everyone knew about the coon now.

And then Maxx found out.

Even as Jack's mind was exploring the ugly ramifications of the equation MAXX + RACCOON = !!, he was screaming, "Sit, Maxx! Sit!"

Maxx sat. For a nanosecond or two. Then the mutt's thin veneer of civilization buckled, and he reverted.

Snarling and barking, Maxx leaped up on the table and made a wild, snapping lunge for the coon. The coon squirmed down to a crouch, hissing, and feinted with its mouthful of very sharp teeth. Maxx parried. They were knocking food dishes in all directions. Glass crashed, and a dozen human voices yelled.

The coon made a break, ran two steps, and swung

around into a defensive crouch again. Maxx dived for its throat. The coon's strong little hands grabbed Maxx's loose neck skin, and the two of them locked in serious combat, turning and tumbling, snarling and hissing. Casseroles flew. A salad bowl skidded across the floor upside down.

Jack grabbed for Maxx, missed, grabbed again. Somebody's teeth sank into his arm. He got two big handfuls of Maxx's silky hide and pulled backwards with his full weight. He kept backing up, yanking Maxx off the table. The weight nearly ripped the dog out of his hands. He began turning in place, twirling, swinging Maxx in a swift circle. The dog yelped in pain. Good old angular momentum took over, and the raccoon went sailing. Jack dropped to the floor, still gripping Maxx, and flung himself on top of the excited dog.

"Stay! Down!" He clung to his dog, his full body weight across Maxx's back to hold him down. Maxx yelped and squirmed and struggled. Slick with blood, chili beans, and potato salad, Maxx was as hard to hold as a greased pig. "You bite me, you worthless mutt, and I'll personally feed you to that coon!"

Jack heard folding chairs clunk and rattle. The sound of yelling voices moved farther and farther away toward the door. Jack could see nothing, but he assumed they were hazing the coon out the door using the metal chairs.

It was bad enough that Jack was in this park on official business. It was bad enough that he wasn't hitting it off with Sarnoff to begin with, and Sarnoff held Maxx in very low regard. It was absolutely terrible that this festive dinner was ruined. Jack abhorred waste, and any waste of food most of all.

What was *really* bad was who had witnessed this debacle.

Marlette.

6

The Dating Game

He felt like a high school kid on a date. A weary, weary, high school kid. Jack offered a hand as Marlette slid off the truck seat and out the passenger-side door. He hit the lock, closed the door, and scooped Marlette's graceful hand up in his. Casually they strolled from the east end of the parking lot toward the far side entrance of the Seaview Motel, the door closest to Marlette's room. He was in no hurry for the night to end, and that was amazing, considering how the night had gone.

Marlette giggled. "Amazing!" *A-my-zing.* "I've never had a night like this one." She snuggled against him.

"Thinking exactly that same thing myself." And he never wanted another one like it, either.

"The guest of honor's presentation after dinner: all the jokes and the gag gifts. And that absolutely silly poem they wrote about him painting windows shut and making the plumbing back up. The people who work in the park are very close. Very—" she fished about a moment for the word "—very family."

"Most parks are that way, particularly those in remote locations. A camaraderie develops. And you usually see its finest flower in the going-away party and the retirement party. Like tonight. The honoree gives goofy gifts—

just cheap doodads—that represent in-house jokes and funny memories, and gets equally goofy gifts in return. But the final words from the shop foreman, telling how much Vern will be missed—they were the real thing."

She stopped at the outer glass door. "I think what impressed me most was how everyone adjusted so quickly. After the raccoon, I mean. As if a raccoon is something natural that happens all the time. The only one butchers was that bald bloke."

"He was furious, all right."

She didn't even hear him. She warbled delightedly. "I watched a couple women straightening up the table, and by the time they had that done, the shop foreman was coming in with buckets of potato salad and things from the restaurant down by the wharf to make up for what was spoiled. There wasn't that much food ruined, actually. Not as much as you'd think. And everyone seemed in jolly good spirits—they all thought it a lark."

Not Warren Sarnoff, Marlette. Not Warren Sarnoff.

She bubbled on. "And the ride back across the water, with the lights and the reflections . . . so beautiful, and peaceful. The perfect end. It was a bonzer do, all around!"

"Glad you enjoyed it." He escorted her inside the glass doors and started up the end staircase.

"Jack? That Vern, the man who's transferring, said all he really expected from life was a mild winter, good beer, and an occasional Superbowl. Tucson had all those. What do you want out of life? What are you working for?"

Jack had to think about that. "They're two different things, wanting and working. I have ample of everything I need. I've got the world's greatest job, and I love it. Everything else I want in life I have, except a family. And I haven't been working on the family aspect. Guess I don't want it badly enough yet."

"You have everything?"

"Abundantly. You see, I'm one of those people who takes the Bible at face value. When God says something in

73

Scripture, that's what He means, in plain language. Jesus promised His people eternal life and life abundantly. I'm His, and He's given me exactly what He promised."

"But you said you want a family, and you don't have that."

"I didn't say 'everything I *want*.' Everything I *need* and a lot of surprises, most of them happy. The kind of life most men would love to lead. That's abundance. What about you? You've traveled fifteen thousand miles to find something. What do *you* want?"

"Plenty! I guess 'abundance' is the word. I want lots of everything. Lashings! This job with Edith Cray is a stepping-stone. America is where the dollars are and foreign models are popular now, and I'm the right age at the right time. I'm going to have it all, Jack!" Her blue eyes sparkled.

"'All' includes God."

"I don't have time. I'm delighted you found your religion—oh, I saw you praying over your food tonight, right enough—but that's not for me. At least not yet."

How should he counter that? Within an hour of midnight is not exactly a time to defend the faith. Paul told Timothy "in season and out of season," but Paul, Jack assumed, was talking about when Timothy was sharp enough to mount a good defense. Jack was as sharp as a drenched paper towel right now.

On the other hand, now was a good time to catch her, when she was tired and less guarded. "I have one last question, then. The whole evening, you never said word number one to Alan Messier. Why?"

She shrugged, suddenly cautious. "Just keeping out of the rain. His missus, you know."

"I smell a bit of berley, Marlette. You were talking to a score of men and their wives. Why not him?"

"You saw him. He was shickered."

"Yeah, he was drunk, but not too far gone to say hello. Earlier you were telling me what a good sort he is." He

74

studied her face, trying to read those ethereal eyes without getting lost in them. "You're afraid of him."

"Hardly, if I don't speak to him."

"Come on, Marlette. Give me the drum."

She paused, hesitated. "The story is, Edith took Ronnie back to the motel that noon."

"Right, and you other three went clamming."

"We did that all right, but it wasn't Edith took Ronnie off. It was Alan."

"Did you actually see him, or is this hearsay—something you only heard?"

"That green felt hat he wears—what's it called?"

"A crusher."

"He was wearing it when he came by. They had something of a row—ugly words, but not loud enough to hear—and he walked off."

"In the written reports, you said Veronica asked Edith to take her back to the motel on her way to the airport. Edith was sending her wardrobe mistress home."

"She did. Alan left, and she did. Ronnie went to the car with Edith. But I saw her with *him,* not Edith, near the bridge as the rest of us were leaving. I know it was him. The hat."

"The cement bridge onto the island." Jack tried to do some fast sorting, but his brain was too tired to reshuffle facts well. "So he, not Edith, was the last to see her alive."

Her voice was that of a small child. "Per'aps."

"And he was intimately involved with her?"

"I'm sure of that. His wife is a fair cow, I trust you noticed." She handed him her room key.

"She seemed perpetually out of sorts, if that's what you mean."

"Alan was considering giving his cheese and kisses the boot."

"Divorcing her?"

"I assume so. And Ronnie was done with Mike Kovik,

75

but he wasn't done with her, so she wanted someone strong. Someone who can stand up to Mike when he gets a snout on." She straightened and brightened as he opened her door. "You said in the truck you wouldn't be coming in, but the offer's still open. I hate to see the evening end so soon."

He smiled and shook his head. Since this was a date, excluding the occasional interrogation he kept slipping into, he ought to kiss her good night. On the other hand, she was still a suspect, though at this hour he simply couldn't imagine why. So he compromised by kissing the back of her hand.

"Good night, Marlette."

"G'night, luv." Glowing like a teenager with a brand new driver's license, she slipped inside. The door clicked shut.

Wearied beyond belief, he strolled past Lauren's kitchenette room, past Ev's small single, toward his own. He could just picture the subject of a nightmare tonight: potato salad.

"Jack?!" Ev's voice sounded exactly like his mom's used to when he sneaked in past curfew.

He twisted to face the voice behind him. "Yes, Mother?"

She stood in her open doorway, her arms crossed tightly in front of her, and she was not a happy camper. "Have a good time?"

"I'm sure you'll hear all about it tomorrow. Trust me." He walked back to her. "How'd it go today?"

"Buy me a drink." It was not a request. She closed the door behind her and headed down the hallway. Meekly he followed. The last thing he wanted to do tonight was go out on another date. Actually the last thing would be to stick pins under his fingernails and then play a guitar, but this was a close next-to-the-last.

She churned down the end staircase and pushed out the glass door into the night. She headed unerringly for his truck, which told him that she had been watching for him to come in and saw where he parked.

Apparently Ev did not know that on cold nights on the road like this, with no kenneling at a motel, Maxx slept in the truck cab. Further, she obviously had no idea how very doggy a truck cab smelled after Maxx spent a night in it. She found out.

Jack sent Maxx to his cage in back, but she rode with her nose out of joint, figuratively and literally, all the way down the road.

It was past eleven. Nothing was open between Route 3 and Northeast Harbor whence he had just come, so he tried east into Bar Harbor. He saw the lights of a lounge in a hotel at this end of town. He pulled in.

The only patrons in the place, a couple in the far corner, were talking nose to nose in near whispers.

The bartender caught Jack's eye. "We close in forty-five minutes."

"I know the feeling. I closed at nine-thirty myself." He ushered Ev to a booth and slid in across from her. He waited until the cocktail waitress, a brassy little number with frizzed hair and short shorts, delivered their order, his orange juice and her port wine. "So how's it going in the world of glamour and haute couture?"

She snorted. "That boy who holds the reflector knows an agent in New York who handles the Avon catalog models, and if I go out with him he'll introduce me. That photographer, Arturo, promises that he'll flatter me with the camera if I go out with him, and if I don't he'll take pictures that make me look forty years old. Clyde just looks at me. Watches me. It's creepy. And a local kid named Timmy wearing clothes that were the latest thing two years ago told me I didn't want to spend my life in this dreary little town and we should go to New York together."

"You're cutting quite a swath."

She rolled her huge doe eyes ceilingward. It was an offhand gesture, but her face was tight, worried.

77

"Want me to pull you off this? Do you want to go home?"

She opened her mouth and closed it. She shook her head. "Yes, I want to go home. But I won't. I don't think I'm in any danger, if you know what I mean. Timmy's nothing, of course. I told him he was the one stuck in this town—I already lived in a big city, and he could stay stuck as far as I'm concerned. I told the photographer he didn't dare—it's his reputation too—and the kid who handles the reflector—"

"What's his name?"

"Roger Ellis. No. Ellison. Anyway, Roger. I didn't tell him anything. I just sort of ignore him."

"Incidentally, you're not getting proposition number thirty-seven, or whatever number you're up to already, from me. But I should kiss you at the door tonight, since we're dating. Just a little advance warning."

She stared at him as if he had just put a tablespoon of Tabasco sauce on her breakfast cereal. "I see. Every man in Sitting Pretty finds me desirable, but you kiss me because it's business."

"They find you desirable not only because you are beautiful but because you are obviously a newcomer in this game. You likely don't know the ropes yet, so you're therefore probably vulnerable to any old line they can spin. Most men—not just the Neanderthals at Sitting Pretty —would take a shot like that, especially since there's nothing to lose and a whole, whole lot to gain."

She studied him awhile in silence, sipping her port, and sighed. "When I first got here I really looked forward to playing spy. And it's fun. I admit it. Eavesdropping. Picking up gossip. One thing about what you just said. Edith is worried that I'll get serious with Arturo, and Harry will hear about it."

"Sitting Pretty's owner, you mean."

She nodded. "That fellow in Hollywood. Edith thinks that since Harry set me up here, I'm his girlfriend, and if he

78

finds out Arturo is—uh—interested in me, he'll fire Arturo. Or refuse to use him. Jealous, you know?"

"And she has a special interest in Arturo?"

"Very special. She pampers him. Favors him. She's not bossy with him the way she is with everyone else. Athalia says Mike Kovik used to be her pet. When she dropped him, he took up with Lauren. Then he dropped Lauren, and Ronnie—Veronica Wayne—took him up. It's a whole hideous mess."

"As I heard it, Ronnie insisted that Edith use him. I assume by that that Edith would not have otherwise."

Ev pondered the comment a moment and nodded. "That sounds right. Edith is really giving him a bad time now that Ronnie's gone. Always finding fault, swearing at him, giving him the less desirable jobs. Apparently Ronnie worked for Edith longer than anyone else in Sitting Pretty except Clyde. Clyde's been with Edith from the start. And Ronnie was getting fed up with it. I don't know why she didn't just quit and work for someone else. Lauren says she could have had a good job anywhere she wanted."

"Do any of these girls have an agent?"

"I don't think so. But they have to, don't they?"

"I don't know. I'll ask. What do they say about you?"

Her cheeks colored, and the pink ran down her neck. Her huge dark eyes and short Amelia Earhart hair made her look young and innocent anyway, but that blush was the topper.

Jack pressed it. "Come on. I know they talk about you. They have to. You're the outsider."

"I heard Marlette and Lauren on the other side of the van. They agree I'm such a dummy at this business it's obvious I never modeled. Therefore I must be that Harry's favorite at the moment, or I wouldn't have gotten this job. Everyone is so sure I'm in a hot romance with this Harry, Jack, and I never met him. I don't even know his last name."

"Neither do I. I have it written down in Hal's notes somewhere."

The dark Jersey-cow-sized eyes studied the tabletop a few long moments. "Jack? Hal said when I took this assignment that it was unusual and we would both be winging it pretty much."

"It's been that. Unusual, I mean. And you've been doing just great winging it."

"Hal said I should do anything the circumstances required. Anything." The eyes rose to met his. "Does that mean I have to—uh—be receptive to—uh—you know . . ."

"Absolutely not! I'm sure Hal wouldn't mean that." Jack thought a moment. "Even if he did, absolutely not. You draw the line wherever you feel comfortable and phooey on Hal."

She bobbed her head suddenly and straightened. "I was pretty sure that's what you'd say. You're very moral. And religious. If Hal suggests anything different, I'll just say you're in charge. Is that all right?"

"Fine, yes. Do." He got another thought. "Besides, if the motives in this case include jealousy, you could be targeted. No. You want to stay clear out of it."

"Good." She drew a deep breath. "I'm really tired. That cold just eats right into you and saps you. That's all I needed to know—how far I had to go." She started to slide out, leaving her port glass half full.

Jack drained his orange juice, scooted out, and followed her toward the door. "Want me to stick around closer? Protection?"

"No." She pushed out the door into the cold night. "No, I'm not worried that way. I just wanted to make sure I didn't have to be nice to Arturo. Or Kovik, for that matter. He has such a hideous temper. Scary."

"How about Clyde?"

Maxx barked enthusiastically as they approached, waking the whole north end of the island.

Jack shushed him, but it did no good.

"Clyde doesn't seem to be interested in girls. At least not us girls."

"Or Edith."

"No. Not intimate."

"He's very protective."

She nodded. "Paternal. It's sort of paternal. I think it's what he gets paid to do, and he carries it to extreme a little."

"Mm." A little? Jack remembered again about getting bowled over by the buffalo. His shoulder still hurt if he drew his elbow way back. He started the motor and backed out of his parking slot. "Any indication he's interested in boys?"

She thought about that a moment, or maybe she was just so tired her brain worked in slow motion. Jack's sure did. "No. No indication of that. Nothing someone might have said or anything."

There were a lot more questions he ought to ask her and observations he ought to draw from her, but his transmission was stuck in neutral. Tomorrow he'd diligently quiz her. They drove back to the Seaview in silence.

When Ev crawled out, Jack put Maxx back in the cab and got a wet tongue in his ear for his trouble. Stupid dog. He slipped Maxx a liver-flavored treat and dragged himself up the end staircase one more time.

Ev did not hand him her room key. She obviously considered herself perfectly capable of unlocking a door. Jack couldn't decide whether he liked the old-world Australian customs better or the new liberated woman.

Strictly for purposes of appearances—they were into some serious undercover work here—he drew her into the good-night kiss he had mentioned. Much to his surprise, it lingered far longer than appearances required, a more expressive gesture than ever he had intended.

She was equally slow breaking it off. She stepped back, looked at him a moment in a way he could not read, and disappeared inside.

He heard the deadbolt click, the night chain rattle.

He did not dream about potato salad that night, or

even raccoons. He dreamed about cold, wet trees with skinny arms, reaching out to suffocate him.

* * *

Acadia National Park in Maine is, yet it isn't. It is very close to the people-packed seaboard megalopolis, yet it isn't in any way urban. Sleepy carriage trails meander through dense forest, some of it ancient and some of it newly risen from the ashes of the Great Fire in 1947.

The park is half of well-populated Mt. Desert Island, yet it isn't much damaged by development. A visitor can still stand at places on its thundering, boulder-pile shores and see no sign of human habitation. Can feel remote without being remote. Can climb its low, glacier-chiseled mountains in glorious isolation. Can prowl Sand Beach in the winter and watch seals and Oldsquaws play offshore. And will probably be alone.

Jack stood on the rocky shore in misty morning light. The dark forest was hard at his back, and the restless sea sloshed among the boulders before him.

He felt enclosed, but Maxx reveled in this country. Maxx, on his long leash this morning, stuffed his cold black nose into a million crannies, investigating a bezillion new aromas. Moist air carries and maintains odors far longer than does dry air—Maxx had days' and days' worth of smells to sort out.

The air felt clammy cool, the sort of air Jack expected on the Maine coast. He picked out at least three different kinds of bird chirps in the trees behind him, but except for juncos he couldn't identify them by ear.

Down on the shore, an abandoned jetty extended fifty feet beyond the tide line. Mosses and lichens picturesquely splashed big patches on its grayed timbers. At its far end, Arturo was photographing Ev as Kovik reloaded his camera at the table behind the reflector. Edith sounded especially crabby today. The other girls huddled in their blankets, waiting. Nothing had changed.

82

Since this shoot was inside the park boundary, John Grayson was baby-sitting. His sandy hair was completely hidden beneath the Smokey Bear flat hat. His small frame seemed custom-made for the gray-and-green ranger uniform. It fit him correctly in every dimension.

Jack felt a spate of envy. He was always tucking in and tailoring his uniform items.

Despite being hidden behind his gold-rimmed glasses, Grayson's eyes glittered in the morning light. He leaned casually against a tree with his hands in his pockets, watching the activity on the jetty, drawing exactly the same pay he would be getting were he in his office pushing paper.

Jack paused beside him. Maxx bounded over to Grayson and shoved his head up against the man's leg, sniffing and licking in one fell swoop. Grayson kept his hands in his pockets. No petting, no friendship. Maxx turned an icy shoulder to the law enforcement specialist and stuffed his nose under a bush.

Jack nodded toward the Atlantic Ocean in general. "Quiet morning. Looks like the weather is breaking for the better. Or am I reading coastal influences wrongly?"

"I'd say they might get some rain this afternoon." Grayson smiled. "So we'll see who's right. It's a crapshoot." He nodded toward the water. "The Italian and the boss lady. They're an item?"

"According to Marlette." He would not mention Ev as a source of information. She was the new girl on the block. She would not logically know much, and Jack could not discount anyone as a possible suspect. Not even Grayson.

Grayson nodded. "You're single, right?"

"Yeah." Why mention he was widowed? It was in his dossier.

"That's why they assigned you to this, I'll bet. So you can date lithe young models in order to get all kinds of information. See, I can't do that. I'm thoroughly married."

Jack nodded. He wasn't about to take that bait. "And for this I get paid. An abundant life I lead." He walked down onto the jetty and felt it creak beneath his feet. Maxx sniffed at a piling so intently Jack had to pause. Impatient, he yanked on the leash. Maxx jogged forward to the next piling.

Jack grinned a good morning to Marlette, all wrapped in her blanket.

She responded with a smoldering glare that caught him completely by surprise.

Nonplussed, he didn't know what to say or do, so he said and did nothing.

Ev was modeling a lovely red dress and big white hat, sort of the kind Little Bo Peep would wear. As much as Ev complained about having to pretend she was a model, she was a natural for the work. Arturo told her what to do, and she did it. She was sashaying now. That was probably not the term, but that's what Jack would call it. She swooped and swirled her long skirt, smiling brightly as she walked toward the photographer. The camera clicked rapidly.

Ev completed her sashay and did another. She beamed at the camera.

Finally Edith called a halt, ragged her about some fancied slight, and beckoned Marlette forward.

Marlette stood up, letting the blanket slide off her shoulders. She shot Jack one last dirty look and stepped out in front of the camera. Ev looked good, but Marlette looked world class. Jack would have thought a pretty girl is a pretty girl, a model is a model. Not so. He could see the difference between the experienced pro and the tyro.

Marlette, too, sashayed toward the camera, but she moved faster through some parts of the stride than others. She did a slow turn that was, nonetheless, fast enough to make her skirts and her long hair flow out to the side. She radiated. She glowed. If she were Cinderella, she wouldn't need a fairy godmother. On her, a gunnysack would have looked like a ball gown.

84

Clyde was watching Jack approach as a lion would watch a crippled lamb. Edith glanced at him and turned away.

He paused behind the reflector.

Ev did not sit down in the chair Marlette vacated nor did she wrap up in a blanket. She came striding purposefully right toward Jack. She must know something important. Her face hardened as she approached. Jack backed up five steps as she came, so they would not be in easy earshot of anyone.

Her voice hissed like an angry cat. "I talked to Hal early this morning. Do you know what he said?" Her demeanor was not friendly.

"What'd he say?" But Jack knew.

"This idea of dragging me into this was not his idea. It was yours!" She was rasping in an excited stage whisper.

Jack glanced beyond her to see if any of the party was picking this up. "Well, I may have mentioned something about—"

"You begged him to bring me in! And you knew I would be freezing my teeth! You knew! And getting sexually harassed! And wet and cold and . . ." At an apparent loss for words, she called him a name.

It startled him that so demure a mild-mannered accountant would even know that word. He raised both hands, a gesture of conciliation. "OK, so I might have suggested you. In fact, I may have even used the word *ideal.* I don't remember exactly. But name-calling isn't going to help us—"

She flung at him an ugly epithet—another phrase he wouldn't have guessed she knew—and planted her delicate, feminine hands suddenly, forcefully, in his chest. She shoved hard.

He lurched backwards awkwardly. He flailed his arms wildly, trying to regain his balance, but the attempt was away too late. His center of gravity already hung suspended out over the water. He dropped like an anchor.

85

The cold water stabbed through his pants and jacket and pierced to his shocked skin. It drenched his nose and mouth and ears and eyes. It turned out the lights. He struggled in the frigid water and with a mighty kick forced his head above the surface. Never in his life—absolutely never —had he ever gotten so deeply and totally chilled so fast.

She was gone. Staring down at him, Maxx, the disrespectful mutt, curled his lip and leered.

Grayson's face appeared. He dropped to one knee and peered smugly, casually, over the side. "And I wouldn't want to be single for the whole world."

7

Loons

Wh4at was going on here? It almost looked like a fire.

In the big open room beyond the visitor center front desk, Vernon Bondi in his gray maintenance uniform shirt and green jeans hovered over an old clunker of a Xerox machine. He held a canister fire extinguisher at ready, the white cone nozzle pointed at the copier.

Stella Smith was feeding sheets into the machine faster than it could copy them. Its brilliant white bar light skated nervously back and forth beneath the lid.

Jack had simply stopped by the visitor center office for a sheriff's report. He wasn't really in the mood to fight a structure fire. He stepped around the waist-high desk and through the double door into the back room. He moved in closer to Stella's shoulder and watched.

He looked at Vernon. "I hesitate to ask what's going on."

Stella kept stuffing the paper through. "One of Vern's last acts before he leaves. This copier has been a pain in the patoot for years. It burns the edges of the copy paper. It doesn't make copies, it makes treasure maps. Then it breaks down. A week after you call the company, they send a man out from Bangor to fix it. It breaks down a day later, and it's another week before he comes—"

"Ever think of getting a new one with year-end money?"

"What year-end money? It's crazy. With all we've spent on repairs for this miserable thing, we could've bought three new ones."

There was a mischievous twinkle in Vern's eye, the same naughty look Jack saw in Maxx every so often. "So this time they're going to *have* to buy a new one."

Stella grinned. "It's down for good if it gets filled up with fire extinguisher powder." She finished the thick deck of papers to be copied. It spit the last of its assignment out into the tray, and she stood erect. "The miserable beast! Now, when we want it to, it won't do it!"

"Do what?" Jack asked. "Catch fire?"

"Get a burned-rubber smell, like something electrical. And then a lot of smoke. And then it won't light up again until that guy comes out and replaces something. So when the smoke appeared, we were going to nail it."

Jack wagged his head. "Boy, I'm sure sorry you guys don't have a structure fire to put out. That's really tough."

Stella smirked. "Oh, all right. Make fun. It was an idea." She brushed her hands off on her hip pockets. "What can I do for you?"

"A sheriff's deputy called me about six this morning. Said he'd drop some reports by here."

Vern wandered off, probably to hang up his fire extinguisher, and Stella led the way out to the lobby. "Not here yet. Little early, wasn't it?" She perched on her stool behind the counter.

"I was up. I try to read the Bible every morning. That's about the only time of day I can just sit down and do it." Jack leaned both elbows on the rangers' side of the counter.

She smiled brightly. "Let me be the first to invite you to our church. First Baptist in Bar Harbor, 9:30 and 11:00, informal worship and study at 6:00 P.M., Bible study Wednesdays at 7:00. We're in Ephesians." Her smile fled. "From your manner and all, I knew you were a Christian. That's why it surprises me that you'd escort that model, that Australian girl."

"That was more business than pleasure." *Liar, liar, pants on fire!* "We didn't even kiss good night." *Semi-liar.*

Stella frowned as she wagged her head. "Very jealous girl. Now there's a jealousy that's excusable when a relationship is new. For instance, the two people are still uncertain about their position with each other. But hers is an ugly kind of jealousy."

"You're gossiping, Stella. It doesn't become you."

"No, I'm not. I'm telling you something you should know. Didn't you notice? Every single time you started talking to another woman, particularly an unmarried one, such as Marie Stover for example, she came running over and inserted herself. Stuck herself into the conversation. Hanging on your arm. Drawing you away. Then you'd be in a group, or with men, and she'd go off flirting behind your back. Over and over."

He shook his head. "No, I didn't notice."

"That's a nice jacket. My daughter has a nylon parka something like it, but hers is blue, not green. New?"

"Just got it this morning." Jack was not about to mention that his denim and sheepskin coat was dripping puddles on the floor in his motel bathroom. Or why.

She leaned forward and studied him closely. "Your hair looks wet."

"Went swimming this morning. Think nothing of it."

She was going to pursue the topic further—he could tell, and he desperately wished she wouldn't—but Sarnoff came waddling out the hall door labeled *Employees Only.*

He smiled grimly. "Oh, good. There you are. Saves Stella the trouble of finding you." On the counter in front of Jack he plunked down three stapled pages of fine print. "Information on rabies. You're required to read and understand it."

"Rabies." Jack stood erect and picked it up. Yep—

three sheets. Yep—fine print. Yep—Hancock County Health Department.

"You were bitten in that melee last night. If we can't trap the raccoon, you'll have to take the shots."

"Wasn't the raccoon that bit me. It was my own stupid dog. And his immunizations are current."

"You don't know that."

"Sure I do." Jack shoved his sleeve up and showed Sarnoff his owie. "Look at the pattern of tooth marks. Too wide for a raccoon."

"Not good enough. I already set the wheels in motion. It's for your own good."

"Right." And that anger that Jack had successfully banked yesterday, with difficulty, flared up anew. He was just about sure, if he asked anyone on Great Cranberry, that no one was bothering to try to catch the raccoon.

The outside doors flew open, and in swaggered the long arm of the law.

"Swaggered" was the only way to describe the man's proud, swinging strut. A Hancock County sheriff's deputy of immense proportions, height as well as width, he wore the full class A regalia, from hat to shiny motorcycle boots. Every kind of gadget under the sun hung off his tool belt— gun, jiffy-loader, key case, extra rounds, cuff case, mace, baton, flashlight, radio. They ought to make a black leather basket-weave-stamped lunchbox to hang on a belt. He'd have one.

He planted himself in front of the counter and scowled at Sarnoff. "Something's hot."

"Or," Sarnoff retorted, "maybe somebody just thinks he's hot."

The come-back delighted Jack. He would not have thought Sarnoff had it in him.

Sarnoff told Stella he was unavailable and, with a cursory nod toward the Hero of Law Enforcement, waddled back to his inner sanctum.

Jack read his name tag. "Deputy Patterson. You called

earlier." He was itching again. And it wasn't even flea season.

The deputy studied Jack. "You're John Prester?"

"*Doctor* Prester. Yes."

The deputy dropped a thin little manila folder on the desk in front of him. "Material relevant to the Wayne murder."

Jack sniffed. "The Health Department puts out more material than that just on rabies."

"It's everything we can release pending further investigation." He stood tall and imposing. "My sergeant is in charge of this case. He expected you to check in with him when you arrived."

Diplomacy. "He's a busy man, I'm sure. Tell him, please, I made the unilateral decision that it would be the wisest use of his time and mine if I sat down with him after I found useful information, rather than before. Coming into this cold, I've been having to play catch-up, and therefore I'd be useless to him."

Turf wars. How he hated them. They were the reason Jack had worked so desperately to get out of the Washington office. He tapped the nearly empty folder. "And what can we do for you to further your investigation? What do you need?"

Mr. Law Enforcement apparently wasn't expecting that question. He stumbled a moment. "We've questioned the people associated with that Sitting Pretty company extensively and can't find a crack to get a wedge in. For starters, we want all your notes on interrogations to date."

"I'll check with my operatives and get back to you. Will a summary do?"

"If it's complete."

"With or without the raccoon?"

And Stella burst out laughing.

"Little in-house joke," Jack explained. "Not all that funny, really. I guess you had to be there to appreciate it." He wiggled a finger toward the Paragon's gun and mused aloud, "You know, if you guys go to nylon instead of that black leather, your tool belt there will weigh fifteen pounds instead of twenty-five."

But it was lost on the deputy, for Patterson's attention was focused, laser-sharp, on the back room. He pointed through the double doors. "Your office is on fire."

Thick white smoke rolled out from under the copier's lid and ran up the wall from the vents behind.

"It's burning!" Stella squealed. She grabbed Jack's hands as she leaped off her stool and danced him in joyous circles around the floor, laughing wildly. "It's burning! It's burning! It's burning!"

Belatedly, almost as an afterthought to the scene, Vern appeared in the back room. He emptied his extinguisher, whooshing and splurting, into the machine. Only after his canister was empty did he pull the copier's plug.

The Paragon of Enforcement just stood at the counter, and for the longest time he couldn't get his mouth to close.

* * *

For once the girls were modeling something useful: slacks, jeans, and windbreakers. They had moved up from the abandoned jetty. Now they were using Jordan Pond as a backdrop.

Jordan Pond, a small lake, was enclosed with trees on two sides, brush on one side, and a broad, sweeping lawn at the south end. With a carpet of smooth green, the neatly trimmed grass united the water's edge with the restaurant called Jordan Pond House. Jordan Pond House specialized in tea and scones, although it served full meals as well. Quite probably, tables and chairs graced the expanse of lawn in the summer, that patrons might dine *al fresco* beside the lovely lake.

This was a new Jordan Pond House, according to Vern. The old restaurant, dating from the park's beginnings, burned some years ago. The old one, he claimed, had simply oozed charm. Its interior, rustic with timbers

and peeled logs, had been wallpapered throughout in genuine paper birchbark, the kind of bark Indians once built
canoes with. As nice as this new restaurant might be, Vern
maintained, it couldn't hold a candle to the old one.

Someone must have held a candle to the old one,
Jack suggested, if it burned down.

Vern, usually the first with a joke, missed it. He
wagged his head gravely. "Electrical."

Jack parked in the Jordan Pond House lot next to
Sitting Pretty's vans. Grayson might think they would get
rain later, but right now a delicate mist drifted in picturesque fingers across the water of the pond beyond the
lawn. Lauren, Athalia, and Marlette stood around as Kovik
arranged Ev the way he wanted.

Jack watched them from the parking lot a few moments while Maxx oiled a big red fire hydrant. Ev was the
one he wanted to talk to, but she was going to be busy for
the next ten or fifteen minutes. Now what? He wandered
that way. Maybe Marlette would offer some clue as to why
she was suddenly and inexplicably mad at him. Marlette
and Kovik were preparing a shot up on the Jordan Pond
House porch.

Athalia pointed to him as he approached. "Edith!
You ought to use Maxx in a couple shots. He'd be perfect
with the windbreakers. Arturo? Isn't that right?"

Fracci turned and studied Maxx a few moments.
"She has the point. With Athalia in the black denim set."
He and Athalia seemed to be the only two people who
thought Jack was an all-right kind of guy.

"I'm not paying extra for that dog." Edith hadn't light-
ened up one ounce.

"No charge." Jack smiled at her, just to show that he
was actually an all-right kind of guy.

"Clyde? Get a model release from him." Edith nodded toward Fracci. Had it been Kovik, would she have
acquiesced?

Jack handed the leash off to Athalia. With a sparkling grin of delight, she began rubbing Maxx behind the ears. He snarfed with sinuses that echoed like the Carlsbad Caverns and, with a hearty belch, began enthusiastically licking her.

His faithful canine companion employed for the next half hour, Jack wandered over to a split-rail fence along the walkway to the restaurant, out of the way of the shoot. He leaned on the rail, both elbows. It creaked loudly. He watched the soft, translucent gray mist lacing itself across the lake on the still air, thickening here and thinning there in exquisite slow motion. Perfect background for windbreaker shots.

A dot on the water near the extreme far shore caught his eye. He watched its attitude a moment and managed to detect the tilt of its head.

"I'm sorry I laughed earlier, when Ev shoved you off the dock." Lauren's voice startled him. She had moved in beside him as softly as the mist. She huddled in her windbreaker, her hands thrust deep in the pockets and her shoulders hunched. That platinum blonde hair seemed to float in the damp air, looking longer than it was because her neck was scrunched down so tight.

"Don't feel too bad. My Loyal Companion there was laughing just as much. Maxx the Wonder Dog. You wonder why you put up with him."

She giggled. "What are you looking at so intently?"

"A loon. That bird out there." He pointed.

"How can you tell it's a loon? Why not a duck? There were ducks on the pond at a shoot yesterday. I forget what kind."

"Buffleheads."

"Oh, yeah." She was looking at him with her head tilted, as if he might have a better career in a circus sideshow.

"You can tell it's a loon by the angle and shape of its head. And you remember those ducks rode higher in the water."

"Sort of. And they had white on them. On the head."
She peered across the pond. The mist was thickening between them and the loon. The loon disappeared. "I never saw a loon before. You did, obviously."

"Launched one."

Now she really was looking at him.

He hastened on. "Loons and grebes are water birds, but they can't just take off from water. They have to get a running start—paddle across the surface with their wings flapping to get up airspeed, and then they lift off."

"Taxi? Like a 747?"

"Exactly. We had a spate of rain at Death Valley one year, about ten years ago, when the loons and grebes were migrating. They would mistake the wet roads down the valley for rivers and land on them. Then they couldn't get off."

"Couldn't paddle along. Taxi." Her expression had changed from tentative curiosity to enthusiasm.

"So what you do, you pick up this grebe by the backside—it's about the size of a cantaloupe—" he made a grebe shape with his hands, miming the action "—and you run full tilt down the road like a ninny holding the stupid grebe aloft, and when you're up to speed you throw it, like this." He mimicked a baseball player returning a hit from deep right field.

She was laughing merrily.

"It flaps its wings and takes off. You've saved another fluffy little life." He settled back against the rail. "But loons are a whole 'nother thing. They're as big as a mallard duck. Another seasonal and I in the park pickup came on a loon one day. Same problem. Mistook the road for water and landed and couldn't get up. Now Trish was about eight months' pregnant—"

"Trish was the seasonal?"

He nodded. "So gallant old me said, 'I'll do the honors.' I picked up the loon by its backside, took off down the road, heaved it . . . and *splack!* Right on its beak.

"Trish put her hand out the window, and I gave it to

her. I drove down the road twenty-five or thirty, and she held it into the wind and gave it a toss . . . and *splack!*"

"Still not fast enough."

"Still not fast enough. So Trish got in the back of the pickup with the bird so she could hold it above the cab in maximum wind. Here we are, ripping down the road at thirty-five with balloon-sized Trish in back holding this loon out. The loon lifted off her hand and flew alongside the truck, by my window. Along comes a motorcycle up the valley, and he is staring, and he is staring, and he is staring. He zips by us, and you can tell his helmet is turning a hundred and eighty degrees, staring. I don't know why he didn't run off the road."

She was laughing hard enough to threaten her mascara. "I don't know whether it's true or not, but I don't care. It's a great story."

"It's true. And the reason you hold them by the backside is their sharp, stabbing beaks. Stilettos. Grebes, but especially loons. Murderous."

The mist had shifted again. He could see that loon at the far end, drifting in lordly disdain. He watched it float in the water and the mist, wrapped in complete serenity. He yearned for serenity. He became aware Lauren was studying him. He glanced at her.

She didn't ask it accusingly or even critically. "Are you gay?"

"No. Why do you ask? Saving time again?"

She giggled appreciatively. "You haven't hit on any of us. I sort of asked around. You know, you could have any girl here. Except Edith, I mean. She's sewed up with Arthur. And maybe Ev. Ev's kind of snooty. I don't know what you see in her, trying to date her."

"She's not that bad."

"You know, Marlette was trying to lay it on us that you two were cozy, but you can never really believe anything she says—we all know that. So Athalia said, 'Knock it off, Marlette. We all know better. He's a gentleman.' And

Marlette got real huffy. She gets furious so easily anyway.

"Then Athalia told her, she said, 'I feel sorry for you. You're so messed up you don't know a decent guy when you meet one.' And I jumped in and agreed with her, and you should have seen Marlette throw a fit then! She could've shot us both on the spot. Anyway, we all noticed that you haven't moved on us." She shrugged, but it was a shrug that expected an answer.

He watched the loon. "The stock answer of a man dedicated to Jesus Christ is, God considers fornication sin. The practicing Christian sticks to God's rules of morality. No fornication, certainly no adultery."

"OK, that's the stock answer. What's yours?"

"That. It's true. God let His son die for me, and in gratitude I live the way God wants me to, at least as much as I can."

She watched him a moment. "There's more to it than that."

"In my case, maybe so—not Christian men in general." Why did she have to push the topic? But then, it wasn't any secret. The loon reversed directions and began moving this way. "My wife was Australian. Sounded like Marlette."

"Past tense."

He nodded.

"Was she pretty?"

"Very. Like Marlette. Marcia wasn't paying attention driving one day, and came up behind a guy in her lane making a left-hand turn. She swerved to miss him. But Australians drive on the left." He stopped. He couldn't trust his voice.

"Like the English do."

"She instinctively swerved left. Into a dump truck the other vehicle had been waiting for." His voice broke. Three years, and he still couldn't talk about it without a hitch. He couldn't bear to look at Lauren yet, so he watched the loon.

He raised his voice a couple decibels to strengthen it. "When we were married, and Marcia would go out of town on a trip, or I would, you put yourself on hold. You know—your wife will return, and the two of you will resume the romance then, and you don't even think about it much while she's gone." He gestured helplessly. "On hold. I guess I'm still on hold. Waiting for her. Waiting patiently till she gets back."

"But she's not coming back." Lauren's voice was soft, sympathetic.

"My head knows that. But my heart's never been on the ball. Very slow to catch on." If he thought about Marcia now he'd dissolve completely. He pointed. "See?"

Hikers on the path at the far end of the pond had made the loon too nervous to sit. It was taking off, flapping madly as it paddle-footed across the water. Leaving a stitched line of splashes behind, it finally lifted away and came flying toward them. As soon as it could clear the trees it veered off to the south and out of sight.

She glanced back at the shoot. "Athalia's still on. We can talk a few minutes yet." She turned her normal blue eyes to him. "I'm going to do it."

"Do what?"

"What's right. Be honest and forthright. You know. I'm going to blow the whistle on Edith. I want my son to grow up seeing me as a person who values what's right. It's important to be an honest person who values what's right, isn't it? I mean, you are."

"It's important if you're doing it for the right reason."

She cocked her head.

"To please God. He abhors evil even while He loves evildoers. Also, I do what's right not so I'll make Brownie points with God but because He took the first step. He's reached out to me, and that's one of the ways I can respond."

She looked confused. Then her face said that she was shining that through for the moment. "I want a truly rich life, Jack. Fame and fortune. Actually, not just money. In fact, not really money. But feeling rich and full. You can't do that if you're mean or you wink at evil. Wrongdoing. You have to be forthright. You know that.

"Anyway, Edith has gotten away with far too much too long, and Athalia agrees. Athalia thinks it won't get anywhere, but she said she'd go along with me. Marlette won't. Her green card's at stake, she says. Edith has all this clout in the trade, and she's been abusing it. I'll probably get blackballed, but I don't care. It has to be done. Look at poor Mike Kovik."

"He doesn't look too poor to me. He's working."

"Not because Edith wants him to. It was Ronnie. He'd be out of a job if it was Edith's choice. But Ronnie insisted, and now he's contracted."

"I hear he's extremely violent at times."

"Oh, my, yes! And he knows how to hit you so the mark doesn't show, not even in a French cut swimsuit. I've known a few weirdos, and I never knew one who's violent like he is."

Jack frowned at her. "He's . . . uh . . ."

"Got strange habits? Yeah. Not many know it. But it sure fried Edith when she found out. I suspect that's why she dumped him." Lauren shrugged. "But that's not any of my business. I don't care about that. It's the other things I'm filing for. And Athalia too, as a witness. You know. Backup."

"Filing a grievance."

"Union first, then the Labor Relations Board. And I don't know—maybe even the Internal Revenue Service. I hear they—"

From afar, Edith called her name.

The IRS? Jack pressed, "What specifically are you and Athalia going to tell them?"

Edith called again, more insistently.

"I'll tell you about it later. Is it true that the Jordan Pond House here has great food?"

"Not only true, they're open weekends, starting noon today. Known especially for their tea and scones, but meals too. May I take you to lunch?"

"Sure!" She beamed. "We'll talk then." And she ran off.

Jack took his time wandering back to the shoot. Kovik was done with Marlette. The beautiful lady had already changed into another jacket, and Thelma Hyde, the new wardrobe mistress, was gathering the shoulders together in back and pinning them.

Jack walked over. He nodded to Thelma. "Good morning, Celestial Lady. And you too, Marlette."

Thelma cackled and pulled half a dozen pins out of her mouth. "Hello, Mr. Prester. There. Hold your head back. How does it hang now?"

"It feels dreadful."

"It's how it looks that counts. I think that will do. Don't twist around too far." She stuffed the pins back in her mouth, gathered up the clothes that had been photographed, and trotted off.

Marlette started to turn, but Jack parked himself directly in front of her. Time to be direct. Honest and forthright. "The only reason you didn't shove me in the ocean this morning is because Evelyn beat you to it. What, pray tell, has engendered your rancor?"

The phrasing seemed to catch her for a moment. She recovered her ire quickly. "I will not be stood up, Mr. Prester."

"It's doctor—criminal psychology—not that it makes any difference. How did—"

"You dumped me off so you could take Evvie out! That is horrible! You seduce me and then drop me! You—"

"Whoa! Sed—"

"You rangers! You think you can just waltz up and take any sheila your heart fancies."

"Like Alan Messier with Veronica."

"Stone the crows! Not them. She did the seducing.

100

The poor back-blocker just wasn't sophisticated enough to see through her. He has such a good heart, and she was . . . that's different. I—"

"You are either twisting things around deliberately or looking at the situation from a warped perspective. You don't—"

"You may take me to lunch. We'll discuss it then."

"I'm already booked for lunch. How about—"

She called him a name that was even less polite in Australia than it was in America. She was glaring not at him but at Lauren.

He had to give her this much—she was quicker at figuring out his social calendar than he was.

With a toss of those gorgeous tresses, she flounced off.

Down by the lakeshore, Fracci was photographing Athalia with Maxx the Wonder Dog. Maxx reached out suddenly and gave Athalia a loud, slurpy kiss with his tongue. She laughed, her eyes squeezed shut, as she scrunched back. Fracci's camera click told Jack he had captured the moment in midlick.

Maxx resumed his regal posing. Fracci stretched an arm to the side and snapped his fingers. Thus cued, Maxx turned his huge, blocky head toward the snap. The camera clicked. Athalia gave him a big hug. The camera clicked.

The mutt was worth pudding when it came to obeying elaborate commands, such as "Sit."

But he was a born showman.

8
Changing Tide

When the day goes to pot, it goes there on a greased pole. Jack mixed those and other metaphors as he toted the runabout's empty gas can up the street to a gas station in Northeast Harbor.

It had all started when he dropped in on the fashion shoot. The whole Sitting Pretty crew, very close to mutiny, was working through lunch. To quote Edith, "We have to reshoot some outfits, as well as finish. This is Friday, and I must be in New York Monday. Must. We're all tired of this gig, but we have to finish it. As soon as we get done here, we're going to return to Northeast Harbor for the reshoot. The girls understand."

Understand indeed.

Lauren slid out of a windbreaker and into a cute T-shirt. She wagged her head. "This is ridiculous! It was Mike who messed us up, but we have to pay."

"How'd he do that?"

"I don't know. How does he do most of his mess-ups? The wrong exposure or something. I don't know. All I know is, we can't use almost a whole day's work." Her blue eyes clouded. "I'm having a terrible time finding a sitter for tomorrow. I didn't know I'd have to work Saturday, and my regular lady's going away." She described in some viciously honest and forthright terms exactly what she thought of Mike Kovik.

And then Edith was barking Lauren's name, shouting orders crossly in all directions. To work, to work.

Did Edith know yet that Lauren was about to lower the boom?

If Jack were a cartoon character, the thought balloon in the first frame of his panel would be blank. The second, though, would have a light bulb above his head. He hurried over to the near van, where Thelma was adjusting a swirly sort of skirt on Evelyn.

Jack caught Ev's eye. She appeared to be toying with the notion of ignoring him. Then she said something to Thelma and came to him.

"I'm still freezing. I hope you notice," she snarled.

"That must be why your nose and ears are blue. Hey, Lauren said something in passing about the IRS. You're a budget analyst of the first water. Can you put together a spreadsheet on Edith's operation? Just this gig. How much she'll probably rake in, how much she's spending—especially how much she's spending."

"I don't have my laptop here."

"I don't need the whole bale. Just the bottom line. Guesstimates. You're watching the operation on the inside. What costs do you see?"

"Well . . ." She looked thoughtful, which was a pleasant change from the snarl. "Without a computer . . ." She bobbed her head, and her dark Amelia Earhart hair fluffed and settled. "I'll have to wangle some hints about how much each person is earning."

"More spy work."

"I'll try."

"Hal can find out how much she's getting from Harry in Hollywood. All we need are expenses and anything she's making—kickbacks, for instance—that Harry wouldn't know about." Jack paused. "One other thing. If I'm going to supposedly sustain an interest in you, try to look pleas-

103

ant, all right? You act like I'm Jack the Ripper."

"Sure, I'll look pleasant. While you put the moves on every other woman here."

"'Put the moves on' is not the applicable term."

"It is to hear Marlette. She assumes you're her personal property, and I haven't seen anything to prove her wrong. You put yourself forward as such a terribly moral person, but that's not the story she tells. You want to two-time both of us, and I'm supposed to look pleasant."

"Look on the bright side. You're getting double pay. Hal and Edith."

She blew a raspberry. "I managed to overhear Clyde and Edith talking about that. Edith called Harry to ask how much I was supposed to be getting, and he said whatever Edith wanted to pay. So she told Clyde 'scale.' And she's deducting my motel expenses because I insisted on a private room. She intimated she would have paid motel costs if I doubled up with someone, but I can't do that if I'm going to be calling Hal and talking to you."

"How about the other girls?"

"She's doing the same to Lauren because Lauren needs the kitchenette, with the baby and all. It's a cute place—a kitchen-dining area and a separate bedroom. Still . . ."

Edith was calling again, crankily, impatiently. She scowled at Jack, at Ev, at the world.

Jack raised his voice and grinned winsomely, he hoped. "So are we friends again?"

Ev smiled brightly and gave him a peck on the cheek. "We're friends." She flounced over to Edith and Fracci, the swirly skirt and the swirly hair all swirling.

Clyde watched Jack as a heron watches a fish, just waiting for it to swim within range of the fearsome beak.

Thwarted, Jack had given up on Sitting Pretty for the moment and decided to go for Messier instead, and his day didn't get any better.

When the Rockefellers owned most of what was now

Acadia National Park, they built an elaborate system of carriage paths that wound through picturesque hills. Equally picturesque were the splendid arched stone bridges they built, enabling the paths to pass safely beneath the major vehicular roads. Closed to motorized traffic now as then, the grass-paved roads were guarded at the main points of access by gatehouses.

The word *gatehouse* suggested a postage-stamp-sized kiosk, possibly manned by an English looking guard in a tall, black bearskin hat. Not. These gatehouses were houses, constructed of the same New England fieldstone as the bridges, with casement windows, spacious rooms, and enough bedrooms to comfortably house a family. One family thus comfortably housed was the Messiers.

After striking out with Sitting Pretty, Jack stopped by Alan Messier's gatehouse and rapped at the door. No one home. Another strikeout.

He could go back and read some of the yard-high stack of paper in his motel room, or he could go out to Great Cranberry and see what was going on about that raccoon. Rabies in a pig's eye. On the other hand, although Jack was pretty sure it was not the raccoon that had bitten him, the thing had really chewed on Maxx. Maxx's rabies tag was good for another year or two, but why not be double safe? Besides, with a few memos, Sarnoff could make his life miserable. And he didn't doubt for a moment that Sarnoff would.

Dandy idea, going out to Cranberry, except that the gas tank was empty. So was the spare can. And that was why he was now trudging around town humbly seeking fuel.

Refueled and raring to go, he managed to back the runabout from its space and get it out of the harbor without hitting anything. Halfway to Great Cranberry it began to rain. He was not wearing his Stetson.

On Great Cranberry Island he learned a number of things:

(1) Locals there considered the coon a public pet.

(2) They were afraid Maxx had given it rabies.

(3) They were angry with the Park Service because they were sure rangers had trapped the coon and taken it away.

(4) Why were they so sure? The raccoon hadn't been around since then.

(5) Where was it taken? No one knew.

(6) Who trapped it? No one remembered.

(7) When? No one noticed.

Jack bought an overpriced bag of tortilla chips and a Pepsi. Then he just stood awhile under the porch roof of the quaint little island store. A local dairy's name was written in glowing neon in the store window behind him. He watched the rain, nibbled his snack, and enjoyed a first class blue funk.

Maxx got bored with exploring the smells at the end of his leash and curled up at Jack's feet, snorting and snarfing in baritone and belching occasionally.

The rain let up finally, so Jack strolled down to the public dock to head back. Sir Francis Maxx, the Old Sea Dog, was by now getting more or less used to life on shipboard and didn't look quite so worried when they sailed.

Jack cast off the line—a ritzy nautical term meaning he remembered to untie the boat before leaving the dock —and nursed the Johnson into a muffled roar. He might mention to Vernon about maybe changing the plug and tuning this thing up. Never mind. Vern's last official act was filling the copier with fire extinguisher powder. Jack cranked it up and whined out into the channel.

The tide was changing. He could see it in the way the sea's surface patterns looped and drew jagged lines across the water. Changing tides.

He thought about Bethany Somebody in high school, back in New Mexico. A nerdish guy named Roger took her out one Saturday, and Monday morning he had all kinds of tales to tell in the boys' bathroom. In tears, Bethany proclaimed her innocence the moment she heard about it and protested bitterly. Too bitterly, some thought. Her reputation shot, she suddenly quit school a week later. It wasn't until their senior year that Roger's penchant for lying became abundantly clear, two years too late for Bethany.

Did Ev actually believe Marlette? It sounded so. He appreciated a tiny bit how Bethany might have felt.

Mount Desert Island loomed ahead. The rain returned when he was a little over halfway there. Maxx reared up on his back legs, his front paws hooked over the gunwale, to watch the road. His ears flapped and blew. He did that out the truck window too.

Off their starboard quarter—another ritzy nautical term—a fast little runabout approached. If it held to its course and Jack held to his, they could conceivably collide. Prudently, Jack angled away. Their courses still converged, but the guy now had plenty of time to see him.

The runabout jacked its speed—it was raising quite a rooster tail now—and came roaring alongside. Suddenly it dipped into a hard, sharp curve and headed right for Jack. The boat's pilot wore a peacoat and a green crusher.

Jack tilted away so abruptly that Maxx yelped. Jack's boat slowed and bobbed. It swayed crazily, virtually in place. He must have turned too hard.

He barely had time to jump. He was in the air, headed for the drink, when he heard the boats collide. As his hands and head hit the water, his boat slammed into his thighs. The blow twisted and flipped him. Debris of some sort pounded him into the water as a hammer drives a nail.

He churned ineffectively in ice water that pierced instantly to the bone, and he couldn't even tell which way was up. He couldn't force his eyes open, and when he finally did—a little—it was equally dark in all directions. If he started kicking, would he drive himself to the bottom or to the surface? Would he float to the top if he lay still? Would he get whacked by a propeller if he approached the surface now? Where was Maxx? The cold water roared and rang in his ears. They hurt terribly.

Jack always put on a flotation device of some sort. Always. Except this time. It occurred to him now, suddenly, stupidly, that he had not.

He couldn't remember if he took a breath before he went under, but it didn't matter—he was out of air now, and now was when it counted. His legs ached so badly where he'd been hit that they refused to kick. His jaw started shivering. He prayed for help. Rather, he tried to, or planned to. He didn't seem to actually be doing it, and help did not seem to be forthcoming.

He waved his arms and legs at random. He could feel a foot slosh the surface. He folded up and pushed in that direction.

His head broke the surface. Fat lot of good that did. With water streaming down his face, he still couldn't breathe. And when he did try to draw a breath, he went under in a wild paroxysm of choking and coughing. He shoved himself back up to air. His legs were so cold and heavy he could barely move them. They hurt excruciatingly. His fingers were going numb.

It took awhile—the better half of forever—to clear his lungs enough to breathe, and even then he couldn't stop coughing. Now he knew how Veronica Wayne could die with her lungs full of air and her airway blocked shut. He tried to call to Maxx, but he couldn't make any sound except a croak. He must pray, but his logical mind intervened. Why pray? God knew where he was. God understood the predicament better than he did. He asked anyway, asked for temporal salvation, his eternal salvation having been already assured. But within moments he started doubting the eternal safety too.

God, help!

No still, small voice offered succor.

He'd better get ashore fast, before he got too cold to move. Maxx was probably already halfway there. Labs are natural and enthusiastic swimmers, with oily, waterproof coats—which was why Maxx always looked so well groomed and glossy. Jack must not try again to call his dog. Maxx might return to him and waste the precious energy he needed to reach safety.

Dark hills, obscured by rain and dusk, obviously marked the nearest land. He started swimming toward them.

It crossed his mind that if this had happened on the other trip, he would have had Marlette with him. Lovely, frail Marlette, in this ice water . . . thank God she was warm and safe!

The polyester lining in his jacket had to be blotting up water like a sponge. Should he shed the heavy jacket because it was weighing him down, or keep it on? Wool retained 85 percent of its insulating effectiveness even when soaked, but how well did polyester do?

He couldn't remember what the survival manuals said to do. He couldn't remember anything at all about cold water survival other than that, if he went under, the mammalian diving reflex would keep his innards alive awhile.

Tell me what to do, God!

Still no small voice spoke.

But he had to do something. He was struggling, making no progress at all that he could see. No matter how strenuously he worked, the hills looked just as far away, or farther. How long had he been in here? A couple minutes at most. His legs and arms paused unbidden, and he sank below the surface. He shoved himself up and out and flipped to his back, gasping. He was so cold he didn't feel cold anymore. His body parts all worked in slow motion, if at all. His ears still roared.

And then he panicked. This was it. This was the real thing. After all the times he had lucked out, rather had been blessed by God—after all the times he had courted danger and managed to skirt it—he was literally and figuratively in over his head this time. He wasn't going to make it ashore. His eyes at water level, the gentle waves breaking across his face, his limbs freezing, his body giving up . . .

Rage shoved panic aside. This wasn't fair! It wasn't his time, it wasn't the place. He was a country boy from New Mexico, who should die of thirst in a desert wilderness, if by the hand of nature, not in icy water two thousand miles from home.

He rolled over to start swimming again but succeeded mostly in just flailing. He went under, shoved himself back up, flailed some more. He might have been able to get his act together enough to swim effectively, but his tortured legs spasmed down and quit. He rolled to his back so he could scull with both arms. Instantly the surface wash filled his ears with icy water. It sloshed in his mouth, up his nose, across his eyes.

Help me, God! I'm dying.
I'm coming home.
And I don't want to yet.

9

Lobster

Jack's right arm locked straight up, tilting his head under. He tried to kick, and his thighs screamed at him and refused. His head popped out of the water. God's still small voice was finally offering some suggestions, but he couldn't make them out. His aching ears roared like a motor in a bathtub.

It occurred to him then that his whole upper body had left the water. His face was no longer at surface level, his eyes were no longer splashed shut by every little ripple. Maxx barked somewhere. If this was death, it was a most curious death.

Even more curious, God's still small voice spoke with a heavy Maine accent. "Quitchur struggling. You're gonna pop me in the kisser if y'ain't careful."

Maxx's eager barking, closer now, rose above the din in Jack's clogged ears.

Jack thunked against a wooden wall. Sharp jerks hoisted him, scraping him against the wood. This was a boat, and strong hands gripped his arms. His hands were too numb, too useless to grip back. Strength that was not his hauled him over a rail. He collapsed, totally spent, onto a wooden floor.

Instantly a hot tongue attacked his face with joyous slurps. Maxx belched in front of his nose.

Beneath a black watch cap, Winthrop Spalding's stark, aged face floated in the near darkness. He was tugging at Jack's belt. "Here. Get these wet blue jeans off. Come on. They ain't doing an ounce of good."

Jack would have liked to help, but he couldn't make his hands function. Spalding yanked off his running shoes and sopping jeans. The old man slipped out of his own yellow slicker bottoms. He had nice warm, wool pants on under them. He pulled the slicker bottoms onto Jack's numb legs, and all Jack could do to help was lift his hips.

"Magggzz . . ." He tried to shove his dog away.

The old man jerked him to sitting, stripped off Jack's jacket, shirt, and T, and wrapped wool blankets around him. He topped the whole costume with his own watch cap, dragging it down hard around Jack's ears and eyebrows. It nearly shoved his eyes shut.

Then this ancient one, who looked as if he ought to be in a nursing home, gripped Jack under the arms and dragged him unceremoniously across the deck. He propped Jack in a corner of a small cabin. Actually, it was half a cabin, two walls and a roof only, with a hot exhaust pipe running up the middle. Jack sat scrunched in the only actual corner.

This lobster boat wasn't much larger, deckwise, than a rowboat, it seemed. The pilot cabin was closed in on two sides only. The roof kept out rain no doubt but did nothing to keep in warmth. A dozen weathered lobster traps were stacked at the stern end, and coils of line lay here and there. Jack had no idea what any of the fixtures and gewgaws did aboard this vessel.

Spalding reached over to a panel above Jack's head. The engine below decks snarfed like Maxx. The exhaust pipe beside Jack vibrated. A cloud of black smoke burped out the back and floated off across the water. And the boat began to move. It was raining.

Casually, effortlessly, Spalding turned his wheel. "Get a look at the numbers on that boat?"

"Nuh, din'."

"Betch it's stolen from Bait Bucket Brewer's. That sure as blazes weren't Bait in it just now."

"B-bai'?"

"Ayuh. Bait Bucket. Cuz that's what he smells like. He runs a boat rental down in Northeast Harbor. Used to run it outa Great Cranberry, till he fin'ly figured out you can't get to Great Cranberry 'cept by boat. Moved over to Mount Desert Island here, and his business grew a million."

"How . . . dyou . . . f-fin' us?"

"'Tweren't hard finding the dog, the racket he was making. Hauled him inboard right away. I started to work a circle looking for you when he ran over to the other side of the boat and jumped in and swam away. Barking like mad. By cracky, there you were, right where he swum to. I pulled him in first and then you."

Jack's Labrador retriever had just retrieved him, and he had been so numbed out in the water that he didn't even know the dog was near.

Amazing grace! Definitely divine intervention. Definitely worth hearty praise. And Jack finally had his wits together enough to offer it.

Winthrop got the boat plowing water in a straight line and pulled a mike off a CB radio above Jack's head.

Jack strained to hear clearly, but his ears still weren't working very well. He derived from the conversation that although Winthrop Spalding had not seen the collision itself, he heard the crash. Because of the time it takes sound to travel, he just so saw Jack's boat going down, ceased what he was doing, and headed for it. As he was approaching, the second boat passed him less than a hundred yards off his bow. He could not get an ID.

The radio voice crackled questions, and Spalding responded in monosyllables, except that the way he said

"Ayuh" was two syllables. Jack couldn't understand a word of it. He was still trying to grasp that Spalding could see well enough in this drizzle and evening gloom to ascertain correctly what had happened and find two dark bobbing heads in that huge piece of ocean, Maxx's barking or no.

Maxx still swarmed all over him. Finally, his face licked past tolerance, Jack flung a leaden arm across the dog's back. "Maxx, f-for pete s-s-sake, s-sit. Down. Long d-down."

The dog curled up against him. Jack perceived that Maxx was snuggling up not for love but for terror. The poor old mutt vibrated like a foot massager, and he wasn't cold.

Spalding hung up his mike. "Here. Get up on your feet and walk around. You won't freeze as fast."

"Can'."

Casually, the old man grabbed him under the arms and hauled him up. "Walk. But don't fall over the side, hear?"

His thighs still hurt incredibly. Both legs felt broken, but they supported him. Strange, that the rain-wet deck felt warm to his bare feet. He lurched to the lobster traps, leaned back on them a moment, lurched back to the partial protection of the cabin. He felt suddenly, intensely, in need of its protection, however flimsy. He huddled in the corner where the two walls met, pressing against them, separating himself from that cold, cruel sea.

Spalding handled the wheel with an easy grace. "They'll get the Coast Guard and the county sheriff onto it, but I don't guess they'll find him. Coast Guard's nowhere 'round—never is when you need it—and by the time the sheriff comes out from town, the guy could have his boat repainted."

He watched Jack a moment. "That OK, what I told 'em about you?"

"Wha'd you s-say?"

"That you was all right. Just a little cold. They wanted

to know if we needed MAST. I said no. It's a lot of tax money, you know."

"M-mast. Helic-c-copter?"

"I can call 'em back if you want one."

"No. No. I'm f-fine." To prove it Jack shoved himself erect and walked around a little. Except for his legs and aching toes and ears, and a chill that had him shivering uncontrollably, everything worked without complaining too much.

Maxx stuck like Velcro to his side. It might be the only time in their lives together that Maxx voluntarily and cheerfully heeled. Jack had better enjoy it while it lasted.

The radio crackled. Spalding picked up the mike and answered with a terse, "Don' see no need." Pause. "Five minutes or so." He hung it up. He turned on his running lights. Dusk arrived early in October this far north.

"This yere's my son's boat. He's in Bangor, so I said I'd pull his traps for him. Got about a third of them. He can pull the rest tomorrow."

Jack walked back and forth a few more times. Every time he stopped walking, the moving deck made him feel a little greener. His mouth was warming up enough that at least he could talk without sounding like a drunk with a speech impediment.

Spalding asked, "Get lobster much in Kansas?"

"Lobster tails with steak."

The old man spat. "Frozen trash from South Africa. I mean real lobster."

"You mean you can eat lobster without steak?"

Spalding chuckled. "Gonna hafta educate you."

Jack tried to walk faster. His legs refused to move faster. The nausea was getting worse.

They entered the outer mouth of Northeast Harbor, and Spalding slowed the boat to a crawl. It bobbed with cruel deliberation on every swell.

The old man studied Jack a moment. "You look worse than when you came aboard."

"Know why I d-drove in from Kansas? Don't like to fly. I get airsick." The shivering was now growing more violent, and Jack realized that was a good sign. He was warming up. Fifteen minutes ago he had been too cold to shiver.

Was Spalding laughing or grimacing? Jack watched him a moment. Neither. The man smiled, but it was a sympathetic expression. "My grandson has the same problem. You'll live."

Jack calculated he was within twenty-five seconds of losing the tortilla chips and Pepsi when Spalding nudged the boat, slick as a greased balloon, up against the finger slips.

Awaiting them there on the slip were a minimum of a dozen volunteer firemen with a gurney. Half a hundred civilians clustered around an aid van with its lights flashing. Everyone in Northeast Harbor was out to see the show. Jack had forgotten how quickly word travels in a small town.

It took Jack maybe ten minutes to convince all those disappointed EMTs that he was one himself and he was refusing treatment. No, he was not going to the emergency room in Ellsworth. No, he was not injured. No, he did not require medical intervention of any sort. "Unless . . . you guys have anything on board for motion sickness?"

They didn't.

Jack signed the refusal form with a hand that would not stop shaking. It rather spoiled the facade of good health.

Spalding had taken his lobster boat out to a mooring buoy in midharbor. Smoothly he rowed a little dinghy ashore. He tied up near where Jack's boat would have tied, were it not at the bottom of the sea. He joined them, with Jack's wet clothes, a big wad of sopping coldness, under his arm.

And then the old man, bless him, rescued Jack yet again. Twice in one night. Spalding poked his arm. "Let's go." And to one of the EMTs, "See you tomorrow, Les. If the sheriff ever shows up, tell him where we are."

"You gonna drive, Winthrop?"

"Ayuh."

"OK. He's in no shape to drive."

"Ayuh."

Not unlike Maxx, Jack heeled, close at Spalding's side, and followed him across the parking lot to an aged beater Ford Pinto.

Winthrop dropped Jack's wet clothes on the floor of the passenger side. He dragged stray clothes and rubber rainpants off the front seat to make room for Jack and stuffed them in the backseat.

"Don't look like much," the old man commented, "but it's got a heater that won't quit." He let Maxx in the back and flopped behind the wheel. His heater roared almost as loudly as the heater in Jack's pickup. Away they went.

Maxx panted heavily against the back of Jack's neck. The warm breath felt good. "Where are we going?"

"My place. I have a place in Seal Harbor. Ever been down to Seal Harbor?"

"Not yet. Give me a minute."

Winthrop cackled. A few minutes later he drove into his front yard (or, in Maine-ese, "dooryard," which he pronounced, approximately, "dwah-yaad"). The car bucked a couple times in a spate of afterfiring when he turned off the ignition.

Jack climbed out stiffly, wearily. His legs hurt so badly he could barely stand, let alone walk. Maxx bounded out of the backseat not on Jack's side but on Winthrop's.

They entered his tiny bungalow, a couple of very small rooms stuck together beneath an ancient looking shingle roof. A hutch filled one corner of the kitchen. A table and two chairs sat in the other corner. The kitchen was hardly big enough to serve as dining room as well. Beyond an arch was a small, cluttered living room—just

117

the sofa filled half of it—and off the kitchen, a little bedroom.

Winthrop's house looked a lot like his car. Lived in. Every square foot of flat surface had something on it. And everything sitting on a flat surface was dusty. Jack would guess that Winthrop lived alone. In the old corner hutch, a lot of collectors' bottles and plates were displayed, or stashed, or simply stacked—much more glassware than the hutch could comfortably accommodate.

On a shelf over the sideboard, a hundred little figurines of dogs crowded together. Scotties, terriers, shepherds, collies, cockers—and there was a black Lab, all grime-coated. Strange, colorful crocheted guess-whats graced the walls, and all the small appliances were protected by crocheted covers. Magazines and brown grocery bags were stacked by the stove, newspapers piled by the sofa in the front room. Through the bedroom doorway Jack could see stacks of things and brown cartons next to the unmade bed.

"So you never ate real lobster." Winthrop pulled off his parka and tossed it in a corner. "Put your stuff in the dryer. Just take that other stuff out."

Jack opened the dryer door. It was full of clothing. He pulled the clothes out, piled them on the floor, emptied his pockets, and put his clothes in, shoes and all. It took him a minute to figure out the controls. The dryer lurched into action. The drum needed greasing.

"Set there." Winthrop waved toward the kitchen table. "Your clothes should be ready by the time we eat."

Jack had to remove unopened mail from the chair seat. He laid it in a stack beside him, wrapped up in his blanket, and sat.

Maxx had disappeared into the living room, probably doing a tour of the house. He returned to Jack's side and plumped down by his chair. Within a minute or two he had fallen asleep, snoring with nasal passages that vibrated like echo chambers.

Jack thought about how close he had come to losing the dog—to losing his own life as well. He shivered, and it wasn't all from cold.

As he moved some old mail off the corner of the table, he noticed on top a Sunday church bulletin. "You go to church?"

"Ayuh."

"Can you recommend one for this Sunday?"

"Here in Seal Harbor is a good'n. My wife liked the one up in Somesville, and she always preferred to go there, and I just never got around to switching. But this one's good. Good Bible preaching. They love the Lord."

Jack smiled. *They love the Lord.* What better accolade can a church receive? He began the complex tasks of drying out his wallet and dismantling his waterlogged revolver. Winthrop didn't have any tissues. Jack used toilet paper. His fingers refused to cooperate. Jobs needing fine coordination, such as backing screws out, seemed to take hours.

Winthrop pared some potatoes and set them to boiling, discoursing on the silliness of leaving the skins on, like these yuppies do. He put aside cooking long enough to make a call at the wall phone by the door.

"Ayuh." Pause. "Ayuh." Pause. "Say, pound and a half?" Pause. "Two. Send Donny over."

He opened a can of peas and dumped them in a pan, extolling the convenience and virtues of canned foods. He put out a couple of plates and some flatware.

The man seemed to move slowly, or hardly at all, yet he accomplished a multitude of little things in a brief time. He wasted no motion, and his movement intrigued Jack.

"Your dog like scraps?"

"I haven't found anything yet he doesn't like."

The man nodded. He dug a couple bowls out of his refrigerator, combined their contents in one, and set it on the floor by Jack's foot. Jack kicked Maxx.

The dog rolled to his belly.

119

"There you go, dog." Winthrop returned to his stove.

Maxx looked at the bowl, and at Jack, for maybe two seconds. Jack nodded. Eagerly he set to, scarfing up whatever it was. He could wake up instantly and thoroughly, under sufficient provocation. He licked the bowl, licked his chops, and belched appreciatively.

Winthrop chuckled. He put on a big pot of plain water and turned the burner to high. He dropped into the other chair at the table. "Used to have a dog. Sort of a mutt. Cunnin' dog, but no particular breed. Not good for anything."

"Who collects the dog figurines up there?" Jack nodded toward the shelf.

"My wife did. She's been dead maybe ten years now. Died early. Of cancer. Worked in the bank. With her paycheck, I could afford to run my lobster boat. Can't make a living off fishing around here, but you can add to a living. Know what I mean?"

Jack nodded.

They talked for fifteen minutes about clamming, scalloping, lobstering, fishing, and crabbing. Jack asked a couple questions about finding the body, since the topics were related, sort of. Winthrop had given his all in the written statement. They got off onto the extreme tides of this part of the country.

"You know," Winthrop rumbled, "if you'd kept swimming the way you were swimming, you woulda been fifteen hours reaching shore."

"You mean fighting tides and currents."

"Ayuh."

"I just headed for what looked like the closest land. How do you know where the currents are going?"

"Well, for starters, you get born here. Then you buy a boat when you're a kid."

"I get the idea." Jack thought awhile. "You said you dragged the body up out of the water because the current would have carried it away. Can you say where the currents would have brought her from?"

"You mean, where she got kilt?"

"Yes. She was dead about four hours. Where would she have been four hours earlier if someone killed her and tossed her in the sea?"

Winthrop raised his bushy eyebrows. "Gotta think about that one."

Someone knocked. Maxx barked, a knee-jerk reaction to anyone at any door. A little kid, probably fearing the big bass-voiced dog, refused to enter. He handed Winthrop a newspaper-wrapped package and scooted.

"My grandson." Somehow, Winthrop made a flat, explanatory statement brim over with pride. He unwrapped the parcel. Two large lobsters, still quite alive, moved slow motion. Their claws were not tied or rubber-banded shut in any way. Unceremoniously Winthrop picked them up and dropped them in the boiling water.

"That was my daughter-in-law I talked to on the phone. My son does some lobstering on the side, weekends mostly. They usually have a half a dozen or so. I send them over clams and crabs every now and then—and get a lobster when I want one."

He sat back down. "Where would she start from?" He studied Jack a few moments, and Jack studied him back. It wasn't staring. It was thoughtful looking. "Within a hundred yards of the bridge."

"The bridge onto the island?"

"Ayuh." The old man scowled. "Then again, maybe not. She was floating. A body generally don't float until it's been in the water awhile. You sure it was only four hours?"

"Her lungs were full of air. Medical examiner says that's why. She wouldn't actually float on the surface, likely, but not on the bottom, either. Free of the bottom. Free moving."

"Mm. Then the bridge, or right beside there." More

121

frowning. "Why would her lungs be full of air? Why not water?"

"She was still alive when she went in, he says. Took a breath, hit the water, the water clogged her mouth and throat, and then the muscles spasmed down. She was partially choked by blood too."

The old man shuddered. "My wife died young. Had so much life in her yet, so many years. But that girl . . ." He shook his head. "That's too young. Too hard a way to go."

He stared into the space beyond Maxx somewhere. Suddenly he snapped back and stood up. He walked to the stove, fished up a lobster with a wooden spoon and grabbed an antenna. He yanked the feeler. The lobster bobbed. He dropped it back in. "Five minutes yet."

Five minutes. Jack walked out to the utility room and opened the dryer. He tested his jeans. If the seams were dry, everything but the shoes was dry. They weren't. But they were dry enough. The elastic in his underwear was the only actually damp part. He put the jeans on last—gave the rivets time to cool off. He paused to bask in the beautiful, beautiful warmth. He tossed his shoes and the nylon parka back in and turned the dryer on again. He didn't think the motel had a public laundry—might as well get the coat as dry as possible. His denim coat was going to be days drying out. He didn't dare put the sheepskin in a dryer.

By the time he made a quickie bathroom trip, Winthrop had melted a small pan of butter and was fishing out a lobster again. He yanked the antenna, and this time it came away in his hand. "Sit."

Jack sat.

Winthrop set out the lobsters, the butter (still in its melting pan—Winthrop did not dwell upon formality) and a big empty bowl. He served up the peas and potatoes. He dug a pair of ordinary hinged two-bar nutcrackers out of his kitchen junk drawer and sat down.

Jack asked a silent blessing on the food, even if it

122

did look absolutely inedible. In fact, if looks were any indication, lobster was poisonous. There it sat on his plate, a full-grown, bright red lobster, all parts intact, an amazing wealth of texture and small detail that you never notice in pictures, its stalked eyes watching Jack's every move.

Winthrop casually cracked his lobster's big claws with the nutcracker and passed it to Jack. Obediently, Jack followed suit.

Maxx, all ears, nose, and eyes, sat on alert by Jack's knee.

"Them rusticators, they think there's some big mystery to getting lobster meat outa its shell. They gotta have the cook split it and crack it and pound on it. Nothing to it, really. All you do is break the joints backwards, like this."

Winthrop gripped the tail in one hand and the carapace in the other and snapped them apart by arching the lobster's back, as a kid would dismantle Tinkertoys. He broke back the telson, that fan of palps at the lobster's tail, and casually pushed the tail meat out from the back.

What amazed Jack most of all was that when he tried the same thing, it worked for him just as well. Usually, when he tried some arcane skill, it never turned out like the demonstration.

Winthrop broke the claws off and the leg joints. He showed how to squeeze meat like toothpaste out of the thin little walking legs. He broke away the carapace. He pointed out the tomalli, the green goo up under where more sensible animals have a heart. Jack's dissections in biology class were never this interesting.

Each white, delicate piece of meat they dipped in the communal pan of butter. The shells they tossed into the big bowl. The empty shells, for some reason, looked as if they took up more total space than the whole lobsters had.

"This is, without equal, the most delectable stuff I've ever eaten in my life." Jack paused to savor a chunk of plump claw meat. "Except the tomalli. The green glop is all yours if you want it."

"You'd like it better if it wasn't green."

"If you think color makes a difference, I'll introduce you to serrano chilis. But the meat is heaven."

Without hesitating, Winthrop scooped the green gunk over onto his plate. Obviously he refused to waste a treat this delicious on some clod who wouldn't appreciate the delicacy.

Maxx was missing out on the whole thing. If Jack didn't like this lobster quite so much, he might have passed a bit to Maxx. No way, José. Let Maxx be content with the unique taste sensation of leftovers.

One ought not to waste a treat this delicious on some clod who wouldn't appreciate the delicacy. This stuff was all Jack's.

10

Trial Run

It wasn't Jack's idea to call a press conference on Saturday morning. But the reporters all wanted something for the Sunday paper, and the Sunday paper went to bed early, and Jack hadn't gotten to bed nearly early enough, and his legs still ached mightily, and his thighs were swollen and black and blue, and his ears hurt when loud noises hit them, and something in the scraps Winthrop fed Maxx had given the dog gas.

In the truck cab all night.

And the press conference was in Ellsworth, half an hour away in that truck cab.

It was not a good morning.

Jack hated press conferences. He found himself managing press releases during that fire on the north rim of the Grand Canyon eight years ago. With TV station choppers flying places they weren't supposed to, and reporters asking inane things without doing their homework, Jack had developed then a bad taste for the press that he harbored yet today. He was being unfair, probably. There must be responsible journalists out there somewhere.

But they sure weren't here. Jack and Marian Hastings, of all people, stood together behind a bank of mikes fielding some incredibly dumb questions. Ms. Hastings was treating it as the crime of the century. Jack tended to get a little flippant and had to keep restraining himself. This was, after all, a murder—serious and grisly business.

What Jack really wanted to do was sit Lauren down and quiz her about the IRS versus Edith Cray, among other things. So far, their exchanges had been casually conversational. Now was the time to turn into a cop and start interrogating her big time. If he did it softly enough, he wouldn't frighten her off. He wanted to quiz Edith too. And he wanted to get into Kovik and Fracci deeper, Kovik especially. And he wanted to shake the aches out of his complaining, put-upon body.

Then the day started breaking right for him. The overcast melted to a thin haze that let some sun and blue sky through. The improved brightness set the autumn trees afire. He got out of Ellsworth well before 8:30 A.M. and truly enjoyed the drive back in the golden morning light. He arrived at the Seaview before the crew had left the parking lot.

Edith was fuming and fussing, trying to herd people into vans and meeting reluctance at every turn. She wheeled on him as he approached. "What do *you* want?"

"And the top of the morning to you too. I want to talk to you, to Lauren, to Kovik, and to Fracci, not necessarily in that order."

"Of course you do." She waved a hand toward the emergent sun. "It's the first decent morning we've had since we got here and you want us all to sit down and chat." She pronounced a word Victorian ladies definitely would not utter.

Clyde had managed to get his bunch together apparently, because his van pulled out and headed down the road. Ev waved to Jack from the passenger-side window as they departed, and he blew her a kiss. After all, they were building a pretense of girlfriend-boyfriend here.

"Where is the shoot this morning?"

126

"Otter Cliff. There are enough evergreens there. We don't have to worry about autumn color."

"Only someone shooting pictures for a midsummer magazine issue would worry about beautiful trees."

"True." She licked her lips. "Mr. Preston. Ronnie's death was tragic." Edith sounded annoyed, not beset by tragedy. "But this project must be completed. My crew will give you our cooperation, but I'm asking your cooperation as well. Don't disrupt our work."

"Fair enough. I've been stationary too long. Maxx and I will go un-gel our blood first. The carriage paths look like the perfect place to run, so we'll take advantage of them. We both need the exercise. And I'll catch you people closer to lunchtime. We can work from there. Will that help?"

"The best of all worlds would be for you to just back off completely until we're finished, but I know better than to expect that. I suppose that will do. Happy running." Without further comment she turned and climbed into the second of the Sitting Pretty vans. Away they went. Edith, at the passenger-side window, did not wave. Jack blew no kisses.

The wise runner donned appropriate running attire (the most fashionable of which looked as if it was made from neon-colored inner tubes), performed a prescribed series of stretching and warm-up exercises, and carefully monitored pulse rate for maximum aerobic effect. Jack and Maxx were not wise runners, nor did Jack ever intend to be. Such wisdom drained all the fun out of it. He parked down by the gatehouse, pocketed the leash, and left his coat in the truck.

They walked the first half mile up the carriage path, Jack and Maxx, and filled their lungs with damp air flavored richly with dying leaves. The wind was picking up overhead and shaking treetops, but it hadn't reached the path yet. Dancing dapples splashed across the trail. They began to jog, a casual, floppy dogtrot. Jack had no idea were he was going, and unwisely he had left the park brochure containing the trail map back in the truck.

A couple of interesting trails crossed the carriage path, and after all this was an island. How could he get too lost? He left the carriage routes and took to hiking trails. Whenever the trail forked, he took the way promising uphill. They topped out on a bulging bluff, where the view was obscured by the forest. Jack upped the pace somewhat, running uphill and down.

As they passed a dark pond, its surface rippled by the breeze, a brace of black ducks lifted off the water. In the duckweed at the far end, a pair of ruddys, like wind-up toys, paddled in tight circles, then disappeared among some cattails. Jack paused to watch a buteo soaring high overhead. It dipped and swooped and turned its back to the sun. Red-tailed hawk. He called Maxx up out of an apparently intriguing ditch and continued on. The day sang to him.

Caught up in the sparkling pleasure of the run, Maxx bounded ahead.

Jack remembered a run many years ago when he worked for concessions at Mount Rainier. He had hiked the Comet Falls trail beyond the falls and beyond the forest, up into Van Trump Park. Bigger than life, filling the sky, the brooding presence of Mt. Rainier rose beyond Van Trump Park as a craggy fortress of rock and snow and everlasting ice.

The park, actually a vast, damp meadow just above treeline, was mostly grass and rock, with a few clumps of subalpine fir scattered here and there. The open space beckoned too strongly to ignore, and Jack had begun to run. It wasn't a legal run—he was off the established trail and running across the open, rock-strewn slope, where hikers and other people ought not go.

An elk herd grazing uphill of him put their noses in the air and ran not away from him but beside him. For

128

several exhilarating, unforgettable minutes, Jack and the elk ran together, less than a hundred yards apart, free and wild, across the broad, bare shoulder of the mighty mountain.

Then the elk dispersed into a patch of subalpine fir among the rocks, and Jack picked up a trace that took him downhill. The run was done. He was back on the established trail and therefore legal again. Older and wiser now, he didn't leave established trails anymore. That had been a foible of his youth. The memory thrilled him yet.

The carriage path cut through a wonderful stand of blazing maple and from there through dark and glowering evergreens—balsam fir? Jack wasn't sure. He had grown up among junipers and ponderosa pine and not much else. Identifying conifers was not his long suit.

He stepped up the pace again. He really ought to get some hard running in before he cooled off, and in another two miles or so they'd be back at the truck—that is, if they were about where he thought they were. These trails were confusing despite the signs.

Old Maxx managed to stay a couple of hundred yards ahead—it was probably a macho thing with him. But his tongue was hanging out now. Good. The dog needed the exercise as much as Jack did.

They crashed down along a series of slippery switchbacks carpeted in wet, slimy leaves, jogged through a little creek drainage, and broke out onto a broad, grassy carriage path. Now where? The path at this point seemed to be running east and west, and Jack wanted to go south. For lack of any clear direction, he turned left and took off at a lazy jog.

Behind him, someone motorized was breaking the no-motorized-vehicles rule. He heard the whine of an approaching moped or small motorbike on the path a few hundred yards back. This posed a dilemma. He was a commissioned federal law officer, and the park operated under federal regs. He had jurisdiction here. He really ought to ticket the biker behind him. But he hated like blue blazes to wreck a beautiful run with a lousy law enforcement procedure.

He'd wait and see who it was. If the miscreant was young, he'd flash his badge, chew the kid out, and chase him or her off the path. If it was an obvious scofflaw, old enough to know better and breaking the law on purpose, he'd write him up.

Overjoyed at the thought of chasing something, Maxx shed every sign of exhaustion and charged away from the path up through the woods, following a deer trail. Jack heard him crash and thrash in the undergrowth. Here was another dilemma. Surely dogs were not allowed off leash. Jack with his illegal mutt was about to write up an illegal biker? He called Maxx.

He entered an S-curve as the biker came up behind him. The motor revved and approached flat out, top speed, which wasn't saying much.

Jack jogged on. He still hadn't resolved his dilemma. The motor came whining. The dumb cluck sounded as if he was going to pass right beside Jack—to practically brush him. That settled it. A guy who played chicken with pedestrians deserved any kind of trouble Jack cared to serve up.

He started to turn, to hail the biker as he passed, when King Kong swung a mighty fist, whanged him below his shoulder blades, knocked him sprawling across the loose leaves. Who invited King Kong in on this? Jack tried to call Maxx, but he had no air to breathe, let alone speak.

For a long moment he lay paralyzed, unable to see, unable to move, unable to breathe. He heard the bike turn and head back this way. He managed to tuck, to protect his head. King Kong kicked him in the back.

Maxx barked and snarled and yelped. The bike raced away with the dog in hot pursuit. Then, off in the distance, Maxx yelped in pain.

Jack tried to straighten. He wondered how much

was broken. It felt like everything was. He still couldn't breathe. How much time had passed? Was there any chance he could reach a park radio or otherwise get somebody out in pursuit? Hah.

He pulled himself to his knees and squatted back on his heels. He arched his back—carefully. Everything worked, albeit reluctantly. He stood up then, but he did not run up the path toward his dog, wherever Maxx was. He walked, and not too steadily.

A hundred yards beyond the S-curve, Maxx was stumbling dejectedly this way. He raised his head as Jack appeared, and the clumsy tail flopped a few wags. He broke into an uninspired trot. His mouth was bloody.

Jack and his dog met in an open stretch of the sun-dappled path, in a sea of crunchy leaves. Maxx obviously wasn't feeling well because Jack said, "Sit," and the dog sat instantly. Maxx considered prompt obedience the first sign of a sick mind.

Jack sat down beside his woebegone pooch and went over him, every inch. No bones broken, but Maxx had been walloped in the ribs. They were tender on the left side. He had taken a big one alongside his head too. His lips, both upper and lower, were broken and bleeding on the left side, and his left cheek was swelling up. Jack checked for broken teeth as best he could, but Maxx fought him. Maxx's trust had been eroded by pain. He didn't want anyone messing with his sore face.

Jack could understand. The biker had to have put Maxx down hard to break his pursuit, for once the dog decided to take someone, he took him. Jack almost said, "Find, Maxx," and decided against it. The dog would probably obey that one, for his pride had been bludgeoned even worse than his face. And what he needed most right now was an uninterrupted six-hour rest.

Jack spent a good five minutes rubbing the dog's chest and ears, cooing to him, praising him, reassuring him. His own back was so stiff he almost didn't make it to his feet. He swatted his left leg, and old Maxx fell in beside. Neither one took the trouble to officially heel.

They took a wrong turn somewhere, for they came out on the road a quarter mile from the gatehouse. It was nearly eleven by the time they crawled into the truck cab. How could a fun run turn into such a trial?

11

Thunder Hole

Every national park and monument, large or small, has a certain look and feel, an ambiance that is uniquely its own. Cognoscenti can study a photo of a few tumbledown stone walls and tell you which Indian ruin it is. They can see a cave formation and identify the cave it is in; glance at the cacti or alpine wildflowers or trees in the foreground of a photo and name, if not the park, at least the area of the country where the photo was taken. Mountain massifs and deserts, lakes and rock outcrops all bear their own stamp.

Jack tried to place Acadia's uniqueness. Grayson had said it in part: if you see a photo of a beach on a summer day, but no swimmer is in the water above the knees, it's Sand Beach. Cold water was part. Marine influences kept the park from being torrid in summer or frigid in winter. That too would form the feel of the place in part. So would the trees, the low, glacier-chiseled mountains with their sloping north sides and abruptly truncated south faces, the rocky shore, the restless sea.

Jack's perceptions were clouded by pain, frustration, and the murder of Veronica Wayne. He was not one to ask if one wanted an unbiased description of Acadia's uniqueness. And yet he liked this dark, somber area in spite of himself.

He of the West, who loved the wide open spaces, could appreciate the delicate tangle of these Northeast woodlands, for he had run through them. He of the spreading skies was coming to appreciate the way the close forest exploded out into the totally open horizon of the Atlantic, stretching clear to Europe. He of desert heat accepted that this Mount Desert, pronounced not *desert* but *dessert* or *d'zairt*, was no less simply because it differed.

As he drove south down the one-way loop road on the east side of the island, he thought of all sorts of snappy comebacks he could have made to those silly questions this morning. *Why can't you ever come up with something clever at the time you need it?*

Most of all he thought about how he should have handled the moped/motorbike thing differently. He had messed that one up completely. He had no idea what the rider looked like, nor what weapon the rider had wielded in his attack. It could have been anything from a baseball bat to a piece of steel fence post. What a fool he had been.

And Maxx had paid as dearly as he for his folly.

He stopped by Sand Beach a few moments just to look at it, despite that he wanted to get to Sitting Pretty before they broke for lunch. Sand Beach happened to be north of Otter Point, and therefore first on the one-way loop.

The beach was a concave arch of sand at the back of a tiny sheltered bay, a hammock slung between rocky heads to either side. A marshy little creek meandered down out of the valley behind it and ran its water in lacy fingers across the sand to the sea. A hundred feet offshore, a flock of Oldsquaws bobbed on the surf.

Jack was the only human being around to watch the water slosh up the sand and drain back, up and back, up and back, up and back.

The wind had picked up considerably since his run. Sand Beach's pinched cove seemed sheltered from it, though. Whitecaps a few hundred yards out showed where the wind dropped from a howl to a crawl.

He returned to his truck and to Maxx sleeping soundly on the passenger seat. As he opened the door, a lady in L. L. Bean Outdoor Chic pulled to a stop beside him and rolled down her window.

"Excuse me, are you a ranger?"

"Come to think of it, yes." This happened ridiculously often. Jack would be standing around in civvies looking unofficial, he thought, and tourists would peg him as a ranger. It never failed to amaze him when it happened. "What can I do for you?"

"I've been driving around this loop for over an hour. How do I get off it?"

Jack had long since learned to hide smiles by pursing his lips and scratching his head. "Well, let's see. Go on down here past Otter Point and around the corner. When the sign says 'Seal Harbor,' turn a hard right. You'll come to a gas station. They'll tell you how to get wherever you want to go from there, and you'll be off the loop."

She looked dubious.

"Try it," he suggested. "Hard right."

She smiled, still uncertain, and drove away.

He climbed in the cab. Maxx never stirred.

If Jack managed to secure a date for lunch, Maxx was going to have to move. Jack could take Lauren out to eat, a rain check on that aborted date yesterday. Information always flowed more smoothly when food was involved. If Lauren was tied up, he'd take Ev and get filled in on what she'd picked up lately.

He left Sand Beach. He passed the parking area for Thunder Hole and continued down to Otter Point. Otter Point, with its Otter Cliffs, was not protected as was Sand Beach. It stood alone against the sea, a mighty hundred-foot headland jutting out into the Atlantic, its face thrust into every wind that came.

135

As he pulled out onto the point, a disgruntled blond giant with a camera and collapsed tripod on his shoulder came trudging this way. Mike Kovik was not with the rest of the crew, obviously. And Jack didn't see the vans. Did this mean he would end up with Kovik for lunch? That was like taking your favorite girl's kid brother to the movies.

Kovik's hair flew about in a wind that could strip paint.

Jack stopped beside Mike and rolled down the window. The cold wind hit him hard in the face. "Looks like they abandoned you."

"Basically, yeah." Kovik eyed him wearily and warily.

"If, like me, you avoid exercise whenever possible, you're welcome to a ride to wherever you're going."

Kovik's voice took on the tone of an adult explaining to a two-year-old why a hot wood stove is off limits. "I'm going up to Thunder Hole. This is a one-way road going in the wrong direction. You just passed it. You'd have to go clear around."

"Doesn't matter to me if it doesn't matter to you."

He shrugged and swung his tripod off his shoulder. "Sure doesn't matter to me."

As Kovik came around to the passenger side, awkwardly maneuvering his tripod, Jack prodded Maxx awake and relegated him to his cage in back. Maxx was not pleased. Jack sympathized.

Jack hopped in and headed his truck on down the road. "Where'd everybody go? I thought they were supposed to be here."

"Beats the tar outa me. I thought so too." Kovik lapsed into silence.

"Were you with them at all this morning?"

"What business is it of yours?"

That was not an answer Jack would have expected, but he'd obviously just pushed some sort of button. He considered his approach a moment and softened his voice a little, keeping things light and casual. "Federal investigator, remember?"

"Yeah, I remember. It'd help if you looked like one, you know. Cowboy hat, cowboy coat. Not exactly authority stuff. Kansas, Marlette said. Not even out West—not cowboy country. Midwest."

"Sure it's out West. 'Gunsmoke,' Matt Dillon—the quintessential TV Western for how many years? Dodge City is in Kansas."

Kovik grunted. "New jacket there, huh?"

"Brand new."

"How long's it gonna take the cowboy coat to dry out, do you think?" Kovik was grinning. Or smirking. Or both.

"Week, probably, the rate it's going. Were you with them at all this morning?"

"Yeah." And his voice sounded bitter. "When Edith closed us down I walked out to get some surf shots. It's pretty spectacular down there. They knew where I was, and they drove off and left me."

"Deliberately, you mean."

He exploded. "Of course, deliberately!" And he called someone an unseemly name.

"Who? Edith?"

"She runs this show, if you haven't noticed. She says, 'Drive on,' they drive on. And nobody cares. You know who was the only one who cried when Ron was killed? The only one?"

"Athalia Adams." Jack turned right off the loop road and headed north.

"Someone told you."

"No. Surmise."

"Oh? So what do you surmise about me?" Kovik was watching Jack without watching him, pretending to look at the road ahead.

"Uncertain, not sure of yourself, but you don't know why. Even frightened, in a way. Angry, but you can't say what you're angry at. You keep a lid on it, but when the lid blows it blows sky high."

"Missed by a mile."

"Nailed it right on. Your body language, your need to cut me down, your uncertainty and frustration about your sexual orientation—you're textbook. Did I mention chronic depression? That too. You probably don't recognize the depression as such, but you feel it as lethargy, a sense of watching time slip by out of control, getting nothing done. A world-weariness. A vague, unfocused feeling of dissatisfaction. Now I'm working on the question of whether your imbalances are severe enough to allow you to kill."

"You're nuts."

"I'm also right."

"You actually get paid to spout this garbage?" Kovik spent the next five minutes—Jack surreptitiously checked his watch, just for curiosity—ranting and railing, explaining why Jack was absolutely totally wrong and Kovik had his life quite well in hand, thank you.

Signs promised the loop drive and Jackson Laboratory. Jack hung a right and put himself back on the one-way loop, headed for Thunder Hole. Kovik's tirade eased.

Jack changed subjects. "You said Edith closed you down. What do you mean?"

"She decided it wasn't happening because it was too windy and called it quits. While Fracci and Clyde were packing things up I walked a hundred feet—less—to take some pictures of the base of the cliff from the top of it. Hundred-foot sheer drop. Good light. It's spectacular, and the waves were breaking well. When I heard the engines rev I started back, and away they went."

"Clyde drives one van. Fracci drives the other?"

"Usually."

"You ever drive?"

"Not much. Sometimes. Depends."

"What does Edith drive?"

Kovik laughed suddenly. "She drives us nuts. That's

138

what she drives. I mean, look at it. Sun for once! It's not raining. She said we'd try again after lunch, and she's so hot to get this shoot finished. We could have another three hours of work done, if she hadn't quit."

"I don't know. It was so windy, Maxx's ears stood straight out when I kenneled him a few minutes ago. Try after lunch where? Do you know?"

"Something about a stone bridge. Know where it is?"

Jack shook his head. "Not exactly. Somewhere along the carriage paths, I'd guess."

"Those grassy trails in the park? You think that's where the stone bridge is?"

"Couple of them, I believe. Lauren will be there, I assume."

"You wanna talk to Lauren? Why?"

"Why not?"

Kovik shrugged. "She sure doesn't show me much, is all."

"You were her lover at one time."

"You better quit surmising and stick to the facts, Prester."

"And her baby—"

"That baby. She doesn't give a hang about the kid. She's using it to get sympathy—and drain some extra bucks out of Edith. That's all. You should have heard her whining about getting a baby-sitter on a Saturday."

Jack carefully modified his voice to mask the anger rising inside him. "Why didn't you help her find a sitter? The baby is your son."

"That's not true!" Kovik let fly with another expletive-laced protest, laying on denial of his paternity not with a brush but with a trowel.

Jack pulled into the Thunder Hole parking area. His pickup was the only vehicle here. "Ever been here before?"

"No. Supposed to be one of the major sights in this park. I want some pictures of it." He jockeyed his unwieldy tripod out the passenger side, but it didn't take him as long

139

as it took Jack to leash up Maxx the Wonder Dog.

The wind came whipping in here almost as hard as it blew on Otter Point, but the dark forest directly behind them mitigated it somewhat. A path with handrails led down to the craggy shore across black, broken, squared-off rock. The rock dropped off abruptly into the sea.

With a roar, a great cloud of white spray rose from within the cliff. Jack followed Kovik down the stepped path across the rock, hanging onto the wet iron rail. Maxx heeled for once. Maxx was not a seaside dog.

Another surging swell entered a great notch in the rock. With a boom it crashed in the hole and exploded into another billowing cloud. Thunder Hole. Right on. Maxx slammed against Jack's knee and stayed there, pressed on like a mailing label.

Jack watched fascinated as the ocean sucked its water back out of the notch. From the seaweed and mussels on the boulders below, Jack determined that this was low tide or nearly so. No sooner had that water rushed out than another swell came crashing in. This one was not quite as great as the first, the boom and cloud not as big. Its water departed with a swirling hiss.

Kovik poked Jack's arm. He had to shout above the noise. "Do me a favor. I need a size reference for one shot. Stay leaning on the rail here, all right?"

"Sure." Jack watched Kovik climb the path toward a vantage point on the granite cliff edge. But then a super colossal wave rushed in and destroyed itself with a roar. Maxx jumped and nearly pushed Jack off balance, so heavily did he press against him. Jack reached down and rubbed the mutt's shoulder. Maxx licked his pant leg. By training if not practice, Maxx was accustomed to gunfire, but dynamite-sized noises were obviously in another league altogether.

Jack stood erect and looked up toward the photo point, expecting Kovik to tell him to get out of here and quit spoiling the scenery.

Kovik was looking off toward the parking area in such a way that it was obvious someone else had arrived. He snatched up his tripod and began collapsing its legs as he disappeared in that direction.

"Maxx, come!" Jack broke into an unsteady lope up the wet, slippery rock path.

Behind them another biggie boomed. Maxx lurched into Jack's leg at just the wrong time. Jack sprawled across the cold, hard rock. His leash suddenly free, Maxx plunged forward and made tracks out of there.

By the time Jack got back on his feet and reached the parking area, the passenger-side door of a white Mercedes Benz was slamming. The driver must have been talking to Kovik. The driver-side window, cracked two inches, rolled shut. Its heavily tinted glass prevented Jack from identifying the driver. The Benz peeled out of the parking area and roared off down the left-hand lane of the one-way loop.

"Maxx! Saddle up!" Jack gestured toward the dog's open cage as he ran for his truck. Make that limped. Clumsily. He had banged his right knee when Maxx knocked him down—stupid dog!—and pain stabbed through it every time it flexed. By the time he reached the truck, got Maxx (at Maxx's insistence) not into the cage but up into the cab, and pulled out onto the road, the Benz, of course, had vanished. And pursuing a Mercedes with a Dodge pickup was like chasing a Thoroughbred with a Shetland pony.

Mumbling unseemly epithets at Maxx all the way, Jack drove up to the north side of the island and the Seaview Motel. He parked at the office door and pointed a finger at Maxx. "You stay put, you dork!"

Maxx slurped his wet tongue once around the finger and made a try at licking Jack's nose. Stupid dog.

Inside, Jack forced a smile at the little red-haired girl on the registration desk. He felt dark and ugly and not the least like smiling. It came as a surprise, and not a pleasant one, how thoroughly Kovik had managed to anger and irritate him. He thought he had his defenses up too. "I'd like to see the registration cards for the Sitting Pretty crew."

"I'm sorry. I can't—"

But he had his badge out and tilted in front of her nose at an angle conducive to clear viewing. "I want to know exactly what vehicles they brought."

"Well . . ." She licked her lips. "I guess there's no secret or anything. No privacy thing. You know. I mean, their cars are parked out there, right in public." She fumbled around in an open file box under the desk for minutes and minutes, it seemed. She brought up a wad of white four-by-sixes and laid them on the counter.

Jack spread them out. He remembered writing down his vehicle make and license when he checked in. These cards would hold the same information. And here it was. White Mercedes Benz, with the license number.

Registered to Edith Cray.

12

Jack Splat

Now here were Jack's kind of people. Despite a thick, gray overcast that had moved in during lunch (Edith was going to be peeved by that) and the windy weather, a slim, healthy looking young couple were out touring the carriage paths on horseback. They waved to him as they passed on their way up a slope and around a bend.

Envy leaped up and danced before his eyes. He ought to go check out a horse himself. It would be so much more fun—and faster too—than walking along these carriage paths. His running shoes squished with every step. His toes ached with the unaccustomed cold. Apparently they still weren't quite recovered from that frigid dunking. Funny that they didn't complain those few hours while the sun was out—the temperature had been about the same. And that's not to mention his bruised back, or thighs, or . . .

Maxx tugged at his leash, begging to follow the horses. Many a mile had Jack ridden, in New Mexico and elsewhere, with Maxx ranging out alongside. The old pooch loved it as much as he.

Sitting Pretty was not at the motel when he checked vehicle registrations. He could search all over the island for the vans, or he could wait at the most likely of the two bridges for them to show up. He had grabbed a quick bite to eat—a lobster roll—and chose the latter. Now here he stood. Waiting.

Would Sitting Pretty set up around a stone bridge if they had to carry stuff in? Not likely. So they'd no doubt use this one, which arched beneath the major highway. Jack had parked his truck unobtrusively off a sidetrack that accessed some farmer's field and walked the quarter mile to the bridge. Edith just might dump the location in favor of some other if she saw his truck there. Edith was like that.

Bored and inexplicably restless, Jack wandered off south down the path. The broad, grassy sward wound in lazy curves, never straight for long, through thick deciduous woodland. Even with the leaves coming down, you couldn't see more than a few feet to either side along this stretch. Jack felt incredibly closed in, and he had not felt like that during his run. Curious.

The map in the park folder showed the carriage path system as roughly a pile of spaghetti with trails looping and crossing in all directions. Again he didn't have the map with him. He'd better not go far, or he'd be hunting his truck with a metal detector.

And here came Ev at a stumbling run. "Jack! Oh, thank God! Jack!" In clear defiance of Edith's edict, she was wearing a Sitting Pretty parka over a pink-flowered summer frock.

Totally winded, she slogged to a stop in front of him. Clearly, she was distraught, for she didn't tell Maxx to quit licking. Between gulps of air she moaned, "I'm lost! I can't find the bridge. A big stone bridge."

"Behind us, just around the bend there. How did you get out here?" Jack yanked on the leash. "Cut it out, Maxx. Heel."

She sighed, still panting. "Being stupid. Edith dropped me off here and went on to get someone else. She said wait. But there aren't any bathrooms here, obviously. And the main road was so close. Right up there, where everyone can see. And I—"

144

"So you stepped around the corner, so to speak, and then accidentally kept going in the wrong direction." Jack started walking back toward the bridge—he hoped, or he was really going to look dumb.

She fell in beside. "So stupid."

"No it wasn't. Look at the sun."

She tilted her face up. "Where?"

"Exactly. The sky is evenly overcast. No way to tell from the sun which way is south. No shadows cast. You can't see buildings or landmarks because of the woods all around. Easiest thing in the world to get turned around wrong, especially if you're accustomed more to cities."

The stone bridge appeared up ahead. Ev wagged her head. *"You're* not lost."

"I didn't wander as far. On purpose. So where is everybody?" A hundred feet from the bridge, Jack stopped. It really was quite picturesque, except for a few miscellaneous cars and pickups that whipped by up on the road now and then. "I don't know." Ev sounded woefully dispirited. "Edith decided we wouldn't spend time eating lunch after all. And it's stupid, after she wasted the whole morning anyway. So she dropped me here and went off to gather up the rest of the crew. She said she'd have Clyde bring us lunches and we could eat while we worked. I expected Clyde and Arturo and everyone to be here by now."

The couple on horseback came up behind them. The man smiled sheepishly. "Can you tell us how to get to Witch Hole Pond?"

Jack smiled back. "No, but I can tell you how to get a lot closer to it. It's near the visitor center, and the VC is up that direction." He waved a hand toward the bridge and beyond.

"Thanks." The couple rode on.

"You said Clyde and Arturo. Where's Kovik?" Jack knew, of course, but he wondered what Ev's impression was.

"Down where we were this morning, I suppose. Edith

145

says he wanted to stay behind and take some scenics. She's pretty upset with him anyway, I guess, for messing up that whole day's shoot."

"How's he supposed to get home?"

Ev shrugged. "Nobody said. I imagine something was arranged when she talked to him, just before we left there."

Oh, really.

They strolled in peace, with leaves rustling beneath their feet and a flock of chickadees working a tree somewhere off to the east, dee-dee-deeing each other over every little find. The wind that rustled the treetops so wildly reached the carriage path here only in fits and bits. An occasional gust would tousle Jack's hair or kick Ev's summer skirt out ahead of her.

Jack pondered his next questions. So Kovik and Edith conversed before they separated. She did not simply go off and leave him without warning or explanation, as he intimated. Kovik felt insecure around Jack for some reason. He would surely not let it appear to Jack, of all people, that he had been summarily abandoned unless that were a lesser embarrassment than what had really happened. "Could you hear anything Kovik and Edith said?"

"No." Ev shook her head, and her dark hair floated. "They were over by the edge of the cliff."

"Mm." Jack knew for a fact that Ev got really nervous around cliffs. His mind drifted away to the time he got knocked off a cliff—a very high cliff—and she climbed down to help him. He thought of her fear then, and the peril of that ledge . . .

Maxx lunged against the leash and nearly ripped it out of Jack's hand. He began to bark and squirrel around, stirring the leaves beneath his paws.

Hooves were thundering this way. From beyond the bridge the young woman on horseback came riding at a full gallop. From the look on her face the world was flat and she had nearly fallen off the edge of it just now. With considerable difficulty she dragged her horse to a halt beside Jack and Ev.

Her mouth moved a couple times before it started forming words. "We found a . . . we think she's dead . . . but we didn't . . . Larry is there. He said—"

"Whoa." Without thinking, Jack gripped the horse's reins at the bit, to keep it in place. "A woman died?"

The girl's head bobbed. "Larry said call the police. I don't know which way a phone is."

"Give your horse its head and let it run back to its barn. It'll take you to a phone as fast as you'll let it. Call the rangers and tell them what you know." He turned her horse loose.

With a perfunctory nod she leaned forward in the saddle and yelled. The horse bolted away, south down the path.

Jack was already at a dead run himself. He released the leash. Maxx bounded ahead. Their feet sounded like a horse's as they raced beneath the bridge and on around the curve. The wet, slippery grass made Jack's footing uncertain, slowing him down.

Up ahead, in the middle of the carriage path, the man named Larry had dismounted. He huddled beside his big bay horse's head, holding its nose in a death grip.

Maxx stood on perfect point, showing Jack the ditch beyond the horse. From it protruded a girl's leg. The hem of a summer-weight skirt flittered in the vagrant gusts.

Larry babbled, "So pretty . . . blonde . . ."

"Marlette!" It exploded out of Jack before he could think. *God, no! Don't let it be her! Please, God!* He skidded to a halt at the edge of the road.

She lay asprawl, as if dumped. There was blood, but not a lot of blood. Blood soaked the upper half of her slim body and all but a few wisps of her platinum blonde shoulder-length hair. It smeared across her face.

Her face had relaxed into the ugly complacency of death, with her eyes, an ordinary shade of blue, fixed on

147

the cloudy sky. Lauren was still so very pretty, her face not at all marred by bludgeoning, as had happened to Veronica Wayne.

A shocking sense of loss engulfed Jack, very nearly the same shock he felt when he saw his Marcia's dead face. It literally floored him. He sat down heavily by the pathside, cocked his knees up, and draped his elbows over them, so he could rest his forehead on his arms.

She had been so eager to do better, to be the best she could be. Morally as well. A rare spirit, lost. But the worst loss by far, the infinite loss—the one that stunned and felled him—was her soul. And in that regard, he was her co-murderer, for despite clear opportunities he had never spoken to her about the work of Jesus Christ.

There was always tomorrow.

Her tomorrows were gone now.

"Jack?" Ev's hand pressed Jack's shoulder. "I know. I feel really queasy too. Oh, Jack! She was so . . ." Ev's voice quit.

Jack lurched to his feet. Time to shift into automatic and turn into a cop, secure the scene, do all the things cops do on automatic so that they don't have to deal with the full ugliness of it right now.

Larry was warning them not to touch anything until the police got there. Ev, bless her, had picked up Maxx's leash to keep him from investigating the remains. She was telling Larry that Jack *was* the police, and . . .

Jack grabbed Larry's horse's reins. "Climb up on the road at the bridge back there and flag down the next car that comes by, either direction. Your wife is on her way to a phone, but you go too."

"No. I don't think I should leave the scene. I don't . . . no."

Jack was reaching for his badge to enforce his request to Larry with a little muscle when Maxx barked. The dog yanked on his leash, lunging against Ev's grip. Jack wheeled to look at what touched Maxx off. A rinky-dink

148

putt-putt motor was headed this way from the north. A very familiar sound, that motor.

A moped rider in baggy pants, a peacoat, and a green crusher came putting around the corner. The rider braked hard, cut a doughnut turning around, and howled off in the other direction. Jack was finally getting a look at his assailant.

Jack shoved Larry aside and swung up onto the guy's horse without touching the stirrups. He was not wholly in the saddle before he was urging the horse after the moped. It was a sluggish beast, slow to get moving. Larry yelled something behind him, but he didn't care. The last time he saw that moped rider, he was in a boat. Jack wouldn't let him get away this time.

Not far ahead, the moped, cranked to the max, howled like a cat with its tail caught in the wringer. Jack got a glimpse of the fellow when the path straightened out enough, and the fellow knew Jack was right behind. He could tell from the way the guy hunched low, getting every ounce out of the dinky little bike that he could, and then some.

Jack kept his knees high on the horse—he sure wasn't going to fish around with his toes looking for stirrups now —and leaned over the dark bay neck. The mane whipped in his eyes and brought tears. Jack had forgotten the sheer power of a horse, the immense inertia of a thousand pounds hurtling up the road.

The moped hung a left suddenly through a break in the fence and onto a little, dirt farm road.

Jack reined the horse around the same corner. The horse stumbled, nearly slipped and fell. It staggered, catching its balance, and came back up to speed. The moped had gained several hundred yards.

Whining along the tree-enshrouded road, the bike was making good time. The horse was blowing loudly, its nostrils roaring. Flecks of foamy sweat and spit blew back into Jack's face. The moped did not tire. It would be going just as fast five miles from now as it went this moment. The horse was already starting to lose steam. Jack slapped the reins hard against the bay's lathered shoulders.

The road left the woods behind and ran straight-line out along the rutted road among open, weedy pastures and fields. They passed a weary little farm with rickety fences and weathered gray outbuildings. Another. If Jack was lucky, one of those farmers would call the cops about the weird drag racers who just went by, and a patrol car would be waiting at the head end of the road.

Nah.

His horse was flagging badly. It was losing all interest in the pursuit.

Half a mile ahead, the dirt road T'd into a major paved highhway. Jack could see traffic on it. And flashing lights!

From the northeast, here came a white official car with the Mars bar merrily dancing red, white, and blue. It slowed and pulled into the dirt road, blocking the moped. The cavalry to the rescue!

The moped dipped to the right and bounded out across an unfenced fallow field. It swung in a wide arc and aimed itself toward the road the cop car had just come down. The cop car kicked into reverse and started backing out the dirt road, but it wasn't going to reach the bike in time.

Jack could ride on to the unfenced field and cut right, or he could turn right here and cross a fenced pasture to that road. The fences around this field were weighed down to half their original height by snarled clumps of wild roses. He opted for the shortcut, reined his horse sharply aside, and yelled.

The big bay gathered itself in one stride and lunged. It barely cleared the fence. It's head high, it thundered out across the field, caught up for the first time in the thrill of the chase. The next fence would be easier. The horse would have time to prepare itself properly.

When the moped bounced onto the paved road, Jack was less than fifty feet behind and coming up on the last fence. He brought in the reins a bit and felt the horse bunch under his knees. As they left the ground, he moved his hands forward, giving the horse its head.

He heard the rose or berry bushes—whatever they were—crash and crackle. His horse dropped out from under him. He made a wild grab for the mane, for the neck, too late. He cleared the fence. The horse didn't.

The world exploded in a cacophony of howling moped, neighing horse, squealing tires, flashing lights, sirens, yelling, and a lot of pain and darkness.

Others would have to take up the chase. Jack was out of the race. He was out of everything. He lay still not by choice but because he could not move, could not think, could not function. The cacophony, somewhat muted, continued to swirl around. Voices tangled together in his ears. He could make nothing out. He drew in great gulps of air just as soon as his tortured ribs could move again.

Strong hands rolled him from his back to his side.

"Behind the back seat," a familiar voice called. "That. Yes." John Grayson?

As the voice protested, Jack hauled himself to an elbow and from thence to sitting. John Grayson knelt beside him, watching him closely. Jack sat on the shoulder of a paved road, half on asphalt and half in gravel. Before him, the bay horse, lathered and sweat soaked, stood disconsolately beside the crushed fence. Ev stomped noisily down into the ditch in front of Jack and handed a blue plastic box to Grayson.

She dropped to her knees and gripped Jack's shoulders with both hands. Her brown eyes, large under any circumstance, were distractingly huge. "We almost ran over you! The horse tossed you out onto the road, and the car almost hit you!"

Jack looked at Grayson. "The horse all right?"

"Not the first horse to breast a fence. Shucks, Prince

151

Charles's horses do it all the time. Yeah, probably. Lost less skin than you did. Here—take your jacket off. It's in shreds."

Shreds indeed. Jack's brand new jacket was, for all practical purposes, missing its left sleeve. He let Ev help him slide out of it. His shirt, miraculously, was still in one piece. Likewise his arm.

Grayson almost smiled. "Well, good. The only scuff, then is along the side of your cheek there. Off the horse, through the air, and *splat*. You got off lucky, Prester."

"Blessed is the word. Not lucky." Jack snorted. "Jack Splat. That's me. What about the—about Lauren?"

Grayson dug a couple foil packets out of his first-aid box. "Ev left some guy named Larry in charge of the scene and climbed up on the road. She flagged Vern down. He just happened to be passing through on the way to Somesville from Bar Harbor, and he radioed me. Sarnoff by chance was within a mile of the bridge, so he took over the crime scene."

"How did you know where we were?"

Grayson shrugged modestly. "I didn't. But there were six possible places you could come popping out. I took this one, and Vern, with Evelyn here, headed up this way to cover the next. I got the Bar Harbor police onto the other possible exits. And there you were." He ripped open one packet and handed the rest to Ev. "Open one, please."

Jack looked at Ev. "Nearly ran over me?"

She bobbed her head as she struggled with the foil. "John went in the ditch to miss you. Then Vern came up behind, let me out, and roared off chasing that guy. I don't know if they caught him."

"Not according to the radio chatter." Grayson pulled a moist wipe out of the foil. As Ev busied herself with the next packet, he dabbed at the side of Jack's face. Whatever was on the wipe stung like bees. "They're still looking, but I bet he gave them the slip. There's just too many places he could go."

152

Jack twisted to look behind him at the other side of the road. It was going to take a winch to haul Grayson's car back up on the pavement. It's sorry little headlighted nose was stuffed down into the tall ditch grass all atilt, and the right hind wheel hung free. Grayson had turned the lights off.

Jack grimaced. "Any abandoned shed, any farm lane, any ditch. That moped is so small it can fit anywhere. Where's Maxx?"

"With Sarnoff. Quit ducking," Grayson snapped. "You got gravel and leaves and every other thing ground into your face."

Maxx and Sarnoff. Jack wondered which would crack first and kill the other.

A tow truck came rumbling up. A grizzled old timer climbed out and meandered over, in no hurry whatever. He wore a green jumpsuit so dark and greasy it would cause an environmental disaster if it got tossed in the sea. "H'lo, John."

"Hello, Graham. How's the daughter?"

"Fine. Doing just fine. This is the third time this month, ain't it, to be pulling one of your park buggies out of a ditch?"

"If we're inconveniencing you, Graham, we can call Sumner over in Bass Harbor."

The old coot sniggered. He nodded to Jack. "You the feller Winthrop fished out of the water this side of Sutton, ain't you?"

Grayson was into his third wipe. "Graham here used to be a scorekeeper for the high school basketball league. Now he tallies mishaps. Can't help himself, I suppose."

"Not mishaps." Graham grinned, revealing yellow teeth. "Tallying grandbabies, John. Got my tenth grandbaby this week. Girl."

Grayson was saying congratulations, but Jack and Ev stared at each other. They blurted out simultaneously, *"The baby!"*

153

13

Song of Roland

Somebody shut that kid up!" Tall, thin, stormy Marian Hastings glared venomously at one of her uniformed officers, a small, rather shy young woman.

The woman didn't move.

Hastings transferred her glare to Ev and Jack, standing in the doorway of Lauren's motel suite.

Behind them, Grayson muttered, "Mother Teresa, I presume."

There was no chance Hastings would have heard his snide put-down above the infant's squall.

A motel crib to the left of the entry filled this corner of the room. In it a baby wailed lustily. The room contained a nice little table-and-chairs at a window, and a small kitchenette unit—stove, sink, and mini-fridge. The facilities were more than adequate for the mother of an infant to function easily. Beyond the crib, an open doorway led to the bedroom.

A swarm of technicals were going over the place with the tools of their trade—little plastic bags, brushes, dusting kits, a host of new gadgets with which Jack had only passing acquaintance at best. Forensics was probably his weakest suit.

Like the eye of a storm, the deputy prosecutor stood

154

in the middle of the kitchen, the only one not bustling about, and directed operations, apparently by means of snarls and sizzling glares.

The female officer stood open-mouthed, totally at a loss. "I've never even baby-sat." She raised her hands helplessly and looked at the crib.

"Then get the kid out of here!" Hastings cast further vile scowls around the room. She democratically included Ev, Jack, and Grayson in her latest scowl. "The murder occurred here. The killer tried to clean up, but we've already found blood spots. We just got here, so don't come in, and don't touch anything."

Jack briefly explored about thirty things he would love to say to the witch and decided against all of them. With perverse pleasure he disobeyed her by scooping the wailing baby out of its crib. He carried it still howling into the bedroom. It was soaked, its diaper soggy, its little shirt wet to the armpits. Its bare feet were very cold. He started exploring dresser drawers in the bedroom.

"Hey!" a tech barked. "Procedures require that you don't touch—"

"I know what procedures require." Jack was barking too.

No clean baby shirts. No cloth diapers. No baby salve. One threadbare baby blanket, but it was clean. In a corner he found a package of disposables with a single diaper remaining. OK. He only needed one for now. He carried it and the miserable child to the bathroom. No baby wipes, so he wet a washcloth. His brain wasn't totally out in left field. He chose a washcloth that was still folded up in the wire holder over the toilet tank—one that had not been touched yet by anyone.

Did Lauren use any sort of emollient when she shaved her legs? No. But here was a spray can of won't-hurt-the-hurt stuff. Jack scanned the ingredients and saw nothing there that would be bad for a baby.

Armed with the accoutrements of motherhood, he

155

took the baby out to the bed to change it. As he stripped the wet shirt off he sensed a presence in the doorway. Ev stood there looking lost.

Above the incessant howl he called, "See if you can find a baby bottle and milk or formula, will you? In the fridge, probably." He removed the soggy diaper. The tiny boy's whole south side was rough as a curry comb with diaper rash. Carefully Jack wiped and sprayed. When his own son was this size he had done his part as a diaper changer. This one was a real mess. He put on the clean, dry diaper. Firmly and tightly he wrapped the little guy, shirtless, in the blanket.

He went back into the kitchenette. The baby was still screaming. Ev was swishing a bottle of something in a pan of water on the stove. He leaned over her shoulder and plucked it out of her hand.

"Thank you." Jack took it still fairly cold and plugged the baby in. The howling disintegrated to fussy slurping. Once the baby got used to the cool, he ate hungrily. Jack walked back into the bedroom and sat on the edge of the bed. Hastings was snapping orders out there in the kitchen, but Jack didn't listen. He had to get his own brain back on line.

Ev leaned in the doorway, frowning. "It didn't have time to warm up much. Aren't you supposed to warm it and test it on your wrist?"

Jack smiled. "What does a bumbling bachelor know, anyway?"

She watched him a minute and smirked. "I think he knows more than he's letting on. I saw some jars of baby food in the fridge."

Jack nodded. "Sucking reflex is the best thing in the world to quiet him and help him feel better. We'll feed him some solid food later."

Ev disappeared suddenly, and Hastings loomed in the doorway. "If you can bring yourself to attend to business, *Mr.* Prester, I can take your statement now."

156

Jack kept his voice low and modulated. It was quite a strain on him. "This is far and away my most important business just now, Ms. Hastings. But we'll discuss priorities later."

"Your business is a police officer, not a nanny."

All right. So they would discuss priorities now. "My chief business is a human being. You say the murder happened here. I'm afraid this little guy may be a witness, though he might have slept through it. His diaper was very wet, which suggests he may have been napping when she returned here, and she didn't disturb him. In any case he's a brand new orphan. And he's helpless. We serve him first. Your statements and conferences and press briefings can wait."

She stared at him, and he held her eye. What was she thinking? He couldn't begin to guess. Her hard, angular features formed a mask, a wall between him and her thoughts. She turned away and disappeared into the next room.

Within a few more minutes the baby finished his bottle and began to fuss, still not satisfied. Jack brought him up to his shoulder and rubbed his back. Time to get back to the business of police officering. He started for the door and stopped.

The petite woman officer came through the door and parked in front of him. "I wasn't going to say anything, but I want you to know. I just learned a very important lesson about being an officer." She smiled bashfully. "And I'm going to take baby-sitting lessons or something."

He looked at her nameplate. "Thank you, Miss Rush." He smiled back. "If you don't feel at ease in a baby-sitting class with a flock of twelve-year-olds, volunteer to rock babies in the nursery at your local hospital. They'll be happy to have the help, and you'll get personal, hands-on training by the best. Besides, it's fun."

Jack let the sobbing, fretting baby slide down his chest until its head snuggled in the curl of his shoulder. A

157

tiny hand pushed up out of the tightly wrapped blanket and gripped his shirt. The small cheek pressed against him. He wrapped his free hand around the baby's shoulders, head, and back and held it firmly, encasing it in safety.

Jack checked in a mirror to make sure. Yes, the baby's eyes were wide open—and terror-stricken.

Ev watched Jack watching the baby. She watched the baby herself. Her voice trembled. "He saw it all, didn't he?"

His heart ached for the little guy. "I think so."

* * *

"Mother of the year." Grayson grimaced. "She left her baby alone in that motel room." He sat wedged in the padded corner of a six-person restaurant booth, his legs splayed under the table and his left arm slung along the little wooden ledge at the top of the wainscoting.

Dinner was over. The waitress, a rather broad-framed, older lady, had cleared the dishes. But this meeting of the minds didn't feel the least bit over yet.

Beside Grayson in the middle of the booth, Ev toyed with the straw in her tall 7-Up. "She couldn't find a babysitter. And no one bothered to help her. No one even tried. They just yelled at her, Edith especially." She looked woebegone.

To her right, Warren Sarnoff stared at his coffee, looking just as droopy.

Jack slouched in the corner opposite Grayson, leaning against the wainscoting too, feeling droopy and sad and woebegone and tired and stiff and sore. His abraded cheek still burned. His back ached where the moped rider had slugged him. He glanced down toward his belt buckle.

The baby was finally getting some rest. It slept soundly, as only babies can, scrunched up on Jack's tummy. Wrapped in a new flannel blanket and new blanket sleepers, it had finally warmed up.

Jack reflected for a moment on Ev's pure delight as they shopped the local mom and pop department store for the baby things. *Oh, Jack! Look at this! And isn't this cute?* over and over. The blanket sleepers never even saw the inside of a shopping bag. As soon as Jack paid for them, Ev put them on the little guy.

Beside Jack to his left, Hastings signaled the waitress for more coffee. "Someone rifled through the bedroom drawers, but they were neat about it. The rummaging wasn't obvious." She glared at Jack. "My tech says it wasn't you. You didn't stir anything around in the drawers."

"I tried not to. But the baby needed something dry. I noticed there wasn't much in the drawers. Most of his clothes were dirty. Big basketful in the bathroom. Lauren was probably planning to do laundry today, before it turned out she had to work."

Ev nodded. "She was really upset when Edith pulled that."

The waitress brought the coffee pot over. Jack shoved his mug down the table for a refill, since she was about it.

Beyond Hastings, Vern Bondi tapped his coffee mug too. He grinned wickedly at Grayson. "Assuming this here feller and that horse had something to do with your car being in the ditch, John, and your boat getting rammed and sunk—and I don't know what else—Prester here's kind of a liability, ain't he?"

Grayson actually laughed out loud. "Tell me about it! And that's not to mention the raccoon."

Vern har-har-harred.

Ev's huge brown doe eyes narrowed to suspicious little slits. "I heard about that raccoon. But what's this about a boat sinking?"

"What boat?" Jack gazed innocently from face to face.

Hastings looked at Ev. "You're on the inside. Did anyone pick a fight with Lauren? Reveal himself or herself as an enemy?"

"No more than usual."

"What's usual?"

Grayson snickered. "Toss half a dozen stray cats in a closet, and they won't fight as much as the Sitting Pretty crew."

"So there were no unusual indications of animosity, no threats, nothing like that."

Ev shook her head. "Nothing like that, that you could point to. No."

Dead end.

Hastings studied Jack, as if his battered face held answers. "Why did the moped rider turn and run?"

"Guilt. Fear."

"And not guilt concerning an unrelated crime, since neither you nor the horseback rider resembled police, and the body wasn't visible from the moped's viewpoint. Which suggests direct involvement with the murderer."

Jack nodded grimly. "Possibly the murderer."

"And you let him walk away."

"Now just hold on there, Miz Hastings!" Vern twisted to face her directly. "Doing your best still don't guarantee success. We did our best, and we were on top of it too. All of us."

Hastings's voice dripped acid. "How would you know what the best is? You're not even in law enforcement. You're a *custodian*." She pronounced *custodian* as if it were a job one step lower than grave robber.

"You bet I am." Vern straightened. One might even say he swelled a bit. "And proud of it. I can do jobs your technical experts couldn't begin to figure out. Proud of being able to drive a pickup anywhere I want too. I stayed with that yay-hoo the whole way, and through some pretty rough wheeling, until he ducked through a narrow break in a stone wall. Couldn't take the truck after him there and sure couldn't keep up on foot. But Chuck and Walter were both on the ball—Bar Harbor cops. They almost caught him even so."

160

Hastings would have made reply, but Sarnoff broke in. "The big question is why he came back to the scene. Why didn't he just split and stay split?"

Ev stirred her 7-Up some more. She still hadn't actually drunk any. "Left something behind?"

Sarnoff shook his head. "Not that we can find, and I called in some techs from Bangor. They're still working on it, but they haven't come up with anything."

"Anything to indicate where she came from?" Jack's body was getting stiff as a dried cowhide, but he didn't want to move and disturb the baby.

"Yes." Sarnoff actually seemed to brighten. "The techs found scattered blood drips. We're guessing she was transported on that moped, probably wrapped up in a tarp or lawn bag. The murderer came down from the north to within sight of the stone bridge. He must have realized what it was—a highway with traffic—and turned around. Blood drips suggest that. He made sure he was out of sight of the bridge before he dumped the body. No clear indication which way he went after that, though we know by surmise."

Jack tried to figure the change in Sarnoff. And it was a profound change too. Nothing about his demeanor now suggested hostility or impatience.

Hastings mulled this a moment. "Assuming he left nothing incriminating behind, why come back? You still didn't answer why he returned."

"Maybe he got confused on all those paths," Ev suggested. "He headed out intending to go home or wherever, got onto one of those loops by mistake, and ended up back down there. Maybe he didn't even realize he was going wrong until he stumbled onto us."

Vern shook his head. "Nah. There are signs."

Ev glanced at Jack. "It can happen."

Jack nodded. "Very instructive, Vern, what was just said. Ev is a stranger to the area. She says she'd have no trouble getting lost." He tactfully avoided mentioning that

Ev was speaking from experience. "To a stranger, the carriage path system is a confusing maze. But you've been here a long time. It's familiar territory to you. Whether you've actually hiked all the paths or not, you know where the system goes. So does John here. He was able to set up blocks instantly at all the carriage path outlets.

"So we can assume the murderer is not familiar with the area. Especially since Sarnoff here says there was nothing incriminating where Lauren was dumped. Either the murderer has absolutely no sense of direction—not likely, or he would never have used the carriage path as the dump in the first place—or he's a stranger."

Sarnoff nodded sagely. "Someone in Sitting Pretty. Ms. Hastings, have we established a time of death yet?"

"Not yet." As if on cue, the phone in her open bag beeped. She hauled it out and pronounced her name in much the same way she had said *custodian.*

The baby squirmed, stretched, and woke up. Jack hauled it up to a shoulder and absently rubbed its back. He sat up straight, flexing his stiff back and ribs, and rearranged himself into a more comfortable position.

A cook stepped out of the kitchen across the room. "Warren? Phone call."

Sarnoff excused himself and disappeared through the swinging doors.

And suddenly Jack understood Warren Sarnoff. Of course! Until the park superintendent secured the scene at the bridge, he had been playing a secondhand role. Strictly supervisory, and not even that to any great extent. He received reports, he provided reports, he delivered reports. Now he was in the thick of it, firsthand and hands on, at the scene, in control—and that made all the difference.

Hastings grunted into her telephone and asked one-word questions. Mostly she just listened.

The baby began fussing, casually at first, and chewing on its fist.

Instantly Ev whipped out a bottle from the new diaper bag in her lap. "Formula? Or juice?"

"That's fine, right there." Jack took the bottle of ghastly white chalk-looking stuff and offered it to the baby. No dice. It squirmed and turned its face everywhere except toward Jack. The little guy wanted Mommy, no substitutes.

With an embarrassed glance at Hastings, Ev brushed the tears out of her eyes.

Hastings shot the baby a disgusted look as she stuffed her phone back in the bag. "Preliminary medical report puts the time of death at around 11:15 A.M. Signs of a struggle. Some scratches and bumps. A blow to the side of the head stunned her. The killer then drove a sharp object into the base of her neck."

Hastings laid a finger on the back of her own neck. "Here, between the first and second vertebrae. The killer then somehow wrapped her up to prevent a blood trail. The wrap didn't leak in the motel, the motel parking lot, or the highway near the motel."

"But it was leaking when they were on the bumpy carriage path. Yeah, that would figure." Vern pursed his lips as if to ask another question. He lapsed into silence.

The baby was winding up into a full scale yowl.

Ev pulled out the bottle of juice and set the diaper bag on the table. "Here. Let me walk him around a little."

Vern didn't seem satisfied. "How'd he seal it up to make it leakproof?"

Jack thought about that just long enough to come up with the one indispensible item in every camper's pack, every motorist's trunk, every plumber's box, every rancher's jacket pocket. "Duct tape."

Vern snorted. "Oh, sure. Now where would he get duct tape?"

"That heavy silver-colored cloth tape? Lauren's kitchen counter." Ev reached across the table, and Jack passed the baby to her. "Lauren wrapped it around her rubber duck shoes. They were tearing along the side."

Vern watched Ev trying to be mother to a baby who knew the real McCoy—and lack thereof. "Why didn't he just leave the body there?"

Everybody looked blank. They all stared absently at Jack.

"I have no idea." He looked from face to face. No help there. "So it may or may not have been premeditated." He shifted in his seat again. His whole torso really ached. "Her murderer could have arrived with her, or he could have been waiting for her."

"You mean stalk her?" Ev was having some success convincing the baby to accept the juice. "That's creepy."

Sarnoff came out of the kitchen and settled back in his seat. "Hastings, did you notify anyone in New York?"

"I told Barry to call down there and get the cops to seal her apartment. She has an apartment in Queens, according to her driver's license."

Sarnoff looked as smug as a fox with goose feathers in its brush. "Well, there weren't any cops on the scene there. This noon I called a friend of mine at New York City Group and asked him to send a team to her apartment."

"Park Service, you mean." Hastings made the NPS sound like grave robbers too.

"That was my friend just now, calling back. Miss Laren's only close kin, it appears, is a sister in Passaic. So he sent one of his rangers over to confirm it and to notify her. Her name is Leslie Stokes. She knew Miss Laren had a baby and says she wants to take it. Give it a home. Social Services lined up a foster family to care for it until the sister comes up. They're sending someone out from Ellsworth to get it."

Jack glanced at Ev. Her eyebrows tightened as she clamped her lower lip in her teeth. She held the baby less than five minutes altogether, and already she didn't want to give it up.

Neither did Jack.

Sarnoff continued, "They found papers in the apartment—the baby's birth certificate and such." He paused. He looked confused, as if he didn't quite believe what he was saying or why it would be that way. "The baby's name is Roland."

Vern blurted, "Who'd ever name a baby *Roland?* Vernon's bad enough."

Hastings nodded agreement. "I read how names have such a lasting influence on a person's life. So important, names. Maybe the adoptive family, or her sister, will change it to something a little better."

Ev planted herself squarely in front of the table. "What's so wrong with Roland, Ms. Hastings? It's a hero's name, and very romantic. Didn't you ever take European lit? 'Song of Roland'?"

Sad was fast overtaking the droopy and woebegone and tired and stiff and sore in Jack. His heart, already heavy, grew nothing but heavier. Quietly he said, "The name Roland is Teutonic. It means 'the fame of the land.'" He hesitated and raised his voice a bit to keep it from cracking. "Fame. It's what Lauren always wanted. The good life. Abundance. Perhaps this little guy will be the one to realize her dream."

14

Black Jack

She looked motherly, being a bit plump, with short dark hair and a broad, warm smile. She was no doubt a nice enough lady, but she had never known Lauren Laren. She was no doubt a tender enough care giver, but she had never gone shopping for Roland, never bought him a warm blanket sleeper. She could feed him and bathe him and rock him to sleep, but she had never seen the dark splash of his mother's blood on the leg and rails of his crib. She knew nothing about his mother's dreams.

In the gloom of late dusk in the restaurant parking lot, Jack handed Roland over to this nice care giver, this foster mother, as the Social Services rep and Ev both looked on.

Tears ran down Ev's cheeks. Ev constantly surprised Jack. Ev, who admitted knowing nothing about babies, had already adopted this one in her heart. Ev, who when she arrived opined that the Sitting Pretty models were all tarts, was mourning Lauren in a half dozen subtle and not-so-subtle ways.

Ev handed the diaper bag to the Social Services rep. She murmured, "Good-bye, Roland," wheeled, and hastened away to a dark corner of the parking lot.

Jack pasted a false smile on his phizz because it

seemed a better thing to display in public than his real feelings.

The social worker offered a hand. "We're very grateful to you, Mr. Prester, for handling the situation so capably. We'll keep you informed."

Jack accepted the handshake. "Thank you. And if you turn up any other relatives, please remember we want to talk to them. We still have no motive and no suspect. We need all the help we can get."

"By all means."

The social worker said some good-bye pleasantries, the foster mother said some good-bye pleasantries, and they climbed into a car with a Maine state seal on the door. As they left the parking lot, the foster mother was strapping Roland into one of those bulky, impersonal, approved car seats. The car's red taillights disappeared out onto Route 3.

Jack glanced down at his new blue parka—the little department store didn't have any his size in green. The wet spot where he'd wiped off baby spit-up didn't show anymore, at least not in this light. He took his time crossing the lot to Ev.

Ev watched him coming and slurped her nose. "I don't know what's the matter with me. There are a million babies."

"But only one was Lauren's. Nothing's the matter with you. You're being normal. Unless you consider being normal a problem."

"Very funny." She wandered off, presumably to the truck since that was the general direction. "I'm sorry. I'm not acting very professional."

He wrapped his arm around her shoulders and drew her in. "Will you stop cutting yourself down? You made all the right moves, especially when we discovered the body. A beautiful job. It's a lousy situation, but it's turning out as well as possible, considering."

She sighed and straightened, stiffened. "You're right.

Life happens. I'm OK now. You know, I've been thinking about who knows about me—I mean, that I'm on the inside. Grayson, that Vern, Mr. Sarnoff, Hastings. Only police types, except Vern, and he won't say anything. It's still all right."

They arrived at the truck. Maxx squirreled around in his cage, yelping and snarfing cheery greetings as if the world were not black just now. Jack gave him a pat in passing and opened the door for Ev.

He was going to hate himself for the next five minutes. "It doesn't matter anymore. You're out of here."

Her head snapped around to him, and her mouth fell open. "What?"

"I'm not going to let you remain in harm's way. Two girls are down and not a thread of motive yet. There may not *be* a motive—it may be by reason of insanity. Jealousy. A stalker. No. There's no compelling reason for you to put yourself at extreme risk."

She parked herself nose to nose with him. "Now look here, Doctor Prester! You just said I'm doing all right."

"And you are. You're doing fine. It's not a matter of how you're doing."

"Think of all the questions Grayson and Hastings asked this afternoon, questions about the inside of the operation that only I could answer. You couldn't even get those answers from the others in Sitting Pretty, because almost certainly one of them is covering up and you don't know which one, so you can't trust any of them. You need me!"

"Not enough to stick you out in front of a murderer. No."

"You were the one who suggested me. You told Hal I was ideal. You said—"

"I didn't realize where this case was going to go. All right! I admit I asked Hal to put you on. I admit I sort of talked him into it. So shove me into the ocean again. I made a mistake, a very big mistake, bringing you in. And

168

now I'm going to rectify it by putting you on the plane tomorrow and bringing you back out."

"Oh, no, you're not!"

"Watch me. Get in." Jack left the door for her to handle by herself and stomped around to his side. He unlocked his door and flopped into the seat. The passenger side door slammed, but Ev wasn't in the cab. She was striding off across the parking lot toward Route 3.

Women! Bah! He cranked the ignition viciously. The motor roared. He backed out of his space and braked to a stop. He took two deep breaths. No, make that three. At the very least. He had to get his own temper under control before he could hope to control Ev. Besides, he was going to slam his truck into something if he wasn't careful.

She was out on the main road and marching west before he had himself staked down solidly enough to go after her. He drove out onto the highway and slowed to a crawl beside her, his flashers blinking.

He rolled down his window. "I apologize."

She marched on, her snoot in the air. "Apology won't cut it."

"Well, that's just too bad, because it's all you're going to get. I will not concede. You can be as mad as you want, I'm not going to let you place yourself at extreme and unnecessary risk."

She stopped and wheeled to face him, so he stopped. On a major highway. At dusk. "It's not your call, Jack. The very first hours we were ever together, in Death Valley, you said it wasn't a matter of a boss and a slave, or however you put it. It was two people working together. Obviously, as soon as things aren't going exactly your way, you instantly think you're the boss after all. Well, you're not. I take orders from Hal the same as you do. He put me on this, not you."

"Then he can take you off it."

"But he won't if I ask him not to. You know that. And I'm going to ask him not to."

169

"Ev, please . . ."

She shook her head. Her flyaway hair flew. "It's personal now. Even if you both take me off it, I'm staying." Her voice broke. She turned west and continued on her way through the blackness.

He slammed his fist on the steering wheel. He was so mad he literally could not see. He wrenched the wheel and pulled off to the side of the road. He let the flashers blink. His mind was roaring, his mind was blank. He leaned his elbow on the open windowsill and propped his head in his hand. With a sigh, he shoved up into first gear and pulled alongside her again.

"You're not trained as a cop, Ev. You're breaking cardinal rule number one: never ever let it get to you. Never let it get personal. It's gotta be a job, not a vendetta, or you lay yourself open to more than just danger."

She walked on.

"Look." He took a new tack. "I'm sorry. I'm handling this very poorly. I want you—"

"And that's another thing wrong with you, Jack." She aimed a finger at him—in fact, her whole arm. "You're a control freak. You handled it badly. *Handled* it! Like if you can just handle it right you can get your own way all the time. Well, I don't handle! Got it?" She marched on.

Headlights came toward them eastbound. Jack pulled way over. A dark pickup whished past. She marched on.

Now what? What must he say and do to get her out of this potentially lethal fix he'd put her into? The Seaview was something short of a mile from the restaurant, and they were almost halfway there. Maybe he should just drive on in and call Hal. Get the jump on her.

Headlights pulled in behind him and slowed. He moved off to the right. A dark pickup—no doubt the one that had just gone by them—shoved itself between him and Ev. And Jack was so angry he hadn't even noticed the guy's brake lights in his mirrors. He had to sharpen up, and fast.

170

The driver, a dark, burly figure in the green of his dashboard lights, called to Ev in baritone. "Got a problem, little lady?"

"Nothing you can help with. Thanks anyway for asking."

"Come on. Get in."

"No, really. It's not that kind of problem."

"It's safe. Trust me. Get in."

Ev ducked quickly behind the dark pickup and came scooting across the road to the right shoulder. Jack slowed enough to keep his truck between her and her rescuer. He leaned across the seat and had the door open when she reached it. Maxx barked enthusiastically in his cage.

She hopped in nimbly and slammed the door. She sat there a moment, her eyes closed and her body rigid.

Jack watched the pickup, but the guy apparently decided to give up. He peeled out, his tires singing, and drove up to someone's lane. He turned around there and roared away eastbound again. As Jack pulled out into the road and headed for the Seaview he kept a close eye on the rearview mirror. He wasn't going to miss the brake lights this time.

He rather hoped Ev would just break down and cry it out. Then he'd be able to reason with her a little better. But no. She maintained the stiff upper lip, stiff lower lip, stiff spine, and stiff attitude all the way home.

He pulled into a slot near their stairway. By the time he could lock up she was halfway to the door.

He'd take care of Maxx later. "Ev, wait!"

She slowed, but she didn't stop.

He ran to catch up and fell in beside her. "I'll walk you to your room. Now listen to me. Once you're inside your room you don't open the door for anyone, do you understand? No matter how harmless it seems. Not Edith, not Athalia, not anybody."

"You're being patronizing again. Paternalistic."

"Stop it! Lauren opened her door!"

171

Ev halted in midstride and stared at the near darkness. Her face tightened and clouded, but she didn't break. She softened, though, in a way, and walked with him without fighting it or trying to forge ahead. She even let him open the door for her. She headed disconsolately upstairs.

"It's about time you got back!" Edith Cray, Queen of Misery, stood arms akimbo at the head of the staircase and watched Ev come. She assiduously ignored Jack at Ev's elbow. "We needed you this afternoon."

"It wasn't my idea," Ev huffed, instantly defensive. "Jack and the park rangers and a county prosecutor have been grilling me for hours. It's not a whole lot of fun, Edith. Especially when it was Lauren. I saw the body. It was awful!"

"Thelma left a white number on your bed. Go put it on. We've altered the schedule. We do the formals tonight under kleigs at Northeast Harbor. Clyde and the harbormaster are working out the wiring."

Ev left Jack's side. As she scurried down the hall, Edith wheeled and told her back, "And for pete's sake, don't wear that jacket. The dress has puff sleeves."

Jack didn't worry that he'd be ignored forever. For one thing, he was too big to miss. For another, there was the curiosity factor.

And the curiosity factor got her. Without greeting or pleasantry, Edith cut to the chase. "So what happened to your face? Fall off your tricycle?"

"Off my pony. Gotta quit playing polo with amateurs. Where were you this morning, Edith?"

"I went through all that with three different law enforcement agencies that I know of."

"I can well imagine. Because of the logistics, the rangers and Hancock County all get to play cops and robbers together. Go through it with me, please."

"I was being bus driver and cattle drover, trying to round up my stupid crew and get them all in the same place at the right time. I have no alibi worth anything. Just driving all over."

"You picked up Kovik down at Otter Cliffs and dropped Ev off at the bridge. Who else did you ferry around?"

It wasn't Otter Cliffs, it was Thunder Hole. If he was very, very lucky, she'd slip up.

He was not lucky at all.

"I didn't see Kovik until nearly noon. I have no idea how the egotistic jerk got back. I didn't plan to use him in the afternoon anyway."

"Then who borrowed your car?"

"The Benz? Nobody borrowed my car. We used the vans."

"When did you last see Lauren?"

"Look, Prester, everyone else has been asking me this stuff. Why can't you people compare notes?"

"When did you last see Lauren?"

"When I dropped her off at the motel to see about her baby. I don't know the time. Ten thirty or so. When I came back to get her, the place was full of cops."

"Did you see the body in the hotel room?"

"No." She pressed her lips together into a thin white line. Her voice dropped a couple decibels, as if from weariness. "I realize you consider me the wicked witch of the west. You might even be crazy enough to consider me a suspect in one or both murders. People have called me worse, believe me. Frankly, I don't care what you think. I do care about finishing this project up tomorrow. And because of incompetence all around me—"

"Present company included, because I ask the same dreary old questions."

"Present company included, because you ask the same dreary old questions. We're going to have to really grunt to wrap this thing. Ron and now Lauren. And you people keeping Evelyn tied up all day . . ." She grimaced. She looked tired. Vulnerable. Not at all like Edith Cray.

173

"Then I'll ask you one last question that maybe isn't too dreary. Did Lauren tell you she filed formal grievances with the union and sent a whistle-blower letter to the IRS?" Edith's face turned from vulnerable to stony. "That is not true." She studied Jack with anthracite eyes. "I was right the first time. You're engaged in a vendetta—a pogrom—against Sitting Pretty and possibly against me in particular."

"Against wrongdoers, perpetrators—murderers in particular—regardless who they might be."

"No. No, Lauren wouldn't think of filing a grievance or writing to the IRS or anything unless someone put it in her head. She was an airhead. A rube. Besides, she had nothing to complain about—or squeal about. I don't coddle my employees, Mr. Preston, but I don't break any regulations either. I doubt I could ever prove it, but I'm willing to bet you were behind it." She nodded knowingly. "And I suppose, in your pogrom, the crowning achievement would be to pin a murder rap on me."

"Or two."

"As I thought."

Ev came down the hall aglow. She had washed her face and artfully applied makeup. The redness and puffiness were gone, or perhaps cleverly masked. And the gown, all soft and white and swishy with interesting sleeves and voluminous skirts, absolutely dazzled. She arranged a blanket over her shoulders as she paused beside them.

"Get in the van." Edith dipped her head toward the stairs.

"I'll take her down to the dock. Meet you there." Jack gave neither Edith nor Ev any room to argue. He turned and crowded in behind Ev, taking care not to step on her hem as they jogged downstairs.

Ev waited until they pushed out the glass door into the dark parking lot. "I hope you aren't expecting to stand at my elbow constantly."

"I expect exactly that. Either I or someone I trust will

174

be with you every minute you're not safely sequestered in your room."

She wheeled on him. "No!"

"Look, I said I wouldn't concede, and I ended up doing it. Now this will be your concession—to let me protect you."

"I think the term is, you'll blow my cover. No."

"We can save the cover. To the rest of the crew it will appear that I am smitten with you. I'm infatuated. And unlike most infatuated suckers, I have a badge that lets me indulge my infatuation. They can't chase me away. Your cover will stay. But your safety comes first."

She swung away and strode toward the truck. "This is ridiculous. As long as I'm with others, I'm safe."

"The murderer struck in broad daylight both times, ostensibly when others were around but in fact when they were not. He's a brilliant opportunist who grabs the first likely chance—and succeeds perfectly. We're not dealing with a random alley mugging that got a little out of hand. This guy is cold and calculating, without a stitch of fear or conscience. Please, Ev. You can't afford to forget for one moment that you're never safe. Never."

He opened the truck door for her and ignored Maxx's happy greeting. Maxx repeated his joysome, cheery hello. Maxx the eternal optimist. Maxx the Good Time Charlie, sore face and all.

When Jack was feeling good he didn't need further buoying, and when he was feeling black, the last thing he wanted was some fool cricket chirping "Cheer up! Cheer up!"

Right now, he didn't even like his dog.

15

Forgiveness

Weird, it was really weird, giving his truck keys to a suspected murderer. Jack handed them to Alan Messier. "You sure this is all right? I hate to see you going out of your way."

"Not out of my way. I've been doing a lot of walking. Getting out. I'll leave the keys with Ellen at the stable."

"It's a long walk from the stable to your house."

"I walk farther most days."

Jack shrugged. "I appreciate it. Thanks."

Alan bobbed his head—the head wearing his green crusher—and got in Jack's truck. He drove Jack's truck away.

Jack turned to Warren Sarnoff. "Any word back on the Laren body?"

"Not yet. They're not fast in Ellsworth the way they are in Bangor or big cities. And they sure as shooting don't like working on a Sunday. Tuesday or Wednesday, probably, before we hear anything at all."

Sarnoff stood on the berm—his white park car sat on the road shoulder—and leaned back against his fender. He crossed his arms and gazed out across fields and pastures, in no hurry to move.

Jack settled himself beside the hood ornament. His

thighs where the boat gunwale or whatever had hit him ached worse today than they had yesterday. On the other hand, his jacket had dried out enough so that he was wearing it this morning. It felt good, being able to get back into his old familiar sheepskin and denim.

Maxx cut a couple doughnuts in front of them, eager to be on his way. His ears sagged as he realized he was going to have to wait. Maxx was not big on waiting unless he could sleep while doing it.

Jack was eager to be on his way too. The horse he had ridden over one fence too many yesterday stood by his shoulder dozing, saddled again after a comfortable night in a farmer's barn, and ready to go. They had left it at the farmer's overnight rather than have to trailer it home. On the phone Jack had promised the stable owner, a woman with a husky, worried-sounding alto voice, that he would return it today.

Sarnoff had driven Alan Messier out here to pick up Jack's truck and drive it down to the stable for him. Did Sarnoff often do little odd jobs like this? Not likely.

He nodded toward Maxx. "Good dog you have there, Prester. Well trained. Obedient."

"*Maxx?*"

"For about half an hour yesterday, it was just the two of us, him and me, securing the scene there. He was good backup—useful. He did everything right. He let me know whenever someone was coming. Kept his nose out of where it shouldn't be. Stood guard when he was supposed to. Excellent police work. I'm impressed."

"You sure we're talking about the same dog? This is a mutt who chases fellow officers and eats evidence."

Sarnoff chuckled, an absolute first for him. "Then I was going to bring your truck up to you. But the message went through three or four people, so by the time Stella got it and radioed me, the directions were all garbled. Nobody knew where it was. I remembered you telling your dog to saddle up—"

"Our first day here, in the parking lot at the VC."

"Right. So I told the dog 'saddle up,' and he trotted off down the road. Led me right to your truck and hopped in the back. Very intelligent dog."

"Well, I'll be. Maxx. Intelligent. Sure goes to show you can't judge a book by its cover."

Maxx was curled up into a huge, fat, tangled dough-nut, gnawing on the root of his own tail, and snorting as he chewed.

"Say." Sarnoff studied a cow in a far pasture. "You said yesterday that Roland means 'fame of the land.' You study names?"

"Mm-hm. Hastings was right. Names mean a great deal. Knowing something about a person's name may on occasion add to understanding that person. Not always, of course. But it's surprising how often it helps. Even with little kids."

"Happen to know right off what 'Warren' means?"

Jack wracked his brain. "I think . . . as I recall, 'de-fender,' as in defending an estate or demesne. More spe-cifically, 'gamekeeper.' Not a bad name at all for a Park Service career man."

Sarnoff seemed vaguely pleased. "Well, back to de-fending. Gotta protect all that paper on my desk."

He launched himself erect, so Jack stood up. They good-byed each other tersely, and Sarnoff drove off.

Maxx rubbed his head up against Jack's leg. *Now can we go?*

"Intelligent, huh?" Jack gave the mutt a quick scratch behind the ears and swung aboard the big bay mare.

"Find, Maxx." He would deliver the horse back to the stable, but he wanted to do some exploring first. He backtracked that fruitless chase, covering, as much as pos-sible, every inch that the moped had covered.

The thick grass and weeds in the fallow field the moped had crossed prevented any useful tracking. Jack got off and walked most of the field, bent over, his eyes scanning the ground. He could see here and there some occasional sign of the two wheels. But if he had to track the bike, not knowing approximately where it had gone, he could never have done it. He was pretty good at tracking too.

Maxx found nothing, but not for want of looking. He shoved his nose in clumps of grass here and there, essentially following the moped track. He seemed to be sticking to business this morning. Sometimes, when he got bored with police tracking, he'd go sniffling off on some bunny trail.

Jack took to the saddle again on the dirt road. Nothing. They came out, eventually, through the hole in the fence onto the carriage path. Jack rode down to the bridge, turned the reluctant horse around, and headed it away from its stable, back up the path.

Maxx paid special attention to the ditch where Lauren had been. Jack had to call him away twice. The area was trampled flat by all the forensics techs and investigators, barren of clues and promise.

He continued back to the turn-off onto the dirt road and passed beyond it. He dismounted now and examined the broad path carefully, foot by foot. The moped had probably come up this way. If Ev was right, and indeed her theory made sense, the rider could have become confused right here at this Y junction. Jack turned aside onto the wrong leg of the Y and mounted again.

A thousand feet along the way, one side of the tree-guarded trail opened out into a couple of backyards. A horse-wire fence separated the carriage path right-of-way from the private land.

And here were garbage cans not twenty feet from the fence. Jack tied the horse, gripped an iron fence post firmly, and swung his legs over the fence. His back hated the maneuver and told him so, but it got him over the wire.

Maxx whined, so Jack pushed down on the top wire, and the dog jumped it. Maxx could not throw his hundred fifteen pounds up over barricades all that well.

Jack lifted lids on the trash cans.

"Bingo."

Beneath the latest paper grocery sack of garbage from under someone's kitchen sink, a blue plastic tarp had been stuffed. Jack put on a pair of thin disposable gloves and pulled the tarp out. Maxx's nose got interested in it instantly, but even Jack could smell the blood. Strips of used duct tape clung to it here and there.

"Hey, you!" A man's voice yelled from the house. "What are you doing?"

"Police matter. Glad you're home!" Jack called. He rolled the tarp up tightly and headed for the house.

A portly, middle-aged fellow with a day's growth of whiskers stood on his back stoop scowling. He watched every move Jack made, but he watched Maxx even more closely. "What's going on?"

"Is this yours?" Jack held the tarp up.

"Nope. Only blue tarp I got is on my RV out front."

"Did you see someone put this in your trash can there?"

"We just got up a short time ago. Sunday's my only day off. Only day I don't have to get up at five."

"How about yesterday?"

"Went to work yesterday."

"How about your wife?"

"She went into town."

Jack displayed his badge, avoided elaborating on just what the police matter was specifically, and took down the fellow's name and address. Sawyer. Rod Sawyer. Jack documented the tarp and got a signed note confirming that Mr. Sawyer had indeed observed him removing this particular tarp from his trash can. Jack wanted all his bases covered when this came to court.

Jack made some small talk and left Mr. Sawyer five minutes later, immensely pleased with his find. The mortal remains of Lauren Laren had been transported how many

180

miles wrapped up in this tarp, on a moped. A moped with such a bulky load would have to elicit some sort of notice from somebody. But that was legwork for another day. Jack hopped back across the fence, helped Maxx across, and hit the saddle again.

A little north of Messier's gatehouse, Jack gave the bay mare her head. He didn't have to ask directions to find the stable. Like a heat-seeking missile, the horse unerringly homed in on her corral, her bored companions, and the oats bin.

They entered the stable yard about ten thirty. Entranced by myriad new smells, Maxx abandoned Jack's side, along with all pretense of being a police dog. He trotted from pillar to post, pausing, grunting, snorting, constantly sniffing. Now and then he'd lift a leg, but by now, after a morning of exploration, that was largely ceremonial.

Jack's truck was parked by a four-horse stock trailer. Home sweet home.

Jack rather expected the worried stable manager to come darting out to kiss her long-lost horse or give it a complete physical. Nothing. He tied the horse's lead line to a rail, flipped the left stirrup up over the seat, and loosened the cinch. Still no stable person.

He removed the bridle and hung it from the saddle horn. He scratched the mare behind her ears under the web halter and wandered over to the corral (or do they call them paddocks back East?) to look at the other horses. The usual motley assortment of rental stock stood about with ears askance, patiently waiting for dinnertime.

"Well, she doesn't look any the worse for wear."

Jack wheeled.

A very hefty young lady, stocky and round-faced, had stepped in beside the bay. She wore jeans and a nylon parka so battered and stained that Jack couldn't tell its color. She had pulled her mouse-brown hair back in a ponytail anchored with a rubber band.

Jack crossed to her and offered a hand. "Ellen Radner? I talked to you on the phone, I believe."

"You said the mare breasted a pasture fence." Her hand was calloused, her grip firm and definite. "That what happened to your face?"

"Matter of fact, yes."

"Something about a high speed chase."

"Yes. Like you used to see on 'Miami Vice,' only without the rock music or turbo sports cars or cigarette boats."

She snickered. "I was a 'Vice' fan—I was in love with the hunks. But I can't imagine them chasing anyone on Molly here."

"I was in love with Lieutenant Castillo's desk. Ever notice? Big as a soccer field and not a solitary thing on it, except his AT&T Merlin. No overdue reports, no letters to answer, no forms in triplicate, no paperwork at all."

"Height of fantasy for a government employee."

"Pure fantasy. They didn't shoot real bullets either." He shrugged and grinned.

Ms. Radner dipped her head toward the horse. "Did she eat?"

"Molly had about a quart of oats last night and another quart this morning. And hay, of course. The farmer didn't have any alfalfa. Just timothy. I checked her over pretty well last night and couldn't find anything wrong."

"And I checked you over just now, watching you. You know what you're doing with horses. I feel a little better about you stealing her." She untied the mare and headed for the corral/paddock.

Jack followed. "The neighbors back in New Mexico always swore I'd end up a horse thief." Should he apologize? Thank her? Uncertain, he said nothing. He pulled the cinch free and dragged the saddle and blanket off Molly's back.

Ms. Radner opened the gate enough to admit the horse, took the halter off, and swatted her. The mare jogged inside to join her companions. The woman continued over to a door in the barn labeled "GEAR." Most Eastern stables would call it TACK.

She opened the door for Jack. "If a dude shows up who obviously doesn't know diddly about horses, I talk him off a horse and onto a bike or moped, depending where he's going. I'm not going to have my horses mistreated."

Jack carried the saddle in and plunked it down on an open rack. His breastbone tickled. "You rent mopeds?"

"Yeah."

He came out and closed the door behind him. "Are you the only moped rental on the island?"

"One in Bar Harbor, but I think they closed for the year. They're pretty much summer tourists, you know."

"Yesterday or the day before, fellow about this tall with a green crusher and yellow slicker."

"You mean did such a person rent a moped?"

Jack nodded.

"Not that I know of. I have a helper on Saturdays, a little junior high girl who loves horses. She's good, really good. She might have let one out. She didn't mention it, though."

"I want to talk to her."

The woman's round face pinched down into a suspicious scowl. "You weren't chasing a moped with my horse, were you?"

"Wouldn't dream of it."

"You . . ." She hesitated before finding a choice name for him from an obviously extensive vocabulary.

He raised his hands helplessly. "Would a moped jump fences?"

She laughed suddenly and wagged her head. "Come on up to the house. I'll write down her name and phone for you."

Jack whipped out his notebook and pen, so she wrote it down right there. He warned her that if someone returned a moped she was not to touch it and must call the park immediately. He thanked her profusely and bade her good day. He called Maxx in and made a beeline for his truck. This little girl in his notebook may well have gazed upon the face of a murderer.

* * *

The little girl wasn't home. Jack knocked a couple times on the door of a pretty, two-story frame house in Seal Harbor. No answer. But half a block down the road, services were just starting in a small white church nestled back among the trees.

Jack ordered Maxx up on his cage roof, the dog's preferred place to be, and walked down to the church. Its bell pealed as he reached the steps up to the front stoop.

Most of the older men wore suits and ties, and some had topcoats. The younger men were dressy casual. By far the majority of the congregation, though, was composed of women. Jack took a pew at the back, not because he felt out of place in his chambray shirt but because he wanted to be first out at the end.

The pastor was one of those contradictions in terms, a jolly thin man. He had to be on the downhill side of sixty, but he bounded around like a high school basketball player. His exuberance gave the lie to the stereotypical dour New England parson.

Jack assumed Marlette was an unbeliever—that she had never accepted Christ. He wondered where she was spiritually, and daydreamed about sitting beside her in church, sharing a hymnbook. He caught himself in his daydream and slapped himself back to business.

They followed the usual order of worship and stuck to the grand old hymns of the faith, the songs Jack loved from his childhood. "How Great Thou Art," "Blessed Assurance," "Power in the Blood."

The congregation made public confession. "We have sinned against You in thought, word, and deed, by what

184

we have done and by what we have left undone." The pastor in the name of Jesus Christ pronounced general forgiveness. Then he launched into his sermon, but Jack didn't hear a word of it.

His mind and heart were still back there on the confession. "Sins of commission." He had lied to Edith Cray. It was an out-and-out lie that he could make waves if she didn't treat her hired help more humanely. The purpose of the lie didn't matter. Telling it did. And what about all those little fibs of convenience, fibs that could have been avoided with a bit of thought?

And sins of omission. Lauren.

Poor lost Lauren. Because Jack didn't care enough to say something.

The enormity of his sins scalded him. Technically, general confession covered it and general absolution erased it. In fact, Jack knew that "general" was nowhere near adequate.

They passed the plate, and Jack couldn't say how much he put in. He didn't notice. He had studied all the theological ramifications of forgiveness. He had the head knowledge down cold—the theory. At this moment, though, his peace of mind, his very life, depended not on theory but on love. Head knowledge couldn't do it. He begged his Lord's forgiveness. His heart craved it.

A promise from God was a promise kept. The Father promised to forgive. It was done, albeit at great price. Jack's head knew that too, but his heart refused to accept so costly a forgiveness that was freely given.

Then they sang the closing hymn, "Just As I Am," and Jack snapped back into worship. He sang the bass line because on this particular hymn he knew the bass as comfortably as the melody. But even more, he knew the message. *Just as I am without one plea, but that Thy blood was shed for me.*

In his tangle of thoughts and guilt, he had forgotten that for a moment. Jesus was enough. Let his heart lag behind. Let his feelings refuse to accept. His feelings didn't control reality. God did. The fact of the matter was, Jesus *had* paid for his errors, and God would not make Jack pay for them as well. Jack had asked sincerely. Therefore he was forgiven.

He was forgiven.

He was forgiven.

So wrapped up was he in this profound realization that the final blessing was invoked and half the congregation out the door before he remembered why he had been sitting in back. He hopped up and squeezed into the line headed outside.

The pastor stood out on the front stoop with a happy smile and a ready hand.

When Jack reached the man he shook hands and asked, "A fourteen-year-old girl named Theresa Haines lives just up the street. Does she worship here?"

The pastor looked perplexed. Probably worshipers —especially strangers with scuffed-up faces—usually didn't ask that sort of thing. "You want to talk to her?"

"I do, very much."

The pastor jammed his two fingers against his teeth and whistled one of those whistles Jack never was able to master, a whistle that warned ships of offshore rocks. "Theresa!" He waved come to someone up the street.

A slim, perky little brown-haired girl turned and came trotting back to the church, her patent leather flats making horsey clip-clop noises on the sidewalk. Her mom and dad and a couple of little brothers stopped and waited for her.

Jack stood aside as other worshipers filed past. They congratulated the pastor so effusively on his message that Jack was sorry he'd missed it.

But he wasn't sorry about where God had led him instead.

Theresa's ponytail bobbed as she halted beside the pastor. She grinned as only a fourteen-year-old can grin, a

186

smile wide enough to slide a ski in sideways.

Jack extended a hand. "Miss Haines? My name is John Prester. I must talk to you a moment."

She looked at him oddly. She glanced back at her parents. They started this way. The pastor was still shaking hands, but he was keeping an eye on Jack.

Jack led her by an elbow down the steps and out under a tree. "Yesterday, a man and woman took Molly and another horse out onto the carriage paths."

She nodded. Her hazel eyes went wide. "You're the ranger who grabbed Molly! Ellen told me about it. That's what happened to your face, right?"

He grinned. "That's right! Very good."

She smiled bashfully. "Ellen was some upset. She was going to hitch up the two-horse trailer and go get her, but the park called and told her it was all right—that you were experienced and all—and then you called. But she was ready to pull wings off flies, she was so mad."

"More important question now. Who took out the moped?"

And she actually turned pale. Her mom and dad arrived then, at just the wrong moment. Jack introduced himself and displayed his badge. He repeated his question. "Who took the moped?"

"Nobody. I didn't check out a moped yesterday. You can look and see. It's not written down in the book."

Jack watched her face a moment. Her eyes flitted nervously about, alighting on just about anything except him. Now what?

The father broke into the conversation. "That girl on the carriage path yesterday—it's all over the TV news. Two deaths in a week. I told Theresa she has to call Ellen today and tell her she's not allowed to work there until this thing is settled. I don't want her out on the trails alone exercising the horses or on her bike riding over there. Or even being at the stable with Ellen up at the house."

"I understand your concern. A wise decision. We're

not even off first base with this one." Jack turned back to Theresa. "You understand how important it is that the truth be told here? We have to catch a murderer before he kills again." He paused a beat, letting her guilty conscience work on her a little. "When I asked about the moped, you lied to me."

"Now look here!" her father roared.

Jack kept his eyes on Theresa. "The truth is more important than you can possibly realize. Tell me about the moped. Please."

"I'm not lying. Really." She cast her big hazel eyes toward her father. "Daddy?"

The man growled, "If she says it's the truth, it's the truth."

Jack whipped out a business card and penciled in the local park phone number. "If you change your mind, Theresa, please call me. And your dad is right. You stick close around home until this is over."

16
Seal of Proof

Anyone who thinks God lacks a sense of humor should watch seals a few minutes.

Seals, along with camels some of God's more droll creations, act funny, look funny, sound funny. Jack paused at the rail of the big seal exhibit at the oceanarium, north annex. Off to his right, the young woman seal keeper stood in big rubber boots throwing fish to the harbor seals. Out on the fake ice floe, or rocks, or whatever the gunnite cement was supposed to be, Marlette and Ev, blonde and brunette, long flowing hair and short flyaway hair, posed fetchingly. All around them, seals cavorted and splashed.

This horrendous mess was taking its toll on Edith. She was blacker and in a fouler mood than ever. From a canvas director's chair, she ordered the keeper to toss fish here or there in the tank. The keeper would. She had excellent aim, in fact. Then Edith would yell at the poor girl because the seals didn't respond to the cues right. They'd pop up out of the water in the wrong place or grab the bait too fast or stay too low in the water. Jack could empathize with the keeper—Maxx didn't obey much better. Edith even snapped at Fracci, the light of her life—if her life had one.

Over by the snack bar, Kovik was loading a camera. Clyde was fiddling around in the back of the van parked in a pedestrian walkway nearby. Only a few visitors wandered about, and they tended to lose interest in the shoot quickly. There is a great deal of boredom to fashion photography, unless seals are involved.

The oceanarium, Jack had heard, had started with an interesting little aquarium in Southwest Harbor. It bought out a complex called Aqualand up here on the extreme north tip of the island and expanded its operations. Now down in Southwest Harbor you could see Maine's sea life, as Maine's sea life looked back at you. Up here you could walk out across genuine saltwater marshes and watch wetland wildlife, a politically correct thing to do, while the wildlife kept a wary eye on you. Over in Bar Harbor you could, courtesy of this same oceanarium, watch baby lobsters at a lobster hatchery. Whether they watched back was a moot point. Jack hadn't done any of that yet, but he couldn't imagine immature crustaceans being as entertaining as these seals.

Jack continued around the exhibit. He leaned both elbows on the rail, settling in beside a wiry little ancient one. "How's it going?"

Winthrop Spalding nodded. "Can't complain. Neither can she" —he bobbed his head toward Edith Cray— "but that sure don't seem to stop her."

"I hear you." Jack pulled twenty-five dollars out of his pocket and handed it to Winthrop. "I appreciate your help, especially on such short notice."

Winthrop eyed the wad before he pocketed it. "Kind of a lot for standing around doing nothing, ain't it?"

"Five hours at five bucks an hour. It's what we agreed on. You're the baby-sitter. It's not what you do. It's having you here in case something goes wrong." Jack watched the seals dart and glide about beneath the surface as the two models carefully got themselves back to shore along a narrow walkway.

"Bathroom break," Ev called.

Athalia joined the two, and all three girls headed off

190

together to the restrooms. Thelma, the wardrobe mistress, trotted after them, laden with clothes and one of those steamer things for blowing away wrinkles.

"They been good about that—about keeping all together," Winthrop mused. "If one of them needs something, the other two stick with her. I told Madam Seagull there that she ought to stay with the girls for her own protection, and she said some stuff to me hot enough to rupture a fifty-five gallon drum. My wife woulda had a heart attack if she heard that coming from a woman's lips."

"Madam Seagull, huh?"

"Look at 'em." Winthrop waved a hand toward a row of gulls perched on the roof of the gift shop. "Loud, noisy, always squabbling, and not getting much done. Pretty, though."

Jack grinned. "That about sums it." He watched Clyde tote a big stage light of some sort over to the snack bar. Clyde could probably heave a hippopotamus twenty feet, if it didn't squirm so much it spoiled its trajectory. A boy in an aqua oceanarium jumpsuit was helping him, mostly by pointing out the electrical outlets. "What do you know about a girl named Theresa Haines?"

"Bill Haines's oldest? Smart little girl. Does real well in school. Honor roll in the paper. Polite. Likes to be liked. Her daddy was in the marines until they turned him loose with a medical discharge. Lost a leg in a training maneuver that went sour—dummy grenade turned out not to be a dummy."

"And Theresa works at the stable. What does Maine have in the way of child labor laws?"

"She don't exactly work there. She just messes around there a lot. Ellen lets her hang around, and if she wants to help with the horses, why, fine. Every girl Theresa's age is horse nuts, but she's more so."

Jack nodded. "When I was in junior high, we guys rode some, but the girls lived and breathed horses. Their

191

idea of a festive party was to go out and vaccinate thirty or forty colts."

"Ayuh. That's Haines's girl. If you're gonna be here for the rest of today, I'll go home and change the oil in my car."

"Sure. I'll call you tonight when I find out tomorrow's schedule. Thanks again."

"My pleasure. Girls this age, they're way too young to die."

"Amen and amen." Jack watched Winthrop head out toward the gate. He lurched erect and wandered over toward the ladies' restrooms.

Here came the girls. They had changed into the next items to be photographed, similar white, picture-T-shirts and tights. Ev looked great in dark pink tights and a shirt with fuchsia blossoms and ruby-throated hummingbirds splayed across the front of it. Athalia looked marvelous in turquoise tights and blue jays cavorting in a spruce bough on her shirt.

But Marlette took Jack's breath away. She wore red tights and silk-screened flowers. Jack noticed in passing that they were blood red roses, with European goldfinches. Her hair fell in lush ringlets down her back. Marcia used to say moist air made her hair curl. Apparently it did the same for Marlette.

Her snit obviously had passed. The moment she spotted him, she burst into the most heart-warming of smiles.

She came bouncing over and latched onto his arm, beaming like the sun that shone somewhere above this muted overcast. "You hired that old man to watch over us, didn't you!"

"Well, yes I did."

Athalia cooed, "That is so romantic! To hire us a bodyguard."

Ev snorted derisively. Apparently her ideas of ro-

192

mance did not reflect Athalia's. Jack liked Athalia's attitude better.

Marlette snuggled up close. "Really, luv! If a murderer came, what could a feeble old pensioner like that do?"

"Be a witness, which means the murderer won't come." They were headed toward the next location, obviously, so Jack fell in among them, his right arm wrapped around Marlette, Ev on his left, and Athalia tagging along lackadaisically at Ev's left. He felt much grander than reality dictated, surrounded by such a bevy of beauties.

"The killer strikes when there are no witnesses, as half a dozen sheriff's deputies are finding out. They're scouring the countryside—even begged folks on TV and in the newspapers to come forward with anything they saw. Nothing."

Marlette bobbed her head. That mane of luxuriant hair moved languidly, seductively. "And as long as all three of us stay together, there would be a witness."

Athalia cackled. "Come on, Marlette. Get a clue. We're all suspects. As long as we stick together, one of us can't kill the other two. Right, Jack?"

"That too."

The next location turned out to be the snack bar. Quick walk. But then everyone stood idle as young Ellison adjusted the reflector to Edith's liking. Edith had already moved her chair to the new spot and plunked down in it.

Marlette scowled at Athalia. "Dead set, the killer's not someone in Sitting Pretty. We might be an odd lot— and some of us stupid as a wombat"—she glared at Ev— "but not killers."

"Why not?" Jack asked.

"We're all fair dinkum—all basically good and caring. I say most people are, except the very few that go crooked."

Athalia pronounced an unladylike word. "If people were so rooty-toot good, Pollyanna, we wouldn't need tamper-proof aspirin bottles, right, Jack?"

Jack was going to say something affirmative—"Good point" or whatever—but Marlette turned on Athalia with a string of invective, in Australian and in Yank, that would burn the ears off a mule-skinner. He glanced at Ev. Ev made a subtle "Wow!" face.

"Shut up, Marlette." Edith waved an arm. "You and Mike over on those stools. Thelma has the shirt with the poinsettias waiting for you. Evelyn, over there." She pointed toward Fracci at the far end of the snack bar.

Jack pulled his parka off and draped it over Athalia's shoulders. He led the girl apart a little way. The cold bit into the sleeves of his chambray shirt. "Tell me something. Did Lauren mention anything to you about filing a grievance?"

Athalia nodded. She stared off across the park, sober, even morose, her veneer of cheer instantly dissolved away. "So useless, you know? She asked us to back her up. To go into it with her."

"She asked all three of you?"

Athalia nodded again and pulled his coat in closer around her. "Marlette refused. She said she couldn't because if she complained she might lose her green card. She'd get blackballed, and she'd have to go back home before her career got started. Evvie said she'd have to talk to her brother first. I guess her brother's a lawyer in Hampton Roads."

"What about you?"

She shrugged heavily, trying to dislodge her load of sorrow. "I couldn't see how it would do a mite of good, and I told her so. Ronnie threatened the same thing, to file with Labor Relations, a day or two before she died. Edith promised to lighten up. Didn't do no good at all. Same old Edith. I so wish I'd said yes to the poor thing." Her dark eyes went wide. "They both died right after they—it couldn't be, could it?"

"It could be coincidence, if that's what you're thinking. Or not. This case is as frustrating as eating pea soup

194

with a fork. There are so many tangled threads, I don't know which end to pull on first." Jack was trying to keep his mind on the conversation, but his eyes kept turning to Marlette. What a gorgeous lady, perched so fetchingly on a snack bar stool.

"Thal?" Edith called. "You next, while the other two change their shirts."

"Nothing doing." Athalia handed Jack's coat back to him and jogged over to the snack bar. "They'll wait for me, and we'll go change together."

Edith fumed about the ten minutes that would lose.

Kovik crouched down to set up his shots.

Fracci snarled, "Women! So excitable."

Athalia posed beside a stool, right by the orange crush machine. "Yeah. We sure do get all excited about nothing. But trouble is, then we turn around and go out with him."

Ev giggled, and Marlette laughed. Fracci marched off in a huff toward the van.

Edith was not amused. "This is your doing, Preston. I told you in the very beginning you were disruptive."

Jack assumed an overblown drawl. "Yup. Trying to keep the girls alive sure puts a kink in the old plowline, don't it?"

Marlette giggled like water dancing in a brook. She attached herself to Jack's side as if with Velcro, so he gave her his jacket.

Winthrop appeared at the gate and ambled this way. He parked beside Jack and watched the goings on as Athalia posed for Kovik.

Jack smiled. "Fastest oil change in New England."

"Decided if I let it go another three hundred and fifty miles, I can change it right on the thousand-mark."

"How many thousand?"

"Coming up on thirty. It'd be a hundred and thirty if the odometer read up that high." Winthrop gazed beyond Athalia. "Put on a lot of 'em driving into Bangor while my wife was in the hospital there, toward the end."

"That the closest hospital?"

"Took her to Eastern Maine Medical Center. They're the best around." Winthrop snapped back into it. He straightened slightly. "This morning sometimes, when they were taking pictures in two different places, I couldn't watch them all at the same time. So I thought I might's well hang around, in case you ran into the same problem."

"Appreciate it."

Marlette purred, "Fair go, luv. We appreciate it too. You're a bonzer gent."

Winthrop glanced at Jack. "That's complimentary, eh?"

"Highly."

Marlette babbled, and Jack listened as Athalia finished. He felt himself grinning inanely and couldn't close his yap down to a more sophisticated smile. Then the three trooped off to the restrooms. Thelma jogged behind them, her arms full of T-shirts.

In the middle of the sidewalk, Clyde fiddled with a big spotlight, apparently trying to fix it.

Kovik headed over to the van. He glanced furtively at Clyde, then opened the passenger door of the van and groped around under the front seat.

Jack muttered in Winthrop's ear to take over. As the old man strolled casually toward the ladies' restroom, Jack walked past the snack bar to the entrance. As soon as no one was noticing, he ducked aside and ran down a looping walkway behind some shrubbery. He wished he had Maxx now, but the dog was out in his cage. You didn't bring a mutt like Maxx into a theme park full of live animals.

He turned again and followed the wide main walkway toward the snack bar. Ahead he could see Edith's back (her director's chair did not have her name stenciled on the back) and Clyde's side. The van sat between Jack and Kovik. Hustling silently—very nearly a contradiction in terms—Jack moved in behind the van and then around the driver's side to the open doors at the rear end. Methodically, slowly, Kovik was gently rubbing one of the cameras with a box about the size that would hold a tennis ball.

"Hi," said Jack.

The bruiser must have jumped a foot. He nearly tossed the box in the air.

Jack whipped his arm forward and swatted the box out of Kovik's hand. It bumped and skidded across the paved walkway.

Kovik's face went blank for a fraction of a second. Then he yelled, "What are you doing, Prester?! What's that box? What were you doing with that box?"

Instantly, the buffalo charged. Jack saw Edith rising out of her seat.

Jack held his hand up, palm out. "Whoa, Clyde! Don't touch the box, for a couple reasons. One, let's dust it for prints and see who's been handling it. Two, it's probably hot."

"Hot?" Clyde paused, looking bewildered.

Edith came charging up. "What's going on?"

Kovik pointed as he shouted. "He was doing something back here with that box! I caught him."

Edith's eyes shot daggers at Jack. "Mike, go get the people in the entrance kiosk to call the sheriff's office. Now!"

"No." Jack tried to keep a close eye on both Kovik and Clyde. Hard to do. "Find someone else, Edith. Kovik here is under arrest. Turn around, Mike, and lace your fingers together on top of your head, please."

"Nonsense. What's the charge?" Edith reached for the box, but Clyde stopped her. "It's hot, he says."

Kovik didn't move.

Jack would give the bozo ten more seconds before he went for his gun. "Malicious mischief, for starters. Your lawyer will want to know what Maine has on the books for industrial espionage too. I'm guessing the box is hot as in radioactive. Sabotage. Clouding your film with radiation."

197

Edith stared at Kovik. Kovik started to protest loudly, explaining how Jack was trying to destroy the whole operation—an accusation that bolstered the conclusion Edith had already mentioned more than once.

But she was ignoring Kovik's *Sturm und Drang*. "Wait a minute. Does that make film look overexposed?"

"Sort of, yes. Washed out."

"Why, you . . ." Edith started pounding on Kovik's fragile ego with a magnificent array of ugly names, her fury building with every blistering epithet. She capped it with "You're dead, little man!"

Kovik's ten seconds were up and then some. Jack started for his gun to enforce his demands. Kovik's face contorted in a rage to exceed Edith's, and Jack perceived that he was just a tad too slow reaching for a weapon. Kovik exploded not at Edith, for the mighty Clyde hovered by her shoulder, but at Jack.

He didn't pull an arm back or take the trouble to aim. Both his fists shot forward at once. One nailed Jack on the sternum and the other moved his midsection inboard two inches. Jack felt himself go airborne.

He landed heavily in a bush. The bush dumped him out onto the paved walkway. No way would he draw a breath for the next five minutes, as stove up as his diaphragm was. And then Kovik was above him and kicking.

Jack rolled. The kicks landed on his bunged-up thighs. Then, inexplicably, Kovik turned aside. Jack rotated another half roll, taking advantage of the ever-so-brief respite, and managed to get his legs under him. They worked in slow motion, considering the speed they ought to be operating at.

He should pull a gun on this joker. But as enraged and out-of-control as Kovik was, Jack might have to shoot him. There had to be a better way. Possibly even losing this fight was a better way. Jack needed his super-intelligent police dog; he really needed him.

He half turned to meet Kovik and got knocked back

another ten feet. Women were screaming. He saw Winthrop sprawled out on the cement.

Here came Kovik, roaring. The burly giant swung again and caught Jack a glancing blow in the neck—enough to knock him against the iron rail protecting the seals from the curious public. Stunned, dizzy, not breathing, Jack sagged on the rail. Only because his elbow was caught between the rail and the gunnite retaining wall did he stay halfway on his feet. The inelegant situation of virtually hanging by his wedged-in arm was not doing a single nice thing for his shoulder.

Kovik was coming. He kept coming. His eyes wide with surprise, he sailed past Jack into the seal enclosure. Directly behind him, Athalia stood with her legs spread wide and her face twisted in fury.

Splaaassssh!

Athalia lunged forward and pressed against the rail. She flung epithets at Kovik as vile as any Edith had come up with and from apparently an even richer vocabulary.

Jack pivoted and hung on the rail, gripping his diaphragm, as he looked over the side. He tried to inhale and couldn't. Kovik thrashed and flailed just below the surface. Jack knew how cold that water was, but his empathy fell well short of pity.

Marlette wrapped her arms around him, babbling worried sounding inanities. At least she cared.

Like a disgruntled walrus, Kovik hauled himself out on the gunnite ice floe in the enclosure.

Jack tried to speak and couldn't. His diaphragm was still locked up.

Athalia pointed to Kovik. "You just stay sittin' right there, creep."

Jack looked at her, held her eye.

She held his eye right back. "You don't grow up on the streets of Atlanta without learning a few little tricks."

"Obviously." Jack had to sort of gasp it, but it was intelligible.

Ev came running up. "I called the sheriff's office."

Marlette latched on tighter. She was asking him how he felt. He really didn't want to tell her. To Ev he grated, "Get Maxx." She raced off.

Edith parked at Jack's elbow. She had picked up the hot little box. She held it by pinching two fingers on alternate corners, and she had removed a fairly large phial of something. She grimaced as she held it up in front of Jack. "This symbol on the label, a circle with those things in it. That means radioactive, right?"

"Right." Jack still gasped.

"He ruined the day's shoot, then. We have to start over." She looked about her. "Let's go, girls. No time to waste."

"Athalia?" Jack croaked. "Thanks. Afraid I'd . . . have to . . . shoot him."

"Wish you had." Edith walked away, putting the phial back in its box.

The girls moved off to line themselves up on the snack bar stools.

Winthrop came doddering over. "Guess I'm getting old. There was a day I woulda took him."

"I didn't . . . do . . . any better."

Somewhere in the hazy reaches of upper Mt. Desert Island, a police siren wailed.

17

Forgiveness, Part 2

They ached so bad you'd think they were broken in little pieces. The moment they stopped moving they stiffened up. They looked terrible, all swollen. And that was just Jack's legs. Then there were his back, neck, his breastbone and ribs, his arm—especially the elbow where he hung up on the rail. Every breath hurt.

He stretched out across the big, cushy bed in Ev's room and didn't bother to take his shoes off, he was so weary. He closed his eyes and listened to the whisper-soft rustle of pencil on paper across the room.

Ev the professional budget analyst was assiduously toiling over that fake spreadsheet Jack had requested. She was taking the assignment very seriously, even say with élan.

Jack did not understand the kind of mind that loved to crunch numbers, and he did not understand women. That made Ev unfathomable twice over.

Jack's room at the Seaview was merely a room, with a bed, a chair that looked as if it had escaped from a cheap diner, a formica shelf pretending it was a desk, the obligatory TV set stuck on the wall, a nightstand, and a framed sheet of paint splashes that was supposedly meant to represent a seashore on a sunny day. So far on this seashore, Jack had not seen many sunny days, literally or figuratively.

His head thudded.

Ev's room was pleasanter by far than Jack's. It had been repainted recently. Instead of the formica thing, it had a charming writing desk by the window, a Queen Anne design with delicate cabriole legs and a tasteful little brass lamp.

"Jack? Do we include the expense of reshooting?"

"No. That was unforeseen."

"Why did Kovik do it?"

"Patterson, that sheriff's deputy, and I grilled him pretty intensely on that—double-teamed him, got him good and nervous, but he wouldn't crack. Then he decided he wanted a lawyer, and we were dead in the water. I didn't want to wait around, so I told Patterson to have at it, and came on back. Basically, he wanted to cause Edith grief without letting her catch on that it was he."

"So she couldn't get him blackballed?"

"Something like that, I guess." If he lay very, very still, fewer things hurt.

"Mm." Her pencil scritched on.

The fake-antique phone on her little desk rang, and every nerve in Jack's body jangled like sleigh bells on a horse.

She answered it and after a bright "Oh! Hello!" uh-huhed and grunted into it a few minutes. Jack heard that pencil going.

"Jack? Want to speak to Hal?"

"Tell him it's my deepest desire to talk to him, but I'm on the verge of hospitalization and can't move my body. Also ask him if he can fax us some more background info on the principals. Especially Marlette's real name. Get Warner in New York to nose around a little, maybe. And see if he can get the people in Bangor to move a little faster on the medical report."

She told her phone, "He'd love to. Here he is."

Rats. Now he was going to have to move. But no. The phone cord was long enough. She put the phone down beside him on the bed and handed him the receiver. He lay there, eyes closed, and listened to Hal describe for his benefit all the figures he had just given Ev with, no doubt, an identical description.

Jack delivered his laundry list of requests, explained why Kovik was in jail awaiting arraignment, and hung up. Since he had the phone right here, and didn't have to move, he dialed the park.

Stella Smith's soft Down East voice answered.

"Jack Prester, Stella. Don't you ever go home?"

She tee-heed. "I've been working Sundays from one o'clock on. I'm glad you called. You have two messages. Ellen Radner is trying to reach you, and Bill Haines. Isn't he the ex-marine in Seal Harbor who ran the full around-the-island marathon last summer with a wooden leg?"

"Wouldn't put it past him. May I have their numbers?"

She gave them to him, and he repeated them aloud for Ev to write down. He didn't want to move his body enough to get his pen and notebook out. He thanked her, exchanged a few pleasantries, and got back to business. To work, to work.

He dialed Ellen Radner first.

She sounded just as big on the phone as she looked in person. "Dr. Prester? You were asking me about mopeds. I heard on the news that the murderer escaped on a moped. Is that true?"

"Alleged murderer. Possible murderer."

She grunted. "OK. So I inventoried my bikes. One is missing."

"What does Theresa have to say about it?"

"I didn't talk to her. She wasn't there. But I told her father what I just told you."

"You can identify it if you see it?"

"I assume so."

"And no one's returned one?"

203

"No. Do you have a license number for the one the killer used? Alleged killer?"

License number. Jack had been close enough at the very end to read a plate, probably. Why hadn't he? It took him a moment of intensive recall to realize why he hadn't. "There was no license plate on the bike. Rider must have taken it off."

"If you don't ride it out on a public thoroughfare, you don't need one. I license all mine simply because you never know where the tourists are going to take them. And they sometimes want to do the loop road on them." The voice hesitated. "You sound terrible. Are you all right?"

"Ms. Radner, if I were a horse, they'd be reaching for a shotgun. Thank you very much for checking your bikes and calling. We appreciate your service immensely."

"Strictly self-serving. I haven't had a single customer since the girl died. Not one, and Saturday and Sunday are my busy days off-season. But my horses keep right on eating. You gotta catch that dude."

"I hear you." He signed off with the equestrian Ms. Radner, Ellen of the Hungry Horses, and dialed the Haines number.

Bill Haines answered tersely in a clipped ex-marine voice.

"Mr. Haines? Dr. Prester. You asked me to call back."

"Yes. Ellen Radner told me a moped is missing, and you were asking Theresa about mopeds. I think you should talk to her."

"I would like to."

Someone knocked brusquely on Ev's door. She got up to answer it.

Jack asked, "May I come by shortly?"

"That would be fine. Yes. What's your drink, Doctor? I'll make sure I have the fixings."

"Orange juice. You mean booze shops are open Sundays in Maine?"

Over at the door, Clyde's voice was rumbling to Ev.

204

Haines loosened up a little and even almost chuckled. Apparently ex-marines were allowed to stand at ease eventually. "No. That's what neighbors are for."

Jack spoke some good cheer and good-byed him.

"Clyde got back with the fresh film, and we're working again. Reshoot at Otter Cliffs and some new stuff." Ev turned out her desk lamp. "Since you're wearing your denim coat again, may I borrow your parka?"

"Sure. Hey. My jack is bolted to the spare tire under the truck bed. Maxx will show you where. Will you go get it and lift me out of here?"

She smiled and wagged her head. "I bet you need it. We came out of the john just as you were flying through the air. And I mean flying. Plop in the bush. You broke the poor bush, you know."

"Alackaday. I'm so sorry."

"And that puny little Mr. Spalding dived right into Kovik. Scored a hit too, before Kovik floored him. He's amazing."

"Yes, he is." Obviously she was going to just stand there jawing, so he abandoned the jack idea and dragged himself up to vertical unaided. It was a chore.

He called the amazing Mr. Spalding and told him Otter Cliffs.

She locked up, and they stopped by his room so he could give her his coat.

Jack knocked on Athalia's door and Marlette's. Athalia bubbled. Pasting Kovik had done wonders for her good nature. Marlette was in a royal snit again. She made it abundantly clear that she barely tolerated Jack's presence. Both girls joined him, though, as part of the safety plan they had implemented. Always together, guarded whenever possible. His harem of lovely lasses all collected, Jack escorted them out to a van.

He let Maxx into the front seat, followed the van down to Otter Cliffs with his truck, entrusted the girls' safety to an amazing little old man waiting at the parking lot in his thirteen-year-old car, and continued on to the Haines residence in Seal Harbor.

Haines opened the door almost before Jack finished knocking. Jack stepped into an austere home, carefully and tastefully decorated in a bare minimalist style. Elaborate wooden moldings along the ceiling and in the archway between the formal dining room and the living room suggested the place dated from the thirties. The paint, wallpaper, and electrical fixtures all suggested it was brand new.

"My wife, Frieda. I don't think you met her at the church."

Jack extended a hand to a plain woman with short, styled hair and a subdued look about her. She looked worried too, or perhaps even fearful. But she smiled and made some noncommittal pleasantry about Jack being welcome. He didn't feel particularly welcome.

"Please sit down." Bill Haines waved toward a billowy, white overstuffed sofa. "What can we get for you? You sure orange juice is it?"

"More than sufficient, if you have it. Or water." Jack folded in stiff jerks, like a carpenter's rule with rusty hinges, and settled himself into one end of the sofa. He'd probably need the sofa arm to pry himself out again. The fluffy upholstery sort of drew him into itself.

Frieda Haines disappeared into the kitchen.

Haines perched himself on the edge of an oversized recliner and propped his elbows on his knees. "I asked Theresa about the missing moped at Ellen's. Theresa said she didn't take it. I knew that. Where would she hide it? I asked her who rented it. She said nobody.

"So I told her, 'If you won't talk to me, you can talk to the cops,' and then I called you. I'm sure she's holding back on something, but I don't know what."

Jack nodded once and quit. His neck hurt. "I got that same impression when I spoke to her at the church."

Haines looked absolutely grim. "I know my daughter

206

pretty well, Doctor. She's not obstinate or devious. She's frightened. And that terrifies me."

"You've been hearing about mopeds on the news, and you're afraid she's tangled up in something potentially lethal."

"Yes. I may have been too harsh when I was questioning her. I was upset and worried. I may have frightened her more—driven her into a hole, if you will. I'm not too good at interacting with my kids yet, but I'm trying."

"I applaud you. Too many fathers don't try. They don't even know they should be trying."

"Oh, I wasn't always like that. During service I was absentee a lot more than I should have been. When I got back from my last overseas tour, Frieda hauled me off to one of those church retreat things. An encounter. They talked there about how important a father is to his kids. He's the one who shapes them, even more than the mother. I never guessed that. Anyway, I've been working hard to spend time with all three of my kids."

Mrs. Haines entered with four orange juices on a tray. She walked, talked, and served like a high-society socialite. For all Jack knew, she was. He managed to launch himself out of the sofa and stand up for her. His thighs howled.

Theresa followed her mom into the room, obviously under direct orders to do so, because she looked like a puppy about to be swatted with a newspaper. Her eyes, normally sparkling, were puffy and red. Her whole face drooped. Even the buoyant ponytail sagged limply. Mrs. Haines sat at the other end of the sofa, and Theresa took an easy chair in the corner opposite Jack.

Jack sat down again. "Ever show horses at the fair, Theresa?"

"Down at Blue Hill. It's just a little fair, but it's fun."

"The little ones are always best. When I was a kid, we'd go to the State Fair in New Mexico for one day to see the big time and ride the really nauseating rides. But we didn't show there. We took our horses to the county fair. Borrow each other's neatsfoot oil, hang out on straw bales for a week, try on each other's hats, just mess around. Maybe flirt a little. Shovel a lot, and fork a lot of straw."

She bobbed her head. "Ellen lets Josie and me both take a horse down. It's a lot of fun. We made Four H posters and stuff."

"Posters. Oh, yeah. I'd forgotten about the posters. The girls would make these posters showing the bot fly life cycle, or labeling all the parts of a horse. So we guys made one too. 'Top of horse. Bottom of horse.' Then Ernie Morales made an instruction poster to go along with it. 'Place rider on top of horse. Place shoes on bottom of horse. Place feed at this end.' The girls accused us of not taking things seriously."

She was smiling, albeit wanly. "That's how the boys are down at Blue Hill too."

"Hey, the girls were right. We guys would slap a saddle on, jump in it, and take off. The girls would fuss around with their horses, really get to know them. The girls were the real horsemen. We were just riders. Ellen knows what she's doing when she hires you girls. You love the horses. We bozos merely use them."

She tensed up instantly at the mention of Ellen Radner.

Jack looked at Haines. He'd noticed it too.

"In fact," Jack continued, "Ellen Radner knows she can trust you girls to pay attention and do things right. Your dad says he talked to you about a missing moped, and you're reluctant to discuss it."

She was clouding up again, ready to cry.

"You know," Jack mused, "when you saw in the paper, or on TV, that a New York model died, it's tragic and it's news, but it wasn't immediate. You didn't know her. I did. The killer snuffed a charming young woman with her head on straight—a woman who wanted to make a difference. Every killer's victim that you read about or see on TV is a complex person with much to offer. We hear about tragic stuff so much, we too often forget that."

He watched her face a moment and went on. "Pretend for a moment that one of your friends was the victim —a girl you ride horses with and know well. Josie, for instance. Perhaps even Ellen herself. Gone forever." He lowered his voice to a gentle purr. "You see the difference?"

She was cracking. He could tell.

He drove the wedge in a little farther. "You have information I need, Theresa. Your father fears for your safety. So do I. The person we're trying to nab has no conscience. No compunctions. He's killed twice. We think he might kill again. We need whatever you can give us, and now."

She glanced at her dad and looked at Jack. "Can I tell you alone? And you promise you won't tell anyone?"

"I promise only so long as it's not a criminal offense or if the privileged information isn't dangerous to your welfare. I won't keep a secret that could harm you personally." He looked at Bill Haines.

The ex-marine, bless him, saw when he wasn't wanted. He stood up. "We should check on dinner. Frieda?" He headed for the dining room archway.

Frieda hustled out before Jack could get his tortured body fully standing. He sank back again.

He stuffed his hands in his pockets and watched her face intently. "What about the moped?"

"I'm scared. And ashamed mostly, I guess."

"That's perfectly all right. You're still a kid, uncertain about life. Not that you're ever certain. I get scared and ashamed, and I'm twenty years older than you are. Talk to me."

"It was Friday night after school, at the stable. Two nights ago. There was this man called, see? And he said he was with a movie company that was coming in to use the park for a movie. You know, on location? And he needed a moped to get around and scout places."

"He used those words? Location and scout?"

209

She nodded. The ponytail bobbed. "And he's all, 'I'm in a big hurry, Miss. Will you leave it out, and my agent will pick it up?' And so of course I'm all, 'Sure!' He sounded so straight."

"Who actually came and got the bike?"

"I don't know. I didn't see. I put it out by the end of the driveway, and I was cleaning stalls, and when I came out it was gone, so I figured he took it."

"And no paperwork on it."

"He said he was in a hurry—he didn't have much time. And I believed him. It was gonna be dark soon, y'know?"

"And he hasn't returned it."

She looked shot down, totally dismal.

"And you didn't tell Ellen about it yet because you're afraid you just lost her bike to a con man."

More nodding. More bouncing ponytail. "I didn't think she'd notice—the bikes are all sort of crowded together in the shed, you know? You can't really see what's there and what's not. And maybe it would come back. You don't know."

"So most of all you're afraid Ellen will hate you."

The tears bubbled up and over and ran down her cheeks. She slurped her nose. "Do you think Ellen will ever forgive me? I really like her, you know."

"I certainly would if it were me. Everyone makes mistakes, myself foremost. Too often I have much to be forgiven for. I'll put in a word for you when I see her. It was an easy mistake, made from a good heart. You wanted to help."

"I feel so bad. And scared."

"You ought to tell your father about it."

She shook her head. The ponytail went into paroxysms. "He wouldn't understand."

"Maybe not, but not for lack of trying. He's worried about your involvement in this case—involvement in a murder. Your involvement is not nearly as dangerous as we feared. The truth will greatly ease his mind."

"You won't tell him?"

"I promised, remember?" Jack smiled. "And of course, if you see the bike anywhere—at the stable, out on the street, in a ditch—don't touch it, and call the park right away. Will you do that?"

"Sure."

"Good. Let's switch subjects." Jack rearranged his body a little. This sofa wasn't so bad, once you got used to it. "I want you to think about the person who talked to you. What did he sound like on the phone? Old? Young? Like he ought to be handsome? What picture comes to mind?"

She pondered that a few moments, staring more at the lamp beyond his Adam's apple than at him. "I don't know. I guess he sounded big. Real big. A big, deep voice. Tough and muscles, you know? And like, pretty old. Yeah, he sounded old. And like he was just getting over a cold. A real deep-down voice and like he was hoarse, kind of."

Clyde Wilkins.

18

Let's Talk, Emma Hoople

Jack rapped on the door. At 10:30 P.M., Edith ought to be home. In fact, she ought to be in bed. He stepped back a bit so that she could see the hall clearly through the fish-eye viewer in her motel room door.

The chain and deadbolt clunked. She opened it a crack. "Preston."

"Ms. Cray. It's late."

"Yes, it is."

"But I'd like to talk to you awhile."

"How long a while?"

"Depends. If you keep your answers short, I promise I'll keep my questions short by only saying every other word."

She looked at him long and hard. She burst out into a bitter laugh. "Come on in. Who needs sleep anyway?" She opened her door fully and moved aside.

Jack stepped inside. "I do, and I'm not getting any. Occupational hazard."

She bolted the door again and led the way into her suite. It was not a kitchenette like Lauren's or a pretty single room like Evelyn's or a dump like Jack's. It sported a sofa, coffee table, wet bar in the far corner, rather Victorian-looking writing desk and chair, a couple of easy chairs, and a separate bedroom.

"Have a seat." She paused by the wet bar. "What's yours?"

"Orange juice." Jack sat in one of the easy chairs. They looked less painful to get up out of than the sofa.

"Screwdriver?"

"Juice, neat."

She was too good a bartender to make fun of him, but her facial expression said, *What a dork.*

Jack was past caring. He was done with the day. And it wasn't done with him yet.

She gave him his tall juice and settled into the chair across from him with her half-gone pale gold something—Scotch and water, perhaps. "I suppose you want to talk about Mike."

"In part. The pogrom you feared from me was eating its way from inside your crew. Why?"

"Not feared, past tense. Fear. Present tense. Although I admit I'm having second thoughts. You stopped him the moment you realized what he was doing."

Jack repeated himself. "Why was he doing it?"

"Revenge, I suppose. For dumping him."

"And you dumped him because of his orientation."

Her eyebrows rose. "You have good sources. It's not common knowledge. He humiliated me, Preston. He used me. Used my power for his own ends. He didn't really love me." Her voice dropped a notch and softened. "He was the light of my life, once upon a time."

So. Edith had a light in her life after all.

"And the light of Lauren's? I understand Roland is his."

"He disavows the child. I seriously question it too." She relaxed somewhat. She flung a long leg up over the arm of her chair and scrunched into its corner, asprawl. The words began to flow faster and smoother. Apparently catharsis felt as good to fashion mavens as to anyone else.

"He gets around, no doubt about it, but not nearly as much as rumors suggest."

"How about with Veronica?"

"Nothing serious. But then nothing Veronica did had serious implications. She was an airhead. A petulant airhead."

"She was going to go home and file a complaint. So was Lauren. Both died. Coincidence?" Jack slouched deliberately, to look less threatening.

"If I killed all my enemies, Preston, New York City would be down to seventeen people. Though I can see how I would be a prime suspect."

"Anyone who survives at Sitting Pretty is a suspect."

"Except Evelyn."

"Even Evelyn. She could have had Veronica dispatched in order to make a place for herself here."

Edith pursed her lips in thought a moment. "I suppose she could. But she's not that hungry for the work. She's here because Harry invited her and Harry wants to put her into the big time, not because she herself wants to make the big time. She's not ambitious enough."

"She looks just fine to me when she's out there sashaying around."

"I've been in this business for years, Preston. The spark isn't there."

"You kept right on rolling when Veronica was killed, and Lauren's death didn't slow the program a moment more than it had to. That's as heartless as sending a sympathy card postage due."

She turned loose that bitter laugh again. "Business, Preston. I'm in business, as are the people who work for me. I never mix business with personal matters."

"I can't believe that. Not the way the people in this company play emotional roulette with each other."

"That's, shall we say, strictly extracurricular. On the shoot it's all business. You've watched us long enough to know that."

214

Jack was not here to argue, unless argument might bear some fruit. He couldn't see any use for it now. He let it by. "What is Clyde's position exactly?"

"My right-hand man. He handles all the details, whatever the details might be."

"Scouts locations?"

"No. I do that. He might suggest where to look, but I make the choices."

"Then why did he rent a moped?"

She stopped in midbreath, probably in midthought. She snorted. "I can't quite picture Clyde on a moped. Do you know how much he weighs? A Harley maybe or the biggest GoldWing they make. But not a piddling motorbike."

"Then I have to assume that's extracurricular too. That you didn't know about it. Right?"

"I think you don't know about it, either. The sheriff's deputies who interrogated me, right after Lauren was found, kept asking about a moped. So yes, I know one is involved in some way. Why you'd connect it to Clyde I have no idea. Your question is very clumsy. At least the deputies came right out with it."

Jack sat and watched her. He didn't stare, he didn't frown. He just watched, as if expecting more, and let the silence do its work. Like a screwdriver prizing the edge up on this side, the edge up on that side, eventually to pop the lid off a paint can, silence almost always opens up an interview subject, given time.

Her foot, slung so casually over the chair arm, began to bob up and down. Her brows knitted closer together. She sipped her drink. Nervously, she tossed the remainder down. "Clyde is indispensable to me when we're out on a shoot. He wouldn't have time to go riding around on a moped or anything else."

"Neither you nor he can verify his whereabouts yesterday when Lauren died."

"I can by inference. I told three different investigators that. I gave him a list of things to get done in order to set up. All those things were done. He couldn't have accomplished all that and still have time to murder people."

Silence.

Jack shifted in his seat. His body clamored for attention, telling him it wanted to lie still and sleep. His brain was simply shutting down. There were things to ask her that his brain refused to come up with. "You planned to return to New York tomorrow."

"Out of the question. Mike saw to that. Very late tomorrow or Tuesday."

"What is your business there that's so urgent?"

"Nothing pertaining to Ronnie or Lauren or anyone else here."

"A whole new project? Or perhaps legal matters."

She scowled. "You keep coming up with these cockamamy notions out of the blue. Legal matters! Honestly." She swung her leg around to proper sitting position and stood up. "Unless you have some matter to discuss seriously, I'd like to get some rest. It's been a harrowing week."

"Amen to that." Jack stayed put, mostly because he had to give his body considerable advance notice before it would move. "I asked you, or blackmailed you, as you prefer to consider it, to see better to the girls' comforts. Nothing has happened. Veronica extracted from you the same sort of promise. You reneged. What's going on? Do you think they're not earning their money unless they suffer? What?"

She paced over to the wet bar and back. "Models are born whiners. I've never known one that wasn't. If they didn't have these complaints, they'd come up with others. Those others might be about money instead of the weather."

Jack got his legs under him. "So you're keeping their minds off more pay by keeping them on misery? Am I hearing that right?" He levered himself vertical.

"I suspect you hear whatever you want to hear. Good night, Mr. Preston."

He whipped his body to a fevered mosey toward the door. "If you would, please, prepare for me a list of the chores you gave Clyde yesterday around midday. Good night, Ms. Carey."

"It's Cray."

"It's Prester."

He left.

Much as his body yearned to arrange itself in a motionless horizontal position for about ten hours, he walked on down the hall past his door to Ev's and knocked.

Moments passed. She let him in. She was wearing loosely-fitting sweats in either shocking pink or fuchsia. Jack never did know the difference between shocking pink and fuchsia—they both rather shocked him. Her vivid sweats made her cheeks rosy and gave her a healthy glow.

She closed the door and threw the bolt. "I'm about done. I can't think of anything more. Maybe you can." She crossed to the desk and gave her spreadsheets a half turn, so that Jack could scan them without craning his neck.

He leaned on the desk and studied her neatly penciled figures.

"So what's the bottom line?"

She pointed impatiently to this entry and that. "Thirty-seven thousand dollars unaccounted for, right there." She scooped up a highlighter pen and swirled a circle around the entry.

He stood erect. "How close is this, do you think?"

"If Hal got accurate figures from Harry, you're looking at Edith's books to within a five percent error."

Jack whistled. He stared at her work a few moments, but he could have learned about as much by examining the train schedule in a Tokyo commuter station. He did not do well with this sort of thing, which is why, at age thirty-four, he still paid his own saintly mother to do his income tax for him. Mom complained every January. Maybe he could hire Ev this year.

He picked up her phone and gently laid his body out

on the foot of her bed. He punched in numbers and pondered the ramifications of a $37,000 oversight.

She gathered her spreadsheets together, tapped their edges, positioned them neatly on her desk. "Who are you calling?"

"American embassy in Sydney."

"Australia?!" She frowned. "What time is it there?"

"Almost eleven tomorrow morning."

"That's so weird. I never could understand how it can be tomorrow somewhere."

"That's OK. I don't understand capital gains. Good morning. May I speak to Frank Harrold, please? Tell him Dr. Prester. Yes, ma'am." He listened to the gentle Aussie accent of this sophisticated Sydney lass a scant step removed from Mother England. She probably paused for tea at four too.

Frank came on, and Jack recalled what he had failed to remember until now—when it was somebody else's dime, the garrulous, outgoing assistant ambassador could talk the ears off Dumbo.

Jack held Frank's cheerful though idle chitchat down to four minutes or so and shifted the topic. "You may have wondered why I'm calling. I'm buried to the neck in a murder investigation here involving an Aussie model, and I'm trying to learn her real name. She goes by the professional name of Marlette."

"You're kidding!"

"Why am I kidding?"

"Marlette? Honey blonde, waist-length hair, and eyes like Crater Lake?"

"With Wizard Island for pupils. How do you know her?" For some vaguely ill-defined reason, Jack was beginning to regret he had placed this call.

"She had a little trouble getting her green card, and I helped her out. Hang on. I'm digging her file out here."

"Frank, I'm calling from a hotel, and you know how hotels inflate phone charges. Dig fast, huh?"

"No sweat, good buddy. It's right here."

"'Good buddy' went out ten years ago on this side of the river, Frank, along with CB-mania."

"Rats. I'm just now getting the hang of radio ten codes too. You mean CB is passé?"

"So's my credit rating after they post this phone bill. What are you looking for?"

"Specifics. You did say you're investigating, didn't you? Got a pencil?"

"Hang on. Pencil, Ev?" He reached out. His back and shoulders ached with the movement.

She handed him the hotel pen and thin little notepad. "Will this do?"

"Go ahead." He rolled to his side on the bed and mashed the receiver down with his ear, so he could write. For the next five minutes he scribbled notes as Frank rattled off the material in his file folder. Jack filled the whole notepad. His spirits, nonebullient to start with, sank lower and lower and flattened out into a little puddle on the floor.

His file info apparently exhausted, Frank started to launch into more chitchat about the current crop of Australian horses and the Melbourne Cup coming up.

Jack cut him off. "Hey, I appreciate this, Frank, I really do! You've helped a lot. But I've gotta make some other calls."

"Yeah, sure. Incidentally, who's this Ev, and why is she in your hotel room?"

That was the other thing about Frank that Jack had forgotten—the man never missed a syllable of anything he heard.

"I'll write you a letter and explain it. Stamps cost fifty cents. Tell Donna I love her. Thanks again, good buddy."

"Come on, Jack, don't be a nerd. 'Good buddy's' been passé for ten years. Give Marlette my best, huh?" How much longer Frank would have gone on was anybody's guess, but he got a call just then on another line and hung up.

Jack hit the button to break the line and lay still a few moments, absorbing what he'd just heard and collecting his frazzled thoughts. He lurched back onto his feet, reassembled the phone, and set it on Ev's delicate little writing desk.

She sat back in her desk chair. "So who's Frank?"

"Childhood friend. His dad was chief ranger at Carlsbad when my dad was the naturalist there. We spent maybe three years as playmates, chasing bats and getting each other into trouble and having a general good time. Kept contact after our fathers transferred. He went into the diplomatic corps, and I went into the Park Service."

"Was he in Australia when you met your wife? Marcia?"

"Yeah. He married an Aussie girl too. Donna. Great lady. When Marcia was killed, I took her body home to Queensland. Frank was there all the way for me. An immense help, Frank and Donna both."

She studied the top of her desk.

Jack could relate—he didn't know what else to say either. So he asked her to fax Hal her figures right away and wished her good night. He stepped outside, the notes in his hand, and listened to her bolt and chain her door.

Across and down the hall, Marlette's door quietly clicked shut.

Jack crossed the hall and rapped on it.

An Aussie voice much less cultured than Frank's secretary's barked, "Go away." *Gow a-why.*

"You were spying, Miss Hoople. Time to talk." Jack paused. "Emma? Want to take a walk?"

She opened her door and glared at him. "Blasted wombat" was perhaps the most innocuous of the string of names she draped upon him.

He smiled. "Peace and joy to you too. We're overdo

220

for some deep discussion. Let's take a walk and compare notes."

"I don't think so." *Oy down't think sow.*

He abandoned the facade of good humor. "Hang it, Marlette, you don't seem to grasp that you're one of the people I'm trying to keep alive. Catching this killer is not just an intellectual exercise. We have to nail him before he kills again. We need to talk. You know things that might help, whether you're aware of it or not, and talk we shall. So do you want to do it casually, walking around under the dismal overcast, or shall I haul you into town and sit you down in a dismal police interrogation cubicle?"

She studied him a few long moments as the glare faded to a mere frown. "It's late."

"Not a problem. Cops stay open all night."

"Why can't we do it in here?"

"Any number of reasons." He let it go at that.

She didn't look any happier, but she seemed to soften a bit. "I'll get my wrap."

She stepped into the little alcove with the bathroom sink and pulled a fur stole off its hanger. With a practiced toss she flipped it over her shoulders. Her television had been turned down low. She switched it off. She slid her bare feet carelessly into a pair of red three-inch spike heels and scooped her room key off her formica shelf/desk. She lived in a dump like Jack's. Her long, supple legs filled out her designer jeans in exactly the right ways. With a plain old sweatshirt that on anyone else would look like a plain old sweatshirt, she bedazzled like the Hope diamond.

Jack paused at his room only long enough to grab his denim jacket. It wasn't much of a match for a fur stole, but a cowboy is a cowboy is a cowboy. They walked downstairs and out into the damp, somber night.

Jack released Maxx from the confines of the truck cab, but he didn't bother with the leash. They weren't going anywhere. He stuffed both hands in his pockets and led off down the road toward the restaurant. It would be closed by now, probably, or nearly so, but it was a destination, and that was all he needed for the moment.

Marlette walked in silence for maybe fifty feet. Then she moved in against him and matched her stride to his, so he walked slower. She wrapped her arm around his waist. Without realizing, he had pulled his hand out of his pocket and found his arm stretching across her shoulders and drawing her closer.

Marlette sounded disappointed. "You searched my room while I was gone and found my passport. That's how you learned my name."

"Nope. A source in Australia. You have a rap sheet long enough to wallpaper a concert hall. You've been—"

"What's a rap sheet?"

"Official list of petty and criminal offenses. Stuff you do time for or at least get probation. You didn't do time, though, apparently. Still, your record is impressive enough that you were nearly denied a green card. Only through the direct intervention of personnel at the U.S. embassy were you able to come to America."

"That's behind me, Jack. That's all behind me. I'm not like that anymore. Besides, those john-hops were a bit over the top, you know? They were claiming I was far worse than I was. You can see I'm giving you the good oil. Not a single problem since I came over here. You can check."

"Sheriff's Department already did. First thing you do with a suspect is look for priors. You're clean in this country."

"So now everybody around here knows all about me. About my past."

"Probably not. At least not yet. The Sheriff's Department uses official channels, which usually take awhile. Now if they actually arrested you and charged you, they'd hold you until they knew Australia didn't want you for anything badly enough to extradite you."

"Ghastly. This whole thing is so ghastly."

"You can say that again." Ghastly. Lauren.

Covering three miles to their one, Maxx romped in the drainage ditch, exploring energetically as he always did when off leash, his nose in high gear. Easy for him. He didn't get pounded on by enraged photographers. On the other hand, he did get pounded by desperate moped riders. Did he ache as badly as Jack did? His face was still a little swollen.

Jack slowed to a stroll. "Tell me about your history of violent acts." They were beyond the circle provided by the motel lights now. Jack could see maybe five or six feet. That was all.

"History. Too right! Ancient history. I was young and mixed up. I had emotional problems. My counselor showed me that they weren't mental problems. I wasn't crazy or anything. I mean, everybody bungs on a blue now and then, right? And then we dug down into my childhood and worked out what was happening, and now I'm right as rain. I don't even get anyone set anymore."

And Jack's ears perked up. He kept his voice casual, careless. "So now and then you'd have it in for some girl."

"What?"

"You'd bear a grudge against her. Have a snout on her."

"Nothing she didn't deserve, believe me. Some of those cows."

"According to your record, you tried to pay one of them back with a cane knife. And another obtained a restraining order against you, which you ignored. You harassed her over a period of four months and on several occasions threatened her with bodily harm."

"There. Perfect example of the record sounding much worse than it was. They made it sound so dire. It wasn't at all that serious. I was confused, not dangerous." She twisted in the darkness to look at him. "I think I know what you're getting at. And that's silly as a bandicoot. Why would I want to harm Ronnie?"

"You tell me."

"No reason at all. Now Clyde, for instance, he didn't like Ronnie one bit. He detested her. And Mike. And who knows what Alan is like when his back is up. And Edith, she had reason. All of them more than I."

"Why would Edith have reason? Losing her star model would really put the mockers on her plans to get done on time. And it did."

Marlette's shoulders heaved in an exaggerated shrug. "I only know Ronnie threatened to jack up on her and even had a place of her own somewhere."

"Veronica had a room or rental apart from the Seaview?"

"So she said. Said it was a place to get away, so Edith couldn't breathe down her neck. But then, who knows? She didn't go there much, if she did. She was always with us—or almost always."

"But you were never there. You don't know where it is."

"No."

"How would she get there? Would it be in walking distance?"

Marlette shook her head, and that wonderful hair moved in the darkness. "Alan took her off somewhere now and again. There, I'd suppose."

The gentle quiet of the night exploded as Maxx bolted up out of the ditch and barked lustily at the darkness behind them. Jack wheeled. He saw nothing.

Marlette seized Jack's arm with a grip that could have ripped King Kong off the Empire State Building. "What is it?"

"Could be an animal. Could be someone following us. Maxx, guard!" Considering the possibilities, Jack pulled Marlette down into the ditch and hunkered low beside her. "Stay down. Way down. Flat." From the small of his back he pulled his gun.

His neck hair bristling, Maxx parked himself squarely

in front of Marlette, facing into the darkness. He growled.

She purred, "That's so romantic! He's guarding *me!*"

"Hey, just because he's a dog doesn't mean he lacks good taste." Now what? Jack wanted to get a look at whatever or whoever was following them, but he didn't dare leave Marlette alone. Unattended out here in the darkness, she'd have as much chance as a caterpillar on a freeway. And he couldn't send Maxx to investigate. He needed Maxx's superior senses right at his side, lest the perp—if indeed it was their perp and not just another worthless raccoon—lie in wait for them undetected.

She plastered herself against him like melted cheese on a nacho. "I'm not afraid when I'm with you. Even when we're up a gum tree."

"Not as far up as it seems. The closest lights are the motel parking lot, so that's where we're going."

"But whoever it is is between us and there."

"So we move forward and force him into the light." Jack stood up. "Stay behind me, hear? Clear behind me."

His weapon ready, Jack started walking slowly, deliberately back toward the motel. Maxx ranged out a little bit ahead. "Good dog, Maxx! Good dog."

A car's headlights approached from behind. Jack pulled his gun in close to his chest. The car whipped past, spewing light along the roadside. Nothing.

"Close your eyes, Marlette. Try to keep your night vision." Here came another car from the west. Jack held his weapon behind, out of sight. The headlights whooshed by, leaving the blackness blacker. Up ahead near the motel, leaves or brush rustled.

An eternity or two later, they entered the ring of sallow light from the motel parking lot. Jack had seen neither form nor shadow. He lowered his weapon to his side. "Maxx, find!"

Maxx bolted forward, sniffing, ranging, tracking. He found the trail instantly, or perhaps he had been on it all along. He jogged directly to the motel door. Jack opened the door for him. His nose to the carpet, Maxx galumphed up the stairs and down the hall. He stopped at room 213 and looked back at Jack.

Jack rapped on the door. "Open up, please. Police matter."

From inside, Clyde Wilkins's sleepy voice mumbled something. Jack put his eye to the fish-eye peephole. He couldn't see into the room, and he didn't expect to, but he could tell that the lights were all off.

More basso profundo rumbling. The chain rattled on the other side. Clyde swung his door wide open and scowled at Marlette. He was dressed in a T-shirt and jockey shorts. "What are you doing out with him? It's late."

"A better question." Jack kept his gun in hand and at his side. "What were you doing out?"

"I haven't been out." Beyond him, Jack could see that his bed was mussed. A disheveled newspaper was spread out on the formica slab. Edith's right-hand man lived in a dump too.

"My dog here says you have." Jack nodded toward Maxx.

The mutt sat parked at Clyde's bare feet, staring up at him.

"May I step inside?"

"I know what's happening." Clyde glowered. "Not without a search warrant. Marlette, go to bed. Alone." He slammed the door.

Marlette twisted her face up and stuck out her tongue at the peep hole. "Papa don't preach." She turned away, looking weary. "The raving ratbag."

"He seems to think he's your chaperon. Or father." Jack felt stymied. Sure he could get a search warrant, but by the time that came through, Clyde could clean up, arrange his clothes, destroy any evidence other than Maxx's nose that he'd left the room at all.

Jack knew without a doubt that Clyde had followed them, because of Maxx. But even if Jack could prove, as

226

perhaps with witnesses, that Clyde had been out and about, so what? Jack and Marlette went for a walk. So did Clyde. Big deal. No crime.

Jack holstered his gun and ambled off toward Marlette's door. The day was done. Sufficient unto the day was the evil thereof.

More than sufficient.

She handed him her key again. "Come on in, eh? We'll talk some more."

He stuffed the key in the lock and shoved the door open for her. "Nah. I feel about as sharp as a rubber ducky. Tomorrow."

"You were in Edith's room," she pouted, "and Evvie's."

"That's when I could still string more than three words together into a coherent sentence. Good night, Marlette."

"Hooroo, luv." And, the feat made easy by those three-inch spikes, she stretched up and kissed him.

Any compunctions Jack felt about kissing murder suspects fled without a whimper. He wrapped his arms around her and let himself float in the sheer joy of the moment. Quite a few moments. Marcia came and went in his mind's eye.

He broke it off with some reluctance. "Good night." He left her in her doorway and walked on down to his room. He heard her door click shut as he opened his.

19

Ill Wind

The Paragon of Law Enforcement, his uniform starched, his boots shiny, the leather doodads on his belt all nicely arranged, sat sipping coffee in a corner booth of the Tidewater Cafe. A hundred other people were doing the same, in a restaurant built for, maybe, seventy-five. Obviously, the Tidewater was the place to be at 8:00 A.M.

Jack smiled at the hostess, who was coming, menu in hand, to tell him to wait, and threaded between the tables to the far corner. He nodded to the Paragon and sat down across from him. "Officer Patterson. Good morning."

"I thought for a minute you'd be late, but you're on time."

"My body is here. My brain will follow in about an hour. How you manage to look crisp at this hour I don't know, especially considering you were awakened in the middle of the night by a hack phone call. I got four hours of sleep, so don't expect any crispness from me." Jack slid a file folder across the table. "The latest from my end, including Marlette's police record in Melbourne and Sydney."

Patterson was good at scanning. You had to give him that. His eyes zipped down the pages, and he had it. "Psychiatric evaluation and treatment in lieu of jail. Extreme possessiveness? Jealousy?"

"Apparently, from the outside looking in. I haven't had time yet to follow up with talks to arresting officers, her counselor, or whatever."

Patterson closed the folder. "You have good sources."

Should Jack mention he stumbled on this by chance? Nah. "On the phone last night I told you what Marlette said —about Miss Wayne perhaps renting another unit in this area. I was hoping you would have some ideas on how to explore it."

The waitress came with coffee and menu. He accepted the coffee and ordered bacon and eggs without looking. She hustled away. The coffee was good enough to fill the Tidewater with customers just on its own.

Patterson sat forward, his elbows on the table. He fairly glowed with smug self-satisfaction. "If we assume Miss Wayne didn't want anyone to know where she was, and yet she'd want to be fairly close to work, she would take a room somewhere near or on the island. But not a motel room, motels being easy to check. Edith could find her without much sweat. Or set Clyde to finding her. Just call around until someone has her registered."

Jack shook his head. "She could use an assumed name."

"Right. But not if she was paying with a credit card, traveler's check, or personal check, and it's doubtful she'd use cash. Unless—" Patterson paused for effect "—she took a room at a bed and breakfast."

Jack nodded. "As sophisticated as she is, Edith probably wouldn't even think of checking bed and breakfasts. Good avenue to explore."

"I already did. Starting about seven, I called around, phoning the most likely ones first. As soon as you've eaten, we'll go visit Aunt Martha's Shoreline B and B."

* * *

If Aunt Martha got much older, Methuselah would drop to second place. She stood maybe five feet if she

229

wore shoes like Marlette's, which she didn't. Osteoporosis had crumpled her up like a wad of paper, and age had plucked two-thirds of the gray hairs in her head. She wore a housedress and apron and honest-to-pete bunny slippers.

Jack noticed that, like so many older folks who are hard of hearing, if she wasn't looking directly at your lips, she pretty much lost what you said.

Her B and B, a two-story frame house right on the shore in Trenton, was pure Victorian inside and out. Gingerbread on the eaves, three colors of paint, flocked wallpaper, the whole nine yards. Out in the parlor, her television set, a strident anachronism, blared like a jet at take-off.

She ushered them inside and closed the door. "Getting some nippy out." She didn't seem the least bit cowed by the towering Paragon with his big black camcorder and all his accoutrements. "Which one of you called this morning?"

"I did, ma'am." Patterson removed his hat. "Deputy Raleigh Patterson." He waved a paw. "John Prester with the Park Service."

Jack how-do-you-doed her, but she was already rotated and headed for the stairs. Aunt Martha wobbled a little and shuffled a little, occasionally tangling in the edge of a florid throw rug. She was a hip fracture just waiting to happen.

She hobbled to the stairs and chugged up them two strides per step. "When I saw on TV that one of those models died, and it was black hair, I just knew it was her. But she asked me not to tell anyone she was here, so I didn't—just in case it wasn't her after all. I suppose it was, wasn't it?" She turned in midflight and looked at Patterson.

"Yes, ma'am. It was. Veronica Wayne."

"Veronica." Up she went again. "That was the name. Veronica Yonkers. I remember because my brother used to live in Yonkers when he worked in New York. That was a while ago. He died in fifty-two."

She topped out on the second floor not the least bit

winded or shaky and opened a door at the end of the upstairs hall. "I gave her her choice of rooms—it's pretty slow now—and she liked this one. It looks out over the water to the island."

Patterson paused in the doorway and whipped out his camcorder. He videotaped the room, panning slowly, as he narrated. He did an admirable job. Jack always missed details that Patterson unerringly picked up on. As Patterson stepped forward to get the wall beside the door, Jack moved into the doorway. The place was essentially undisturbed. No murders had occurred here, no mayhem. He pulled on a pair of thin rubber gloves.

Aunt Martha kept up a running commentary on how hard it was to find nice roomers in the autumn and how very nice the Yonkers girl had seemed. She assured them she didn't take in roomers with children, because of all the furnishings that were so easily broken, like the ewer and basin over there, for example, which had been her grandmother's, and besides . . .

Patterson videotaped as Jack explored drawers, pulling each one open wide so that Patterson could record that it was empty. Jack paused by the window. He could see the cement bridge from here, the bridge where, ostensibly, Veronica Wayne was killed. He left philosophizing about the irony for some other time and opened the closet. A few tops hung there, and a pair of jeans thrown over a coat hanger. He described them for the audio.

"Whoa." Jack reached into the back to a shelf partially hidden beside the door. Handling it by two fingers, he pulled a green felt crusher out into the light of day. It appeared new and virtually unworn.

Patterson's tape, probably perfect to this point, no doubt was spoiled a bit, for the camcorder bobbed a little as he dug a big bag out of his pocket for Jack. Under the all-seeing eye of the camera, Jack bagged and documented their find.

Aunt Martha obviously didn't know she was recorded

231

for posterity. She kept talking, and Jack prodded her now and then with a grunt or question.

"Do you want to see her box too?" Aunt Martha's rumpled little body still leaned in the doorway.

Jack turned to her. "What box?"

"She kept a box of papers, but she didn't want to keep it in her room. I've forgotten the reason. It's out on the porch. That's it. She wanted to keep it cool, she said, so the Xerox would last longer. That's it."

Jack looked at Patterson. "And if someone comes snooping through the room, they won't find it."

Patterson nodded grimly.

Downstairs, Patterson got on the phone to set up a full-scale forensic search by a Fun and Fiber crew.

Aunt Martha had tottered clear down the stairs by then. She led them to the pantry out back, a little airlock between the kitchen and the back stoop.

"That box there." She pointed to a cardboard archive box. "Actually, I'm glad you two came. It's too heavy for me to lift, and I'm getting a crate of apples one of these days soon. Apple season, you know. I always can apples for pies. The box is in the way. Not that I begrudge that poor dead girl the space, of course."

Jack waited while Patterson mumbled something about batteries and plugged his camera into a wall socket beside the stove. Then Jack picked up the box and carried it in to the kitchen table as the camcorder whirred away.

He lifted the lid and began a narrative. "I see on top a pile of file folders . . ."

In the very bottom lay a big stack of magazines. They appeared unused except for cryptic notes penned in margins. All dollar amounts in the tens of thousands. Did these magazines contain layouts that were the product of Edith or of Veronica or of both? Jack would put Ev on them. She could make sense in a hurry of the strange notations.

Penciled on the file folder tabs were familiar names. Jack opened the heaviest, labeled *Edith.* Dozens of loose slips of paper, some of them pages from scratch pads, some of them envelopes and other random bits, bulged in a compressed stack in the middle. Each was dated. Each offered some little insider's observation into the intimate and financial life of Edith Cray.

Jack was certain that if he arranged all these tidbits by subject, they would detail her relationships with everyone in Sitting Pretty. And he couldn't wait to do it.

At the back of the folder were crammed nearly half an inch of Xerox copies of landscape computer printouts. Apparently as Veronica added material she simply shoved everything in the folder forward and slipped the new data in behind. The newest were at the very back. The latest spreadsheet looked incredibly like the ones Ev had built, though not all the blanks were filled in. It would appear that Veronica's information was mostly picked up from here and there. Ev, a trained analyst, could make learned deductions and guesstimates.

A dozen folders, most of them slim, were labeled with names Jack did not know. But here was *Clyde. Athalia. Marlette. Lauren. Mike. Arthur. Sup't.*

Superintendent? Yep, Sarnoff, but she couldn't remember his name. The only slip in the folder described a run-in between Sarnoff and Clyde. Jack felt in good company. Clearly everybody, from highest to lowest, had run-ins with Clyde.

Marlette. Almost all the slips in this one were of a personal nature and all derogatory. One, dated a week ago, said "Emma Hoople! Ha ha ha."

Here was a folder Jack dreaded opening. *Alan.* The slips of paper in this one, all properly dated, were more on the order of "Dear Diary" entries than exposés of arguments and peccadillos. She documented their first kiss, and how she had engineered it to seem an accident. A lengthy note filling two six-by-nine sheets detailed their first intimate moments.

Patterson had abandoned his taping. He stood at

Jack's side reading over his shoulder. He wagged his head. "The poor sucker never had a chance." And Jack knew that Patterson didn't mean Veronica.

"Sin is sin, Raleigh. And there's almost always a way out—flee, if nothing else. Reading between the lines here, and knowing a little something about personality types, I wonder how much he squirmed trying to get away."

Patterson wagged his tonsorially splendid head. "A very beautiful woman finds you desirable. That's powerful."

Marlette.

Beware.

The Paragon sat down in a rickety chair that threatened any moment to dump his seventh or eighth of a ton. Jack sat down across from him on a chair no sturdier. They studied each other in a mammoth thinking spree as Aunt Martha prattled on.

Presently, bemoaning the folly of these modern flavored blends, and how terrible vanilla roast tastes, the lady put herself to work building a pot of coffee.

Patterson scratched his great square jaw. "None of this would pass muster as evidence in a court of law."

"The printouts, maybe, if they could be verified."

"Big if. Could she be working undercover for some agency?"

"Possibly, but I doubt it. The phrasing, especially the Messier entries, is too personal. And the stuff on Marlette is more petulance than evidence. Even some of the stuff on Edith."

"My first inclination too."

Aunt Martha talked on, apparently unaware of the conversation behind her.

"Blackmail?" Jack suggested.

"She might have threatened someone or let them know she was gathering data on them. But if she's a threat to you, why kill her before you've found the hard evidence? Do you think anyone knew this was here?"

"We could talk to everyone concerned and mention

this stuff without letting on that we have it. See who squirms."

Patterson bobbed his head. "Good idea."

Aunt Martha set three stained coffee mugs out on the table.

"Ma'am," Patterson asked, "did the girl ever bring a man up to her room?"

"Oh, no. I told you, she was very nice."

"Did she have her own key to get in?"

"Key? Yes. She worked late sometimes, and I go to bed around eight. It was easiest if she let herself in."

And Veronica could invite in Alan Messier or a pack of barking dogs or a brass quintet without dear old Aunt Martha ever hearing.

And then the lady added, "She didn't even have anyone coming around to take her to and from work. She walked down to the bridge and got picked up there."

"In what sort of vehicle?"

Aunt Martha pondered that a moment and shook her head. "Too far away to see. My eyes aren't what they used to be."

They had coffee then with the lady and heard how disgusting it is to add milk—or, horror of horrors, two percent—to your coffee, when everyone knows coffee was meant for cream. Her idea of cream was condensed milk straight from the can, which she served in a holstein-cow-shaped pitcher. They put the box upstairs for the forensics crew and exited the moment it was polite to do so.

The Fiber Folk arrived in the police forensics van as Jack and Patterson were bidding Aunt Martha adieu on the front porch. Patterson introduced everyone all around, and the techs disappeared inside. Aunt Martha babbled enthusiastically on their heels.

The overcast was breaking. Sunlight burst through a patch of pearlescent blue sky and torched the pink-orange maple tree in Aunt Martha's frontyard. A vagrant breeze set the flames to dancing.

235

"Tell me something." Jack looked at Patterson. "With two down and counting, why doesn't the sheriff's office set up a bodyguard for the models?"

"I suggested it. My sergeant says the prosecutor's office is taking care of it."

"Really." Jack let it go. They made arrangements for who got what when and who asked which people what questions. They both took notes, which was a very law enforcement thing to do. Patterson headed off who knew where, and Jack climbed into his truck. Maxx licked his ear in greeting. Stupid dog.

Jack stopped by the Seaview to check for messages. He had one, from Ev: "Cadillac Mountain."

He got back in the truck and disobeyed Warren Sarnoff. Sarnoff forbade dogs on Cadillac, and here went Maxx, all the way to the tippy top. But then Maxx was an intelligent police officer; Sarnoff himself had said so.

Sitting Pretty's vans and two other cars were the only vehicles in the parking area on the summit of Cadillac. According to the literature, this bald granite dome was the highest thing on the Atlantic Coast north of Argentina. Jack smirked. At fifteen hundred feet, it wouldn't even pass muster as a foothill out West.

Despite the emergent sun, a cold, cutting wind whipped up over the hilltop. The few deciduous trees among the evergreens up here had lost nearly all their leaves. Jack put Maxx on leash and started up the asphalt trail toward an overlook.

Ahead of him a portly gentleman, balding and obviously of retirement age or close to it, waddled up the gentle path.

Beside the man, his little gray-haired wife chided, "Abe, you are so out of shape."

"No, I'm not. It's the altitude," he puffed. "Thin oxygen."

On the brow of the hill, Athalia was just coming off a session. Marlette and Ev moved out onto the ledge. A few

236

distant islands and the North Atlantic spread out magnificently beyond them. Arturo was doing the photographic honors. Kovik was under bond to stay in the area. Jack hoped the Sheriff's Department was keeping an eye on him.

Jack paused, open-mouthed. Their baby-sitter today was Alan Messier. In full class A uniform, he stood apart, watching, looking bored, looking nervous. Why would Grayson put Messier on this?

Winthrop Spalding kept to himself over by a park bench. He looked as if he were a million miles away. Jack would bet he didn't miss a thing. Jack nodded casually toward him. Spalding gave a single slight nod in return.

Jack stood there awhile admiring Marlette.

No matter what she wore, she looked gorgeous. Put her in a clown suit, and she'd look glamorous. Put her in Ninja warrior black, and she'd look glamorous. Right now the wind picked up her acres of golden hair and tossed it across her shoulder.

Athalia grabbed a blanket and came jogging down the path. How she managed to trot in those tall spike heels mystified him.

Ah, well. He had set a precedent when he first arrived. Might as well uphold it. He pulled his coat off and held it for her.

She yanked off the blanket and wrapped the coat around her shoulders. Her small, slim fist wadded it closed in front of her. "Thank you! Good morning, Jack. Hello, Maxx." She stooped to rub the dog vigorously behind his ears.

"Good morning. How's it going?" Jack wheeled and walked beside her toward the vans.

"SOP. Froze like a fish stick."

"The dress looks familiar."

"It's the clothes we shot down at that dock, where Evvie pushed you in. The film was ruined." Athalia giggled. "You know in the coyote and roadrunner cartoons, where the coyote runs off a cliff and then he just sort of hangs in space until he realizes where he is, and then he falls? Then *zoom,* straight down. You were like that. You just sort of hung there a minute looking surprised and then *zoom.*"

"Zoom and splash. Don't forget the splash."

"Zoom and splash." She cackled. "I guess it wasn't funny at the time, specially to you, but it sure did brighten my day."

"It's an ill wind that blows nobody good."

Thelma Hyde climbed out of the van clutching a filmy red number Jack also vaguely remembered.

Athalia looked at it. "You sure she wants that one?"

"That's what the sheet says."

Athalia shrugged. She handed Jack his coat and climbed into the van.

Thelma slid the side door shut.

Jack pulled his coat back on. "From what the girls have said—perhaps even little comments made on the side—and from what Edith says or does, why do you think the former wardrobe mistress quit in the middle of the project?"

"I'm not a gossip, Mr. Prester."

"I'm not asking you to be. This is an official police inquiry."

"Oh, yes. I keep forgetting that." She frowned at the asphalt. "Part of it was money, I think. She might have been expecting an allowance or something on the road— or pay—and not getting it." Thelma glanced at the closed van and walked off fifty feet to the other side of the parking area. She lowered her voice. "Mostly, I'd guess it was Edith's high-handed control and her penny-pinching."

"For instance?"

"The hotel arrangements. The woman was expected to double up with Athalia, and she didn't like that."

"You mean share a motel room."

Thelma nodded. "So Athalia ended up sharing with

the Wayne girl, since Lauren needed a place of her own."

Blobs of dark conifers upholstered a chain of little islands in the sea beyond them. The wind cut through Jack's coat. He could imagine how it bit into Thelma's nylon Sitting Pretty parka.

"But the Wayne girl wasn't there much," he prodded.

"I spent a lot of time talking to that charming little Laren girl. Actually, Mr. Prester, I don't think she was as old as she let on to be. The way she was so uncertain under the surface. So vulnerable."

"You have good instincts. She was underage."

"I thought so! You're right, the Wayne girl wasn't there much. Lauren said that the Wayne girl flat out refused to live with a black and moved out. It hurt Athalia terribly, but she doesn't let on. She says she's used to that kind of . . . but you can tell it hurts."

"Where did Veronica move out to?"

"I have no idea. Another motel, I suppose. I don't think anyone else knew, either. Although Clyde must have. He brought her to work now and then."

"What was Clyde's relationship with the Wayne girl? Did Lauren have any insights into that?"

"Are you sure this isn't just idle gossip?"

"Positive. I'm trying to figure out how this crew interacted with Miss Wayne, and I'm getting very confused."

"I don't blame you. It's very confusing. Clyde does what Edith wants, but he doesn't pay any attention to her. Do you know what I mean? He lets her—her idiosyncrasies just roll right off him, like water off a duck's back. And she's hard to work with at times. But Lauren said he treated the Wayne girl very tenderly. Differently. Like he cared. And the girl hurt him frequently with cutting remarks and things."

"Toyed with his emotions? Cat with mouse?"

Thelma pondered that a moment. "Yes, I believe that's what it would be, though Lauren never described it that way."

From the van, Athalia called, "Where'd ever'body go?"

Jack started back to her. "Thelma was naming off islands for me." He skinned out of his jacket. "This is a habit I should never have started."

Athalia hung it over her shoulders and wrapped it around her. "But since you did, I ain' going to be polite enough to say, 'Aw shucks, you shouldn't.'"

"Not if you're smart. This wind would shave the hair off a musk-ox." The cold stabbed through him.

"Ain't no musk-ox dumb enough to stand out in this wind." Athalia started back toward the brow of the hill. "Just us delicate little ladies is that stupid. So what islands did you learn?"

Trapped in his lie, Jack dredged through what he remembered from the park map. "For example, Bald Porcupine. Now just envision it. A bald porcupine. All sorts of ramifications."

Athalia cackled. "There's a place on the Navajo reservation called Burnt Water."

"Same mind-set. When were you on the res?"

"Shoot last year for a catalog. Ever hear of Pueblo Traders?"

"Yeah. My mom likes them. Was this with Edith?"

"No, an independent outfit. I was loose. Edith didn't have anything for me at the time. Edith doesn't like it when we take an outside gig. Overexposure, she says. She wants to shape our destinies. I prefer money to destiny, myself."

Jack chuckled. "Why not just quit Edith and strike out on your own?"

"She has the big ones. Like this one."

Out here on the ragged edge of the mountaintop, the wind fairly screamed. Alan Messier watched from the lee side of a gnarled and stunted pine. Jack huddled in beside him as Athalia continued out to join her cohorts in haute couture.

Arturo stood up straight. Ev and Marlette instantly

240

lost their enchanting smiles. As one they dived for Athalia. Marlette was half a second quicker; she seized the coat even before Athalia was fully out of it and wrapped it around herself. Scowling, Ev took consolation prize—a blanket. Its tails whipped about in the wind. The two of them headed for the van with Winthrop close beside.

How should he approach this with Messier? As it turned out, when he and Patterson divvied up the interrogation, he took Messier and Patterson got Marlette. He tried to wangle Marlette and failed. Patterson was obviously the superior wangler. Bummer. Perhaps he'd try jolting Messier's socks off. That sometimes worked when nothing else did.

He stuffed his freezing hands into his pockets. "I have it on good authority that Veronica considered you a lightweight in the romance department."

Messier turned and gaped at him. Already Jack had achieved an admirably high level of shock value.

Jack turned the screws a bit tighter. "And you gave her a green felt crusher like yours—as a token, so to speak."

The ultimate question at hand was, Does Messier know about the box of incriminating notes? And the answer from the look on his face was, Probably not.

His dumbfounded stare melted into an expression of pure, malevolent hatred. "You know about her room."

"Bingo. What do *you* know about it?"

"Her landlady might have both feet in the grave, but she can still talk. Talks constantly. I told Veronica the old lady was a snoop."

Jack moved in closer. He was getting just plain cold. Maxx curled up in a knot at his feet and laid his chin on Jack's shoe. "This is probably beyond your capacity to believe, Alan, but I'm not out to skewer you."

"Then you can quit assuming what everyone else assumes—that Ronnie and I had a thing going."

"According to Veronica herself, you did."

His face melted into an expression Jack couldn't decipher. Then it went blank, a solid wall between Jack and the man's thoughts. Messier stared off at Athalia being charming in a filmy red dress and an Arctic gale.

The silence maneuver wouldn't work now. Messier obviously wanted silence. He had lapsed into it. How to get him talking? Jack explored a couple of ways to go and decided on the simplest and easiest. Ask him.

"What are you thinking right now?"

"Nothing you'd understand."

"I didn't ask you to explain it in terms I can understand. Just say what's on your mind."

"She was evil. She was so evil, Prester."

"I've heard some say that all women are."

"She'd look at you, and you'd just melt."

Marlette.

Messier's voice sounded bitter. "And you'd think, 'What's a harmless little flirtation going to hurt? I'm strong.'"

Marlette.

"She seemed dumb—really out of it. And then you'd get a notion deep down that maybe she was brilliant and was just leading you along." Messier glanced at Jack. "So who has the tapes now?"

"Tapes?" Jack tried to pretend there really were such things and he was only being cute. "What tapes?"

Messier's face shifted from sullen to sad. "I should've known. I thought it was strange that she wouldn't stay at the motel. And at first I thought it was cute, kind of, that she was afraid of the dark. Then I got to thinking, 'What if she's some kind of nut, and she's got a tape running or something? What if she's thinking extortion?' And then I told myself, 'Naw, not her.' Big laugh. I should never have said that first word to her. To any of them."

The balding fellow with the paunch came waddling over, his wife on his arm. He frowned at Jack. "Whatcha doing without your coat?"

"Freezing."

The fellow dismissed Jack as the nimcompoop that

242

he was, to be standing out in this wind in shirtsleeves, and addressed the ranger. "Wot kind of boyd is up here?"

"Several kinds." Alan shifted from distraught to patient instantly. He was a good ranger. "What did it look like?"

"I didn't see it. But I know it was a boyd. I heard it choyp."

Jack moved off a couple feet and tried with limited success to smother a grin. This was Alan's baby. Maxx followed lackadaisically.

"Maybe if you can get a sighting on it—a visual—I can help you."

"See, Abe? I told you." The wife tugged on Abe's arm, and the two headed back toward the parking lot.

Jack turned back to Messier. "If he heard what I heard, it's not a boyd. It's a red squirrel up in that hemlock by the port-a-john."

Ev, Marlette, and Thelma came slogging up the path into the wind. The girls were wearing new outfits, but Marlette still had Jack's coat.

The Aussie lass came over to them and latched onto Jack's arm. She gave Messier a tense, perfunctory hello and pressed in against Jack. "Come talk to me, luv."

Jack tossed a hasty "Excuse us" over his shoulder as she dragged him across the slope. Now how was he going to explain to her that she was on Patterson's list, not his?

She cooed, "That Ellison lad told me about the nicest little restaurant. Let's go there for lunch, eh? We'll order a lobster roll."

"I'm not so sure you don't have a date with Officer Patterson. He said he wants to talk to you."

"That officious bloke! He can't talk to me if he can't find us, right-o? I'll be done here in fifteen minutes. Less. There's a good fellow!" She handed him his jacket and pranced off in outrageously high heels to join the rest of her party out in the cold, cold wind.

20

Flower Power

His formica non-desk was covered with slips of paper in little stacks. His floor was covered with bits of paper. No fool he—he had gathered up a plastic grocery bag full of rocks from a graded construction site across the road. A dirty, round river rock sat on top of each little pile, lest some vagrant breeze from a hastily opened door undo all his sorting. When Ev got back, Jack would ask her to analyze the markings in that stack of magazines.

Here in his room Jack was piecing together the history and habits of Sitting Pretty as seen through the eyes of its most senior model.

Veronica Wayne had a remarkably astute grasp of Edith's financial activities, both overt and covert. Veronica had noticed things: that Edith never tipped in restaurants, that she avoided picking up the tab whenever possible, including hotel bills, that she argued long and loud over insignificant expenses. With dates and amounts, Veronica documented occasions when Edith padded expenses and falsified bills. If these slips could be verified, Edith could indeed be up to her neck in IRS worries.

According to Veronica, Edith used Clyde the way most cold sufferers use Kleenex. Veronica did not record Clyde's attitude and reactions to Edith's imperiousness. In fact, she recorded almost nothing of anyone's feelings save her own. She wrote down exactly when someone hurt her feelings or slighted her. She never mentioned others' hurts and slights.

And those little bits of paper revealed in stunning clarity the personality of the model herself. Veronica Wayne, spoiled and petulant, despised most people instantly and everyone eventually. She considered herself above the other models and smarter than Edith. She held men in universal disdain. In an ugly little memo to herself, jotted on the back of a candy wrapper, she boasted of being able to steal any man from any woman, given sufficient provocation. "I think I've proven that sufficiently just now," she wrote. It was dated three days before she died.

Marlette, too, could be in hot water with the IRS, if you believed the little chits. Veronica documented occasions when Marlette accepted money under the table from Edith. She tattled on Marlette's illegal driver's license and phony ID. Apparently, Marlette more than once entered Canada under false pretenses. It was all there on paper.

Some of Veronica's petty grievances against Marlette, though, were laughable, if you didn't remember that murder was involved here. She had no use at all for Lauren and the baby. She voiced nothing but smug contempt for the bumbling, socially inept Clyde. Her file on Athalia was scant, and in reading what few entries there were, Jack suspected why: Veronica Wayne did not consider a black worth thinking about, much less writing about.

And he picked up a strong thread of bravado in her entries regarding Alan Messier too. How much of these documentations reflected reality, and how many were fictionalized? Might Veronica Wayne have been writing the equivalent of a pulp romance novel on bits of paper? Alan Messier wanted Jack to think he was never actually involved with her. Reading the current of fantasy beneath the surface of these incriminating exposés, Jack could almost believe him.

Someone thumped loudly on his door. Checking to make sure all his rocks were in place, Jack answered it.

Officer Patterson strode in. He stopped and looked around. "Find anything?"

"Lots of things. I have a two-liter of Pepsi here. Want some?"

"Sure." Patterson flopped into the non-easy chair. "The lab got some readable prints off that hat—off the ribbon band inside."

"Messier and Wayne." Jack dumped ice in the motel's plastic cup.

"Marlette and Wayne."

Jack stared at him.

"Crazy, isn't it?" Patterson shook his head. "Those people don't make mistakes, either, at least not of that caliber."

Jack poured Patterson's and poured himself one as well, no ice. He squatted on the non-comfortable bed and tucked his legs in. His thighs still hurt when he stretched his leg muscles. "I was talking to her at lunch."

"So that's where she was! She's my interview, remember?"

"And welcome to her. We weren't talking business— not my business, anyway. Mostly citizenship stuff. I married an Australian and went through all the immigration hoops, so she was asking me a couple hundred pounds of questions."

"She's thinking of immigrating?"

Jack nodded. His neck still hurt.

"The hard way by applying for citizenship or the easy way by marrying in?"

"Whatever works."

"A prison term for murder would ice that idea down."

Jack's heart thumped and collapsed itself into a prune. And that was silly. She didn't mean that much to him. But she was so beautiful . . . and her voice . . .

Patterson rolled on. "You were saying this morning

at breakfast that you have an operative who built a dummy spreadsheet on Cray. My people want to see it—to compare it to the Xeroxes in the Wayne file."

"And I want Xeroxes of those Xeroxes to build the park's case. Can we make the swap tomorrow? I don't have ready access to her room. I'll have to run down to the office and get a key."

"She's here?"

Jack nodded.

"Evelyn? It'd have to be Evelyn. She's too pretty to be that smart." Patterson grimaced. "Gotta watch what I say. Some broad will blow the whistle for sexual harassment."

Jack permitted himself a smile. It wasn't really all that funny. He knew lots of cops who were walking fearful. "What other prints and such did your people come up with? Who visited her?"

"Not much. Aunt Martha's a good housekeeper. Vacuums in all the corners. The only prints on the box are the victim's and Aunt Martha's. Auntie's are smeared somewhat."

"Tried to pick it up and couldn't."

Patterson bobbed his head.

Jack pondered a moment. He hated like anything to admit defeat, especially to Patterson, but . . . "I talked to Messier a little this morning. I don't think he knows about the box, but it was inconclusive. You want to take a try at him?"

"Sure." Patterson drained his Pepsi and lurched to his feet. He stretched his back and glanced at the chair from which he'd just risen.

"Gives me a stiff back too." *So do moped riders.* Jack unfolded and got on his feet. "Say. Where's Kovik? Do you know?"

"Supposed to be right here in the motel. In fact, he's next on my list."

"Want backup? He explodes like sweaty dynamite. And you don't have Athalia to bail you out."

Patterson smirked. "I can't believe you put that in your statement."

"Why shouldn't I? It was the truth. She's powerhouse."

"I'll manage. Even without the chick." With a final macho swagger, Patterson bade Jack good day, approximately, and disappeared down the hall.

A moment later, he came back. "Where's Marlette this afternoon?"

"Thunder Hole, she said."

"Think I'll do that first. Leave Kovik for later." He left again.

Jack stood awhile in his doorway, studying the paper all over his room. He hung the sign on his door telling the maid not to do his room and walked out to the truck.

With an eager spate of barking, Maxx hopped down off the cage in back and swarmed all over him. Jack rubbed his ears and opened the passenger door for him. The mutt jumped in, and they drove into downtown Bar Harbor together.

He parked by the newspaper office and walked down the street to the first shop he came across. He asked the sales clerk about green crushers. She regarded his request with snooty disdain and sent him to the sporting goods store around the corner.

There on the shelf at Art's Sporting Goods and Army/ Navy Surplus were a whole stack of felt crusher hats in green, brown, and international orange, each in its own plastic bag. They were the only thing in this end of the store thus encased, and therefore the only items not covered with dust. To look like the real McCoy, a genuine sporting goods store has to be cluttered and dirty.

Jack bought one, despite that "one size fits all" almost always meant "one size fits all but me."

He picked up some dog treats from a countertop display at checkout ("Army surplus dog treats?" "Why not? Soldiers wear dog tags.") and headed back to the truck.

He gave Maxx a treat. "So how do you like these? I understand actual soldiers eat them."

Maxx gobbled his tidbit and acted absolutely delighted.

"Big deal. This morning you were absolutely delighted that you were getting dog food again too. You have the taste of a slug."

From a booth he phoned the visitor center. No messages. Jack climbed stiffly into his truck and got licked in the ear. Stupid dog. He drove down to Seal Harbor.

Winthrop Spalding was digging in his flower beds by his house. The old car he used was parked in the driveway. Another, same year and model, sat on blocks beside the little garage. Jack pulled his truck up onto the curb to get it farther off the street and wandered across Winthrop's dwah-yaad.

The old fellow nodded. "The chief ranger's baby-sitting, so I figured I had a few hours to do this while the weather's OK."

"Do what?"

"Dig my wife's glads. She used to plant gladiolus every spring, and I sort of just kept it up. They make a nice show around July and August."

"I bet. Can I help?"

"If you want. Don't step on that stuff. That's hollyhocks. And those are astilbe there by the rhody." He drove a potato fork into the ground and lifted.

Jack grabbed a tuft of beige lanceolate leaves and pulled gently. A wide, flat bulb popped out of the loosened dirt. Winthrop moved his fork over six inches and lifted again. With the two of them working in concert, the job took less than ten minutes. Jack helped Winthrop scissor off the dried leaves and the spidery roots.

The old man seemed content in himself. He spoke little, and what small talk they made was mostly weather related. They ended up with a basketload of huge corms

("My wife set me straight on that. They aren't bulbs, she said.") and a plastic bucket half full of tiny cormlets, neat white beads that had sprouted from the root nodes.

Winthrop stowed the basket in his crowded little pantry. "The glads kind of got me started. Guess I didn't want that part of her to die too. The next year I planted the hollyhocks and tried cosmos. That worked pretty good, so I put in some marigolds the next summer. It's sort of been growing since then. Now the flowers start with the crocus in March and end with the cushion mums over there." He pointed to a row of dense, low, pink, orange, and yellow flower clumps.

"Beautiful."

Winthrop closed his door. He didn't bother to lock it. "Somehow ended up doing the church's planting too. Flowers and perennial shrubs. It's something I can do for God. Suits me." There was a satisfaction in his voice—not a prideful pride but rather a sense of importance.

"Tell me—the white and purple stuff I see around town, that's flowering kale, right?"

Winthrop nodded. "I think I might try some of that next year. Run a row of it along the far side of the driveway there." He half smiled. "Bet you didn't stop by to dig glads."

"When I saw John Grayson take over I figured you'd be home. I was wondering if I could borrow you a few hours."

"Ayuh."

"That moped. You know about the moped."

"Ayuh."

"Where would the rider ditch it if he wanted to get rid of it? I thought we might drive around a little and you could suggest some places. You know nooks and crannies a whole lot better than I do."

"Something that big and heavy, if I wanted to get rid of it I'd dump it in the water."

"But not at the cement bridge. Someone might see it beneath the surface."

"Ayuh. There's surely lots of other places." Winthrop followed Jack down to the truck.

Jack ostracized Maxx to the truckbed. Winthrop hopped in, not the least stiff or tired after all the digging. Jack felt older than Winthrop acted.

"Where shall we start?" Jack torched off the motor.

"Do you know about where Chuck and Walt lost him?"

"I know exactly where, from the incident report."

Chuck and Walt knew how to file an incident report. From their written description, Jack could drive right up to the spot. He and Maxx and Winthrop looked around the area, but it had been looked around by a couple of dozen eyes before theirs. Jack whistled Maxx up into the bed and took off slowly.

"We're assuming the fellow's new to the area and doesn't know his way around well," Jack explained, "but we could be wrong. And no witnesses. The Bar Harbor police and some sheriff's deputies practically went door to door, hoping someone noticed the bike. Nothing."

"Try out that way." Winthrop pointed to a dirt drive that crossed this paved road. Half abandoned and not maintained, the road wound through trees and overgrown shrubbery to the seashore.

"Silted in some." Winthrop got out, and they walked the cobble beach.

Jack saw a starfish out a few yards. This was a charming spot, and the lack of tracks suggested no one came out here.

Neither had a moped.

They tried an abandoned boat launch. Winthrop led him to a boathouse in which were stored some nice little yachts. They checked inside and out—any place accessible to a moped. Nope.

Winthrop stood on the jetty out beyond the boathouse and stared off at a ragged little island in the distance. "We're going about this wrong."

"I'm open to any suggestion."

"You're saying the feller's a stranger. But you just about have to know about these places we've been looking. You don't likely just stumble on them. It has to be a place he'd stumble onto."

"Sounds good so far."

"Let's start back at the beginning again."

Jack called Maxx in and headed for the truck. "The Bar Harbor police already tried to track him. They borrowed someone who's apparently a known poacher and a good woodsman."

"Oh. Curly. Ayuh. If Curly couldn't track it, it can't be tracked."

Ten minutes later they stood again on the spot where they had begun the pursuit of wild geese.

"Now if I was desperate to ditch my bike and didn't know the area, where would I go?" Winthrop wandered off.

Jack fell in behind. Why hadn't he thought of this? Get inside the mind of the biker and second-guess him.

Jack let Winthrop do the leading. The bike rider would likely take this way rather than that because it afforded better cover. He would probably follow this trail because it was clear enough to see if you're moving fast. He could go this way or that—both ways are paved—but this way doesn't have any houses visible, and that one does. They turned down a side road for no reason other than that it seemed an attractive way to go.

They came out suddenly into an open amphitheater sort of field. Jack thought at first it was an abandoned gravel pit into which people had dumped dozens of old cars and washing machines.

"Forgot this was here," Winthrop mused. "Bar Harbor's original dump. Hasn't been used for forty years that I know of."

252

"The auto hulks are all so old they're geologic. There's a Packard."

"Used to be lots more of them. But people with more money than brains haul 'em off to restore them."

"Maxx, find!" Had the dog been picking up any scent at all of the biker? For that matter, did the biker come anywhere near here? As far as Jack knew, they were still hot on the trail of wild geese.

Maxx trotted off in his search mode, working circles, sticking his nose everywhere, ranging wide.

Jack and Winthrop both searched the stony ground for any sign of their moped, but the dirt was too chewed up. Kids came here a lot with ATVs and dirt bikes. They'd cut doughnuts all over the place. Ruts and gouges and talus slopes marked where they climbed the steep walls of the dump. If a moped were somehow secreted here, some kid would surely have found it.

Maxx parked himself in front of the Packard Jack had noticed, and barked.

The blunt, boxy hulk was gutted. The hood was missing. No doubt the motor too, for boldly flowering yellow composites—some kind of sunflower—billowed out of the engine compartment. It gave a new dimension to Flower Power. A few remarkably large bushes now grew inside where once its owners rode proudly. Great holes gaped in its rusted roof and the B post had rusted away completely. The ceiling upholstery hung in a few wispy shreds. The car no longer possessed seats, a steering wheel, or floorboards. But down inside, beneath one of its interior bushes and a pile of leaves, it did indeed contain a carefully hidden moped.

21

Jackhammer

This one-panel cartoon depicted an older couple sitting under a tree on a blanket with a picnic lunch. The woman was seated cross-legged facing the viewer, and the man sat across from her with his back to the viewer. She was saying, "Of course, dear. It isn't a picnic without ants." And approaching them from beyond the hill behind her came carpenter ants with mandibles the size of McDonald's arches.

Jack saw that cartoon when he was perhaps ten years old. Twenty-four years later, it still was vivid in his mind. To this day he felt uncomfortable whenever someone suggested he might want to enjoy a picnic.

He didn't care for insects, either.

All that was about to change, however, because Marlette was dressed in attire appropriate for a picnic, and the girls were posing around a picnic table. This gorgeous new mental association was fast replacing the ancient cartoon. Jack was ready for a picnic.

Edith had abandoned Thunder Hole as being too windy. Now she had set up out on Thompson Island, that stepping-stone bit of land between the mainland and Mt. Desert Island. The major road onto Mt. Desert—the only road onto Mt. Desert—cut right down the middle, and traffic whizzed by constantly.

They stayed away from the information center and set up instead in two picnic spaces down on the shore. In the picturesque background of distant trees and seaside meadows and the saltwater narrows, a small island perched. Open water couldn't be seen from here. The shorelines of both the island and the mainland were too convoluted. It was an interesting area that, in the camera lens, could be saltwater, river, or lake.

This Thompson Island picnic area lay within yards of where Veronica Wayne ostensibly died. He had seen it from the window of that room she had rented. The murderer surely ought to be nervous here.

Did anyone realize that the garishly painted Victorian two-story on the far shore was Aunt Martha's? The girls didn't behave any differently. Edith was the same old Edith. The Ellison kid looked just as harried as always, but he was doing a somewhat better job of reflecting light onto the girls' faces than he used to. Practice makes perfect. If Clyde picked Veronica up in the morning, he surely knew where she stayed. Clyde, though, was off somewhere on an errand, the dog fetching still another paper and pair of slippers for the mistress.

Jack really wanted to see Alan Messier's reactions and mannerisms. Messier absolutely did know about that house over there. But Patterson had swept him away for an intense interrogation session. John Grayson stood around in Messier's stead. So much for Jack's attempt to find someone looking guilty.

Jack watched the shoot a few moments and crossed to John. On leash, Maxx heeled, more or less, lackadaisically. Out here in this grassy picnic area, there weren't a lot of places to explore with his nose, and Maxx was bored already.

Grayson smiled. "You're in luck. The girls are really

going to have to work to shove you into the water from here."

"I'm sure if they're bent far enough out of shape at me, they'll manage. Besides, Maxx will be happy to help. It's as windy here as it was on Cadillac."

"Almost. I'd say Edith pulled a boner. Thunder Hole's a little more protected. But I doubt she's going to get away from it today. Weather's too unsettled."

An artificial smile pasted rigidly on her face, Ev caught and held Jack's eye. She gave him a tiny, tiny dip of the head.

Fracci relaxed, pried his camera off his face, and walked away. Smiles evaporated instantly, and the girls dived for blankets. Correction. Ev and Athalia dived for blankets. Marlette dived for Jack. She came hustling to him and latched onto his arm. Obviously, she expected his jacket.

Thelma called her name, but Marlette ignored her. "Let's go for a stroll, luv. We've twenty minutes until I have to work. Edith's using Evvie and Thal next."

With difficulty Jack extricated his arm from her grip. "I'd love to, but I want to talk to Evelyn first." He kissed his finger and tapped it on her forehead. He walked away quickly before his mind changed itself for him. It had a habit of doing that when he was around Marlette.

Ev looked past his shoulder at Marlette as he joined her. They greeted each other cheerfully, Ev in her blanket, and she took his arm. They walked off away from the group.

Edith called to her to stay near, and she responded over her shoulder.

She hissed at him in undertone. "Well, well. I'm surprised you resisted temptation there."

"Know how you sound? You sound jealous."

"Who, me? I'm not jealous. I'm livid. I have information for you, and you took that slut to lunch today instead."

"She wants to immigrate. We found the moped."

"Where?"

"In a dump, cleverly disguised as a Packard. I'll tell you about it. What do you have for me?"

She frowned, but she let it by. "They were talking about Veronica earlier today. Reminiscing. They didn't have much to say about her that was positive."

"I gathered that. She seems a vindictive, petty sort."

"That's the least of it. She set traps for people she didn't like."

"And she disliked everybody."

"You got it. For instance, she wanted to get Lauren for some reason. This was on a shoot in August, and they were rooming together. Lauren didn't have the baby with her that time. After dark, Veronica put a coffee table and a stool and some other things out in the middle of the room and then took the light bulbs out of the lamps."

"So Lauren would trip and possibly hurt herself."

"As soon as Lauren realized the trap, she worked her way over to the refrigerator and opened it. She used the fridge light to clear the floor and replace the bulbs, and apparently Veronica *really* got mad."

"Clever."

"Not to Veronica. If Veronica were still alive, you could probably arrest her for Lauren's murder." Ev glanced back nervously.

Jack turned them around. He stopped. From here they could see the crew, but they were far enough away to talk. "Anyone have a particular reason to do her? Seriously burned in some trap, maybe?"

"No one mentioned anything you could read that way, and they were talking about some really disgusting things Veronica did. They seem to take it philosophically. You know: 'That's just the way Ronnie was.' Also, Veronica was a kleptomaniac."

"Steal from stores or from other people?"

"Other people. Sometimes expensive things, sometimes worthless things. No one seems to be able to figure out why she took things she did."

"Any specific examples?"

Ev brows puckered and hovered close above her huge doe eyes. "I'm going to have to write this up in my report tonight, right?"

"Yeah, you should."

"Then I ought to try to remember better." She pressed her lovely mouth into a tight little line. "I remember one. A girl named Chris—this was a few months ago, I guess— got a cheap plastic bracelet with a frog on it. She likes frogs, and her boyfriend saw this dumb little thing at a carnival. Chris liked it because of the sentiment, you know? It was worth a dollar, maybe. It disappeared, and Chris thought she'd lost it somehow. Then it fell out of Ronnie's bag. Chris was madder than if Ronnie had stolen a diamond necklace."

"Did all the things she pilfered have sentimental value?"

Ev pulled her blanket closer around. The overcast was thickening. "You know, that might be. Nobody this afternoon thought of that, but it sounds right. She'd take things that the girls' boyfriends had given them, or that meant something special. I'll ask around." She glanced up at him. "And I'll be sneaky."

"That's a good spy. Anything else?"

She shook her head, and her hair did its Amelia Earhart bit. "Nothing else about the relationship between Veronica and the girls."

"Try to get at least a casual list of things she took, especially from people here present. Not just recently. We're looking for sources of resentment, and they could perhaps fester a long time."

"OK."

"Sounds like it's going all right, then."

"Marlette's being a little snot. Really nasty to me. But Edith keeps a lid on her pretty much." She tried to make it sound off-handed, but he could hear the tension—possibly even fear.

"Edith? Protective?"

"Sure, 'cause it's disruptive. We can't have anything disrupting the job."

"Oh, yeah. Disruptive." He searched the crew in the distance. "Where's Marlette?"

"Up there with . . . I don't see her."

"Personal business, maybe?"

"We've been careful not to separate. Athalia wouldn't let her go off by herself. Athalia takes this stay-together thing really seriously."

"So do you, I hope."

"Honestly, Jack. You treat me like a child."

"No, like a potential murder victim. I'm still kicking myself for asking Hal to bring you into this. I should have anticipated this could happen. I should have thought past the end of my nose, and I didn't. If anything happened to you . . . " His voice quit on him.

"You'd feel guilty forever. Yeah, yeah, yeah. Well, don't forget I was the one who insisted on staying with it. You wanted to send me home."

"I still do." He started back toward the crew.

"Well, forget it. I'm just now starting to be accepted. Athalia and I are getting really close, and she knows a lot about everyone here. She can probably give me plenty for the list of things Veronica pilfered too."

Edith turned this way and hollered Ev's name. Ev left his arm and bolted ahead at a run. Why was she so eager to please Edith? The image. Her cover. That was it. She was the struggling model grateful for this opportunity. She crabbed at Jack in private, but she played the role to the hilt in public. She disappeared into the van.

Jack continued on over to Grayson. "Where's Marlette?"

Grayson shrugged. "Around somewhere close. Has to be. In a van, probably."

259

"You weren't keeping a close eye on her?"

"I'm baby-sitting the furniture, not the people."

"I thought we were watching so that the murderer doesn't find another opportunity to strike when no one is looking."

Grayson waved a hand. "You're paranoid. What could go wrong here?"

"What went wrong here twice already?" Jack called, "Edith? Where's Marlette?"

"Mr. Preston, I'm getting a little bored with you."

"Same to ya, Miz Carvey."

Athalia popped out of a van in designer jeans and a loose, swirly little top with puffy sleeves, very feminine. "Isn't she with you, Jack? She headed your way."

Jack unsnapped the leash. "Maxx! Find. Find Marlette."

Grayson snorted. "He doesn't understand that."

"Probably not, but giving him impossible jobs keeps him busy. You don't mind, do you?"

"Yeah. He's off leash."

"That he is."

Maxx had trotted off in the same direction Jack and Ev had gone, but he wasn't following Ev's trace. He was twenty feet west of where Jack and Ev had walked. Jack followed him, and his stomach tightened into ugly knots. He had seen Marlette only moments ago. Not enough time had elapsed for anything really gruesome to happen. He glanced back. Athalia and Ev stood close together watching him.

Actually, they were watching Maxx as he cut circles, his nose to the ground. Maxx was not a good scent hunter. His nose was nowhere near the equal of a trained bloodhound's. He was a total loss on an old scent, a dry terrain. But this trail was moments old in damp grass. The scent was writ large, like a broad-tip Magic Marker instead of ballpoint pen.

Jack heard a coarse whisper, "Shoo. Go away!" *Gow awhy!*

Maxx's thick, ungainly tail flailed as he disappeared behind a big information panel identifying the trees and birds one would most likely see during a picnic. He barked cheerfully.

Jack swung around the other side of the panel and barked too. "What in blue blazes do you think you're doing?"

Marlette's eyes like flames scorched him. "If I want to take a walk, that's my concern. You just go busy yourself with your little snip." She flounced off around the far end of the sign and marched away toward the others, her lovely, delicate nose high.

Maxx squirreled around, snuffling. He yapped.

"Maxx, heel." Jack fell in beside her. "The rule about not separating is for your sake, cookie, not mine. You're in mortal danger, literally, and you go prowling in the weeds. Marlette, you set yourself up for a murder just now. If our attacker wanted to, he could have done you. Can't you get that through your pretty head?"

"Honestly, Jack," she mocked, "you treat me like a child."

She'd been listening to them. To Jack and Ev. Eavesdropping.

Maxx turned around, looked off the way they had come, and sat down abruptly.

Jack didn't waste much time pondering what that might mean. "Ev! Athalia!" he called. "Come take Marlette back with you, please. John?" He gave a come-hither swoop with his arm.

Ev and Athalia started in this direction. The moment John began to move, Jack turned and followed his dog. "Maxx, find." Just to be on the safe side, he drew his weapon now. Drawing it later doesn't count for much if now is when you need it.

Maxx didn't bother sniffling around at this end of the picnic ground. Springloaded, he bounded back to the information sign where Marlette had been cowering. He trotted off into a weedy, brushy thicket separating some of the more intimate picnic sites. He followed his nose to the men's restroom and stood at the door.

Jack shoved it open for him. In all his five years, Maxx had never figured out that some doors latch, some doors swing, and he could handle the swinging ones. He walked instantly to the handicapped stall on the end. His single sharp bark reverberated like a twenty-one-gun salute through the boxy room and made Jack's ears ring.

Grayson entered, his weapon aimed at the ceiling.

The stall doors opened inward, Jack noticed. He pushed on the handicapped stall door. Latched. No feet showed underneath. Jack grimaced to Grayson and got a grimace back. As Grayson silently stepped into the stall beside, Jack motioned Maxx to heel.

Vibrating like a jackhammer, Maxx obeyed instantly. How the mutt did love hard-core cop stuff! And somehow he always knew when business was serious. Well, almost always.

It was time for Jack to do a little jackhammering of his own. He moved out in front of the handicapped stall, reared back, and stomped the door at its latch, throwing his whole weight into it.

The door flew open. The metal latch, or part of it, chinged into the far wall like a bullet. The door slammed against the wall, slammed shut, slammed open again in a matter of a second.

Jack found himself leveling his sights on Clyde.

The buffalo stood on the throne, squatted low so that he would show neither above nor below the stall door and divider. He cried out, an inarticulate "Aaah!," and popped his hands into the air.

Maxx growled, just to remind everyone he was on the job.

John Grayson was standing on the seat next door now, his gun leveled on Wilkins as well. Jack dipped his head. Watching Maxx as a duckling would watch a hawk, Clyde thumped down off his perch and stepped out into the washroom.

"Turn around."

He did.

"Hands on your head, fin—" Jack didn't have to finish the instruction. Clyde plopped his massive paws on top of his head and laced his fingers together. Quite obviously, he'd done this more than once.

Grayson was still on him. So was Maxx.

Jack could safely stuff his gun in his right hip pocket now. With his left hand he grabbed the fingers on the top of Clyde's head and squeezed them together hard. With his right he went over Clyde top to bottom. No weapons, no suspicious nonweapons such as screwdrivers, no incriminating tidbits of any sort.

"Where's your sidearm, Clyde?"

"Edith told me to leave it in my room."

"Why?"

"I dunno."

In a way, Jack was disappointed.

In fact, he found himself sorely disappointed that Clyde hadn't put up a fight. For suddenly, Jack wanted intensely to cut loose on somebody. He wanted a good, big, solid piece of damning evidence no jury in the world could misinterpret. He yearned for vengeance, for Lauren, for Roland, and yes, for himself. *Vengeance is mine, saith the Lord,* but Jack wanted some too. He wanted to vent his frustration, his hatred, his fury, his sense of injustice gone berserk. He who prided himself on his superior reason and self-control was no more rational just now than was his dog.

Clyde blurted, "I was in here on business. Harmless business. I just got back from downtown. I wasn't doing nothing wrong. Nothing."

Grayson purred, "Yeah, sure, Wilkins. And when we

describe to the judge how you were positioned behind there, he'll buy your story, no strings."

Jack was carrying his portacuffs, a strip of vinyl that looked like a kid's plastic toy and could hold a horse. Literally. Jack had hobbled a horse with them once, just out of curiosity. Applied too tight, they would cut grooves like plow furrows into a luckless miscreant's wrists, but they did the job.

Grayson, though, carried the real McCoy, the new and improved steel cuffs with a hinge instead of connecting links. He tossed them to Jack, and Jack locked Clyde down as the buffalo continued ranting his protests.

They Miranda-ed him, just to be on the safe side, but they both knew they couldn't really hold him long or pin much on him other than maybe, on the outside, a stalking charge. Besides, Jack had other worries, possibly greater worries.

Marlette, airhead one minute and conniving siren the next, was a loose cannon. All she had to do was get mad, and she could spill too much to the wrong ears without realizing it. Marlette had overheard. Now she knew that Ev was a spy.

22

The Autumn of His Discontent

In the near darkness of the unlighted hallway, the eagle folded her wings across the front of her, a position of doubt and defiance more than comfort, and watched the unfolding scene beyond the one-way glass. Jack stood beside her, his hands in his pockets.

On the other side of the window, in a brightly lit cubicle, Patterson and Grayson took turns barking questions at Clyde Wilkins. The three sat on dull gray steel chairs at a dull gray steel table with Clyde conveniently facing this way. Patterson, nearly Clyde's equal for sheer bulk, crowded the buffalo's right. Grayson, looking like a Chihuahua in a pack of bulldogs, sat at his left.

"I'd say he's our man." Deputy Prosecutor Hastings murmured, even though this hallway was soundproofed. They heard the voices in the cubicle through a speaker system. The people in the cubicle heard nothing from the hallway.

"If he is, he's an Academy Award quality actor." Jack found himself muttering also, just because she did. "Watch his hands and feet, and the way his mouth tightens. He really gets nervous when they're talking about Veronica or Edith. But not about Lauren or Marlette. I don't think he's holding back on anything regarding Lauren. I don't think he did her."

"You're saying we have two different killers out loose?"

"I'm saying I doubt Clyde is directly responsible for Lauren's death. Better than even chance he wasn't responsible for Veronica's either, therefore."

"You're wrong."

"That's beside the point. The point is, you have nothing to bring an indictment with. Curling up on a toilet seat is weird but not incriminating."

"He didn't come out when you told him to."

"We didn't tell him to."

She cut loose with an expletive loud enough to rattle the one-way window and glared at him. "How do you expect me to do my job when you flub yours? That's the first thing you should have done."

"It would have spoiled the surprise."

Beyond them in that little room, Clyde was saying all over again that he didn't know anything about a moped. He was in and out of the area on Saturday gathering up things for the shoot. Neither Grayson nor Patterson were mentioning the bike was actually taken Friday night. Clyde didn't try to alibi Friday night or otherwise mention Friday in any way. Jack doubted Clyde was clever enough to keep talking about it without slipping up, but so far the buffalo was keeping his ponies in all the right corrals.

The eagle grumbled, "We'll have to let him go. I'll assign someone to keep tabs on him."

"Speaking of which. I asked Raleigh in there why the Sheriff's Department didn't put a guard on the surviving models, and he said you were taking care of it."

"I am."

"No one's doing it."

"They don't need to anymore. We have our man. We'll keep an eye on him until we can nail down something definite."

Jack had assumed that bringing Clyde in and working on him awhile would assuage his anger. Not so. In fact, his fury and frustration boiled hotter, if anything. And as he stood there and thought about it awhile, the fire burned against this woman standing beside him.

Hastings turned to leave.

"Just a minute." Jack grabbed her elbow and stopped her. "Let's see if I have this right. You pretty much knew you ought to look out for the girls' safety. The sheriff's deputy suggested specifically that it ought to be done. But you didn't do it."

"I'm busy. It got put aside."

"No." Jack held her eye with his, so she would see his anger and frustration. "You told Raleigh it was taken care of, and he had no reason to believe otherwise. No one would."

"Prester, I don't have time to—"

Jack cut her off, and he hardly ever did that. "Putting a close watch on the girls is expensive and silent and invisible. It doesn't draw media attention. But another murder would toss Acadia right back into the national spotlight. You're not interested in being silent and invisible. You want all those microphones in front of your face and your name in the papers."

"If you're intimating what I think you're intimating, I'll skewer you dead for slander."

Jack pressed on. "You're immune to censure. If the murders are over with, no problem. If another girl dies, you simply plead you made an error of judgment, and you're off the hook. You might get a dirty look or two, but no one's going to remember for long. No one's going to call you on it, and you have another tragedy to handle."

"Prester, you breathe a word of that lunacy and I'll—"

He cut her off again. "The more killings this guy attempts, the greater the chance he'll slip up and we'll catch him. The odds are all in your favor, aren't they!"

She yanked her elbow free, and only then did Jack realize how tightly he had been gripping it. She marched away and left him there sizzling. If he was wrong, why didn't she bother to deny it?

He picked up the house phone and punched an extension number. In the cubicle, Raleigh answered. "Deputy Patterson."

"Need me here?"

"Nope."

"I'm going back out to the island then."

"OK." Raleigh didn't even glance at the window as he hung up.

Jack walked out into the cold gray, still too furious to think, let alone think clearly. More or less numbly, he climbed into his truck and fought off Maxx's attack-with-a-friendly-weapon.

He wiped the dog spit off his cheek and drove south out of Ellsworth onto Mt. Desert Island. This was Monday afternoon, and his back still hurt from getting walloped by that biker on Saturday morning. Maxx had lost his stiffness, and his face was the same size on both sides again, but Jack was in no shape to drive clear home to Kansas.

No matter. He'd have to stop in D.C. anyway and check in with Hal. Whatever possessed him to lose his cool with Hastings? His mind flitted from thought to thought, including thoughts of petty, endearing, volatile, gorgeous Marlette. Emma Hoople. Actually, he liked the name Emma just fine, and he was sorry she didn't.

The crew was still out on Thompson Island, so he pulled into the picnic area parking lot. He ought to put Maxx on leash, but he didn't care enough to bother. He climbed out and walked down the shore to the set-up. Maxx ranged out around him.

On the grassy sward, Winthrop Spalding sat on a lobster trap whittling with a pocket knife at a peg of some sort. In his yellow slicker, a nondescript pullover sweater, rubber boots, and that faded watch cap, he looked vividly, authentically, indelibly Down East. Edith was taking forever posing all three girls around him.

Jack grinned. "So they sucked you into show business, eh?"

Winthrop snorted, but he didn't seem particularly displeased to be thus surrounded by beauty. "Local color, they say."

"And of the brightest hue. Hey, I want to thank you for being able to take over here on such short notice. I appreciate it."

"Happy to. Nothing else pressing to do."

"OK, let's go. Arturo?" Edith walked over and flopped wearily into her director's chair.

Arturo dropped to one knee and started shooting.

Jack crossed to Edith. "Yesterday I asked for a list of the chores you gave Clyde to do Saturday."

"I haven't had time."

"It's not an option, Ms. Cray."

She looked crushed. Defeated. Jack had never seen any trace of defeat in her before. It unnerved him.

She turned baleful eyes to him. "You just carted my right arm off to jail. You arrested my photographer. I admit if anyone deserves arresting, he does. Still. Now you want paperwork. Lists. I hire my paperwork done, Mr. Preston. All of it. Clyde was the paper shuffler on location here. I'm sorry. I have neither the time nor the inclination. So sue me."

"Sue, no. Arrest, possibly, for obstructing the investigation. But I'd much prefer cooperation. I trust you'll come through on that."

She looked at him then. Just looked. It wasn't a hostile glare or an approving stare. He could see no emotion in her face at all. Whatever she was thinking now she had masked completely.

Winthrop whittled quietly at his peg, looking absolutely content. His was the only contented visage in this outfit, Jack's included. Well, Maxx's too. Maxx was usually content, and occasionally bored, but hardly ever troubled.

Jack tried another tack. "Are you aware that Clyde has been stalking Marlette?"

"Nonsense."

"People ask me why I put up with a dog when I'm traveling. Dogs are a nuisance, even little ones, and Maxx is a world class nuisance. They forget he's a working dog. He tells me things I can learn no other way. Maxx told me that when Marlette and I went out for a stroll a couple nights ago, Clyde followed us and then tried to evade detection. This afternoon it happened again. Clyde wasn't just stopping by that restroom, Ms. Cray. He was lurking in the bushes near Marlette, and he retreated to the restroom, again to evade detection."

"You believe a dog." She made it sound as if Jack was equally convinced there is a tooth fairy.

"Maxx can lie like a rug, but only when I accuse him of something. When it's police work, he's honest and trustworthy." Jack dropped down to a squat near her left knee, facing her, so that his face would hover in front of hers below eye level.

"And his testimony is admissible in court," she sneered. "One woof for yes, two for no."

"That's very clever of you, Ms. Cray, shifting the topic from Clyde to Maxx. The question is Clyde. Have there been other incidents in which Clyde has pursued or stalked women?"

"No. You've seen his police record. Clean."

"Beyond the record. You probably know him better than anyone else."

"No."

"Why did you tell him to ditch his gun?"

"Because of you. He has a tendency to go for it a little too quickly when you're around, and I was afraid an unseemly incident would put us even farther behind."

"'Unseemly incident.' Blow each other away. Yeah, I guess you could call it that." Jack could go in half a dozen directions from here. Where next? "That house over there

270

on the shore, the rather garish one. Use it in any shots?"

"What house?" She did not snap her head around toward Aunt Martha's or otherwise indicate she had ever noticed it.

Jack pointed.

She looked, neither lingering too long nor cutting the glance too short. "Too far away."

Fracci snapped his fingers at Marlette, and she altered the angle of her head. What bothered Jack about that? Of course! Fracci had made precisely that same gesture the day he used Maxx over by Jordan Pond. Exactly the same snap of the fingers. It's one thing to cue a dog like that, quite another to summarily dismiss a human being that way. No "Please," no "Thank you," no sign of respect. By no stretch of the imagination could anyone in Christendom call Marlette a dog.

Jack watched Fracci work a few moments longer and turned away. It's not Christian to loathe a person for being how God made him.

A lot of non-Christian thoughts kept bugging him lately, everything from his thirst for vengeance to Marlette to this irritation with Fracci. He felt under pressure, vaguely dissatisfied with everything in life, covered by a big, fat, ugly black cloud. He wanted the whole affair to be over with, and he was fast reaching a point where he didn't care whether it was a satisfactory conclusion or not.

Just over with. Please, Lord. Done, God. Finis.

Apparently Fracci decided he had completed this particular take, because he abruptly walked away. The girls broke formation instantly. Mrs. Hyde came bounding down out of a van and called to Ev and Athalia. She hustled over to Marlette and stuffed a sandwich in the girl's hand. She warned her she would have to change shortly and jogged back to the parking lot.

Jack headed for Marlette. Obviously she was going to snub him and play hard to get, but then she seemed to think better of it. She allowed him to drape his coat over her shoulders.

"Miss Hoople," he began, just to keep it on a semi-formal basis, "we must talk."

"That's all? Talk?"

"For now, that's plenty." He drew her aside, away from the seated Edith Cray, away even from Winthrop Spalding. The spry old fellow stood up and casually walked over to the van, tending the sheep. Maxx developed a weird fascination for a clump of wild rosebushes. He snuffled and poked around the base of them in the futile pursuit of some small mammal or bird. He hardly ever came close to catching anything.

Jack wrapped his arm around Marlette to pull her in closer. "I take it from the sandwich there that you'll be working into the evening again."

"The *last* evening. Finish here, then that cliff thing . . . what is it?"

"Otter Cliffs?"

"The very thing. In the morning, and then the blue and gold pants ensembles at Thunder Hole, and we're done. All done!"

"And you'll be glad to get home."

She rolled her eyes. Gorgeous blue eyes hundreds and hundreds of feet deep.

He lowered his voice. "You were spying on Evelyn and me earlier. Any particular reason?"

"I took a walk. You saw me."

"No, I didn't see you, which tells me you were sneaking around spying."

"That's my affair."

"No, it's mine, because I care about you." He stopped her and turned her to him. "I really do, Marlette, and you don't seem to mind placing yourself in jeopardy. It worries me more than you can imagine."

"Really?" *Railly?* She looked positively smug.

"You were listening to Evelyn and me earlier. What do you think?"

"About Evvie and you? I don't know what you two are cooking up, but it's probably interesting. You're con artists or something, right? Going to work a scam on Edith? That would be a bonzer turn! Or revenue agents. That'd be just as fine. A fair cow, that woman. She deserves anything you two pull off on her."

Jack pondered a moment. He had not expected that assumption on her part, but it fit well. She would surely keep her mouth shut if she thought that, by keeping silent, Edith might get burned. He had best just let that particular sleeping dog lie.

Marlette gripped his arm. "Are there snakes here?"

"Little ones."

"Not . . . you know."

"Not at all like Australia. Most of your snakes are elapids—cobra family. Most of ours are harmless. All of the ones up here are. That doesn't mean you should go hiking out across the boonies, you know. Not until we've caught our man."

"I thought you did. Clyde." She snuggled against him and matched her stride to his.

Jack wondered if she'd forgotten the sandwich in her free hand. "He's a suspect, that's all."

"Mm." She persisted. "You have snakes out West, though, where you live. Right? "

"Lots of them."

"Ever been bitten?"

"Nope. Almost lost a senator to one, though."

She watched him, her eyes dancing.

"Hovenweep." How he loved walking beside her!

"Where?"

"Hovenweep. A National Monument conserving certain Indian ruins, among other things. Near Mesa Verde."

"Do they have rattlesnakes? Like in those mystery books?"

273

"Mystery books." Jack frowned. "Oh. Tony Hiller-man?"

"That's it. I couldn't think of his name. I read one called *Coyote Waits*. It had snakes in it."

"So does Hovenweep."

"Did you ever catch one?" She tried to eat her sandwich and talk at the same time. It wasn't working well. She choked.

"That's one of the things you do when you're a ranger. Remove problem snakes. I was doing an SCA stint in high school. Hovenweep has a perpetual snake problem, but it seemed worse that spring. People were seeing them on the trail every now and then. So we decided we'd just fill the winter den with cement, and they'd all go away."

"Did they?"

"The maintenance crew cemented it up solid. The snakes sort of disappeared, and we didn't see a single one over the summer. Everyone was congratulating each other." Jack paused. "Then autumn arrived, and the snakes came home for the winter."

"Oh, I see! The den was closed up, right?"

"Right. So instead of all disappearing down that hole, as per usual, they basked on the trails and tried to den up under houses, and in the restrooms—the restroom doors didn't have thresholds. We had snakes all over the place."

"How gruesome!" The gruesomeness, though, wasn't visibly affecting her appetite.

Jack rather envied her that sandwich. "It would've stayed pretty low key, but the regional director and some bigwigs announced they were coming. Big publicity spread to pitch SCA to some Washington people. Senators, some reps. Here comes the party to see the area. So we sent a kid a hundred yards ahead of them to chase the snakes off the trail. Would have worked all right, but he missed one. The senator, a fiftyish man, was walking along talking about how great nature is when this buzzer raises its head right up in front of his foot. Scared the willikers out of him.

For the rest of the walking tour he followed at the rear and asked why we were bothering to preserve this depressing wilderness anyway."

"Are the snakes still there?"

"Nah. We were supposed to be doing trail maintenance, but we ended up trapping snakes. We all got pretty good at it. Caught a hundred and ninety-three in the last two weeks. Took them all out in the back country and turned them loose. It killed two birds with one stone, you might say. The rangers had been having trouble with deer poachers, so they publicized where all the snakes were going. Haven't had any trespassers since."

She tittered delightfully and popped the last of her sandwich in her mouth. "Such pesky things, snakes."

"Speaking of pests—" Jack gave her his handkerchief to use as a napkin "—has Clyde been pestering you?"

"What's pestering? He stays close around. He looks at me funny sometimes."

"Funny how?" Jack was fast losing interest in the subject. He hated ruining this warm, close conversation with a discussion of Clyde.

"I don't know. Strange." *Oy down't now. Strynge.*

"He relate to any of the other girls that way? Did he look at Veronica funny? Or Lauren?"

"He looks at everybody funny, except you. You he glowers at. He really has a snout on you for some reason."

"That's OK. I'm not all that thrilled with him either."

She giggled like a brook dancing through a rocky streambed.

And then Mrs. Hyde was calling Marlette in earnest. To work, to work.

Jack turned her around and headed back. When they reached the van he pulled his jacket off her back. She turned, planted a fast, wet kiss on his cheek, and climbed inside.

Winthrop studied that cheek a moment and grunted. "I'm gonna hafta start giving the ladies my coat, I s'pose."

Jack put his jacket on. "She's actually in love with the dog. She's just using me to get to Maxx."

"Then I hafta get a dog. What am I gonna do with a dog when they go back to the city?"

Maxx joined them and gave Winthrop's unsuspecting hand a juicy lick.

"Feed him scraps. Look how quickly Maxx became your buddy. Dogs bribe so easy."

Winthrop chuckled quietly. "Naw, I'll do without a dog. Content just the way I am."

Content. Jack's mind grabbed the thought and juggled it. Content.

Winthrop Spalding had everything he needed—his God, a quiet life, enough of everything necessary, a grandson. Essentially, Winthrop Spalding truly possessed the abundant life.

Jack was not content by any means. He hungered for something, and he couldn't define or articulate what it was. And look at all these people, scrabbling for more and more. Seizing. Grasping. Reaching. Even Lauren, poor Lauren, yearned for the abundant life.

But Winthrop, in his elegant simplicity, had achieved it.

23

Hat Trick

When Jewish writers under the aegis of the Holy Spirit assembled the Scriptures, they had no really good word for "paperwork." For lack of a better term, therefore, they used the words "fire and brimstone."

Well, all right, maybe he was overstating it a bit. But here he stood in the doorway of his motel room, staring at the prospect of hours and hours of paperwork. And already it was nearly eight in the evening.

He had not been keeping up with the supplementals that charted what he had done each day. He had not kept up with summaries of interviews or of the backup documentation of physical evidence such as that blue tarp, other than that done when the evidence was first obtained. He had a lot of catch-up to do. He rather envied Ev her ability to assemble arcane paperwork in record time.

With a can of Pepsi and a heavy sigh, he pulled a non-easy chair over to the featureless formica slab and sat down. This would go so much faster if he had a cute little desk and a brass lamp like Ev's. First he wrote up all the notes and explanations that would require Ev's initial or signature as well as his. That didn't take long, since she was preparing her own reports.

Then he started his individual stuff, the things that

277

would not be reflected in Grayson's reports or Patterson's. It went excruciatingly slowly. As he wrote down this bit and that—page after page of terse notes—strange, ugly little thoughts nagged at him, possible solutions to the puzzle at hand. Eventually he gave up his pitiful semblance of getting anything done and simply sat back to think. His sore back complained about being sprawled in the non-easy chair, but he didn't move.

With chatter and moans, the girls arrived back. They filled the hallway outside his room with giggles. He didn't hear Edith among them, but then she wasn't a giggler.

He stood stiffly and stretched his back. Then he scooped up the stuff needing Ev's signature and headed down to her room. Physically and emotionally he felt ninety years old. He rapped on her door and stepped back so she could see him in the peephole.

A muffled "Just a moment" kept him standing there a couple of minutes. Ev's notion of a moment was pretty much like his father's. Jack's mom had created a cottage industry out of waiting for that man.

Ev popped the door open, and he stepped inside.

Her eyes, normally the size of English walnuts, had widened to tennis balls. She slammed the door. "Am I glad you came! Edith has one of those green felt hats!"

"How do you know?"

"Edith brought the three of us back in the Mercedes. Athalia sat up front beside her, and Marlette and I were in the backseat. I saw it sort of sticking out from under the driver's seat."

"Like it was stuffed under the seat?"

"Right, only she stuffed it too far under, and it showed a little in back. I'm sure that's what it was, Jack, but I didn't want to draw attention to it so I tried not to look at it—know what I mean? I didn't want Marlette to notice it."

"You get an A in spy school." He thought about it a moment. This would not in any way muddy up the theories

278

that were starting to form in his mind, and it added weight to a couple of them.

Ev moved in against him suddenly and wrapped her arms around his ribs. He pulled her in tight with an avuncular bearhug and pressed her tousled head to his shoulder with one hand. It was exactly the sort of way he had held little Roland. Only the size proportions differed.

"Marlette is being mean, Jack. She is so mean. It's getting to me. I don't want it to, but it is. I'm sorry."

"Mean how?"

"Nasty words and stuff, but . . . well, for instance, when I was getting out of the car here tonight, I was stepping out, and she jabbed me with a hatpin or something. I yelped, and Edith said, 'Watch your step,' as if I were clumsy."

Jack knew he ought to be taking Ev's word at face value, but he couldn't imagine someone doing that without provocation. "Marlette show hostility toward anyone else that way?"

"Nobody else has yelped. I didn't notice anything. No."

"Might she suspect you're a spy?"

"Spying on what? Unless she's feeling guilty about something." Ev did not ease her hug, so Jack maintained his.

"Ev? Why were they using the Benz?"

"One of the vans wouldn't start. It's still parked out at the picnic area. Edith wanted to us to split up, and she'd take us in two loads in the other van—it's just crammed full of stuff now—but we wouldn't let her. We stayed together."

"Good for you!"

She clung a few more minutes, then straightened and stepped back.

"You all right?"

She nodded. Her dark hair floated.

He left her then and stopped by Edith's to ask for a

key to the ailing van. Edith sent him to Arturo. He asked Arturo, and the Italian provided it along with a lengthy explanation of what, he was convinced, was wrong. Arturo knew as much about auto mechanics as he knew about astrophysics.

Jack got the same carefree, exuberant greeting from Maxx that he got in the morning at dog-food time, or in the afternoon at treat time, or any other time. He shoved the mutt over to his own side of the truck seat and drove out to Thompson Island.

The ghastly hue of pole lights illuminated the restroom island and a large freestanding sign telling where you are as compared to where the park is. The van was the only vehicle in the lot.

Maxx stood up on all four feet and barked at the windshield.

The dog did some inscrutable things, but barking at a stationary vehicle was not one of them. Jack killed his lights, slid out, and waited a moment until his eyes adjusted to the dimness. He pulled his gun and murmured, "Maxx, find."

The dog bounded forward. A shadow figure ran off toward the woods beyond the van.

"Maxx! Take him!" Jack followed as best he could, but the dog was three times faster than he—three times faster than the prowler too. Somewhere off in the trees, Jack heard the dog snarl and a male voice yell.

Jack hated these woods. Cautiously he moved in among the trees, from weird half-light into total blackness. Bushes rattled and branches snapped with every step he took. Tree limbs scratched him, and cold, bony, arboreal fingers clutched at him. They caught his ankles and tried to trip him. He struggled inches at a time through the vicious tangle, headed toward the snarling.

"Your dog bit me!" Mike Kovik's voice roared in the blackness just ahead. "Get him off me!"

Why hadn't Jack brought the flashlight from under

280

his seat? What an ultra-moron! "Maxx, guard." He waited for a beat. "You can stand up. Put your hands on your head, lace your fingers together, and walk out toward the lights. Reach for a weapon or make any unseemly moves, and I pull the trigger before Maxx can get to you."

"I didn't do anything, Preston."

"Good boy. Just keep it up. Walk."

Kovik could be whipping out a bow and arrow, stringing the bow, nocking the arrow, and taking aim for all Jack knew. He could see absolutely, totally nothing. He was breaking every rule in the book, at least in the chapter on taking down perps. A bare branch like a disapproving schoolteacher switched him across the knuckles. He moved two feet farther and got slapped in the eye by another. He followed Kovik by ear, for the hulking photographer crashed through the woods as noisily as did Jack. What was that movie where men glided soundlessly through thick Eastern woodlands? *Last of the Mohicans.* That was it. It's easy to slip through the trees like a will-o-the-wisp in the movies. Just have the second unit director turn off the sound system.

Ten feet ahead, Kovik stepped out into the light. He was wearing a crusher, although with these pole lamps you couldn't tell colors. His huge ham hands mashed the crown down against his head. At last untrammeled by the underbrush, Maxx ranged out beside him, guarding, ready to spring. Kovik kept a constant and wary—terrified—eye on him.

"Over by the shore there, two picnic tables side by side, about six feet apart. Go sit down." What would Jack do next? To be honest, Kovik hadn't done anything wrong. For that matter, neither had Clyde, technically speaking. There were just all these strange people skulking around, usually under cover of darkness, and a disproportionate number of them wore those goofy hats.

Kovik sat down carefully, slowly, on the inside seat of one of the picnic tables.

Jack perched just as carefully on the seat of the table

across from Kovik. He lowered his weapon until it rested on his thigh, pointed not toward Kovik but toward the darkness beyond the shore. "Maxx, sit. Guard."

The dog's big black bottom plopped into the grass beside Jack's table. Even in this eerie, muted chartreuse from the parking area lights, you could see that the grass in the picnic area had really taken a beating over the summer and was only now starting to recover. The damp smell of the sea, the odor that leaves a funny seafood taste in your mouth, drenched the darkness around them. Every minute or less, headlights and taillights whipped by whistling, darting across the little island from bridge to bridge, intent on business elsewhere.

"Can I take my hands down now?"

"No. You look like a ninny to every passing motorist, and it serves you right. I hate squirreling around in those woods after dark." Jack studied him a moment, deciding which way to start. "You and Veronica Wayne were an item, as were you and Edith previously. Veronica insisted you be a part of this project, and Edith acquiesced. However, after Veronica was gone, Edith did not drop you. Even when you messed up—on purpose, as we've since learned—Edith kept you on. Therefore I deduce that you have something on Edith. You're holding some dark secret over her head. Let's talk about it."

"You're overdeducing."

"You accused me of misreading your personality structure too, remember? This was during our conversation Saturday, when you intimated that Edith drove off and left you without explanation, out on Otter Cliff. The truth is she talked to you before she drove away. From that I surmise that whatever actually passed between you two was more embarrassing—or more damaging—than the fiction that you'd been abandoned. You despise me and fear me —yet you would have me believe a woman dumped you, something that a man's ego doesn't do well with. A man certainly doesn't want another man to know that."

"If you know so much, you tell me."

"I know only the generalities. I'm asking you about the specifics."

"Yeah, well, you don't know any of this. You're just guessing—shooting at ducks in the dark—and hoping I'll spill my guts. Well, there's nothing to spill."

Jack stared at him. Good old Maxx was staring at him too. Maxx sometimes got bored with guard duty when there were more important things to be doing, such as sleeping or licking between his toes, but tonight he was right on top of it.

Kovik's nerves started betraying him. You could see it in the way he started acting uncomfortable, the way his hands seemed to want to do anything except rest on top of his head. "You don't understand. You can't begin to understand."

"I've been doing pretty well so far."

More silence.

"She uses people, Preston. She takes whatever she wants, gets a boost up in her career, and then throws them away. She does it to everybody. She threw me away."

Silence.

"I didn't kill her, but I wanted to. I wanted to so bad it hurt."

"What went on between you and Edith out at Otter Cliff?"

Kovik studied Jack's face, weighing words or options or pain. Who knows? "Edith." He snorted. "Sooner or later she finds out everything. She knew about my outbursts—found out about those. It's funny, though. I never blew up on her. I never hit her once. She's bigger than me. Than anyone, I guess. I don't mean size. She's not bigger than I am, obviously. But she's . . . bigger. She stares at you with those iceberg eyes, and she just grows until you're afraid of her."

Silence.

"Otter Cliff." Kovik took his hands down off his head

in order to rub his face with both of them. Jack doubted he even realized he did it. "Edith knew Veronica had soured on me, and she accused me of hurting her. Edith said I lost my temper with Veronica, like I do sometimes, and accidentally killed her, so I threw her off the bridge."

"Why did she drive off and leave you?"

"To show me she had the upper hand. She does stuff like that. She's so convinced I did it, she thinks all she has to do is mention her suspicions to the cops and they'll run right out and arrest me. She thinks she has this power over me, and that was a little demonstration."

"So who took pity afterwards and picked you up in the Benz? Edith again?"

Kovik smirked. "Pity? Edith?"

"Then who?"

"I forget."

"Why'd you run just now?"

"Someone messing around the van in the dark?" He grimaced. "Looks suspicious, and I thought I could slip away before you saw me. I didn't think you'd come chasing me."

"What are you doing here tonight?"

"Arturo said the van broke down so I came out to see if I could do something."

"Do something." Jack watched the man's hands and decided Kovik was probably telling the truth. "Do what? Wreck it completely?"

"Fix it."

"Sure. After you sabotaged Edith's project here."

"Whether that van runs or not isn't going to affect her project anymore. Just seeing if I could fix it. Arturo told me what he thought was wrong. He's full of rose fertilizer. He doesn't know the cam shaft from the steering wheel."

Time for some empathy. Jack nodded. "I got the same general impression listening to him. He has the mechanical skills of an imaginative four-year-old. You walk out here?"

"Yeah." Kovik was chuckling. "The only vehicle I have keys for is this one."

Jack straightened. "When you saw my truck pull up, you ran. That doesn't say much for your presumed innocence. But you weren't actually caught in the middle of doing anything. I forget—what's the Latin phrase?"

"*In flagrante delicto.*"

"That's it. So for my peace of mind, let me check you for unfriendly weapons and let's go look at the van." Jack waved his gun barrel a little.

Kovik stood up, turned away from Jack and put his hands back up there. There was nothing wrong with the guy's smarts.

He was clean.

Jack holstered his gun at the small of his back. "So what are the symptoms?" He took off toward the van, and Kovik came along, keeping a nervous eye on the dog.

"Coughing, dying, won't start and stay running. It's been missing and acting strangled for a while, but Edith wanted to get it home if she could."

"Carburetor?"

"Maybe. Or I was thinking fuel filter."

Jack sat in the driver's seat with one leg flopped out onto the ground. He started it and stopped it and revved it on command, as Kovik poked at things under the opened hood. It was the classic masculine bonding ritual, a thing boys do from about the age of ten on up. Kovik flopped on his back and rapped on the fuel line underneath with his pocket knife.

Jack got his four-cell out from under his seat, now that he was probably finishing thrashing around through the black woods, and dug into the big jump box just behind the cab in his truck bed.

"I grew up in New Mexico and live in Kansas now. Lots of wide open spaces. I know all about losing a water pump in the middle of nowhere, so I keep spares of the basics." He handed Kovik a fuel filter. "This fits my Ram.

How close does it come to fitting the van?"

Not exact, apparently, but close enough. As Jack held the light and loaned the tools and for another five-minutes pressed his thumbs over the open gas line, Kovik changed the fuel filter. It was actually quite a feat in a parking lot in the middle of the night.

Kovik hopped into the driver's seat and touched it off. The motor started reluctantly, coughed, sputtered, and kicked into a welcome, unmitigated roar. He dropped it back on idle. It didn't run smoothly, but it ran. The roughness probably had nothing at all to do with its recent ailment. Jack had noticed without really noticing that the other van needed a tune-up just as badly.

Beneath that crusher, Kovik's huge, golden-bear face opened into a disarming grin. Every massive inch of him spoke *We did it!*. He sprawled in the driver's seat, one foot on the brake, with the air of a victor. Now was the time to hit him with questions, while his guard was down.

Jack stood in the open van door and leaned against the B post. "Apparently Veronica Wayne left the motel and rented separate quarters somewhere. Do you know where?"

Kovik took it without a bobble, smooth as bacon drippings. "No. You might ask Clyde. He'd prob'ly know."

"You were her boyfriend. You didn't know?"

"*Was* her boyfriend. She was developing a new relationship. That might be why she took the other place—to get away from all of us."

"From you."

"From me too, yeah."

"Tell me about her and Alan Messier."

"You know about that." He heaved his massive ham shoulders. "Sure you'd know. You're investigating. You probably won't believe this, but Messier and I got along pretty well. The day before Ronnie died, in fact, he and I had a couple beers together."

"Friendly, you mean? Together at a bar?"

"Yeah. Boasted. Told each other lies. Only I don't

think he was lying. He was—you see, Ronnie was, well . . ."
He stopped.

Jack gave him the silence he needed to string his thoughts together.

Kovik stared at the steering post a few moments. "Whenever you were with Ronnie, you had this feeling that she was glancing over your shoulder, looking for the next man in her life. You never had all her attention, not completely. So I wasn't too surprised when she zeroed in on Messier. He was—you know—restless. Looking around. She sensed that. Like a lion picks out the weakling in the herd. *Bam.* She had him."

"The word I hear is that she led him astray."

"Yeah. Their flaming romance wasn't all that flaming. They only got together once."

"Once is all it takes to be an adulterer."

Kovik nodded. "And it scared him. I don't think he really meant all that to happen. That night when we were talking, he said he was thinking about breaking it off before anything more happened. He didn't want to be a—you know—is *sinner* the word?"

"The perfect word. What would have been her reaction if he told her he was ending their involvement?"

Kovik smirked. "Ronnie dumped everybody. Nobody dumped Ronnie. Nobody. Know what I mean?"

"Would she react violently?"

"She'd react any way it took to change his mind."

"Who told you she was tipped off the bridge?"

He frowned at the steering wheel and shrugged. "Just sort of common knowledge. Lauren said that's the last place she was seen alive. Edith, I think. Or maybe Marlette. She loves gossip. I don't remember." He handled that one without getting nervous or acting cautious too.

"What are you holding over Edith's head?"

Kovik grinned wickedly. "If I told you—that is, if there actually was anything like that—then I couldn't hold it over her head anymore, right?"

"So you're withholding information in an official investigation."

"What's to withhold? You're the one who says I know dirty secrets, not me."

"If I find out I'm right, Mike, I'll nail you." Jack waved a hand toward Maxx, who was minutely examining the base of a shrub with his nose. "Or send in my goon here."

Kovik watched Maxx for a moment, and his facial expression told Jack that for a second he actually believed the goon threat. He chuckled again, a man insufferably proud of himself. "I'll tell Edith she owes you a fuel filter."

"See you later." Jack stepped back and swung the van door shut.

Kovik popped it into reverse and scooted backwards in a big arc. He roared off into the night, across the bridge southbound toward Acadia.

Jack stood there a short while pondering the images in his mind of the bulky photographer. Kovik probably did not often get one up on Edith, particularly something this positive. In fact, Jack doubted there was ever an abundance of positive associations between those two—or between Edith and anyone.

He headed toward his truck, thinking of the earnest Lauren and the tiny Roland and the stunning Marlette. He paused in the sickly light of the pole lamps to glance at the information panels. The first paragraph seized his eye and shook him.

The name *Acadia,* it said, came from a Micmac Indian word meaning "plenty" or "abundance."

24

Hit the Road, Jack

Every place on the face of the earth can boast of blue sky sooner or later, but Jack was beginning to wonder about Acadia. Wonder no more. Tuesday morning dawned bright and clear. He took Maxx down to the water's edge behind the motel for his first romp of the day and enjoyed the crunchy crispness of his first hard frost in a long time. The frost provided an extra touch of crystalline glory to an already spectacular day. Jack prowled the shore to seaward as Maxx explored to landward. Maxx was a land dog, not a sea dog.

Glistening water met glowing sky at a muted, hazy boundary. The trees of the distant shore shrank back, giving center stage to the brilliant pas de deux of sea and sunlight. Jack basked. He let the sunshine flood him and nearly blind him. He had been without the joy of sun for far too long.

At this point along the rocky shore, the low tide washed across a mix of rocks and sand. Jack recognized blue mussels, starfish (species undetermined), periwinkles (he thought), barnacles, and sedate little limpets plastered to the rocks. He knew that if only he could look more carefully with an educated eye, he would find hundreds of different organisms, filling to abundance a habitat that was totally alien to him.

He called Maxx to him and returned to the motel parking lot.

Edith was herding her weary models into the van Kovik had just repaired, even as Clyde was loading boxes and clothes bags into the other vehicle. Edith did not appear grateful or relieved or in any way emotionally buoyed. Were she reduced to using wheelbarrows, she probably would be wearing that same dogged look of grim determination. She was entering the homestretch and still running hard.

Ev waved to him from the van, and he grinned and waved back. He felt good this morning, for the first time in days. The convoy headed off toward Otter Cliff.

He turned toward his truck and stopped. Kovik was standing over by the motel's side door, watching Sitting Pretty disappear beyond the curve. Jack walked over to him.

Kovik nodded toward Jack's pickup. "Four wheel drive, right? Oversize engine?"

"Nah. You're looking at the pace car for a tractor pull. Zero to sixty eventually."

"Yeah, I've heard them all." Kovik interrupted himself with another of his big, throaty chuckles. "The only car passed by its own exhaust."

"At the drag strip they time me with a calendar."

The chuckle again. "Never heard that one." Kovik stared off for a moment toward the empty road. A car whizzed by, breaking his gaze. "Edith has had a long-standing habit of spending more than she makes. She's usually having to scramble to meet loan payments to some jerk or other."

"That's the basis of your dirty little secrets on her?"

"Secrets? What secrets? I just thought you might want to know she's a patsy for loan sharks. Check into her credit rating sometime."

"I'll do that." Jack didn't say he assumed it had already been done.

"You might want to get yourself a fuel filter too. I wouldn't bet money on Edith replacing that one."

"A word to the wise is sufficient. I'll stop at that auto parts store on the way down to Otter Point."

"That where they're going this morning? Edith didn't say. You know, if it wasn't for the cops telling me I have to stick around, I'd be out of here long already. Feels strange, watching them go out and sitting here doing nothing."

"Sort of figured that." Jack stood about a little longer, but Kovik seemed out of things to say.

The blond bear mumbled some sort of good-bye and walked off toward the main motel door.

The drive down to Otter Point, a stop at the auto parts store notwithstanding, was just gorgeous. No longer hampered by drizzle and cloud cover, the autumn color did its level best to out-perform the dazzling dance of sea and sun. The frost had melted, but the sparkling wetness it left behind heightened the greens and browns of the ground covers.

Jack took an extra minute to check out Sand Beach. Wave after wave of heavy surf rolled in, despite that this arch of pale beige was well protected. A raft of ducks bobbed on the swells just offshore. How could they do that without feeling queasy?

Winthrop had mentioned that heavy seas could come in although the storm that caused them be a hundred miles offshore. He said they might also follow an abrupt change of weather, or sometimes precede it. Jack wondered which this was.

And he thought about Marlette. The southern part of Australia from whence she hailed enjoyed some change of seasons, but they did not experience this overabundant wealth of beauty. He wondered if she appreciated the area she was in right now, and its glory. She could enjoy the natural beauty of this place—of any place in the States—if only she could understand it better. Perhaps after this gig he could buy her binoculars, a bird book, maybe a picture tree guide, and help her get acquainted with nature.

He'd done that with his Marcia. When they met, Marcia knew only what she had learned in high school general science, and Jack had never been to Australia before. Field guides in hand, they had gone forth together to explore and discover—the reef, the Queensland rain forest, the dry interior, the Gulf country. In the process of discovery they had fallen in love.

Yes! That was what he'd do, just as soon as this case was cleared. Only one cloud darkened this happy picture. Conceivably, Marlette was mired at least peripherally in the murders.

Jack parked in the Otter Cliffs lot beside the vans and put Maxx on leash. The air was what the Aussies would call "fresh"—meaning colder than an Eskimo's lawn mower—but with a bright sun and no wind, it didn't seem cold today.

The girls were posed out near the lip of the cliff much as they had been posed previously. They were reenacting ruined takes with the same clothes, the same positions, the same backdrop. The smiles today seemed brighter, though. Perhaps it was just the brightness of the day. Nobody needed Ellison and his reflector this morning, but he was positioning it all the same.

The surf roared against the cliff below, a constant distant cacophony. The contrast intrigued Jack—that churning, howling war between sea and land below them and the serene sweetness of the girls posing against the placid blue sky. He wandered over to John Grayson in his gray and greens, leaning against a post of the fence that kept tourists on the established path.

Jack nodded toward Clyde. "Our stalker is behaving himself, I trust."

"Hasn't changed one iota. Good morning." Even the cool and laid-back John Grayson seemed cheerier today.

"Good morning! I see you put Alan Messier back in harness a day or two ago. How's he doing?"

"OK. He's a binge drinker. When he's on the juice, he's on it. When he gets off the juice, he's off it. He just came off it."

"What behavioral changes does the juice make?"

"He gets truculent, hard to talk to. Withdraws. Snaps at people he shouldn't be snapping at."

Jack nodded. "What about guilt and Alan Messier? Can you speak to that?"

"Hadn't thought of it in that particular way. Guilt and Alan. Yes." Grayson pondered the question only a moment. "He doesn't handle guilt at all well. In fact—" he studied the horizon as he assembled words "—I'd guess— strictly a guess, mind you—that guilt could be the trigger for the binges. Not just this time but on at least one previous occasion I can think of. I'm not too familiar with his private life, but I'd say guilt is at least one of the triggers."

"Fairly typical pattern, then, but it's nice to hear it come from direct observation instead of assumptions."

Out on the cliff's edge, the three models broke their poses and headed this way. They did not seem in such a hurry to snatch up blankets, attesting to the penetrating warmth of the October sun.

Jack hurried out to Ev before his feet accidentally detoured over to Marlette. He turned her around by both her hands, then wrapped an arm around her shoulder. They headed back toward the vans.

He let Maxx's leash out more. The dog was enjoying the day as much as everyone else did. "I want an exhaustive credit check on Edith. Not just the usual but also tax infractions and penalties other than IRS, bank records, et cetera, et cetera. Can you handle that kind of thing?"

"Credit check." She stopped, and her pause was a wise move. They were getting too close to other ears. "You mean a deep one. In an official capacity. Yeah. I'll call Hal's secretary and get the phone numbers. Official investigations can use avenues ordinary people can't tap into. Know what I mean? It'll mean a hefty phone bill at the hotel."

Jack turned himself to her and took her hands in his, as if they were enjoying the intimate tête-à-tête of two people plunged headlong into the heady pleasure of discovering one another. "Hal's as generous as Santa Claus. I'm sure he'll—"

She blew a particularly messy raspberry. "In other words, you want places she'd spend money other than this project."

"I was assuming someone else was doing a credit check kind of thing, but that's not a safe assumption. Besides, if you do it too, you might uncover something other people didn't find. I'll ask Deputy Patterson what the sheriff's office has come up with and request he dig deeper. With both of you working on it, we should find any goodies there are to find."

"Want me to do this for everybody here?"

A little bell went *ting*. "Sure! Also Veronica and Lauren."

She snorted. "You're not asking for much."

"Edith foremost and the others as you can. How about Alan Messier?"

"Why not? All right. I'll start with the credit ratings and work on the other stuff an item at a time." She stared at his Adam's apple a moment. "You know, the easiest way to do this—the credit check part—is to sit down with the loan manager at a local bank and let the bank's computer and fax do the work."

"And better you than I, because you know what questions to ask and what sources to go for. I'll set up some ruse for Edith that gives you a couple hours at the bank."

"How about: I'm considering buying a house up here?"

"Perfect! For Harry and you. Edith won't dare begrudge you a couple hours at the bank if it's for her boss and you. I'll call Hal and ask him to clue Harry in."

Her giant eyes sparkled. "I'm getting a real kick out of this, even though I'm freezing solid. This spying is great."

He was kind of hoping to hear an apology for getting shoved into the icy drink, but it didn't happen. "Glad you're having a good time in spite of the cold." He grinned and nodded toward the vans. "You're being paged."

Edith was snarling something at Ev, and Thelma Hyde was calling sweetly.

Jack escorted his spy back to the parking lot.

As they approached, Athalia swung the van door open and stuck her head out. "Thelma, I'm supposed to have that strawberry number next, I thought."

"Oh, dear." Thelma frowned. "This whole day has been running rough as a cob. Let's go look." She stuffed a couple hangers full of leisure wear into Ev's hand and followed Athalia over to the rear of the other van. They began rummaging, gray head and black together, and mumbling.

Ev stepped up inside the near van. The door clunked shut.

If Kovik had not gotten their second van back on the road, what would they have used for a dressing room? Out at the theme park with the seals, they used the restrooms, but here at Otter Cliff—

The wall of the van went *whump!* from the inside. From within, women's voices shrieked and yammered like cats fighting in an alley. Maxx yanked at his leash and barked. Jack let go, in surprise more than anything else. He fumbled with the handle on the side van door and hauled it open. Snarling, Maxx leaped instantly into the van. Jack stomped up inside behind him.

Ev wasn't doing any shrieking because Marlette's hands around her throat were choking her wind off. Marlette was doing all the shrieking—in fact, an excellent job of distraught, continual shrieking. Her golden hair flew as she jerked rapidly back and forth, doing her level best to either punch Ev's head through the van wall or strangle

295

her. The only garbled words Jack could discern were "He's mine!" *Haze moin!*

Maxx, in a display of gentlemanly behavior Jack would not have expected, refrained from using his teeth and jaws on Marlette, as he would any male perp. He flung his hundred and fifteen pounds between the women and prized them apart. Even in his consternation, Jack admired the dog's restraint, for the mutt did love a brouhaha.

Jack wrapped his arms around Marlette from the back, gripped his hands together, and threw his own weight backwards. His ears rang from the din of Marlette's pitiful howls, Ev's strangulated cries, and Maxx's howling snarls, all reverberating in this enclosed space.

Marlette separated from Ev because she had no choice. She snapped her head backwards and cracked Jack in the cheek. She missed his nose by millimeters. Her forearms flailed, though the upper arms were pinned tightly beneath Jack's grasp. She kicked wildly and arched her body. Jack tucked his face away from her and dragged her down to the cluttered floor. She thrashed, struggling with every inch of her body.

Marlette's screams abated to moans of misery, Maxx limited himself to occasional happy yelps, and Ev's major sound was simply air, noisily moving in and out her lungs.

Polished cordovan uniform shoes scuffed by Jack's nose. Grayson. Jack could feel the difference in Marlette's struggling as Grayson's grip supplanted his.

And Jack despised himself. He despised Ev for somehow provoking this attack. He despised Marlette for letting herself be suckered into it. He despised Grayson for placing her under arrest. The joy of the day fled beneath a black cloud of his own making.

Eventually she ran out of steam. Jack squeezed aside against the clutter of the place so that Grayson could haul her to her feet. The ranger escorted her out the door, and she did not resist. Dry sobs racked her.

Ev sat on a disheveled pile of clothes, crying lustily.

Jack took her elbows in his hands and drew her to her feet. He wrapped both arms around her and held her, hoping she would quiet down quickly. The more she cried, the worse Marlette looked.

The van doorway darkened. Edith stared at him and Ev, wagging her head. She exploded in a lengthy diatribe against Ev, Marlette, and the world in general and disappeared back out into the sunshine.

"She was trying to murder me!" Shuddering sobs still jolted through Ev every now and then. "She just pounced on me and tried to kill me!"

"What in the world did you say to her?!"

"Nothing, Jack. I stepped inside, and she was on me. She was screaming. I didn't say a word. I didn't even see her."

"Come on, Ev! Unprovoked?" He thought about the jealousy he'd heard in her occasionally, but he figured it politic not to mention that aloud.

She pushed against him suddenly, shoved him back a step. "You jerk! You supreme jerk! You don't even believe me!"

"Yes, I do!" No, he didn't, not completely.

She stared at him with those doe eyes, all wet and red and swollen from weeping. Finger marks showed up vividly on her throat even in this muted light. "I know what's happening! Of course!"

"Ev, what—"

"Your dead wife! You told me about your Marcia. She sounded like Marlette, didn't she! That awful accent! And I bet she even looked like her some. You think you're in love with Marlette, but you're in love with your dead wife! That's what's going on!"

Fury flared up inside him. "Who do you think you are, second guessing a psychologist! You don't have the slight—"

"Oh, don't I! Don't you dare throw your degrees in

my face! If this was some client, you'd see it in a second. But it's you, so you're blind!"

"Ev—"

But she was throwing her hands up in the air, literally, and sobbing anew. "You are such a . . . a . . . a . . . a pitiful, deluded *jerk!*" She stormed out into the sunshine, abandoning him to the empty silence.

Maxx cheerily licked his hand and wrist, leaving a swath of spit deep enough to float a canoe. Jack shoved the overzealous cur aside, furious and frustrated to distraction. Sure, he had down times, but he'd never had it this bad since Marcia died. Ev and Marlette and Marcia all boggled together in his addled mind.

Outside, Ev yelled. His cloud of gloom deepened instantly. The very last thing he needed was another go-round like this one. Edith yelled. Ev yelled again. So did Athalia. What was going on? He stepped down from the semi-darkness of the van into light that forced him to squint.

Dazed, John Grayson sat on the asphalt, his gold-rimmed glasses in a sorry little tangle three feet away. Athalia lay sprawled on her back, her arms waving aimlessly. Clyde the buffalo was lumbering off under a full head of steam toward the loop road. Marlette? Ev ran over to kneel by Athalia. Beside the other van, Edith raged and stormed and howled in a frustration that sounded every bit as intense as Jack's.

"Where's Marlette?" Jack didn't know which direction to head first.

"Who cares?" Ev, still tear-streaked, screamed at him. "Your precious Aussie flower just hit the road, Jack! She decided she didn't want to go to jail again. *Again,* you hear?"

"Maxx! Find Marlette!" It worked once. He'd try it again.

Maxx went roaring off after Clyde. Either Maxx got the name wrong, or he was onto something.

Marlette! How could she . . ?

In adult Sunday school, all students nodded soberly and agreed that when adversity strikes, you earnestly call upon the Lord first and then let Him lead you. The Christian party line, easy to say in the calm deliberation of a Bible lesson as the participants coolly discuss options. Out here in the raw, cold world, with violence exploding and threatening all around, and life happening a lot faster than you can manage, it wasn't so simple.

Jack remembered at the outset to call earnestly upon the Lord. But he was letting a goofy Labrador retriever do the leading.

25

Jack and Jail

Sunshine dappled the road beneath flame-red maples. A blue jay flashed his brilliance from tree to tree across Jack's line of sight. How sparkling and bright this all was. How dark and dull his heart felt.

Marlette.

Where Maxx had gone he had no idea. Where Clyde and Marlette might be eluded him. He was running blindly, full tilt, clockwise along the one-way loop road. At least he was moving with the traffic.

A little red Honda rounded the curve behind him and passed. The brake lights flashed on, even as it disappeared around the bend ahead. Jack was losing his first wind and felt no sign of getting his second. He huffed and puffed. His feet slowed despite direct orders to the contrary.

There was Marlette—she had flagged the Honda. Clyde was galumphing up behind her, a slow second in this insane footrace. Maxx yapped joyfully beside the car. He had found Marlette.

When Warren Sarnoff climbed out of the Honda, Jack remembered that more than once he'd seen the superintendent drive that particular little car. Sarnoff looked back at Jack, down at Maxx, over at Clyde. Marlette shoved at Sarnoff's arm, vainly trying to squeeze him back in his driver's-side door. She ran around to the other side of the car, a persistent and desperate hitchhiker. The passenger-side door was locked.

She spied Jack and cried out, "Don't take me to jail!" shaking her head. Her glorious mane flowed back and forth. She ran off into the woods. Instantly she came running back. Jack had seen the high wire fence partially obscured by brush; apparently she had not. She was obviously a city girl. It was easily climbed, but she didn't try to climb it. She ran across the road to the south, like a terrified rabbit hard pressed by hounds. Didn't she know that the rocky shore would bar her way?

Clyde bellowed and took off after her. Was he pursuing her or protecting her?

Sarnoff yelled to Jack, asking what was going on, but Jack paid no attention. He ran south, following the two. Maxx, caught up in the thrill of the chase, took off after Clyde and Marlette. He wasn't chasing them—he was joining them in their frenzied run.

Jack plunged almost immediately into the dense woodland he loathed so much. The brush slowed him to a frantic mosey. He pushed and elbowed and ducked and at one point crawled five feet on hands and knees. How did the buffalo manage to make such good time when he was bulkier by far than Jack?

Marlette's startled voice yipped. Jack saw daylight ahead. In moments he broke out onto the open shore. Gleaming sea prevented any further flight to the south. Dark boulders and jagged shelves of rock at the water's edge separated sea and forest. Marlette had moved out among the rocks in her mindless fleeing. Now she stood terrified, her back to the sea and her face toward Jack, with nowhere to go.

Clyde wheeled and placed his hulk between Marlette and Jack. He skewered Jack with a menacing glare. "She didn't do nothing. It was that Brant. She didn't do nothing."

Jack pulled to a halt on a grassy little patch just short of the bare rocks. Wild roses blocked his way on either side. Scraggly and unpruned, they didn't look promising now. But hundreds of dead flower heads, the rosehips that so delight lovers of vitamin C, proclaimed that these sparse, thorny bushes had bloomed gloriously.

Jack took a deep breath, one of many for which his aching lungs clamored, and straightened. "The finger marks on Evelyn's neck suggest otherwise, Clyde. Stand aside. This is between Marlette and us."

"Leave her alone."

"Believe it or not, I'm on her side. You're only making things worse."

Marlette whimpered something Jack did not discern.

She repeated it. "I just know you're going to send me to jail! You're so sure."

Clyde seemed to accept reality. He couldn't stand aside without sticking his feet in among the jumbled boulders to his right, but he did appear to soften.

Maxx bounded over to Marlette and stood beside her, yapping hopefully. *Look! I found her, like you asked. Won't you look?*

Jack heard someone—Sarnoff, presumably—thrashing through the woods behind him. He moved forward toward Marlette.

Big mistake.

Clyde didn't attack—he simply threw himself at Jack. Like a ball into tenpins, he bowled Jack aside.

Jack flew into a rosebush. He threw his arms across his face to protect it and rolled. A thousand needles jabbed and clawed at every inch not protected by his denim and sheepskin. Even his legs got ripped. He dragged himself to his feet. He yanked his weapon, but he couldn't use it, couldn't even aim it. Marlette was struggling away from him across the rocks and ledges, slipping and floundering, right beyond Clyde in Jack's line of fire. He holstered his sidearm and took off running.

"Maxx! Take Clyde. Take him down!"

But Maxx was struggling too. He wasn't doing much better than Marlette on these slippery rocks. With a startled yelp he scrambled ineffectively as his hindquarters slid down between two boulders. His head jerked and lunged forward as he tried to unwedge his back end from among the rocks. Jack didn't have time to help free him.

If Clyde knew much about martial arts, Jack was dead in the water. He'd had some training, but his only brown belt was on his summerweight polyester dress slacks. Still he had to try something.

Clyde might be big and burly, but Jack was faster by far. As he came running up behind Clyde, the buffalo wheeled to meet him. Jack rotated three hundred sixty to gain momentum and lashed out with a foot.

Clyde did not know much about martial arts. If he saw it coming, he mounted no defense. Jack's foot sent him sprawling. The only other moves in Jack's meager arsenal were a flying kick and a double-twist where he sometimes managed to throw his kung fu instructor over his head, but he didn't need them. Here came Maxx, a day late and a dollar short.

Maxx took Clyde, as ordered, now that Clyde was already down.

"Marlette!" Jack hurried after her.

She ran back into the woods, still frantic to escape. Jack heard her thrash and crash. Reluctantly, he followed after, as all those twiggy fingers grabbed at him. He called to her, over and over.

She broke out onto the road fifty feet ahead of him and took off running. Either her sense of direction was as lousy as his mom's, or she had some escape plan in mind, because she headed off against the one-way, back toward Otter Cliffs.

Whoa! Here beside Sarnoff's red Honda sat one of the Sitting Pretty vans and Grayson's white cop car, the PARK RANGER decal emblazoning its door, its light bar flashing. Marlette grabbed the driver's door of the prowl car. Locked. She dived wildly for the van, but now Jack had her, had her arm in a death grip, had the whole grisly puzzle worked out.

He held her tightly, pressing her against his tortured lungs and his aching, aching heart.

Her struggling abated by degrees. "No, oh, no," she moaned over and over. "I don't . . . don't want . . . to go to jail."

He had tapped into his second wind and was doing pretty well now—she was far more out of breath than he. The sweat rolled down his face, and if a little of that was tears, who would notice? His voice remained steady despite his anguish. "You attacked Ev out of jealousy."

The head against his shoulder bobbed, affirmative. He could smell her sweat in her hair. It was a clean smell, a healthy smell in contrast to the foul, unhealthy mental aberrations going on down below that magnificent mane.

Ev and Edith, of all people, came popping out of the woods. Sarnoff, gasping and gulping air, staggered out behind them. He and Grayson were bringing Clyde, with Maxx keeping a close eye on the handcuffed buffalo.

Jack watched his dog a moment and marveled at how well Sarnoff and the dog worked together. Clearly, Sarnoff was directing the operation, and Maxx was following his cues. Quite probably, Grayson was legally blind without his glasses.

Better late than never, a Sheriff's Department patrol pickup pulled up by Grayson's car. Patterson the Paragon climbed out. He stopped in midstride and looked from face to face.

The party came to a sort of casual stop at the patrol car. Everyone stood around glancing at each other's face and avoiding each other's eyes.

Jack continued talking to Marlette. "You were jealous of Veronica Wayne as well, and for even better reason. She stole Alan Messier from you."

Her head snapped up. She turned her outrageously blue eyes to him. "No! She couldn't unless I let her!"

He kept a tight grip on her. "Among her papers was a note to herself a few days before her death: 'I can steal any man. I've proven that sufficiently just now.' She took Alan away from you."

"Ridiculous!"

"In her closet was a green crusher, the kind of hat Alan wears. Her fingerprints were on it—and yours. I saw those hats for sale in the sporting goods store. They come from the store in a plastic bag. When Alan gave it to you, a memento, it was still in the bag, so his fingerprints weren't there. Veronica had a nasty habit of stealing sentimental keepsakes from other girls. She stole your hat. It had double significance for her—a sentimental token from Alan to you, and the trophy of her conquest."

"Evvie told you to say this, didn't she! It's her! Send *her* to jail!"

He hung onto her, kept his arms wrapped tightly around hers. "Ev? You said Edith had a crusher stuffed under her car seat. Could Marlette have put it there?"

"I don't see how. Wait! Yes! We got in the car, and then I said, 'Wait a minute,' and ran back to the table and got my Styrofoam cup. It still had some coffee in it, and I didn't want to leave it. It was only a minute. She was alone in the backseat then."

"And you didn't spot the hat until you returned and got back in."

"Right. The hat was about at Marlette's feet. She could have. It could have been in her big makeup tote, and she stuffed it under there." She stared at Marlette. "But why?"

"To get rid of it, fearing it might be found on her. Hers was supposed to have been stolen."

Grayson frowned. Or maybe he was squinting without his glasses. "So she bought another green hat after Veronica stole hers and wore it out on the boat?"

"And on the moped." Jack dropped his head to direct his words to Marlette. "You told me Clyde despised Veronica. The truth is, Clyde idolized her, and everyone knew it. Why would you lie about something like that, something of no direct consequence to you, unless you were trying to divert attention away from yourself?"

Edith stepped forward. Kovik claimed she was bigger than he. Not now. Crushed, defeated, sorrowed, she no longer commanded a presence by sheer force of personality. Now she commanded attention as a broken person to be pitied.

"You're right. She ripped Clyde's heart right out of him. Brutal, the way she treated him." Her voice sounded very, very weary. "I'm sorry, Preston. This is . . . devastating. Marlette, I can't—" She exploded, but the explosion was a muted little puff of foul words, not the avalanche of blue that Edith usually unleashed. "You have such promise, Marlette. And Ronnie was the best. And Lauren . . ." Her pained eyes rose to meet Jack's. "Why Lauren?"

"Knew the truth. Saw what happened. I don't know. We'll find out."

Edith shuddered. "Evelyn? We have one sequence left, the stuff at Thunder Hole. I can't use Athalia. She has a mouse under her eye the size of a baseball. No way to hide it—it sticks out from any angle. Will you help me finish this? Please? I'll scratch three of the outfits and just use yours. It won't take long."

And Ev showed what she was made of. She pressed her lips together only briefly. "Sure. I'll drive." She looked guiltily at Patterson. "I'll be driving the wrong way up the one-way road. It's only a couple hundred yards. We'll pick up Arturo and go do that. OK?"

Patterson snorted.

Grinning brightly, Ev took that for an OK. She hopped into the van behind the wheel. Edith crawled in the passenger side and wearily snapped her seatbelt. She leaned her head back against the headrest and closed her eyes. Ev swung the van around and drove up the road and around the bend hugging the shoulder.

Suddenly Jack felt very proud of her. His heart ached for Marlette, but it was Ev who ran the course. Whatever he asked of Ev she delivered. And now, despite the cold and rain and misery she had endured, she was going this extra mile for a woman she did not particularly like, simply because the woman needed her so desperately. She who did not yet know Christ was acting more the Christian than he had.

"Well." Patterson reached to the back of his belt. A snap popped and he hauled out his cuffs.

Sarnoff raised a hand. "When I was a buck ranger at Yosemite, we broke up a drug ring. That was thirty-one years ago, and it's the last time I got to use these. My turn." From his pocket he brought out a pair of handcuffs, the old style cuffs with a short length of chrome-plated chain between the bracelets. He snapped them onto Marlette with a flourish. The gentle little clicks tore at Jack's heart.

Patterson nodded. "You can Miranda her or I will." He turned to Jack. "Clever thinking, the thing about the hat. Logical. I never would've thought of it."

Grayson unlocked his car and dug a clipboard out of the front seat. "We need some info before you take her away." The car had one of those miserable tinny computer voices. Over and over it whined, "The door is ajar. The door is ajar."

He handed the clipboard to Sarnoff. "What about the boat? It was Marlette out in that boat that sank ours, right?"

"We'll bill her for it." Sarnoff grinned at Patterson. Easy for him to smile—his heart wasn't broken. "At least, now you can interrogate a cute looking woman instead of Clyde there. Nice change. Get to know her."

Patterson shook his head. "Miss Marlette and I are well acquainted. I talked to her Saturday for hours—late lunch."

A voice called from up the road. Arturo was jogging

this way, asking what the bleep was going on in an Italian accent thick enough to float a brick.

A flood of contradictory thoughts washed over Jack. *"Oh, God!"* But he wasn't swearing. He was calling upon the only Person in the universe who could save Evelyn Brant now. *"Oh, no, please, God!"*

Patterson scowled at him.

Jack ran for the ranger patrol car. "Edith! Ev is alone with Edith!"

He didn't even wait for Maxx. He threw himself in the driver's seat and let the door slam shut on its own as he wrenched the wheel and stomped the accelerator. He turned the car in a tight arc and headed the wrong way up the one-way road.

Ev was alone with Edith.

Jack Prester, smart guy. He knew all the answers. He guessed all the puzzles. Only this time he guessed wrong. Patterson just said he was with Marlette during the hour that Lauren died. Why didn't Jack check alibis and place people during that Saturday? Because he thought someone else was doing it. And everyone else thought someone else was doing it.

By process of conjecture and elimination he had narrowed the suspects to either Marlette or Edith.

And now Ev was alone with Edith.

Oh, God, please, God, cover for my fatal blunder! Don't let Edith hurt her!

At this speed, if he hit someone going properly clockwise, the vehicles would weld together. He should flip the siren switch, but he didn't dare take his eyes off the road or his hands off the wheel to seek it out. *Please, God!* He couldn't pray intelligently. He was babbling, inarticulate. He passed the Otter Cliff turnout.

Then his next-to-the-worst fear materialized. Here came a tourist's recreational vehicle meandering down the road. Jack laid on his horn and swerved right. The RV swerved right and went into the ditch. Jack did not, thank

God! He roared on up the road, lights still flashing.

He twisted the wheel savagely and skidded the car into the Thunder Hole parking lot far too fast. The van sat empty on the far side of the lot. His own car lost traction and swapped ends, the tires screeching. Rear-end-first it broadsided the Sitting Pretty van, flinging his head back against the protective rest. He wanted to leap out instantly, but he sat dazed for a moment unable to move.

Where . . . ?

Then he threw himself out the door and ran toward Thunder Hole. With a magnificent roar, a white plume rose above the rocks ahead and sparkled in the sunshine. He paused at the first viewpoint on the bare, flat ledge.

Ev and Edith had fused into one grappling, struggling, wavering form. Jack discovered his sidearm in his hands, but he certainly could not use it. He could as easily put a bullet in Ev's heart as Edith's. Almost in slow motion they were bending and swaying against the iron pipe railing beside the hole. Jack lurched into motion again.

He wasn't watching where he went. He hit wet rock, and his foot slid out from under him. He dropped onto his left knee. The inertia of motion came into play, and he fell face forward down across the slippery granite. His gun went off in his hands, but it didn't sound nearly as loud as the roar of another incoming wave in the hole. White spray shot upward.

He thought he heard Ev scream, but all he could really hear was the surf. He shoved himself up to his knees. The left one gave and sent him sprawling again.

Ev now struggled with her back to Edith in that grotesque pas de deux, with both of Edith's hands around her throat. Ev was gripping Edith's wrists. Suddenly she snapped forward, her dark hair flying. She kept folding until her head nearly reached the ground, and Edith was curled over her back trying to hang on. Ev let go of Edith's wrists and reached between her legs to grab one of Edith's ankles. She yanked, pulling Edith's leg forward between her own.

Edith let go. She had no choice. She peeled off Ev, falling backwards against the pipe rail. She hit her head on the pipe—Jack saw it jerk, but he could hear nothing but surf. Headfirst, she slid gracelessly between the top and middle rail. She dangled over the side by that one leg, head down, as another bolt of spray exploded upward.

Jack was on his feet now. He heard Ev wail, "Nooo!" as she clung desperately to that leg.

Both women were soaking wet from the spray. Edith's leg must be as slippery as the rocks. She hung upside down over the hole for a long, tantalizing moment.

Jack ran at a hobble down the ledge. He was certain he could get there in time. He watched Edith slipping from Ev's frantic grasp. But he could do it—he could grab her and keep her from sliding to her death.

He dived headlong at Edith, arms outstretched, hands open. He missed by less than half a second, less than half a yard. As he slammed into the granite he saw her shoe, just beyond his fingertips, disappear over the side.

26

Apple Jack

They didn't trust Jack at the helm of a boat, and who could blame them? Look what happened the last time. So he rode out to Great Cranberry in the mail boat, one of perhaps three dozen passengers on the little interisland vessel. Maxx stood with his front legs draped over the stern transom, inhaled exhaust fumes, and barked at seagulls.

Ev, in her white angora sweater and designer jeans, cut as dazzling a figure as Marlette ever did. She commented more than once on the rustic charm of the islands and this mail boat.

Rustic charm? The boat was a dinky little launch with a broad, open stern and a ridiculously tiny wheelhouse up front. Of old-fashioned straked wood, it needed painting. Passengers sat on hard, wooden, built-in benches on either side in the stern. Two dozen sacks of groceries were stashed in the extreme aft. Cryptic names in broad-tip Magic Marker identified each sack: *Pug, Compt, Smith, Joe.* Supplies for the Cranberry islanders. The engine howled in monotone as they ground their way across the open reach and docked at Great Cranberry.

When the load of passengers arrived at the community building, several men in blue jeans were setting up an antiquated sound system on the low stage in the main room. This crew in plaid shirts must be the dance band Sarnoff mentioned. With a couple of guitars, a keyboard, and a set of drums, it was definitely not Glenn Miller. They were clowning around a lot. Jack couldn't hear the joking, but a fellow in a scraggly T-shirt pawed on the stage, stomping out a slow four-four beat.

One of his buddies picked up a dead mike and yelled, "Patchy the Pinto, folks. Ain't he great? OK, Patchy, now count to thirteen."

The room was set up for a potluck again, and Jack wondered if they ever configured it for anything else. Women put out foil-covered bowls and mysterious casseroles. Chips and dips appeared. Jack added his ten pounds of apples to the plethora of desserts on the east end of the food tables.

Stella Smith sidled up to him and laid a hand on his shoulder. "Jack Prester! This potluck tonight is in your honor. You and Evelyn. The guest of honor doesn't have to bring food. You know that."

"Good evening, Stella. That's not how I heard it. Warren specifically said this celebration was in Maxx's honor, and Ev and I could come along if we wanted to."

She giggled. "Well, consider yourselves guests too."

"Thank you. But this guest ended up with twenty-five pounds of apples from a roadside stand in Trenton. It's apple season in case you didn't notice. And he's sure not going to eat all those apples before they spoil. Help me out here, OK?"

She laughed, and her sparkling eyes matched the gleam of her white hair.

"Prester." John Grayson tapped Jack's arm.

Jack turned. Beside John stood Alan Messier. Jack would feel distinctly uncomfortable were he Messier in this place at this time, but Alan didn't seem bothered at all. The four of them shook hands, Ev included, and Messier's grip was firm and friendly.

Maxx, bored to tears, curled up on Jack's shoe and

312

stretched his chin out across the floor. Falling asleep at the party held in his honor was probably a faux pas, but that was Maxx's problem, not Jack's.

"You worked out what happened, Warren says. Tell us, can you?" Grayson watched Jack intently from behind new glasses.

Jack pursed his lips, assembling his thoughts. Where to begin?

"Veronica Wayne had been with Edith longer than any other model. She not only was aware of Edith's financial shortcuts and illegalities—paying people under the table, for instance, and siphoning off funds—she documented them. How Edith learned Veronica was onto her I've no idea, but several people mentioned her reputation for finding out everything eventually. I doubt she knew about the documentation, or she would have up-ended the earth itself to destroy the solid evidence."

He was drawing an audience. A dozen people stood around, all ears. He noticed Winthrop Spalding among them.

He continued. "Reputation is everything in Edith's business, but even more important was Edith's difficult financial straits. When Veronica got fed up with this assignment, she threatened to go home to New York and file grievances. Edith recognized that it was no idle threat. Veronica could bury her.

"She decided to capitalize on the blossoming relationship between Veronica and Messier. Green crushers like Alan's are very easy to come by. Edith ostensibly dropped Veronica off at the bridge to meet him. In reality, she accompanied Veronica onto the bridge, put on the hat, clubbed her enemy, and tossed her over the side.

"Kovik thought he heard from Edith that the bridge was the murder site, but he couldn't remember for sure. He assumed it was common knowledge. It wasn't.

"Lauren posed another problem. Somehow she found out about enough of Edith's dealings that she, too, threat-

313

ened to reveal them. Her idea of going to the IRS struck the deepest fear. Edith had killed once with impunity in broad daylight. Emboldened, she struck again."

Maxx stretched out on his side for some serious snoozing, his hulking shoulder firmly pinning Jack's foot.

"I see!" Ev's eyes were the size of kiwi fruit. "But too many people knew she was taking Lauren back to her room, so she decided to dump the body somewhere else."

"Exactly. To avoid being placed with Lauren at the motel. She wanted it to appear that Lauren had been killed out on the carriage path."

Ev wagged her head incredulously. "So she dropped me off out there too, to establish that the models were being left off at the bridge."

Grayson tipped one corner of his mouth up. It wasn't a smile. "That was pretty clever. Showed foresight."

Jack nodded. "Premeditation to the max."

The dog on his foot stirred. Jack looked down and smiled. "Watch when you say his name while he's asleep." Softly, he called, "Maa-axx."

The dog's tail thumped the floor lightly.

Ev giggled.

Back to the subject at hand. "Edith probably didn't know that no one can clean up a murder site thoroughly enough to escape forensic detection, but she tried. She was quick and efficient and as cold as a penguin's toenails."

Ev snorted. "She did everything that way."

"She had her faithful servant Clyde arrange for the moped—and cleverly too. She used that and an inexpensive plastic tarp to convey the body, then stuffed the tarp in a convenient trash can. But she became confused on the maze of trails. Got turned around."

Sarnoff was standing there listening too. "We know the rest of that part. But why did she attack you?"

"I threatened her myself. Idle threats. Pure bluff. But she took them seriously, enough so that she acted to either destroy me or discourage me. The moped was opportunistic. She already had it, so she used it."

Winthrop Spalding chuckled. "And it wasn't a big job to steal one of Bait Barrel's boats. He never locks 'em up."

Jack smiled, but the smile faded instantly. "She probably wouldn't have feared me nearly so much if she wasn't already under a lot of fear and stress for doing Veronica." With a ton of black Lab lying on it, Jack's foot was going to sleep.

Messier asked, "Isn't this all circumstantial? Marlette had just as much opportunity. So did Athalia, for that matter."

Sarnoff rumbled, "Assuming one person committed both murders—not a bad assumption—Patterson eliminated Marlette as a suspect by interrogating her during or near the time of Lauren's murder. Someone should have been taking a close look at where people were that day. No one did. It never even occurred to me to have someone investigate alibis, because I was so thoroughly sure it had already been the first thing done."

Jack cautiously pulled his foot out from beneath Maxx's shoulder. "That's the fatal flaw in a case like this, where three different agencies are involved. Everyone assumes George is doing it. Ev, tell them what happened at Thunder Hole."

She looked somewhat embarrassed to suddenly become the center of attention. "Well, uh . . . after Edith and I left that scene with Marlette and all—in the van—uh . . . I started to pull into the parking lot to get Arturo. She said, 'Forget Arturo. There are a couple cameras in the styro case. Let's just go do it.' So I kept on going up to the other parking lot.

"We got out. She said the spray would get the costume wet, so we should set up the shot in what I was already wearing, and then I'd change while she got out the camera. It sounded right. We walked down to the railing,

315

clear down. I don't know why I turned when I did. I heard stones rattle or something. And there was Edith holding a boulder the size of a volleyball over her head. She smashed it down at me, but I managed to duck in time. Then she just came at me and tried to shove me over the rail. I would never have guessed she was so strong. Jack, I still don't know why she tried to kill me."

"You said you thought that fake spreadsheet you worked out was correct to within five percent, remember? She saw it, recognized its accuracy, and believed you somehow had obtained her most secret records. She had to get rid of you."

"But she didn't know I was a spy. I'm sure she didn't. There's no way she could know about those fake books."

"Sure there is. She had access to your room. Remember? Saturday evening while you were out, she left a white dress for you on your bed. Later, she must have gone into your room again for some other reason and saw the spreadsheets on your desk, complete with a big pink highlighter circle around the embezzled sum."

Ev stared off into space, mulling this. Suddenly she gasped. "Roland!"

Jack snapped his head around. The plump foster mother stood beyond Grayson, beaming, and she held Roland. The baby wore a snuggly blue blanket sleeper Jack had not seen before.

Ev shoved past the men and cooed at the baby. "I thought you'd be in Passaic now, little man."

The foster mom smiled. "The sister has three kids of her own. She decided she couldn't handle this fourth one, and my husband and I have grown some attached to him. He's such a sweetie. We've started the paperwork to make him our own." She nodded toward John. "Mr. Grayson here invited us."

Ev wheeled and enveloped Grayson in a super hug.

Stupidly, ridiculously, Jack felt a sharp twinge of jealousy.

Ev glowed. "That was so thoughtful! Thank you!"

Grayson glowed too.

Sarnoff was nodding knowingly. "Patterson says that without anyone to protect anymore, Clyde's starting to open up. He's really torn apart. He was devoted. You know, like British butlers in the movies."

"That's so sad." Ev scooped Roland into her arms. "Edith treated him like dirt."

Jack nodded agreement. "Hung him out to dry when we arrested him on Thompson Island. No lawyer, no bail, no nothing."

Sarnoff rolled on. "He'll go down as an accessory, but if he gives them all the evidence they want, he'll probably get off fairly light. Anyway, that's what Patterson says."

"Was he stalking Marlette?" Jack asked.

"According to Athalia Adams, he took a strong, possessive interest in women—a protector, stalker, observer, whatever—but never approached them or came on to them. She said for Clyde that behavior was normal and harmless, and no one paid any attention to it."

Jack studied the sleeping mutt at his feet. "Probably should've invited Athalia tonight."

"We did." Grayson smiled. "She couldn't come because she's off on another modeling job."

"I thought her eye was swelled shut."

"It is. She's modeling just her hands. Jewelry. Crazy, isn't it? You ever hear of a hand model?"

Ev asked guardedly, "Where's Marlette? Gone home to Australia?"

"Nope." Jack shook his head. "Went to Dallas."

"Texas?!"

"Yeah. Looking for a job there. She wants to work in the States, she said. She finally recognized that she's got some serious problems, and someone recommended a psych clinic in Dallas."

Maxx rolled to his belly. He wasn't what you'd call awake, but his ears flopped forward.

317

Over by the food table, people laughed and yelled. Jack heard apples hitting the floor, *plup-plup-lupplup plup!*

Maxx snarfed, his cavernous sinuses echoing, and lurched to his feet.

And then Stella's voice came through above the general ruction, loud and clear. "Oh, no! Get that raccoon out of here!"

	DATE DUE	

OPPORTUNITIES

in

Retailing Careers

REVISED EDITION

ROSLYN DOLBER

VGM Career Books

Chicago   New York   San Francisco   Lisbon   London   Madrid   Mexico City
Milan   New Delhi   San Juan   Seoul   Singapore   Sydney   Toronto

Library of Congress Cataloging-in-Publication Data

Dolber, Roslyn.
      Opportunities in retailing careers / Roslyn Dolber.—Rev. ed.
         p.   cm. — (VGM opportunities series)
      ISBN 0-07-140602-6
      1. Retail trade—Vocational guidance.   I. Title.   II. Series.

    HF5429.29 .D65   2003
    381'.1'02373—dc21   2002514112

1 2 3 4 5 6 7 8 9 0   LBM/LBM   2 1 0 9 8 7 6 5 4 3

ISBN 0-07-140602-6

Interior design by Rattray Design

McGraw-Hill books are available at special quantity discounts to use as premiums and sales promotions, or for use in corporate training programs. For more information, please write to the Director of Special Sales, Professional Publishing, McGraw-Hill, Two Penn Plaza, New York, NY 10121-2298. Or contact your local bookstore.

This book is printed on acid-free paper.

Contents

Foreword

My feet still throb whenever I think about the rock-hard terrazzo floors I encountered on my first job in retail. This was back in high school, when I admittedly was less interested in a retailing career than in saving enough of my paycheck to buy the world's coolest prom dress. Yet for years after, whenever I gave a fleeting thought to retail, that first painful experience and those unforgiving floors were the boundaries of what I recalled.

Which only goes to show how little I knew about anything.

A career in today's fast-paced world of retailing can take you in countless different and exciting directions—far and fast. From merchandising and buying to systems and logistics . . . from store operations to store planning and design . . . from credit management to data analysis and processing . . . from marketing and promotions to E-commerce and strategic planning. The range of career opportunities in retailing today is virtually unlimited, as are the challenges that await someone who's looking for a career track that bypasses the ordinary.

Few professions come with more individual responsibility right from the outset than does retailing. It's not unusual, for instance, for an assistant buyer with less than a year on the job to be managing his or her own multibillion-dollar business—making decisions that have a direct impact on the company's bottom line. Nor is it extraordinary for an executive trainee in a store's organization to be managing a sales department inside of six months, or running a store inside of five years. Success can come early in retail, and there are as many opportunities to move up into the ranks of management as there are paths to get there.

A career in retailing may not be for everyone, of course. Certainly, it's not for the faint of heart. Nor is it for those who prefer predictability, because if there is one constant in retailing, that constant is change.

Retail companies and managements change. Customer preferences change. Popular brands and vendors change. Retail demographics change. Trends and styles change. Technology changes. The economy changes. Manufacturing and distribution channels change. Marketing and sales promotion strategies change. The look and design of store interiors change. The competitive environment changes. Whichever way you look, the retail sector is awash in a constant sea of change. Yet that's what keeps it vibrant and makes it exciting and challenging—anything but boring for those who have enough vision, gumption, and confidence to see the unprecedented possibilities a career in retailing has to offer.

At Federated Department Stores, we spend a lot of time on college campuses looking for the next generation of retail leaders—the merchants and managers of tomorrow who will be running our Macy's, Bloomingdale's, Bon Marche, Rich's, Lazarus, and Goldsmith's stores, as well as our merchandising/product development, credit, and systems and operations support divisions. We do this because it won't make any difference if we have the best merchandise in our stores or offer the best values if we don't also invest in the best people—and then give them the opportunity and support they need to do the best job.

There's a whole world of career options opening up before you. Take the time to investigate those that appeal to you. Decide what you want to get out of your working life, and what you want to put into it. Choose carefully because in all likelihood you'll be living with your decision for a long time. But above all, don't rule out any career options based on what you *think* you know. When it comes to a profession such as retailing, there's a good chance you may not know the half of it!

Carol A. Sanger
Vice President/Corporate Communications and External Affairs
Federated Department Stores, Inc.

INTRODUCTION

CAN YOU IMAGINE yourself in a career that is exciting and challenging? In an industry with enormous prospects for growth? One that will reward your skills, creativity, and imagination? Would you like to be part of a multibillion-dollar industry that requires long-range planning and daily involvement with people, technology, and merchandise? Are you eager to learn about forecasting, pricing, advertising, management, and computer operations? Are you able to work and communicate with others and use decision-making skills? Would you also like to be able to see the results of your efforts every day?

Then be sure to learn more about the business of retailing, the nation's second-largest industry and one that will allow you to put your knowledge and experience to work just about anywhere in the world. Retailing is a people business, and it is one of the most labor-intensive industries in the country.

Retailing is the sale of goods or services to customers through retail stores, catalogs or mail-order services, TV, and computers. The retailer is the intermediary between the producer of the goods and the purchaser. Manufacturers rely heavily on retailers for the sale of their merchandise. It is often said that retailing simply means having the right items at the right price at the right time.

The typical flow of merchandise is from the manufacturer (and sometimes the next step is a wholesaler) to the retailer to the customer. Retailing is an industry that changes rapidly in response to the needs of its customers. These days many of the old stores and familiar names are gone, casualties of the mergers and acquisitions of the 1980s. Yet new types of stores have sprung up to keep this industry alive and well. It's harder than ever now to divide stores neatly into specialty shops and department stores. The lines are somewhat blurred, as some discounters go upscale and many department stores reduce prices.

The field of retailing is in a state of constant change because of the flow of new products and the exciting new ways of presenting these products to the public. Shoppers can make their purchases in stores, through catalogs, via websites, or by watching TV. There are a great many career opportunities for you to learn about in retailing. Promising futures can be found in organizations of all sizes and all kinds—department stores, specialty shops, buying offices, variety stores, TV merchandising programs, catalog houses, direct mail, and online operations. There are firms selling all kinds of goods from apparel to fashion items, furniture, food, and automobiles. There are careers in retailing for those who want to be their own boss, want to be involved with the latest technology, want to work in a large firm, want to perform any variety of tasks, and want to become specialists. Many diverse careers are available. Marketing and sales jobs will grow 24 percent by the year 2005, and the majority of those jobs will be concentrated in the retail world. Retail employers will need two million more workers for retail careers. Now that a large segment of our population—the baby boomers—is well into its peak earning years, demographics indicate an increased demand for retail services. A wide choice of career opportunities is in place to offer rapid career growth and advancement.

You may be interested to learn that more than half of the people employed in retailing are female. A high percentage of women are employed in buying and selling and are moving up more swiftly than ever to management spots. Salaries and benefits compare favorably with other industries. Women have traditionally enjoyed the flexible hours the industry has offered, especially if they prefer part-time or holiday season schedules. And the world of retailing has long offered opportunities to all, regardless of sex, race, or background.

In the past, it was not unusual for retail employees to work extremely long hours, sometimes up to sixty- or sixty-five-hour schedules each week, often working late nights and Saturdays. Fortunately, retailing employment practices have changed dramatically. Many retailers have adjusted the typical workweek to thirty-five to forty hours, with fewer evening hours. Do keep in mind that it is now common for retail stores to be open on weekends, so working on a Saturday or Sunday is considered typical, although weekend schedules are frequently rotated among employees. However, middle-management and management executives generally work more hours than those employees who are hired on a precise weekly schedule, such as stock or sales workers.

Learn about every kind of opportunity that is available and consider the wide range of exciting choices before you decide where you may fit. Remember that once you are trained as a retailer, you can move from one type of retail operation to another, find job openings in other parts of the country, or even open your own retail business. And retailing is never dull—it is alive with change.

Fashion Retailing

If you would like to become one of the fast-moving and enthusiastic workers who choose the fashion items that we will all be shopping for in the coming seasons, consider the world of fashion retailing. Such jobs are available in the thousands of stores located nationwide. You might find a job in a boutique, department or specialty store, or in one of the many buying offices and discount shops that sell apparel and fashion-related items. Jobs can also be found in firms that produce catalogs and fashion bulletins, as well as on TV networks and websites that offer all sorts of merchandise for sale. The growing focus on fashion has created a huge need for men and women with an interest in the fashion field. Retailers large and small are more involved with fashion merchandise than ever.

The retail field offers an enormous array of opportunities for ambitious workers. Beginning sales associates can move into career paths such as:

- Buying and merchandising
- Regional and corporate management
- Inventory control
- Distribution
- Finance
- Marketing
- Sales promotion/public relations
- Human resources

- Information systems
- E-commerce

Because retail outlets are so plentiful throughout America, beginning career opportunities are readily available. Merchandising activities are the heart of retail stores, and the principles of merchandising can be learned. Aside from any required specialized training, other qualities also are necessary for a successful career in retailing. For example, it is important that you are outgoing and enjoy working with a great variety of people. Energy, stamina, and the ability to work under stress are essential traits, as are good leadership abilities and self-confidence. Having a facility with numbers and details and being well organized are further requirements for the person eager to enter this world. In fashion retailing, excellent grooming and a keen interest in fashion are mandatory.

You may have to work long hours, but your hard work will not go unrewarded. You will be recognized for your efforts and have a chance to see the direct results. Your benefits will be career advancement and financial compensation that matches your productivity. And if you are willing to consider relocating, you may have additional opportunities in retailing. Indeed, if you are unwilling to consider a move, chances are you'll remain in a "holding pattern" at your current job title until the person above you moves on, thus opening a spot for you. Retail opportunity will be found in every region, in urban and suburban centers, throughout the United States and even abroad.

Are you generally interested in fashion—from the newest trends in clothing to cosmetics to home furnishings? Are you flexible and easy to deal with? Do you enjoy working with people every day rather than working by yourself? Are you able to communicate well and do you enjoy public contact? Do you find constant changes and trends in fashion exciting? Does adventure appeal to you? Would you enjoy exploring new market items? The retail world operates at a fast pace, so those in it need to think and move quickly. If you feel prepared to work hard and tolerate long hours, pressure, and deadlines, the dynamic world of fashion retailing may hold a career for you.

The retailing industry in America has always been imaginative and innovative. American retailers dreamed up shopping malls and discount stores, catalogs, and television and E-commerce merchandising. And in the twenty-first century, we can expect America's shopping malls to become leisure and entertainment centers, as well as major retail centers, in an effort to attract more and more shoppers. Stores already have more flexible business hours, offering late-night and weekend shopping to accommodate working people.

You might have thought retailing simply meant keeping the shelves well stocked and waiting for customers to come in and select the desired items. Well, retailing has come a long way from that concept. The high-tech invasion has already begun. In fact, many large retailers now own or lease their own satellite communications systems. They handle inventory and pricing with lasers and run their businesses with high-powered computer systems. Retailers have upgraded their technology so they can serve customers faster. Firms such as Eddie Bauer, J. Crew, Lands' End, and L.L.Bean have sophisticated websites for customers' purchases. Retail employees with information technology skills will be in demand.

Electronic retailing will allow us to shop in the luxury and privacy of our own homes. And with the population growth continuing well into the twenty-first century and millions of two-income families with more disposable income than ever, it is predicted that retailing will remain one of the nation's top growth industries. Retailing is big business, and it is modern business.

The retail industry currently employs more than twenty million people, or one out of every five American workers. According to the U.S. Department of Labor, retail employment is expected to increase to twenty-four million workers by the year 2005.

The excitement, the challenge, and the careers are there for you.

1

How It Began:
A Brief Overview of Retailing

It's hard to imagine that cave dwellers of the Stone Age were involved with trade, but experts on early cultures tell us that it is so. It was probably as simple as trading one kind of animal skin for some food or a piece of flint to be used in hunting. However, that might have been the very start of retailing. We know that trade in ancient marketplaces existed in early Greece, Egypt, and Rome thousands of years ago.

The Indians of North America used their own barter system successfully—exchanging furs they trapped for food and liquor or other needed goods. The simple barter system of olden days has become very different and very sophisticated. In 1668 Canada's Hudson's Bay Company searched for new sources of beaver pelts and began the North American idea of merchandising. American retailing has not always been as vast and diversified as it is now. It has grown dramatically in the last few hundred years and has changed with the major forces of modern technology, communications, and cultural ideas to become the important career field that it is today. Simply stated, retailing is the delivery of goods or services to consumers. Let's take a look at how the world of retailing developed.

The Early Years

With the coming of the Industrial Revolution in the late 1700s, goods could be manufactured in ample quantities to satisfy the increasing demand of our young and growing nation.

Development of the cotton gin and the steam engine gave jobs to many, making it possible for more income to be spent on new goods. Soon factories sprouted up to replace the traditional small shop where items were made by hand. Mass production of goods began. The development of the railroad aided in the growth of towns and cities in the West; and, of course, the merchandise followed the settlers. Retailing has always grown rapidly in the most heavily populated areas. Marketplaces were developed to handle the flow of the merchandise. There is no doubt that retailing played a vital role in our early system of trade.

As retail trading centers expanded, merchants discovered the importance of assigning the buying duties to someone else to allow the retail store owner to concentrate on other tasks. Thus the buyer of merchandise became responsible for selecting what and how much of each item to buy and at what prices the items should be sold. The buyer became the specialist whose primary job was getting the merchandise to the customer.

As the United States expanded westward, the trading post was the ideal place to trade goods and also information. Wagon trains needed the goods and news of the frontier, and trading posts were sought out by the wagon trains as they made their way westward.

The forerunner of today's road salesperson was the Yankee peddler, a person of great importance to the frontierspeople. The peddler visited less-populated frontier settlements, bringing a wide assortment of much-needed merchandise to pioneer families by wagon, boat, or horseback. The peddler's offerings sometimes included such luxuries as bits of laces and trims or fancy pins and hair combs, as well as staples. Goods were often traded as well as sold.

The General Store

The development of the general store provided customers with a wider assortment and wonderful variety of goods. Everything from farm equipment and tools to gunpowder, whiskey, food, and even eyeglasses was offered for sale, often on a credit basis. Most of the settlers' basic needs could be satisfied in the general store, and that included hearing local gossip, news, and politics. General stores served an important function as the local gathering place as well as a center of trade. In fact, general stores still exist in rural areas of the country, performing the same functions as their earlier counterparts.

Specialty Stores

By the middle of the nineteenth century, more sophisticated retail stores were developing as the size of the country and the population grew. The Industrial Revolution had reached our shores. Retailers became interested in specializing in certain kinds of goods rather than stocking the haphazard assortment of items offered in the general stores. With the growth of cities it became necessary to stock more specialized merchandise. The larger towns and cities began to have a collection of specialty stores. These shops offered customers only one line of merchandise, such as shoes or hats, or one service, such as delivery or gift wrapping. The specialty store soon emerged as the major form of retailing, and stores cropped up next to each other, forming downtown centers. Merchandise and services were now available to the customers within blocks of each other. With the help of public transportation, shoppers were now able to ride downtown and take care of all their shopping needs.

During this expansive period, many of the great retailers began the operations that established the basis of American retailing: Sears Roebuck and Company in Minneapolis, J. L. Hudson in Detroit, Filene's in Boston, and Abraham & Straus in Brooklyn.

Modern Retailing

The retail world has experienced a great deal of change and growth, particularly in the types of stores that have surfaced. A description of these stores follows.

The Chain Store

In the late nineteenth century, the Great Atlantic and Pacific Tea Company (A & P) and F. W. Woolworth Company were among the first to introduce retailing to the nation on a grand scale. Buyers for these great chains purchased merchandise for several stores, rather than locating goods for just one retail unit. As you might imagine, in the early days of retailing, the buyers for these chains dealt with the difficulties of limited production of goods, very unpredictable deliveries, and manufacturers who were not really able to mass-produce items with ease.

By the turn of the century, ready-made women's apparel finally started to appear in stores, along with the already popular children's and men's factory-made clothing. Women's ready-to-wear was launched as chains placed large orders for garments and were able to sell them at very affordable prices. Ready-to-wear items became very popular and were no longer considered to be for the lower classes, who could not afford to have custom-made clothing. To this day, fashion apparel and accessory items account for a significant percentage of retail sales, and they remain an exciting and ever-changing part of the retail industry.

The Resident Buying Office

With their mass purchasing power and main offices headquartered in the heart of the market, the strength of the chain stores became apparent. It seemed logical that an organization was needed that could supply its members with current market information, represent member stores in dealing with manufacturers, and pool several orders to get the lower-price benefits of mass merchandising.

Resident buying offices developed in the early days of retailing in New York City, the most important market. The resident buyer would visit the central marketplace and make merchandise selections and purchases for the store owner, who could not leave the store. Placing orders for the store owner was the major job of the resident buyer. As the number of product lines increased, the retailer had a harder time keeping up with the new advances in fibers and fabrics and manufacturing techniques. It made more sense to rely on the resident buyer for expertise in market trends and new developments, as well as for placing orders.

Before long, resident buyers established themselves as important links between the manufacturer and the retailer, who might only occasionally visit the central marketplace. The resident buyer became the representative for the retailer and acted as the retail store's advocate. In addition, the resident buyer's ability to purchase merchandise in volume became an important feature of the buying office. Most retail operations could not compete with the vast purchasing ability of the store chains without pooling their purchasing power. Volume buying by the resident buying office allowed them to take advantage of lower prices.

Resident buying offices have become very important to the member stores they serve for the wide range of services they offer, including their original function of placing orders for the retailer.

The Department Store

A new and departmentalized type of retailing surfaced in the late nineteenth century, as more and more people began to live in or near large cities. These developments heralded the emergence of the department store, in which a wide range of apparel and non-apparel items was sold. Although all the goods were sold in one large store, each department was run by its own buyer. It was as though customers had many different specialty shops all in one building, offering much more than a general store could. It was now possible for customers to shop for clothing, furniture, tools, and fashion accessories under one roof. An important feature of the department store was the provision of services: credit, tailoring and alterations, wrapping and delivery, and layaway plans. Some of the early department stores of the nineteenth century are firms you may be familiar with: Wanamaker's, Macy's, and Marshall Field's.

Department store retailing became popular, growing considerably after 1900 and expanding even further with the concept of branch stores. Today just about every American city, large and small, can boast a department store or branch store. The period from 1920 to 1945 was one of great prosperity and growth for department stores.

With the end of World War II and the trend of migration to the suburbs, department store growth slowed, but smaller branch stores cropped up in the new centers of population. The main store, or flagship store, was still responsible for the greatest assortment of stock and the greatest volume of sales. It was quickly observed that small inadequate branches would not do for the shoppers in the suburbs. They, too, wanted the full range of items the main stores carried. So large and modern branch stores were designed and built across the country, often generating sales greater than those of the main store. And today's department stores still offer individual "departments" and sell a wide variety of merchandise, from apparel to furniture to gourmet foods.

The Supermarket

The concept of the supermarket grew out of the Great Depression of the 1930s. With money scarce, supermarket owners lured in the public with low food prices, in contrast to the higher prices and smaller selections offered in the neighborhood food shops. Supermarkets were mainly self-service operations, where customers were able to buy many kinds of goods in one store. Meat, dairy, and vegetables were available, as were drugs and beauty aids, hardware, and small home improvement items. The supermarket was like a department store for food and related merchandise, offering self-service selections and low markup to the public.

Suburban Shopping Centers

Millions of Americans moved to suburbia shortly after World War II. The growth of the suburbs was dramatic. As retail centers followed the population, it was only natural that suburban shopping centers became part of the retailing picture. The 1950s brought American shoppers this major retailing development.

The suburban shopping centers offered stiff competition to the downtown shopping areas. Wise downtown retailers opened branch stores in the suburban centers, anticipating the trend away from downtown. With vast parking areas at no charge, new and exciting stores—even restaurants and movie theaters to attract customers—the suburban shopping center certainly reflected the tastes of suburban American families.

Discount Stores

As mentioned above, a great shift of population from the cities to the suburbs occurred when World War II ended. The young couples who were now new home owners needed everything for their homes: large and small appliances, furniture, lawn and garden equipment, and tools. The idea of a discount style of purchasing—buying items at less than retail prices, usually with few or no extra services—was an immediate hit.

Discount store owners were able to keep their costs down by doing business in low-rent, low-maintenance locations and by trying to reduce the cost of sales help and markups. Suburban consumers quickly accepted these "no-frills" settings in an effort to save money on every purchase. And the idea of shopping at discount became as acceptable as buying groceries in the cut-rate supermarkets.

Mass Marketers

The development of mass marketers has changed the face of retailing. Indeed, stores like Wal-Mart and Target now account for a huge percentage of all the mass retail volume in the country.

Wal-Mart, the world's largest retailer, with sales of more than $191 billion in 2001, seems unstoppable. Its strength at one time was in hard goods and consumables, rather than in fashion items, but that has changed. Because of the volume it commands, Wal-Mart can undercut just about any other retailer on the prices of basic products.

Sam Walton, Wal-Mart's founder, began his career as a management trainee at JCPenney. Just five years later, in 1945, he opened his first Wal-Mart store. Wal-Mart's growth has been remarkable, as just a decade ago the firm was ringing up a mere $4.6 billion in annual sales. The firm now operates more than four thousand stores under a variety of names: Wal-Mart, Sam's Club, Hypermarket USA, and Byd's Warehouse Outlets, with branches in Argentina, Brazil, Canada, China, Germany, Mexico, and Puerto Rico.

Target stores are often called the "discount stores of tomorrow." They offer great presentation of timely fashion merchandise. What sets Target apart from other discounters is an upscale image and a focus on trendy merchandise, comparable with specialty stores like the Gap, Limited, and moderate-priced department stores, rather than with traditional discounters. This thirteen-hundred-plus store chain, owned by the Dayton Hudson Corporation, also offers hard goods, but its real strength is in home and apparel items. Target's presentation of merchandise is clean, and the stores have wide shopping aisles with clear signage for easy shopping. Moreover, customer service is one of Target's main attractions. The employees refer to the customers as "guests" and treat them accordingly.

While the impressive names of Wal-Mart, Sears, and Target stores often dominate retailing news, the discount store has been gaining an enviable share of the market. Surveys indicate that the typical off-price shopper is between eighteen and thirty-four years old and is generally a working woman with children. Most of these shoppers believe they find good value with low prices at the discount stores, and they are contributing to their growth.

Since World War II the number and size of discount stores have grown considerably.

Franchise Operations

Although they first appeared as early as the 1890s, franchise operations became quite popular in the 1950s. A franchise operation is a business (or sponsor) that allows a franchisee to have operating rights. You are probably familiar with many of the service franchises that are popular nationwide such as Dairy Queen, McDonald's, Holiday Inn, and Hertz Rent a Car.

A strong working relationship exists between the sponsor and the franchisee. The franchisee pays a fee up front to the sponsor and then continues to pay the sponsor royalties based on sales. In return the franchisee gets the product, training, and an extensive local or national advertising campaign. The advertising and marketing benefits alone can make this sort of venture very profitable to the franchisee.

The McDonald's Corporation might be one of the best-known food franchisers of all time, with more than ten thousand individual retail stores worldwide. Today starting a franchise with McDonald's would cost in the range of $500,000. But there are hundreds of other franchising operations to consider. You can get started in some of these businesses with as little as $10,000 start-up money.

In some situations, sponsors may even lend you part of the start-up fee.

Boutiques

Boutique stores cropped up in London in the 1960s. These small shops featured unique kinds of items, often handcrafted or one-of-a-kind pieces, in attractive settings that lured customers with their special ambience and decor.

It did not take long for boutiques to become established in this country within larger stores, such as Macy's or Henri Bendel in New York City, conveying the charm and unique feeling that the boutique atmosphere provides. This concept charged the retail environment with an excitement that still holds strong today. Many new businesses and entrepreneurs have blossomed in the boutique trend. An entrepreneur is someone who starts a new business, such as a retail store, and is responsible for the store's profits as well as losses. Enterprising men and women took advantage of their entrepreneurial skills to bring to the customer innovative merchandise and a high level of service.

Hypermarkets

Beginning in the late 1980s, we got a glimpse of the future direction of retailing—hypermarkets. Hypermarkets are giant supermarkets and discount stores all rolled into one great shopping adventure. Long popular in Europe, these sprawling "malls without walls" are now popular in the United States. American and European retailers are betting that shoppers will like the low prices and the chance to find just about everything under one roof—and a huge roof at that. Customers are lining up in stores the size of five football fields with two dozen checkout lanes to purchase their garden supplies, TV sets, groceries, and clothing. The blend of food, apparel, and general merchandise is important to the future growth of retailing. The new American hypermarkets, mainly in the South and the West, are also offering shoppers restaurants, beauty salons, oil changes for their autos, and supervised playrooms for their toddlers.

In the last decade, Wal-Mart has opened Hypermart USA and Kmart has launched American Fare. These hypermarket businesses offer lower prices because they have the ability to make larger and more frequent purchases of merchandise. And they are counting on the business of price-conscious customers who are not able to resist the blend of good prices and good services.

Warehouse Clubs

Shopping clubs are another destination of choice for consumers making their weekly or monthly stock-up shopping trip. Wholesale clubs, which charge a fee for membership to the general public and to small businesspeople, have become a real trend. Clubs like Costco and Sam's Warehouse are the fastest-growing retail segment in the country. It's generally a self-service environment without delivery service, advertising, or amenities. With an annual membership, shoppers have access to national brand names at low prices.

The warehouse club environment is quickly reshaping how consumer goods are packaged and sold. Many shoppers are learning that they can easily do without the frills. "Value" is the operative word, and retail analysts believe that warehouse retailing is here to stay, as shoppers show their loyalty to operations springing up around the nation.

Concrete floors, stacked displays, and bag-it-yourself checkout counters have not deterred shoppers, and no-frills shopping is not only acceptable, but trendy. In the 1990s Americans were in a discount mindset, where it was considered appropriate to be frugal. Shoppers realize that they just don't need the extras. The clubs offer price and value—an unbeatable combination.

Market research has shown that higher-income and larger households shop the clubs most frequently. And grocery-related sales make up more than half of the warehouse club sales. A recent opinion research study indicated that shoppers thought clubs were "a fine place to shop." Somehow, the warehouse environment has managed to avoid what plagues most supermarkets—the sense that this is a boring place to spend your dollars.

Specialty Superstores

The specialty superstore features a selection of goods at very low prices in just one product area. Toys 'R' Us is a wonderful example of such an operation, and it is growing rapidly all across the United States. The most popular categories of specialty superstore tend to be in the areas of toys, health and beauty aids, children's apparel, consumer electronics, and office supplies.

Malls

Millions of visitors, in addition to millions of shoppers, travel from the world over just to get a taste of these exciting retail destinations. Some of these malls are modest in size, with just a few dozen retail stores. Other malls, however, boast hundreds of stores, offering a spectacular number of choices. For example, Grapevine Mills has 1.1 million square feet of shopping and is one of the major tourist attractions in Dallas. Sawgrass Mills, with 1.9 million square feet, draws twenty million visitors each year to Fort Lauderdale and is the second most popular tourist attraction in Florida, after Disneyland. And the largest of U.S. malls, the Mall of America in Bloomington, Minnesota—with more than five hundred specialty stores, four department stores, fifty restaurants, fourteen movie theaters, and more—welcomes forty-two million guests each year!

Retailing on the Internet

The Internet, the world's largest computer network, is becoming retailing's best marketing tool and has become one of retailing's fastest-growing areas.

In many ways, the online explosion has changed the way we make our purchases. This new trend in electronic commerce (or E-commerce) is opening many doors for new and exciting job opportunities. E-commerce, also referred to as E-tailing, came into its own in the 1998 Christmas season. Sales skyrocketed and, in many cases, exceeded expectations. Electronic commerce shows no signs of slowing.

There will be jobs for workers who can build websites and manage the distribution of merchandise for profitable online sales. Currently, many traditional buyers have the responsibility for buying goods for websites, but more and more, the industry searches for applicants who specialize in *online* retailing and can create seamless paths between websites and support systems. Anyone with an interest in information technology will be sought after.

Traditional retailing continues to bring in huge amounts of consumer dollars, but E-tailing, or electronic retailing, offers overwhelming opportunities.

Retail stores (brick-and-mortar) are certainly here to stay. But "click-and-mortar," which is a blend of online and traditional retailing, is new. Click-and-mortar retailing involves retail stores and E-tail sites. Macy's, J. Crew, and Toys 'R' Us are some examples of operations that have both retail units and E-tail sites.

The projection for 2003 is that online retail sales will grow to $108 billion. For most shoppers, convenience is the big draw for online purchasing, perhaps more than price.

Amazon.com, the major online bookseller founded and run by Jeff Bezos, has now become the biggest music retailer and has moved into toys as well. Amazon.com set the standard with its early online experience.

When Web retailing surfaced, many in the industry thought shoppers would soon disappear from the stores. Instead, shoppers began to use the Internet for researching and buying products, but they also have continued to shop in stores and to order from catalogs.

Research by Shop.org found that shoppers who use multiple channels—stores, online, catalogs—spend more. It's now impossible to ignore the impact of the Internet. Online retailing is growing up and has proven itself for millions of shoppers.

Retail Kiosks

An outstanding industry projection is that by 2006 twenty-three million shoppers might be buying goods and services through retail kiosks.

Merchants such as Crate & Barrel, the Gap, Staples, and Barnes & Noble have started to assist shoppers with kiosks. With advances in technology, highly reliable kiosks are now becoming available to consumers.

Younger shoppers are most familiar with kiosk technology. Studies show that 90 percent of six- to seventeen-year-olds have computer access, so these tech-savvy consumers are perfect customers for kiosk use.

Vans, a California-based retailer of clothing, footwear, and accessories, aims for the young in-line skater and skateboarder market. In addition to its E-tailing, Vans touch-screen kiosks give information on athletic events, tours, contests, and any news of interest to the average Vans customer—a fourteen-year-old male—thus providing yet another channel or source of information for the shopper.

Successful retailers must stay on top of consumer trends: past, current, and future. This is particularly important for retailers of fashion items, where styles and trends are constantly changing from season to season. Small independent store owners can keep up-to-date on fashion changes by reading fashion magazines and trade and business journals. By determining as closely as possible what customers will want to buy, retailers can satisfy shoppers' needs and be profitable. Those profits can also go a long way in contributing to the success of the retailer and the community the retail store serves.

The Next Phase

Many in the industry predict that M-commerce, such as through wireless phone lines, will be the next phase that shoppers will be introduced to, as more brands announce plans to boost their sales with the use of mobile technology. Smart marketers who can see the benefits of this technology will be ahead of the game.

Of course, retailers must reflect current trends, regardless of the type of merchandise that is sold. Window and counter displays, along with advertising and store promotions, let the customer know the type of merchandise being offered and that the retailer is aware of the latest styles. Retailing in America has grown from a simple system of trading to a multibillion-dollar industry that employs millions of workers. This past century has brought about dramatic changes. However, the uppermost goal of the retailer still remains the same: to meet the needs of the all-important customer. Shoppers now have the luxury of a mixed approach to making their purchases, and retailing still remains a question of finding the most desirable items and selling them at the best prices.

Customers and Consumers

We are all customers and consumers. We are in and out of all types of retail stores each day searching for basics that we need or looking for some new and different luxury that we don't need, but want.

At the start of the 1950s, there was a major emphasis on the consumer in the field of retailing. This emphasis has continued. The concept of consumerism is centered on the idea that the needs and desires of the consumer are of great importance. As a result of sensitivity to this kind of thinking, most retailers offer us products for sale along with some kind of service for those products. Whether we buy a small appliance, such as a radio or VCR unit, or something as large and as costly as an automobile or a refrigerator, we expect to have those items serviced when necessary. Some major retailers are well known for their outstanding ability to provide service for their products, such as Sears or JCPenney. Smaller retailers that cannot afford to offer extensive service operations must rely on the manufacturers to handle the servicing.

Most stores are very interested in building strong customer relations, and toward this end they maintain customer service departments. These units handle a number of conveniences for the customer, such as gift wrapping, layaway plans, deferred payments, and delivery of merchandise, in addition to the servicing of merchandise purchased at the store.

Major manufacturers, particularly of household appliances, often insert a return-by-mail postcard in their products. Users are asked a variety of questions about how and why they decided to buy a particular item and what their reactions to it are. These candid responses offered by consumers after they purchase and use the product are valuable to the manufacturer.

Kinds of Customers

Most customers want to be first with the newest trend or fad, whether in clothing or cars. But each one of us shops quite differently, and it is helpful to understand what kinds of customers might be in retail stores. Here is a breakdown of categories of shoppers. (Note: the *customer* is defined as the purchaser of goods or services, while the *consumer* is the person who actually uses those goods or services. In this book, the words are used interchangeably.)

Innovative Customer

This shopper wants to be first with the newest product. He or she enjoys being a trendsetter, being the first to wear the latest fad item, or owning the most advanced appliance or auto.

Comparison Shopper

This shopper spends time checking prices in various stores. He or she will also compare the quality of the products, seeing what the name brands offer. Comparison shoppers are concerned with getting the best buy for their money. If good prices and good services are offered, the comparison shopper will probably return to make the purchase.

Impulse Buyer

This shopper makes a quick decision to buy items. These are often fairly inexpensive items rather than "big-ticket" or higher-priced items. Supermarket checkout counters are the ideal location for such impulse merchandise. Think about all the racks of magazines, candies, gums, and other novelties that are stocked right near the cashier.

The Follower

This shopper usually buys the established bestsellers. Such customers make their purchases with care and generally need to feel quite satisfied with their choices before they will actually buy them. They often rely on the recommendations of family or friends.

2

Careers in Retailing

A career in the retail world calls for a competitive person with a range of qualities:

- The ability to get along with coworkers and to develop an understanding of customers' wants and needs
- The ability to adapt to the constantly changing global marketplace
- The ability to be self-motivated and a self-starter; to be decisive and make quick, calculated decisions
- The ability to analyze data, predict trends, solve problems, and be technically current
- The ability to work well under pressure

Large retail organizations have several areas you need to learn about. Although the exact positions may vary from store to store, you should familiarize yourself with these retail job titles:

Sales and Marketing
Personal shopper
Sales associate
Sales manager
Department manager
Special events director

Operations
Stock clerk
Operations coordinator
Associate store manager

Concept and Design
Visual merchandiser
Display director
Store planner
Technical designer
Product developer

Buying and Merchandising
Buyer
Merchandiser
Divisional merchandise manager

Administration
Personnel or human resources manager
Information technology manager
District manager
Store manager
Divisional merchandise manager
General merchandise manager

Elements of Retail Operations

Regardless of the size of a retail store, keeping it afloat requires certain basic operations. The same responsibilities handled by two or three employees in a small store will be handled by a greater number of workers in a larger store. But these tasks will differ in quantity only, not in kind. So regardless of the size of the retail store, there are five important functions of retailing that are essential to all retail operations. They are:

1. **Operations/store management**—providing services for the customer, maintaining the store's appearance and arranging for the receipt, storage, and delivery of merchandise
2. **Sales promotion**—designing and creating means of selling the goods and encouraging customers to shop in the store
3. **Personnel or human resources**—selecting, training, placing, evaluating, and promoting employees
4. **Finance or control**—keeping tabs on profits, losses, and all other details of the financial area
5. **Merchandising**—planning, buying, and selling the goods

Good work experience in any of these areas may lead to a specialized career for you in later years. Each of the five areas offers interesting opportunities. What follows is an overview of each segment. Consider how well you might fit into any of the areas described, including the support areas that would be part of any large retailing firm.

Operations/Store Management

The store management function is responsible for maintaining the store's physical plant, warehousing and delivering merchandise, operating and maintaining the store's supplies, providing various customer services, and maintaining store security.

A successful store operations executive is generally interested in organizing, supervising, and directing people. Store operations workers attempt to ensure the smooth running of every department. An understanding of systems and procedures is necessary, in addition to a real sense of service to the organization.

Sales Promotion

The promotion division incorporates talents in writing, drawing and graphics, window and store display, and publicity. Every retail firm needs to promote itself and does so by communicating with customers in a variety of ways. Advertising, publicity, special features and events, and even the creative use of window and interior displays can provide information, generate excitement, and establish a strong reputation for a store.

Large operations use their advertising or promotion departments to design events, fashion shows, or themes that the entire store can get involved in. Getting the message out to the public about the merchandise or the services of the retailer is important to keep the customer interested in and aware of that firm.

Promotion generally includes the advertising department, which is responsible for advertising in all forms. Its function is to get customers to shop in the store. Advertising can be done through newspaper or magazine ads, radio and TV announcements, or special promotions. On the advertising staff you might find copywriters, artists, or direct mail specialists.

Retail stores sponsor many events and community activities. The public relations department usually handles these. It attempts to get as much free publicity for the organization as possible, which might include sponsoring fashion shows or events for charitable causes.

The display or visual merchandising department makes sure the windows and interior and exterior of the stores are attractive, and that all merchandise is presented in the most appealing manner. This unit also has responsibility for the signs, decorations, or any other visual items that any department might require. Imagination and creativity in addition to specific talents in writing, drawing, and illustration are needed, as well as an interest in putting ideas into shape. The sales promotion area offers exciting, creative opportunities to men and women.

Personnel or Human Resources

This division has the responsibility of locating, interviewing, selecting, training, placing, and promoting workers, as well as keeping accurate personnel records. The selection of workers must be efficient, particularly during peak periods, such as the Christmas season, when many extra workers need to be hired and trained. Training programs for all new workers are designed and implemented through the personnel unit. It is also responsible for employee activities, benefits, and welfare information, such as details on retirement plans, dental and medical insurance, and pension and profit sharing. Labor-market relations and wage and salary administration are other tasks performed by personnel workers. Many large operations have employee counseling available to assist workers with health, personal, and family problems that can affect their productivity on the job.

The size of the personnel department is generally determined by the size of the retail operation: volume of sales, number of departments or stores, and services that are offered.

Finance or Control

The treasurer's or controller's unit is responsible for the organization's assets and for ensuring financial soundness. A close check must be maintained on monies coming in and expenditures paid out. Workers in this department tally vital statistics that indicate the firm's financial position. They set up systems for use in the stores, calculate payrolls, determine taxes due, and maintain essential records for the organization. As keepers of the store's resources, control workers must work with great accuracy and precision.

More than half of the sales made in department stores are handled on credit. The credit and collection workers are important to the operation of this department. They interview applicants, check credit ratings, recommend various types of charge plans, bill charge customers, authorize deferred payments, and handle collection of overdue bills.

The recent computerization of many areas—payroll, inventory, sales, customer invoicing, credit and collection—has eliminated much of the tedious and time-consuming reporting. Anyone with an interest in computers should be aware that men and women with a background in this area are in demand.

To be successful in the financial area, a worker needs facility and training in math and accounting principles, understanding of financial reports, and the ability to interpret economic data. An ability to accurately perform detailed work is important, as is being a well-organized and careful worker.

Merchandising

A successful retailer must buy and merchandise goods effectively. The buyer is the key person in this important process.

The Buyer

The buyer must be aware of the customer's needs and search out and purchase those items, making sure they can be sold at a profit. The buyer also has to be aware of new items and trends in styles and design. And the buyer must always motivate the sales force to sell more and more goods. The goal always is to top the record of the past season.

The buyer's job requires spending time away from the store to visit various markets and search for merchandise to sell. These may be traditional markets such as New York, Chicago, or Los Angeles, or more exotic ones like India, China, or Sri Lanka. Travel is a large part of the job for most buyers.

The candidate with good organizational skills, math ability, a high degree of enthusiasm, energy and stamina, good decision-making skills, and an interest in anticipating what the public will want can have excellent opportunities in merchandising.

The Merchandise Manager

The merchandise manager, as the head of the merchandising function, establishes policy and sets goals. Being upper management's representative to the buyers, the merchandise manager holds a position of great importance that includes a very close working relationship with all buyers. Buyers rely on their merchandise manager to alert them to current business trends, give them advice about various departmental problems, help with future planning and forecasting, and suggest effective sales promotion and advertising strategies. Merchandise managers should be well informed on the contents of each buyer's reports to try to spot future trends or weaknesses in the merchandise collection. And they must coordinate the efforts of all of the buyers in the organization, so that a uniform image is presented to the customer. As always, the merchandise manager keeps his or her eyes open to spot unusual talent for promotion, help the growth of the business, and provide an incentive for all workers. This top executive position requires a great deal of background and experience in the retail field.

The merchandise manager may have several divisional merchandise managers as assistants, each of whom is a specialist in a particular kind of merchandise.

Retail Technologies

Technology has become an important part of the daily functions of a retail business. Every sale represents a series of technology-supported processes that previously were done manually.

State-of-the-art information systems technologies help retailers cut costs, reduce inefficiencies, and enhance sales. They also allow retailers to use databases that contain details about customers' shopping preferences.

Retail technologies have streamlined the ordering and delivering of goods to stores. New hardware and software technology has improved all aspects of business; from planning and ordering to cash and credit processing, new technologies have changed the way retailers do business.

Retailing and information systems may seem like an odd combination, but it is vital to retailing's future. Managing and analyzing data from sales is critical to setting up departments and stocking the right merchandise. Efficiently moving goods from the supplier to the warehouse to the retail store is critical.

Retailing Career Path

The following positions and estimated salaries will give you a good idea of a possible career path in retailing.

Position	Salary Range	Description
Management Trainee	$26,000–$32,000	A chance to learn store operations, product mix, and the basics of merchandising
Assistant Manager	$32,000–$37,000, plus bonus	Responsible for a specific department or a combination of several areas
Store Manager	$37,000–$85,000, plus bonus	Responsible for all operations and departments in the store
District Manager	$70,000 and up, plus bonus	Liaison between the store and regional groups; responsible for a group of stores in a particular area
Regional Manager	$90,000 and up, plus bonus	Manages a group of stores in a geographic region, often crossing several states
Divisional Vice President	$150,000 and up, plus bonus	Title is generally found in a large retail organization, such as a department store; usually responsible for certain types of departments within the stores, such as hard goods or children's lines

Support Services

In large department stores, there are several service offices that assist the buyers in a variety of ways.

Testing Office

Large, profitable chains, such as JCPenney or Sears, can afford to staff a testing office. Some stores maintain their own laboratories, but many other organizations use independent testing services when necessary. A buyer may wish to examine a product before deciding to purchase it. In some areas testing may be considered a standard procedure. Many shoppers rely heavily on the claims made by the testing department for products ranging from clothing to appliances. The tests set specifications and standards for the items being tested, eliminate defective items, and help inform consumers of the benefits of certain products. For example, rugs that are stain and mildew resistant or fabric that won't fade or deteriorate in the washing machine have all been tested strenuously before being sold to the public with that particular claim. As customers are paying more and more attention to their consumer rights, this area appears to be expanding and more important than ever before.

The Fashion Office

This kind of office is often found in larger department stores that focus on the sale of fashion apparel and accessories. As fashion becomes more important to the consumer, almost every retail sales department has a fashion interest. Having the right color of toaster or microwave oven in stock is as critical to the appliance buyer as the right color of hosiery is to the accessories buyer.

The efforts of the fashion office begin with a prediction of the next season's trends. This requires researching the current market and forecasting the next year's styles, as well as having a solid understanding of fibers, fabrics, leathers, and furs. Information that the fashion coordinator, the head of the fashion department, collects while visiting markets is then passed on to buyers. Hem lengths, silhouette, and color combinations are reported as early as possible to assist the buyers with their decisions. It is important that the sales force, which has contact with the customers, be well informed of the latest fashion news. The sales force can learn about fashion happenings in group meetings, by reading bulletins or newsletters, or by attending fashion shows. The fashion office plays a major role in coordinating those shows, from selecting the merchandise, writing the commentary, and staging the fashion show. Fashion-minded retailers know the importance of having a sales force that is knowledgeable and up-to-date in fashion information and is able to help increase sales by suggesting complementary accessories to customers.

The fashion coordinator is responsible for the coordination of all fashion merchandise in all departments and for staging fashion shows to help keep the store's personnel informed and current. He or she must also create a coordinated fashion image for the entire store.

In this way customers are presented with a single fashion message, which helps them coordinate their own purchases in every department. A customer buying a suit in one department should also be able to buy matching accessories with the appropriate style and color in other areas of the store.

Control Office

Workers in this office gather information from the stock inventories and sales figures and supply the buyers with daily details about up-to-the-minute inventories, sales, purchases, and other vital information. This gives the buyer and upper-level executives useful data to help them make merchandising and buying plans. In small stores, the buyer is often responsible for gathering and tallying these kinds of records without the help of the unit control staff.

Comparison Shopping

This office has a staff of shoppers who compare the merchandise, assortment, prices, and services offered to customers with those of the competing stores. They also study the competition's advertising. Results of these comparisons are then reported to the buyer. Sometimes comparison shoppers are able to buy and bring in unique and unusual merchandise that other retailers are offering, or an item of similar quality that is priced lower than at their own store. They have the authority to purchase the item and bring it back to the store for review. Comparison shoppers must operate with a shopper's point of view in the best interest of the consumer. The quality of the store's services is also checked by comparison shopping unit members. They make note of the attitude and manner of the sales staff and may pretend to be customers to assess the quality of the store workers.

This information is all very helpful to the buyers. In smaller organizations, an assistant buyer may perform some of these tasks.

Here is a breakdown of the typical division of responsibility in a large retail organization.

Room at the Top

The demands of a retail organization are extremely varied, and so are the qualities needed for success in the field. You should be aware of the following characteristics that retailers say are essential for beginners to have:

- Ability to communicate well, both written and spoken
- Ability to deal with many people
- Enthusiasm
- Creativity
- Willingness to accept responsibility
- Ability to supervise and have leadership potential
- Physical and emotional stamina
- Ability to tolerate pressure

There is always room at the top of the retailing career ladder for ambitious workers, as the retail field offers countless opportunities for hardworking and dedicated men and women. People are truly the most important feature of this industry. Good workers can make the difference between a successful or failing retail business.

Retailing today is undergoing more changes than ever before. The industry is clearly responding to the needs and demands of its customers—and retail shoppers are savvy shoppers. They know that they have many choices, from superstores to more personal boutiques, from specialty chains to discount stores. Currently retailers generate excitement to attract men, women, and children of all ages. The retail settings of today are a world away from the retail stores of a generation ago. No matter which aspect of the retail world appeals to you, you can be sure that challenge and excitement await you.

There are few industries that are as important to our country's economy as retailing. The strength of the retail sector is one of the primary measures of our business health. You are wise to consider a career path that contributes to our nation's strength and provides great personal rewards as well. In fact, the retail sector is one of the major sources of jobs in the U.S. economy, representing more than 20 percent of all jobs.

A note of caution: anyone interested in pursuing a retail career should be aware of the severe limitations that face those with a record of shoplifting.

Retail organizations keep detailed security records for many years. This does not mean that you are a risk only if you have a police record, as you may be part of a retailer's own security file. Because shoplifting has caused such a major loss of income for stores, this crime is treated very seriously. When applicants apply for retail positions, security records are carefully checked, often going back for as many as six or seven years. You are considered a security risk if your name is on file for any sort of security reason.

If this presents a problem for you, be sure to discuss your situation openly with a placement counselor so that he or she can give you more information on how to deal with this.

3

EXECUTIVE TRAINING PROGRAMS

IT TAKES A great range of skills and an assortment of very highly motivated workers to keep America's retail world on the go. And, of course, this means a broad range of possible careers for anyone with an interest in retailing.

In general, larger retail operations may offer more executive and supervisory opportunities. In smaller stores, the owner and one or two employees may be responsible for all operations—planning, buying, receiving, pricing, advertising, display, and selling—even the handling of inventory accounts and credit records. However, in a retail firm employing hundreds of workers, specialized departments take care of the wide array of tasks that are needed to run the stores. Executives and supervisors are important in their roles of directing and delegating work in each area. Most large retailers offer an executive training program for men and women with college backgrounds to groom them for executive positions.

In the retail industry, top-level executives are responsible for setting policies and establishing objectives. Mid-level managers are responsible for carrying out these policies.

An Opportunity to Learn

Each retail firm has its special method of training new workers. Generally the more formal training programs are found in larger retail organizations. Executive trainee programs typically last anywhere from two to twelve months in most organizations. Trainees are usually exposed to the full gamut of retailing, from buying to security. At JCPenney, for example, the training covers logistics, presentations, advertising, marketing, sales leadership, and human resources. Whatever type of program is offered, the goal is to give the beginner enough information and direction so that he or she can eventually take on the duties of an assistant buyer. In some instances, trainees move into other areas that will be described later. The training is a wonderful introduction to the techniques and principles of the executive retailer's world, and every effort is made to enable the trainee to be productive as early as possible. The training is offered in several ways:

- **Formal training program.** This type of training simulates a classroom situation where training experts give assignments to the trainees. Generally classroom sessions are held in the morning, with an opportunity to be on the sales floor or in the receiving areas or stockrooms of the store in the afternoon.
- **On-the-job training program.** In this situation the trainee is assigned to a suitable entry-level job, and all learning takes place on that job. The employee, under the guidance of senior workers, learns through actually doing tasks— very much learning by hands-on experience.
- **Job rotation program.** In a program like this, the trainee is assigned to one job for a particular period of time and

then is moved on to other assignments. This ensures that the trainee gets a broad view of the overall operation, while also having a chance to actually experience working in each area.

Whatever type of training program is used, it will surely start with information about the company's policies and goals and then go on to discuss store organization and management, buying procedures, sources of supply, and basic merchandising math. The next step is actually assigning trainees to store departments, so that it is possible for them to see the flow of merchandise and begin to understand how important "the sale" is to the total picture of retailing. Major department stores offer this very demanding, but very desirable, entry position as part of the executive training program. Those who acquire one of these competitive spots have been selected because of their potential executive ability. Most executive trainees are groomed for careers in merchandising or operations.

Getting a Trainee Spot

The retailer who hires you for the executive training program will want to prepare you in all aspects of the retail operation to develop your management skills. Those hired for executive training programs are carefully selected from community colleges, four-year colleges, and graduate schools offering degrees in retailing, merchandising, or business management.

While competing for positions in executive training programs, candidates are closely scrutinized by retail recruiters. Frequently recruiters interview students on college campuses and then invite the students of their choice to visit their stores for second interviews with other store executives. Applicants are assessed on their communication skills, how well they present themselves, school and work records, extracurricular activities, demonstrated leadership abilities, level of energy and enthusiasm, and how much interest they are able to express about a career in retailing.

The Trainee Program

Once hired, trainees are started on a rigorous program that may include evening or weekend hours. Each retailer has a different program, so the length of such activities depends entirely on the particular store. Executive training programs often start in the summer, right after graduation. Some stores add new training groups in September or February to handle midyear graduates.

Smaller retailers can add new workers in an informal training setting at any time of the year. Executive trainees work hard while they are part of the training program, earning a salary from the start.

During the first days or weeks in a program, trainees may be busy meeting members of the firm's management team, including the president of the firm. They may visit branch stores and learn all about the divisions in each unit. They will probably have the opportunity to listen to managers talk about how each division operates and how all of the areas of the operation coordinate their efforts. It also will be necessary to be trained in selling procedures and to spend time on the selling floor.

Once the trainee is assigned to a particular department, he or she has a chance to meet the buyer and the assistant buyer and observe how they do their jobs. Trainees may be rotated to several different selling departments, thus getting a full range of merchandise experiences.

Part of the training period will probably include spending time in the operations area working next to employees in the shipping department or the receiving room, or in the control unit observing the billing process or the auditing team. After six to twelve months, the trainee may be ready for an assignment as an assistant buyer, if he or she has a merchandising interest. Of course, assignments depend on the availability of such openings, and they may be in the main store or in a branch store.

During the entire training program, the personnel department evaluates the trainees. The training director and supervisor review each trainee's performance, and progress and productivity are noted carefully.

Although the goal of each executive training program is to prepare candidates for executive positions in the future and to help them develop managerial and leadership skills, each organization's policy varies. In some programs it is typical for a trainee to land a buyer's job two to three years after graduating from training. In other cases it may take longer. For example, the retail management program at Sears lasts for nine months and is set up on a rotational schedule. It is designed to offer about 250 trainees a hands-on experience in a variety of areas. After an orientation that gives details about their role as sales managers, the trainees are rotated through sales and support departments. They eventually get a taste of shipping, finance, visual merchandising, personnel, and customer service. Trainees learn at any one of the eight training centers Sears runs across the country. After this training period, the associates are assigned to manage a group of twenty to forty junior associates. Of course, promotions will always depend on individual performance and motivation.

Executive training programs offer a wonderful beginning to those with a strong interest in retailing. But they are not for everyone, nor are they the only routes to a retailing career. A good first step would be to pinpoint your area of interest. For instance, try to determine which type of operation attracts you the most: a larger or smaller store, a chain or a specialty store, a discount operation, or a more exclusive boutique. Learn as much as you can about each and decide what career opportunities they offer that appeal to you.

4

THE BUYER: A KEY POSITION

BUYERS' JOBS ARE never really the same. The type of organization they work for determines their responsibilities. However, it is the responsibility of all buyers, and their assistants, to make wise buying decisions that will be profitable for their organizations. Some of the more common buying positions are discussed below.

The Assistant Buyer

The job of the assistant buyer is to help the buyer in every way. The duties of an assistant buyer are determined by each buyer, so the job can vary greatly even within the same retail organization. A solid working relationship between every assistant buyer and buyer is essential for success. Because the responsibilities of a buyer are so vast, a buyer for a large store or for several departments needs the help of one or more assistants. The assistant buyer can handle a variety of clerical details and free the buyer to handle duties such as visiting markets and purchasing goods. The assistant buyer is really an understudy for the buyer. He or she learns to assume the managerial functions of the department when the buyer is not available.

The assistant also helps the buyer with many buying and merchandising tasks, such as merchandise control, handling customer service, supervising the sales force, assisting in buying selections, writing orders, receiving merchandise deliveries, and promoting goods. Working as an assistant provides a splendid opportunity to observe the buyer at work and learn the routines and responsibilities by helping to do them, as busy buyers frequently need to delegate authority to their assistants. Promotion to the buyer level typically occurs after two to three years.

In large retail department stores, most assistant buyers get their jobs as a result of completing the executive training program or on-the-job training within that department. This way, by observing the buyer and participating in all of his or her duties, an assistant can quickly learn about the major components of the retail business: selling, customers, merchandise, and the marketplace.

Sales and Salespeople

An assistant can help a buyer to supervise, instruct, and schedule the work hours for the salespeople in the department. He or she will consult with the buyer to determine sales quotas and then relay that information to the sales staff, motivating salespeople to fill the daily/weekly sales quotas. The assistant buyer will also inform salespeople about new items in the department and how to present that merchandise to customers, work closely with newly hired salespeople to introduce them to policies and routines of the department, and work with the more difficult customers if the salesperson needs such assistance.

Customer Relations

Assistant buyers can help buyers handle customer service problems, such as returns/exchanges; take responsibility for filling mail or telephone requests or special orders; and keep alert to what customers are buying and what they are saying about the merchandise selection in that department.

Merchandise

As for the merchandise itself, assistant buyers can help the buyer in a number of ways. They can be responsible for and keep records of all markups and markdowns of merchandise and suggest merchandise that might be considered for the department, commenting on colors, sizes, and styles. They will keep the buyer up-to-date on the status of stock and sales when he or she is not in the store. Assistant buyers also present new merchandise for display and coordinate that merchandise for promotional ads, supervise inventory counts of merchandise, follow up on merchandise to ensure proper deliveries, and review incoming merchandise as it arrives from the receiving department to determine that colors, sizes, quantities, and styles are correct. Additionally, assistant buyers will check merchandise for damage or defects and arrange to have items marked with the proper prices, have merchandise delivered to the selling floor or to the stockroom, and make sure that there is always adequate stock on the selling floor. Finally, they will handle items that need to be returned to manufacturers, make sure that all department displays are attractive and eye-catching, and review and analyze sales reports to alert the buyer to the fast and slow sellers in the department each day.

The Marketplace

The assistant buyer can also go with the buyer on buying trips to local or major markets, such as New York City or Los Angeles, or go alone to a market to review trends and report back to the buyer.

The job of the assistant buyer is generally the first of the middle-management positions in a retail store, and it is demanding and varied work. Some retail organizations have an associate buyer title for experienced assistant buyers who act as the right hand to the buyers in all aspects of the buying function. However, in many firms, the next level after assistant buyer is the position of buyer itself.

The Buyer

The buyer is a critical executive in the merchandising flow of any retail organization. The job of a buyer requires many unique and diverse talents, in addition to formal training. Years ago it was quite common to start out as a stock clerk and work up through the ranks to become a buyer. Today colleges nationwide offer well-established merchandising, retailing, or marketing programs that provide retail recruiters with an excellent source of trainees. A college education is a necessity for those seriously considering a career as a buyer. Many of the management and decision-making skills a buyer needs on a daily basis are taught in college programs, along with the basics of merchandising math, computer, and retailing skills. Courses in marketing, salesmanship, and personnel management are considered very important by retailers. Many retailers also consider strong liberal arts graduates to be excellent candidates. Although the trend is now clearly in favor of graduates of four-year college programs, some recruiters will consider associate degree graduates. Usually, the candidate of choice is one with a bachelor's degree. Candidates with a master's degree in business or marketing are strong applicants.

Keep in mind that the job of a buyer is filled with excitement, pressure, and hard work, and it can bring a great deal of personal and financial satisfaction. This position is responsible for planning, sales, and inventory and merchandise selection, as well as writing orders and promoting the goods. It means working closely with manufacturers and, in some firms, handling online activities. Many retailers are convinced that the destiny of their organization lies in the hands of its buyers. Without the proper selection of merchandise, retail stores would flounder. The job of the buyer is a critical one, and buyers need to:

- **Be good communicators**—write clear reports and bulletins, conduct and/or participate in meetings, and interact well with bosses and suppliers and people they supervise
- **Have analytical ability**—handle figures easily and be able to think in numbers
- **Deal well with others**—command respect and motivate their staff, accept direction and advice from superiors, develop strong working relationships with manufacturers and wholesalers in the marketplace, and understand their customers
- **Be enthusiastic**—transmit that enthusiasm to coworkers and others on the merchandising team
- **Be alert and sensitive to changes**—keep pace with industry trends

- **Think creatively**—visualize how new and different kinds of merchandise and products can become innovative ways for people to deal with their problems
- **Have physical stamina**—handle the daily pressure, fast pace, competition, and frequent changes of the retail industry
- **Be flexible**—quickly adapt to changes and adjust to new and different work situations

Here are brief descriptions of the skills considered necessary for successful buyers to have and for you to think about developing.

Communication Skills

Buyers are always dealing with other people. They work closely with their assistants, manage and supervise their sales team, meet regularly with their superiors, and are routinely involved with manufacturers and wholesalers. They clearly present their ideas and feelings and must be able to fully articulate their views in many daily situations, including writing memos and bulletins. A most important quality is the ability to communicate; it is an ongoing job for the retail buyer.

Enthusiasm

Enthusiasm is contagious. It can inspire trainees and motivate a sluggish sales force. It has been known to generate excitement for a product or an organization right down to the customer. The buyer communicates his or her enthusiasm to others and gets people to work together. Retail recruiters seek many qualities in candidates, and enthusiasm is often very high on their list. Successful buyers have the ability to build a solid team of cooperative workers and foster enthusiasm.

Decision-Making Ability

Round-the-clock decisions are part of a buyer's typical day. Analyzing and assessing events and making judgments, often on the spot, require strong analytical and decision-making abilities. Buyers grapple with decisions about what styles or trends will be popular, what colors to purchase, from which vendors and at what prices to buy, when to reorder merchandise, as well as how to best promote the goods. Buyers are faced with endless decisions, and they must be able to anticipate what customers will want to buy months in advance.

Commitment

Buyers need to be totally dedicated to their job and to hard work. They work long and irregular hours in retail stores and often are away from home because of travel obligations related to their work. At Christmastime, a peak period in the world of retailing, they may work many late nights and weekends. Only genuinely determined and committed buyers can handle these pressures.

Delegating Work

Buyers can become successful managers of people if they understand how to delegate tasks to others. Deciding who should be assigned to do a particular job is critical to the smooth operation of a busy department. Care must be taken to select the right person for the assignment, so that each worker's talents and experience are maximized. A sensitive buyer will choose the best worker for the assignment and then continue to train that worker for additional responsibilities. Clear and specific instructions need to be given so that the worker understands all expectations. The competent buyer allows time for questions and is available to teach the methods and routines of the store. Of course, it is also necessary for the buyer to check on the worker's progress, offer suggestions for improvement, or even assist the worker in finishing a task. The retail buyer must be a master of good human relations.

Leadership

Supervising, managing, directing, delegating work, training, making decisions that involve hundreds of thousands of dollars—buyers learn to be leaders in their fields by attempting to be innovative, command respect, and be sensitive to others. The need for strong leadership potential is essential in the development of successful buyers.

The Buyer's Duties in a Large Retail Organization

It is clear that the buyer is a key person in retailing and has an important and responsible job. A successful buyer's time is filled with excitement and pressure, plenty of hard work, and satisfaction. Buyers for large department and specialty stores have the crucial role of selecting and buying those goods from the manufacturers for the main store and the branch stores, so that they will be available to customers at just the right time. And this all takes place in a very organized way. The daily routine of a store buyer is as varied as researching a vendor to grooming new sales help. Besides the selection and purchase of goods, buyers have regular contact with each of the branch stores and are very concerned with the sales and profits of their departments. They must also pay close attention to advertising, delivery, and warehousing of stock, and attempt to find ways to lower losses due to damage or theft.

The tasks of the buyer will vary depending upon which kind of retail operation he or she works for. Nonetheless, all buyers are a vital part of the merchandising team and share the following responsibilities.

Planning

The buyer prepares a market plan based on his or her knowledge of market trends and careful examination of the sales for the past year for each department he or she is responsible for.

Buying

The buyer's goal is to purchase the correct merchandise at the right price for the customers once a buying plan has been approved. The buyer needs to research manufacturers locally and abroad and select the best-made items to be shipped to the store at the proper time of year. Buyers tend to spend the majority of their time handling this activity. They are very knowledgeable about what goods to buy, what colors and styles will sell well, and how much should be purchased. They then need to follow up with the manufacturers to make sure that the items will be delivered at the determined time and in good condition. Buyers are responsible for offering merchandise that customers will want to buy.

Pricing and Profit

The buyer tries to get the lowest possible price for goods and then tries to sell them at the best markup so the department will make a profit. In addition, buyers mark down items that are slow sellers in an effort to help improve sales. Buyers make sure that stock records of merchandise are accurate and supervise the actual count of all inventories two times a year. They also ensure that salespeople as well as customers properly handle all stock within their department to lower the possibility of damaged goods.

Selling

The sales and sales force of a department are the buyer's responsibility. The buyer ensures that there is an adequate and knowledgeable sales staff, and he or she plans meetings to talk about new merchandise, appropriate sales techniques, and new trends that customers will be asking about, as well as new or unusual items that will be added to the department. The buyer must also be aware of the latest in displays for attractive arrangements of merchandise and pass on to the sales help information on how to set up and display goods.

Most stores have done away with selling as a buyer's responsibility. With the large numbers of branch stores that department and specialty store buyers must be accountable for, it becomes very difficult to supervise salespeople so far from the main store. A wise and effective buyer does not necessarily make the best sales supervisor. It may make good sense to hire an expert in each area. As buyers spend more and more time in the markets to keep up with the fast pace of style and fashion changes, there is less time to devote to the selling function. The wide use of computers now allows buyers to speedily analyze customer demand, so direct contact between the buyer and the public may be of less importance today than it was in the past. This thinking will probably vary from firm to firm.

Sales Promotion

Buyers assist in the promotion of merchandise by carefully coordinating displays, choosing certain items to be featured in the store's windows or advertising, and, of course, making sure that all goods that are promoted are in stock in a wide assortment of sizes and colors.

Relationships with Vendors

The resources (the wholesalers and manufacturers) that buyers rely on for getting their merchandise are called vendors. It is important for the buyer to establish a strong businesslike relationship with all vendors so that issues and problems can be discussed promptly and candidly. Buyers often pass customers' wants on to the vendor, who can then try to be the first in supplying that buyer with an item that may be a big seller.

Branch Visits

It is very important for the buyer to visit the branch stores. Even though this is a time-consuming task, it is the only way the buyer can get a firsthand look at all stock and its display. There is also the chance to talk with both salespeople and customers and to hear about their requests and complaints.

Receiving

The buyer is often in close touch with a store's receiving area, where all merchandise is delivered from the vendors. Buyers' orders need to be checked to determine if the proper styles, sizes, colors, and quantities have arrived. Buyers then authorize the financial department to make payments for the goods.

Difficulties can easily occur in the flow of merchandise from the receiving department to the selling floor. Therefore skilled buyers often develop strong relationships with receiving room workers to avoid in-store delay of goods.

Housekeeping and Stock Display

It is the buyer's duty to make sure that all merchandise is attractively arranged and placed conveniently for the customer. Items must be neatly hung or folded on clean counters, tables, or display fixtures. Signs and price tags must be accurate and easy for customers to read. Fitting rooms and the surrounding department area must always be neat and inviting.

As the head of any department, the buyer can always measure success in terms of how profitable that particular department is. Buyers constantly compete against their own sales and profits records and try to make the current season the best ever. But mistakes do happen. Markdowns and clearance racks are often evidence that buyers misjudged the merchandise they thought their customers would be eager to buy. Sometimes a special promotion or sale helps attract attention and move the merchandise. The last resort of any buyer is to put the items on clearance, which means dropping the prices of the goods to encourage quick sales. This reduces the department's profits, but at least it is a way to make room for the new season's goods and bring some money into the department. As you can imagine, buyers try to avoid having too much merchandise on clearance racks. Skillful buyers also try to determine what went wrong with their merchandise and why the items did not sell so that they can avoid repeating the same buying errors.

Much of the stimulation of the buyer's job is gained from the diversity and challenge of each day's work. Buyers who are successful in small departments can often move into larger areas of buying responsibilities and thus increased earnings. Many buyers are responsible for several busy departments, gaining these additional responsibilities only after years of experience. Once again, the traditional route is from training to an assistant buyer, a position that can last from two to four years, depending on your own ability and potential and the policies of your employer. Once you have been promoted to a full buyer, you can be sure that your boss has confidence in your judgment and that you have demonstrated expertise in your area of specialization.

Small Store Buyer

Many men and women own and operate independent retail stores that keep us supplied with everything from groceries to hardware. You can see examples of this type of retailer everywhere from small rural areas to large urban settings. Buyers for small stores generally handle a wide variety of tasks. These might include the researching and purchasing of items; display, promotion, and advertising of items; selling; servicing the customer; and the hiring, firing, and training of sales help. Often these people act as the store owner or store manager as well as the buyer.

Buyers for small, independent stores make visits to manufacturers in the local markets and major market centers. The buyer selects the assortment of merchandise—colors, sizes, styles, prices, quantities—and places the order with the vendor. The buyer then follows up on all orders to avoid possible problems and stay alert to the delivery dates of all goods. It is common for small store owners to hire the services of a resident buying office.

Department Store Buyer

In a department store, the buyer works very closely with a merchandise manager for guidance in selecting the appropriate goods for the department. The buyer also establishes a buying plan—often involving great sums of money—and converts that plan into units of merchandise that will be profitable for his or her department. It is essential for the buyer to keep a well-balanced assortment of goods in stock in the department. The buyer must also be keenly aware of customer preferences. Buyers in department stores spend time visiting markets, both local and foreign, and keeping on top of the very latest trends. They work closely with their branch stores and, of course, are responsible for the selling activity of their own departments.

Specialty Store Buyer

In small specialty-store operations, the duties of the buyer are much like those of the department store buyer. As all business in the specialty store depends mainly on the needs of local customers, the specialty store buyer must be sure to meet them. Often a specialty store carries a very particular type of merchandise and the buyer concentrates on a specialized market, such as junior sportswear or children's and infants' wear. It is necessary to work closely with the manager of each of the stores to help establish the desired assortment of merchandise and price ranges. Specialty store buyers are truly experts in their specialized line of goods.

Chain Store Buyer

The chain store system is one of the most vital features of our retail economy. A chain store operation is an organization with several or even hundreds of retail stores that sell the same merchandise and are centrally owned and managed. Simply stated, it is the distribution of goods through more than one retail outlet.

This can include everything from a two- or three-store operation in your local area to huge retailing units of thousands of stores located throughout the nation. Examples of this type of organization are Sears and Toys 'R' Us.

After World War I ended in 1918, retail chains began to grow in importance, along with the country's population and the ability to mass-produce goods for the consumer. Chain stores followed the nation's move to the suburbs and opened stores in shopping centers. Many organizations developed throughout the country, building stores coast to coast. Others stayed within a particular region of the country or clustered around a major city such as Los Angeles or Boston. These chains are generally well known to consumers: JCPenney, Lowe's, Home Depot, and Crate & Barrel. To this day, retail chains account for a very important avenue of merchandise distribution.

Central planning, buying, and merchandising of all goods are the major features of all retail chains. The buyers for the chains are usually located in the main headquarters in a major central market, so they can be in close touch with vendors—the manufacturers and wholesalers. New York City is the home office of many buyers for retail chains. These buyers often work far away from the stores they buy for and have no selling responsibility for the goods they purchase. In this setup, the selling function is completely separate from the buying function. Buyers have little or no contact with the sales staff. The buyer for a chain store operation generally has no direct contact with the store but spends the greatest amount of his or her time in selecting and purchasing merchandise. Responsibilities such as inventory, reordering goods, and managing the sales help are the job of the managers of each store.

This represents a major difference between chain store buyers and department store buyers. In the chain store, the store manager, not the buyer, supervises the selling process.

Chain store buyers can place huge orders with vendors because they buy for so many stores. As a result these buyers are very important and powerful in the marketplace. They are essentially specialists in a particular market or category of merchandise, such as housewares, lingerie, or shoes. They spend a great deal of their time each day making sure their stores receive quick delivery of goods that have been ordered, handling stock fill-ins, and arranging for the lowest prices for the goods they wish to buy. Chain store buyers may develop programs with manufacturers to produce special lines of goods that will be manufactured for that chain alone, because of the vast number of orders that can be placed. This is known as *private label* or *private brand* merchandise. These buyers must be very knowledgeable about their customers all over the country, because they might have the responsibility of buying the same item for people in Alaska as well as in Hawaii or Puerto Rico. Tastes, seasons, and climate must be taken into account for such a wide geographic range of customers.

Market and Product Knowledge

The chain store buyer is truly a specialist in a very specific kind of retail operation, and he or she needs very special skills to perform well. Unlike the department or specialty store buyer, the chain store buyer has no responsibilities on the selling floor, devoting instead the major portion of his or her time to the buying function. As a result, this buyer develops an expert knowledge of the market that he or she is purchasing for. Strong working relationships with vendors must be developed so that the most capable and flexible manufacturers are used to handle the great volume of merchandise that is ordered. Backup or substitute vendors are important to know about, so that reorders can be filled if the original vendor is unable to supply the buyer with additional amounts of goods as needed.

Buyers for large chains often work directly with the manufacturer and get involved in the styling and design of a product—even the design and selection of the fabric. Of course, this requires a great deal of knowledge on the part of the buyer, as well as a solid understanding of customers, wants, and preferences. Because buyers have no selling responsibilities, they spend the bulk of their time researching and learning about the goods they buy. They have the opportunity to really become experts in one or more fields of merchandise classification.

Communications

Even though the chain store buyer does not have the opportunity to be in close touch with salespeople or customers, it is essential that the lines of contact with the selling department be kept wide open. By writing bulletins that describe new merchandise, trends, sales techniques, or display ideas, the chain store buyer has a means of explaining to the sales department what department store buyers would routinely discuss in a weekly meeting. Not having this personal contact with the department does free up a considerable amount of time for the chain store buyer. However, it forces the buyer to convey all necessary information in writing that is simple, clear, and direct. The use of computers has been a great help in assisting buyers with their bulletins and reports.

Forecasting Trends

It is difficult to predict what large numbers of customers in a wide variety of geographic locations will want to buy in any season. Not having direct contact with the sales staff and the customers makes forecasting this information even harder. Chain store buyers purchasing staple or basic items can rely on the sales reports of past seasons and make predictions with ease. However, chain store buying of fashion merchandise is never easy. Often the buyer is aided by gauging the good-selling seasonal items in one region of the country. Certain kinds of summer clothing may be selling well in Atlanta in March. Buyers may conclude that the same big-selling items will be well received in New York City in May and June and place orders for that merchandise. The fact that seasons arrive at different times in different parts of the country can be a great help to the chain store buyer, although it is not a foolproof method of determining what will sell well.

Retailers learned a long time ago that central buying—having a group of buyers responsible for the buying for enormous numbers of retail stores—substantially reduces the cost of merchandise.

Benefits of a Career in Buying

In addition to the daily challenges and excitement that come with this career choice, a retail buyer can expect other benefits as well.

Personal Development

A job as a buyer offers men and women the opportunity to constantly interact with a wide variety of other professionals every day. There is the ongoing opportunity to deal with all levels of the merchandising and management team, as well as with a broad range of suppliers, manufacturers, assistants, and store personnel. This calls for the ability to get along well with many types of personalities and to think clearly and make accurate decisions involving large sums of money. It is said that no two days are alike in the life of a buyer. It is an exciting and fast-moving job.

Travel

A buyer always needs to know the latest in trends, product innovations, and sources. Buyers frequently travel to trade shows, fairs, and distant markets, both at home and abroad. For some, this need to travel may be burdensome, but for others it is considered one of the wonderful benefits of the profession.

Financial Reward

Salary is always an important factor in the choice of a career. A buyer's income is good, often above the average of comparable positions in other industries. The most important thing to bear in mind is that the buyer's salary is generally related to his or her level of achievement. Most often, it is based on the buyer's own efforts and is measured on the department's sales and profits.

Career Advancement

After mastering the demanding routines of buying for one or more categories of merchandise, you may be one of the talented people promoted to divisional merchandise manager (DMM). The DMM is in charge of a group of related departments and oversees and coordinates the buyers of those departments. This person works to see that the team provides quality and value to customers. Merchandise must be in keeping with the image of the retailer. Excellent relationships with the buying team are essential. In many ways DMMs act as consultants, teachers, directors, and counselors. They share the knowledge and expertise they have gained over the years with their group of buyers, who rely heavily on their advice and counsel. These merchandise managers have complete control over the amount of money their buyers will spend, and they therefore try to guide them to innovative and profitable projects. They work closely with the store's other DMMs and compete with them for a share of the customer's sales. As it is for buyers, surpassing last season's sales and profits is the goal of merchandise managers.

An innovative merchandise manager might push for new areas in the store or special departments that might add a different approach or a trendy new outlook to the division. For those who believe they can help make a division's business grow, it would be worthwhile to consider this position once they have completed the other required steps. An enterprising spirit and a keen business sense as well as an ability to direct and lead others are essential.

Merchandise managers work very closely with their buyers, helping them plan their visits to various markets and teaching them how to turn their purchases into profits. They need to be familiar with each of the departments in their division. They have to keep up with the many new manufacturers and suppliers and let buyers know about new items and trends that may be important in promoting sales within each department. DMMs always look for new and different sources of merchandise or services. This might mean devoting a great deal of time to travel and research. The demands on the DMM's time and expertise are enormous, but the financial rewards generally measure up to the effort put forth. Working as a divisional merchandise manager gives you the opportunity to run your division as if it were your own business. It enables you to develop a team of professionals, all working toward the goal of a profitable and exciting division.

All divisional merchandise managers report to the general merchandise manager (GMM), who has the authority for all merchandising operations in the retail store, typically oversees an average sales volume of $25 million or more, and employs several hundred workers.

Keep in Mind

Most of the skills needed to succeed in retailing are needed to succeed in any industry. Retailers develop excellent skills in:

- Problem-solving and decision-making
- Teamwork
- Commitment to customer service
- Interacting effectively with various personalities
- Good work ethics

- Initiative
- Communication
- Cross-cultural awareness

The job of a buyer is a hard one. It is common for buyers to work long and irregular hours, be away from home because of travel commitments, and take paperwork home with them. They work in a pressured atmosphere, always trying to beat the sales and profit record of the last year. And, of course, being responsible for running a profitable department means being accountable for spending huge sums of the firm's money. A career as a buyer requires strong interest in business as well as in people. It is surely a demanding position, but one that also brings excitement, financial rewards, and great personal challenge.

5

RESIDENT AND CENTRAL BUYING OFFICES

STORES OFTEN UTILIZE the services of resident and/or central buying offices, which assist stores and their buyers in staying current with trends in the marketplace and maintaining adequate levels of stock.

The Resident Buying Office

A resident buying office is an organization that represents member stores and has its own group of buyers. Located in a major market, the resident buying office provides help to the buyers of its member stores, keeping them well informed with a steady flow of market information. The workers who represent the resident buying office are called *resident buyers* or *market reps.*

Resident buyers are buying specialists who act as assistants or advisers to the member stores. They are responsible for all aspects of merchandising and promotion and become representatives in the market for the stores that use the services of the buying office.

Resident buying offices are both large and small. There are one- or two-person offices with just several store accounts. Others represent several hundred clients and support large staffs, with separate divisions for specific goods, such as children's wear, housewares, or coats and suits. Some resident buying offices work only for specialty stores that deal in a single kind of merchandise, such as furs, millinery, or shoes. Whatever the service provided, the resident buying offices offer retail stores the buying specialists and expertise that the stores could otherwise not have access to. New York City houses the largest number of resident buying offices, as it represents the major fashion market in the country for apparel, accessories, home furnishings, and appliances. Los Angeles is the second most important fashion market, and Chicago and Atlanta are also very important. The organization of the resident buying office usually resembles that of the member store. There are one or more resident buyers or market reps, depending upon the size of the market, for each classification of merchandise.

The resident buyer thoroughly investigates the entire market he or she is responsible for, looking for new sources of merchandise, visiting manufacturers, and providing the member stores with the information gathered. As you might imagine, the resident buyer needs to be on top of the latest fashions and aware of all trends and style changes.

The resident buyer and the store buyer need to work closely to determine what the current trends are and what the customers will want. They attempt to look into new sources of merchandise to locate unique and interesting items, as well as basic goods for their customers.

Resident buying offices save the store buyers time and money by performing the following important range of services.

Market Coverage and Reporting

Resident buyers regularly research and report on all new developments in the wholesale markets and issue special reports to describe their findings. This vital marketplace news saves the store buyers a lot of time and legwork when they arrive in the market. The resident buyers collect information about the newest and the best-selling items and send it to the member-store buyers. The data sent might include details of interest to management or fashion directors, as well as information for the store buyers.

Buying Clinics

Resident buyers arrange for the leading resources in the market-place to be shown to all buyers at buying clinics. This provides a wonderful opportunity for all the buyers to share their ideas about the new lines being presented. Buying clinics also help stores select important fashion themes for each season.

Office Facilities

Clerical help is provided to store buyers who make regular trips to wholesale markets. Trade newspapers, such as *Women's Wear Daily* for women's fashion news or *Home Furnishings Daily* for the home furnishings industry, also publish the arrival of these buyers after the resident buying office assembles this information. This news alerts the manufacturers, who are always eager to know which buyers are in town on buying trips.

Buying for Member Stores

At the request of the member store, the resident buyer can order merchandise for the store buyer if the store buyer does not plan a necessary market trip.

It is considered quite routine for the resident buyer to visit manufacturers with the store buyer as often as necessary. This is a great service to the store buyer, who can then build on the good working relationships the resident buyer has developed with vendors in the market.

Group Buys

Arranging for group buying is a very important function of the resident buying office. It can help save member stores large amounts of money, as they can reap the price benefits from purchasing in quantity. It is also possible for the resident buyer to negotiate for better freight rates and delivery dates, free advertising, display materials, or even exclusive private-label merchandise as a result of placing a large group order.

Follow-Up Assistance

Resident buyers have ongoing contact with the manufacturer. They review the orders placed by the member stores and then follow up on prompt delivery schedules with the manufacturer. Resident buyers are also responsible for handling any adjustments or complaints that may arise between the stores and the manufacturer.

Fashion Office Services

The fashion director and the staff in the resident buyer's fashion office supply complete fashion information to store members. This might include ideas for special events, themes for fashion shows, catalogs pinpointing seasonal events, fashion promotion kits with details about advertising, publicity, or ideas for public relations events. This is the same kind of fashion activity that any department store or large specialty store would use to promote its goods. Smaller resident buying offices cannot afford this sort of service, but fashion offices can be found in most of the larger resident buying firms.

The fashion office also stages the fashion shows, generally held during market weeks when the store buyers are all together. Current style and fashion details can be shown to buyers of fashion items. Fashion clinics are also provided to help the store buyers in choosing merchandise and planning special promotions. Current fashion news is relayed to store buyers in periodic bulletins that detail the latest in fabric, color, and style trends.

Foreign Market Purchases

Many of the larger resident buying offices have a foreign department to help with the flow of merchandise coming in from foreign countries. In addition to handling a range of buying and follow-through services, a foreign department can be helpful to store buyers, often assisting them in developing ideas for purchasing merchandise abroad.

Personal Services

The store buyers, who are usually visitors from out of town, may come to the central marketplace with requests for hotel, theater, and travel reservations. As a courtesy to its store members, the resident buyer or an assistant in the buying office arranges these personal items.

In summary, the major role of the resident buying office is to research the market, buy the merchandise (after obtaining permission of the member store buyer to do so), and help promote the merchandise.

The resident buyer must keep his or her store buyer apprised of what is happening in the market at all times. The resident buyer works with buyers from all over the country, helping them by informing them as well as assisting them in promoting the new merchandise.

Unlike the long hours involved in retail store buying, the workweek of the resident buyer is more traditional. He or she works five days a week, with Saturday and Sunday free and usually no late nights. Resident buying offices are generally organized in such a way that visiting store buyers work closely with a resident buying office representative who services all their needs.

The assistant buyer in the resident buying office usually begins with on-the-job training. By following up on a buyer's activities, the assistant buyer has a chance to place reorders and special orders, handle transfers of merchandise, and eventually open orders. In large resident buying offices, buyers may have one or more assistants. In smaller firms, an assistant buyer may report to and work closely with several buyers.

The services offered by a resident buying office are varied. The most important advantage is the time and money the store buyer saves. He or she receives a continuous flow of essential market information from the resident buyer regarding new goods and new resources at the best prices.

The Central Buying Office

A central buying office represents its own chain of stores and is responsible for centrally purchasing goods for each of its stores. It is truly the center of the chain store operation. The chain's retail units have no opportunity to participate in that part of the merchandising process. There are some interesting entry-level spots for you to consider.

Distributor/Planner Trainee

This is an excellent start for people with strong math and analytical skills who are well organized and attentive to details. This worker determines the allocation of merchandise to the various branches of the chain. The trainee keeps track of thousands of units of merchandise and assigns varying amounts of stock to the stores, which may number in the hundreds. Generally this precision work is helped a great deal with computer printouts and unit control records, which indicate what is on hand and what is needed in each store. A good memory can be a great asset in this job. The ability to deal with many people, usually by telephone, E-mail, or fax, is important as well. From this position, one might be promoted to a head distributor/planner or an assistant buyer. This spot is an entry-level position in most central buying offices.

Buyer's Clerk

This is an excellent starting position for anyone with good clerical skills and an ability to work with figures. The buyer's clerk is responsible for carefully handling the many clerical records that supply the buyer with essential information needed to make buying decisions. He or she answers telephones, takes messages, makes appointments for the buyer, follows up on shipments of merchandise that have been purchased, and might even handle problems related to damaged items or late shipments. This worker has contact with the buyer and the assistant buyer or may be assigned to report to more than one buyer. It is an on-the-job training spot that offers a splendid overview of the buying function and could lead to advancement to an assistant buyer and a buyer in the future.

You must be well organized, able to deal precisely with details, and work well with many other people to handle this job successfully. Buyer's clerk positions are usually available as entry-level jobs in both central and resident buying offices.

Assistant Buyer Trainee

This entry-level job is also found in both central and resident buying offices. It is a fine starting spot for anyone with a future interest in a career as a buyer. Fast-moving, on-the-job training requires the assistant to help the buyer in many ways. When doing followup tasks with the buyer, the assistant begins to learn all about the major resources in the marketplace, eventually being able to place special orders and reorders for the buyer. There is heavy emphasis on keeping precise records, following up on goods, and keeping in close touch with the manufacturers and with the stores the merchandise will eventually be delivered to.

After some time on the job, the assistant may go with the buyer to the manufacturer's showrooms to view collections of merchandise. Later, the assistant may begin to be responsible for a section of the market under the buyer's supervision and for handling the information bulletins that are sent to the stores.

In large resident and central buying offices, each buyer has at least one assistant buyer to rely on. In smaller offices, several buyers may share the services of a single assistant. The assistant buyer in a buying office tends to work more traditional days and hours than retail store workers. Evening and weekend work in buying offices is unusual. Salaries in buying offices reflect this, in that they are often lower than starting salaries in the stores. You would need to have the same skills as a buyer's clerk to compete for this assignment, as well as the ability to work well under pressure and manage several ongoing tasks at the same time.

Assistant buyers are generally eager to observe and learn as much as possible as they move up the career ladder to the position of buyer.

6

Nonstore Retailing

A CAREER IN retailing does not necessarily limit you to working in a store. There are many exciting career opportunities available working for mail-order houses, direct marketing, or mailing list operations.

Mail-Order Houses

A mail-order house is simply a retail business that sells to customers through the mail, usually with a catalog. This has been an important type of retailing for nearly one hundred years. You are probably familiar with some major companies that are well known for their substantial mail-order business—JCPenney, Spiegel, and Victoria's Secret, for example. These firms offer a vast range of merchandise to consumers. All selection and delivery is handled through the mail, although it is also possible for customers to phone in their orders.

At one time, mail-order retailing was the most important form of retailing available to rural customers living in outlying areas. The Montgomery Ward and Sears catalogs can be credited with launching this trend of shopping through the mails to rural customers in the late 1800s. At the turn of the century, Sears was distributing three million catalogs to farmers and small-town residents all across America. And once the U.S. Postal Service began parcel post in 1913, Sears received five times the number of mail orders it had the year before. Today, men and women who are interested in shopping with ease in the comfort of their home or office rely on catalogs of every description.

Specialized mail-order businesses also supply customers with goods that are very specific and unique. Everything from gourmet foods to fine craft-working tools, records and videos to garden equipment, can be purchased by mail from more than ten thousand different mail-order firms. Most department and specialty stores send out catalogs regularly, particularly during the Christmas holiday season. They also routinely send direct-mail inserts in monthly bills to their credit customers to describe merchandise promotions.

Catalogs were responsible for the direct marketing explosion of the 1980s, and its success has continued into the twenty-first century. More than half of our country's population has made catalog purchases. Shoppers seem to enjoy the convenience of making leisurely selections from attractive catalogs that offer a great array of interesting products. In some cases the photo and accompanying description of an item offers more details about that product and its benefits than a salesperson could provide. For many consumers, catalog shopping has become a delightful way to fulfill their shopping needs.

Retail Direct Marketers

Traditional retailers, such as Saks and Neiman Marcus, jumped on the direct marketing bandwagon years ago, offering elegant catalogs filled with high-priced specialty goods. In some cases the items are exclusive and offered only through the catalog. Interestingly enough, some major catalog firms, such as Eddie Bauer, are doing the reverse. These businesses are opening retail stores to complement their catalog sales. Research has shown that those who receive catalogs are more likely to shop in the store that sends the catalog to them. And catalog receivers spend twice as much as others in in-store sales! It's estimated that about one-third of all mail-order sales are generated by retailers with mail-order departments.

The Development of Mail Order

America was still largely rural in the 1800s. The idea of selling goods by mail became a possibility when the great transcontinental railroad was completed, and the country had a postal system that included rural, free delivery. Montgomery Ward set up shop in Chicago, which was the railroad center of the country at that time. Chicago quickly became the mail-order headquarters of America when the main offices of Sears and Spiegel established themselves there as well. The large mail-order operations were profitable from the start, although in the earliest days of the mail-order, many retailers believed that customers would never want to order items that they could not see in person.

Mail-order operations have continued to maintain an outstanding record of loyal customers and solid sales. This concept of retailing is firmly a part of the shopping style of many people. It is no longer the domain of the small town or rural customer. Mail-order customers appreciate the ease and timesaving benefits; the excellent quality of merchandise, value, and service; the huge range of merchandise and services; and the competitive prices, which are a result of the vast purchasing power of the mail-order firms.

Mail-order retailing has offered the public a convenient kind of shopping for general merchandise as well as for more unusual items. The mail-order industry has developed a fine reputation for delivering quality goods. Many such firms frequently offer liberal return policies, and customers now find that delivery can be arranged within forty-eight to seventy-two hours. Of course, the customer pays delivery charges, but many working people do not mind paying extra for this convenient type of shopping.

Mail-Order Copywriter

Mail-order companies provide excellent training to anyone with writing skills. Consider inquiring about entry-level openings at retail stores, catalog houses, magazines, and advertising agencies. If you love to write and think that your words can take the place of a salesperson in promoting a product, consider becoming a direct-mail copywriter. Getting your message to the consumer and convincing him or her to respond to your product or service is a challenging and rewarding task.

Direct Marketing

Direct marketing refers to the method of offering customers products or services through a variety of advertising media—mail, radio, TV, telephone, newspapers, or magazines. It gets an ad *directly* to the customer in the hopes of getting an immediate response. Those responses can take different forms. A catalog sent in the mail asks the reader to place a mail, fax, or phone order. In some situations, especially where expensive goods or services are being offered, a two-step process occurs. Interested people are sent additional information to review and are then called again, perhaps even more than once, in an effort to finalize the sale.

Regardless of the form the response takes—telephone, mail, or fax—it can be measured. This means that the success rate of every direct marketing campaign is known as soon as all responses are tallied. A large response signifies a successful campaign, while less than the predicted response level means the campaign failed. Direct marketing is sales, pure and simple. It is response advertising via the mail, in a magazine, on the radio, or on TV—all geared to making a sale.

In the past, direct mail was the most important direct marketing medium. Although direct mail is still a very effective tool, other media have sprung up as important direct marketing techniques. Ads placed in newspapers and magazines, particularly the colorful ones inserted in Sunday editions, make it easy and fun for readers to respond. TV commercials sell us everything from fine jewelry to children's toys. The telephone has established itself as a solid direct marketing medium. Everything from an ad on the cover of a matchbook to the insert in your monthly utility bill carries a message urging you for a direct response. Consider the fact that about 24 percent of all consumer purchases are made as a result of direct marketing.

Direct marketing offers many career opportunities. In large part, the expansion of direct marketing services is the result of our changing lifestyle. More and more working women are demanding greater conveniences and services. There is also much more credit available to the public than ever before. College students and entry-level workers are able to establish credit lines with ease.

And, of course, customers value the luxury of not having to travel to stores and deal with parking and bad weather, the lack of courteous sales help in retail stores, and the crowds that make it necessary to stand in lines to get served, try merchandise on, or pay for goods.

Kinds of Companies

More organizations than you can imagine are involved in the direct marketing area, either directly or through subsidiaries. For example, the Greyhound Corporation owns a company that sells gourmet steaks by mail, while General Mills owns four mail-order catalog companies. Plus, more than half of the largest ad agencies in the United States have direct marketing subsidiaries. Here are areas where you are apt to find direct marketing activities:

- Advertising agencies
- Sales promotion firms
- Mail-order companies
- Large retail firms
- Utilities companies
- Educational, political, and public interest groups
- Airlines
- Insurance companies
- Banks
- Magazine, book, and record companies
- Federal, state, and local agencies

Are you interested in investigating specific firms? Look through magazines or trade journals in your particular field of interest. Make a note of the firms offering products or information and contact those companies. You can probably investigate any kind of business and locate organizations involved in direct marketing in that field.

Kinds of Jobs

Job responsibilities vary from one organization to the next, so it is difficult to provide standardized job titles and descriptions. Review the following job descriptions to get a feeling of what the industry may have to offer you. Remember that with each passing year, new techniques and new technology will surely result in new job titles.

Traffic

This excellent entry-level area can give the aspiring creative applicant or potential account executive a chance to get his or her feet wet in the agency business. The traffic coordinator is responsible for coordinating the parts of a total advertising project with each of the agency's departments. It takes a well-organized person who is good with details and can follow up.

Account Executive

Account executives are responsible for liaison with the client and are also involved in market strategy and coordinating the various other areas related to advertising and marketing. It is helpful for account executives to have a background that includes marketing, business principles, advertising, or communications courses.

Creative

The creative department usually consists of copywriters and graphic artists. Copywriters need to have a love of words and the ability to communicate clearly. Write as much as you can and take as many writing courses as your school offers. The more you have written, the more you will have to offer a prospective employer in your sample portfolio. Copywriters need to have a thorough knowledge of the target audience—what it wants and why it buys.

For a career as a copywriter, you might start off as an assistant or a junior copywriter. You could then advance to a copywriter, senior copywriter, copy supervisor, or director. Candidates with art talent can find positions as artists or layout artists. They work closely with the copywriters in developing the creative concept and joining the copy to the graphic image. A portfolio of samples of your art talent is a must.

Media Buying and Production

Media includes mail, print, broadcast, electronic media, and telephone. A background in communications, liberal arts, or broadcast may be a plus to a potential employer. The arrival of the new electronic media, such as cable TV, home shopping channels, and shopping on computer from home, means that you have to be completely up-to-date with all of the new advances in this area.

Media people work with all departments. They take charge of the selection and the purchasing of space and time and analyze the results of ad campaigns. Media orders must be coordinated with brokers and publications and placed just at the right time. Candidates for a job in media need to be good negotiators when bargaining for print space or broadcast time.

Production workers must be detail-oriented and able to work under the constant pressure of deadlines. They are responsible for working with suppliers, such as printers and art studios. They must see that all the parts of the message are complete, that colors are accurate, and that there are no errors in the copy or mistakes that will be embarrassing to the advertiser.

Research

For a job in research you need to take courses in research methodology, statistics, psychology, and sociology. Unlike some other areas of the direct response marketing industry, an M.B.A. would be very valuable to ensure a career in this field. Careers could start at the assistant level and bring you up to senior management.

Mailing List Operations

Once the direct-mail ad or catalog has been completed, it must reach the appropriate audience. To do that, the marketer must have a mailing list of potential customers. The best mailing piece will not succeed if it does not target the proper prospects. Anyone with a facility for numbers, research, computers, or sales will find opportunities in the following areas of mailing list operations.

List Brokers

The list broker helps the marketer select the lists that will work best for the product or the message that needs to be sent. The broker helps plan the mailing, analyze the responses, and forecast for future mailings. He or she may even help the client determine marketing strategies. The expertise of a list buyer is measured on the success rate of his or her recommendations. Entry-level jobs include administrative assistant or assistant account manager. You then move up the career ladder to a senior account manager or account supervisor.

List Manager

The list manager rents lists. The manager performs a sales function for the list owner and is concerned with marketing the list and the related clerical detail work. A marketing background is very helpful, as are good communications skills.

List Compilers

These workers develop lists by getting data from a variety of commercial and public sources, such as directories or voter registration lists. List compilers can specialize in business and professional markets or consumer markets. Very large list compilers actually possess databases with marketing-related information of millions of individuals and households all across the nation!

Customers appreciate the value of nonstore shopping. With twenty-four-hour phone and fax ordering services and delivery times shortened to just two or three days—and express delivery for an additional fee if customers are willing to pay the price—shoppers have truly begun to put their faith in firms that do business by mail. Where mail-order companies were once considered shady and their merchandise thought to be substandard, annual sales of goods and services through direct marketing are now well over $200 billion annually.

Getting Started in Nonstore Retailing

If you would like to get more details about careers in nonstore retailing, don't hesitate to do so. Many cities have direct marketing associations you can contact for further information. Use your telephone directory for addresses. They may even offer job placement services. You can also write to the Direct Marketing Association, 1120 Avenue of the Americas, Thirteenth Floor, New York, New York 10036, for information about careers in direct marketing and scholarship programs for college students.

Use your library to research books and magazines for the field, including *Direct* and *DM News*. *DM News* is a weekly publication with classified ads for positions in the field. It will give you a glimpse of what qualifications employers are seeking and the current salary ranges.

7

ADDITIONAL RETAIL CAREER OPPORTUNITIES

WE HAVE ALREADY covered retail careers in large stores and through the mail. This chapter describes some other related opportunities for a career in retail.

Small Store Ownership

Many dream of running their own retail store, and it is an opportunity that is open to decisive and creative people willing to work hard. Retail entrepreneurs must serve in a variety of roles, often handling the buying, receiving, and marking of merchandise; sales; store maintenance; and, of course, the financing of the operation. Successfully opening and running your own small store can be difficult, perhaps more difficult than most people realize. The failure rate for small retail stores is quite high. There are many important decisions that must be made long before your store becomes a reality.

One of the most important, of course, is location. Will the store be opened in a suburban mall, a shopping center, or in the downtown area? You will need to find out about your competition and market and about product demand for the merchandise or service you intend to offer. Are you thinking of a discount or off-price operation or a top-of-the-line store? What will your merchandise and your pricing policy reflect, and will your store's location support it?

Financing is another critical area. You will have to determine how much capital you will need to get started with a full inventory of goods, adequate money for payroll, and rent. And then you'll have to figure out where the initial investment will come from— banks, friends, family, your own savings, or a small business administration loan.

Once you have decided whether you will own your business independently or will be part of a partnership, corporation, or franchise, you will have to decide who will be responsible for publicity, advertising, special promotions, inventory, receiving of goods, and security. Will you be able to handle all of these duties? Are you good at handling all of them? Will you have the time to do so? Do you have the experience to be responsible for them?

And don't forget about personnel and management. Will personal selling and customer service play an important role in your business? Will there be close employee supervision, or will you delegate many of the duties?

The following skills and experiences are essential before you consider becoming an entrepreneur:

- Three to five years of work experience in a mid- to large-size retail organization
- Understanding of or actual work experience in a small store operation, observing all aspects of merchandising goods

- Ongoing assistance from both a lawyer and an accountant for counsel and guidance on many issues
- Familiarity with material available from the Small Business Administration (U.S. Department of Commerce) that provides detailed information about steps to be taken when considering opening a small store
- Self-knowledge and a thorough understanding of your skills and attributes, including commitment, knowledge, and dedication to an exciting and fast-paced venture

It should be clear that starting your own business is not an easy task. When small retail stores fail, it is primarily because of lack of retailing experience, lack of knowledge about the product or service, or inadequate record-keeping and financial experience.

The owner of the retail business is the most important part of the business. It is essential that he or she have the same qualities that successful retail employees need:

- Good decision-making abilities
- Leadership potential
- Ability to accept responsibility
- Good communication skills
- Commitment and dedication
- Stamina and tolerance for long and irregular work hours
- Initiative and self-starting ability

Being accountable for a retail store involves competency in the many activities necessary to maintain it. It is likely that the small store owner will get involved in some or all of these activities. He or she should really be a jack-of-all-trades to be able to delegate and supervise these duties:

- Market research and sales forecasting
- Planning and budgeting
- Buying of merchandise
- Inventory control
- Pricing of merchandise
- Hiring, training, and supervising of workers
- Employee scheduling
- Advertising, publicity, display, and promotions
- Customer service and customer relations

Thinking of Your Own Business?

Does owning and operating your own retail store still appeal to you? More and more people are becoming small store owners, or entrepreneurs, after getting solid experience in the retail area. Operating your own small store often means that you are merchandise manager, buyer, financial expert, public relations (PR) director, and personnel head all rolled into one. You might also be the security guard, housekeeper, and janitor. Once the business begins to show profits, it is possible to hire other workers and delegate some of these duties. But you must be prepared for a lean period in the first few years. It takes time for a store to develop customer loyalty and gain a reputation in the community. Your financial obligations will remain constant, and you will be expected to have the capital to pay for all expenses, even during the slower times. As has already been stated, new retail businesses generally have a low rate of survival. If you can make it through the first two years, the chances of long-term survival are considerably better, and the rewards are many.

Can you picture yourself owning your own store and being your own boss? It is a great feeling to succeed, but success doesn't "just happen" to the lucky ones. It is important for the small store owner to learn all about successfully starting and managing a business.

How to Begin

If opening your own store is your dream, are you confused about how to get started? Don't be. Join the ranks of others who take advantage of the growing numbers of workshops and courses that are now available all across the country. Adult education courses of this sort are offered in high schools and community colleges. Almost every business school and many specialized schools with programs in merchandising, retailing, or business have courses relating to independent business ventures. Short seminars and workshops on small business operations can help you learn everything from how to raise venture capital for the new business to how to write a business plan.

Take the first step. Learn how you can be successful. But don't even think about starting your own business without having solid retail work experience first.

More Career Positions

There are many more areas of retailing to explore as you think about your career. Here are some other positions you might want to consider.

Fashion Coordinator

The job of fashion coordinator is one of the most coveted positions in the world of retailing. As the name indicates, the fashion coordinator makes sure that all fashion departments are up-to-date on the latest fashion information. Fashion coordinators can be style-setters, so they must have their own sense of fashion and good taste. The retail fashion coordinator alerts and advises buyers and their managers to the latest trends and developments in the fashion world. He or she works very closely with the store's advertising and promotion departments. And, of course, the fashion coordinator is responsible for the fashion shows run by the stores. He or she is involved in selecting clothing and accessories, styling the outfits, working with models, writing the commentary, and arranging for publicity.

Frequently the fashion coordinator works with local high schools or colleges to form a college board that appeals to young, fashion-conscious shoppers. The fashion coordinator needs to be familiar with wholesale and retail markets to get a sense of what is new and trendy in fashion and quickly relay that information to the store. He or she also suggests how customers can coordinate or accessorize merchandise from one department with items from another department. In this way, a store can present a unified look—or fashion story—to the customer. For example, the fashion coordinator attempts to make sure that there are shoes, handbags, and hosiery to coordinate with apparel sold in different areas of the store's fashion departments.

This is a busy job, and it requires knowledge of fashion merchandising and broad retail experience. A highly developed sense of fashion and good taste are essential. The job requires being sensitive and open to what is brand new and ahead of the times, as well as having a strong interest in color, design, and fabrics. The fashion coordinator represents the store, so he or she has to look and sound the part. The public component of this position demands excellent dress, grooming, and communications skills.

A fashion coordinator is likely to be an expert in home furnishings, as well as in fashion apparel. If there is no interior design department in the store, the fashion coordinator may also have the job of putting together model rooms and coordinating the latest styles of furnishings, fabrics, and room accessories. Most customers love to view model rooms. It inspires them to consider new ways of redecorating their homes or apartments, and it always spurs new sales in the home furnishings areas.

If you are interested in the job of fashion coordinator, be forewarned—it is highly competitive. Unless you are a top-notch candidate with an extensive fashion merchandising background, it may be extremely unrealistic for you to consider starting off in this position. But if your heart is set on becoming a fashion coordinator, you can look beyond retail stores for jobs in advertising agencies, buying offices, pattern companies, fiber and textile firms, and large clothing manufacturing companies.

Assistant to the Fashion Coordinator

The logical entry job for anyone who aspires to become a fashion coordinator is assistant to a fashion coordinator. It is possible to be hired in any type of retail store or the other areas where fashion coordinators work. Beginner's duties are generally clerical in nature, and strong word processing and clerical skills are an asset. There is a huge volume of detail and follow-up work that the fashion coordinator delegates to an assistant, but this is a good way to learn all about the position.

Assistants do everything: make appointments, make telephone contacts, book models, deal with the fashion press, deliver and pick up garments that will be photographed, run errands, and make sure things run smoothly and on schedule for the fashion coordinator. There are opportunities for the assistant to work closely with the coordinator: putting on fashion shows or other promotional events, writing fashion bulletins, and spending time in the market observing trends and styles.

You must look and act the part to be considered for these very scarce and competitive spots. Excellent grooming and fashion sense are a necessity. Poise, a polished manner, and a good speaking voice are also essential. To successfully represent the fashion coordinator and the store, the assistant must be a model of good taste and style.

The Future of Retailing

The retailing industry can point with great pride to its role in the growth of our country and our economy. And the future of retailing seems bright. That means a great deal to retailers, as millions of shoppers seek more and more merchandise. The potential is there for you to play a vital role in servicing the consumer while forging ahead in a great variety of dynamic careers.

Business experts predict that there will be a major shift in the retail world. Expect to see a surge of vertical malls in bigger cities, retail-restaurant combinations, and a growth in nontraditional shopping environments in places such as office buildings and train and airport terminals. The forecast calls for a great expansion of national specialty and discount chains, probably at the expense of department stores and smaller, local merchants.

Retail consultants also believe that there is a greater movement toward *mass merchandising*. According to the publisher of *Fashion Network Report*, "The void in moderate-priced fashion that department stores have abandoned will grow even larger. The biggest growth is not coming from the silk-wearers, but from the polyester-wearers." We should see a retail mix that combines the convenience of both mail-order shopping online and TV home shopping with the strengths of the more traditional stores. Showroom catalog stores might loom large, with customers selecting their purchases from a display of floor samples. In such a setting, a mere swipe of a credit card will finalize the sale and initiate an automatic delivery system within forty-eight hours. The retail industry will continue to implement new technologies, specifically in nonstore retailing—online and home shopping and interactive kiosks. These dynamic changes make retailing a cutting edge career choice for the twenty-first century.

Television and Video Retailing

Selling goods on TV to people in their homes has taken a giant leap upscale. In addition to the mass merchandise items that have long dominated the airwaves, glamorous and more costly items are now available. For example, today we often see a fashion director on TV giving us information about the latest European and American designer collections.

Home shopping executives generally target an audience in its thirties and forties. But they are also targeting the twentysomething Generation X-ers. This audience differs considerably from the older population who provided the bulk of the buying power in the industry's first decade. There has been a corresponding hike in the quality and price of home shopping items as the industry moves from budget goods to high-fashion fare.

Current sales are ringing up several billion dollars per year. Although it represents only a small segment of the estimated $245 billion spent on apparel and jewelry in the 1990s, home shopping is more than likely to be retailing's fastest-growing sector. Giant retailers such as Macy's and Nordstrom are willing to try their luck and test upscale home shopping ventures. And the industry leaders, QVC and the Home Shopping Network, are starting new channels aimed at more affluent audiences.

As the number of two-career families increases, and as they grow increasingly impatient with what they perceive as the poor service and poor security in shopping malls, more and more customers may be willing to give home shopping a try. You may wonder, just who offers excellent customer service in cyberspace?

In 2001 a study of one hundred online merchants were reviewed in these areas: merchandising, checkout process, communication, and overall shopping experience. Among the top ten were Nordstrom, JCPenney, Lands' End, and Kmart.

Some critics contend that certain types of products cannot be sold on TV. Customers want to touch and feel the fabric of higher-priced garments. Moreover, there is apparently a high return rate from home shopping customers, who complain about the fit or quality of the items they have purchased. These are problems that creative retailers are looking to resolve, as home shopping is simply too big and too important for the retail industry to ignore.

The Senior Market

The market for seniors, customers who are fifty and older, is also ripe for action. This group now represents a large market, one with lots of disposable income. A research project on the shopping habits of older consumers, commissioned by the International Mass Retailing Association, discovered that many retailers are not doing enough to catch the attention or the dollars of the fifty-plus group. Every eight seconds, another American turns fifty, and in 1996 the oldest of the baby boomers became fifty years of age. The United States now has eighty-five million people over the age of fifty—twice the population of all of Canada—and this group of seniors spends almost half of all consumer dollars. They also control 81 percent of all the financial assets in the country. They buy more than half of all the luxury cars and can afford 83 percent of luxury travel bookings. They look, feel, and think as though they were younger than their actual age. With their leisure time and dollars to spend, retailers need to be more thoughtful about capturing this segment of the population, the members of which are not necessarily concerned about passing savings on to their children and tend to be more materialistic than were the Depression-generation seniors, now in their eighties.

One firm specializing in research on older Americans has the following suggestions for those retailers who want to capitalize on the increased spending power of senior consumers:

- Offer senior labels for immediate customer service
- Improve store signs with larger and easier to read type
- Increase in-store demonstrations and sampling
- Display brochures with product information
- Redo packages with easy-to-grip handles
- Add seating throughout the stores
- Station security guards in visible locations throughout the store and parking areas
- Have a public address system that gives clear messages
- Play music that is appropriate and not annoying
- Make sales staff available to handle special requests
- Offer more in-store services, such as food courts, video rentals, photo processing, mailing facilities, and other business services

Private-Label Apparel

Alfani, Charter Club, and Savile Row are names for Macy's store-brand clothes, what is referred to in the industry as *private-label apparel* or *private brand*. They are increasingly popular with retailers because they are so profitable.

Private-label clothing is generally a great deal for consumers, too. Items look, feel, and fit like the name brands, often because the manufacturer of name-brand apparel makes them. Yet the prices are lower, as retailers determine what materials to use and what to charge. Sometimes it's quite apparent that a store's merchandise is private-label. Firms such as the Gap, Ann Taylor, Talbot's, and Sears have built their business on their own labels. Nordstrom uses another approach, contracting with manufacturers like Hickey-Freeman to make its own line of menswear items exclusively for Nordstrom's stores.

Private brands allow stores to customize their product and offer exceptional values. For example, at Federated Department Stores, private brands account for about 15 percent of total sales, and that is more than $2 billion.

Private-brand product development means taking a trend or an idea and seeing it through to becoming merchandise on the selling floor. It entails conceptualizing, designing, sourcing, and marketing the new item. A brief glimpse of the process follows:

1. Forecasters predict trends and colors.
2. Development meetings are held with designers to create items.
3. Pricing and production sequences are set.
4. Samples are made and shown to buyers.
5. Buyers make commitments by writing orders.

6. Items are fitted and tested.
7. Production of the items begins.
8. Merchandise is shipped.
9. Stores promote and sell.
10. Sales are analyzed to measure success of items.

Large Sizes

As the size of the average American has increased throughout the past century, retailers have placed more emphasis on the plus-size industry, targeting women sized fourteen to twenty-four. At least one-third of the women in this country wear size fourteen or larger, according to New York City–based Plus Designers Council. This was a long-neglected segment of the market, and because these consumers finally are being offered fashions that they want to wear, they are buying more than $10 billion worth of large-size apparel items. Plus-size women have waited a long time for flattering, attractive, quality merchandise, and they now represent a very receptive market. After decades of being ignored by manufacturers, this profitable segment is now being catered to by firms such as Liz Claiborne and Jones New York. And major retailers, such as Macy's, Saks Fifth Avenue, and Bloomingdale's, are jumping on this bandwagon and enlarging or opening plus-size departments in their stores.

8

GETTING READY FOR
A CAREER IN RETAILING

No matter where you live, the best way for you to begin a retailing career and provide yourself with the best all-around training is by getting a job in sales or in some related beginning-level position. An entry-level or sales position will allow you to test the water and determine if this fascinating world might hold a place for you. Plan to continue your education beyond high school. Whether you get an academic or a business degree, additional schooling will open opportunities to you. Coursework should include marketing, communications, finance, management, merchandising, computer technology and information systems.

Most retail career-level positions from store manager to corporate executive are attained with a college degree. Most colleges and universities offer programs ranging from associate degrees to master's degrees in retailing, retail management, retail merchandising, marketing, and fashion/apparel merchandising. See Appendix A for schools offering these programs, or visit the National Retail Federation website at nrf.com.

Where to Begin

One place to start might be a summer or part-time sales job, or even a temporary assignment during the peak retail period at the Christmas season. This generally starts right after Thanksgiving and lasts until Christmas Day. Working during the Christmas season will provide you with a great deal of exposure and a taste of this fast-moving industry at its busiest time. Never underestimate the value of sales experience. It puts you in direct contact with the customers and gives you a chance to observe stock routines and learn how inventory records are kept. You will learn to operate a cash register, write up sales, and handle refunds and exchanges. You will also keep counters and shelves neat and arrange merchandise displays. You will discover which items the customers are buying and why. And as you begin to gain product knowledge, you will learn what information you should—or should not—pass on to the customers.

Also, don't say no to a stock job. You can gain valuable experience in a retail store by learning to keep an inventory of what merchandise has sold so that it can be reordered. You will be helping the sales staff by keeping the empty shelves and counters on the sales floor filled with goods as they arrive in the stockroom or warehouse from the manufacturer.

Learning to keep accurate records of the flow of items from the stockroom to the selling floor may be part of your stock job as well. In many retail stores, electronic data processing equipment is used to help collect this information. If you have responsibility for the stock in branch stores, you will have telephone contact with those stores to coordinate shipping and receiving of goods. You can also expect to have contact with salespeople, clerical and stock workers from branch stores, assistant buyers, and buyers.

A stock job is frequently the first step on the retail ladder and might be considered by high school graduates who are attending college at night or someone waiting to enter an executive training program. This might be the perfect job for summer or part-time work while you are still in school. The vast amount of merchandise that large and smaller stores receive must all be recorded, ticketed, and distributed in an orderly system. As the stock person in this process, you can play a major part in the prompt and efficient handling of these tasks.

Investigate Your Options

Become familiar with the retail stores in your local area. Talk with salespeople and merchants to find out what they do on their jobs and what training and experience they have. Consider the various types of stores that you might think of working for: chain, department, specialty, or small independent stores. Approach the store of your choice to see if part-time or summer entry-level jobs are available. You could begin as a salesperson, cashier, or stock clerk. While on the job, you will have the opportunity to observe the overall picture of the organization and see the range of other jobs that people have and how they are done.

If you can take merchandising or business courses while still in high school, do so. Learn about college programs in retailing, marketing, or merchandising with the help of your guidance counselor or librarian.

Work experience in any type of retail store is valuable and transferable. Once you have learned retailing techniques, you can move from a larger operation to a smaller one, from a discount store to a department store, from a firm in Boston to one in Colorado. There are retail stores everywhere. You might even begin to think of opening your own store someday.

Get the Right Education

If you are interested in a retail career, you should consider studying the following subjects:

- **Retail math**—to learn the fundamentals of arithmetic and problem-solving techniques
- **Marketing**—to understand how trading relationships are established and maintained in a sophisticated and changing economy
- **Advertising**—to familiarize you with the communication within the marketplace that gives consumers information about merchandise
- **Management**—to introduce you to the concepts of managing people and situations
- **Retail management**—to allow you to learn basic principles of retailing and retail store organization
- **Retail buying**—to provide you with an overview of the techniques, problems, and policies of a retail organization
- **Computers**—to be up-to-date on the impact and effect the computer has had in retail activities and to understand the advantages and uses of the computer in business

- **Textiles**—to become familiar with the various types of fabrics, fibers, and finishes available to the consumer
- **Fashion merchandising**—to get to know the language of fashion and understand its impact on the consumer

The computer is a vital information source for retailers who must rely on current and accurate data. A store's merchandise is its most valuable asset. Knowing what stock is on hand, what is needed, and when to buy more and from which manufacturer requires great coordination of information. The computer is able to gather data from many departments and many locations with great speed and can print easy-to-read reports. It is therefore important that you take advantage of any computer training you can get. It will serve you well in your career in retailing.

A wide range of other business-related and liberal arts courses are equally important. Retail recruiters are always seeking well-rounded, liberally educated people who have a keen interest in business and the education or experience that will support a career in retailing or merchandising. Retailing offers promising careers in fulfilling the needs of the public. It is an industry that demands many skills and a broad educational background.

Co-Op or Work-Study

Many colleges that offer retailing or merchandising programs also offer cooperative work-study programs as part of the preparation. This enables students to work in a retail setting as part of the college curriculum. Sometimes academic credit is given for this work, but the student is always paid the typical retail wage. It is a perfect opportunity to explore retailing and decide whether you want to consider it as a career. It is the time to apply classroom theory to actual on-the-job experiences. Students are generally evaluated on their co-op experience by their work supervisor and then discuss the evaluation with their school career counselor. It is an unusual opportunity to take advantage of an experienced retailer's expertise while you are still a student.

Below is a sample co-op evaluation form used by the retail employers of one school. Note the broad range of items that are assessed by a supervisor. Students have the opportunity to learn a great deal about the operation of a retail store, including: reviewing sales techniques and store procedures, writing up sales, operating a cash register, handling customer service, setting up displays, getting stockroom experience, following and taking directions, receiving and marking merchandise, developing product knowledge, helping with clerical details, helping with housekeeping duties, scheduling salespeople, and developing personnel relationships.

Employer's Evaluation of a Co-op Student

NAME: _____   POSITION: _____

DATE STARTED: _____   DATE TERMINATED: _____

NAME OF FIRM: _____

Signature of Personnel Officer/Supervisor: _____

Title: _____

Date: _____

Your cooperation in returning this evaluation quickly will be greatly appreciated. Co-op is a requirement for graduation. For the student to receive credit for the experience, the evaluation must be on file by that date.

On the following scale, please rate the student on the standards of performance expected by your company. Also, where appropriate, please document your rating with comments.

	Performs above standard	Performs to standard	Performs below standard some of the time	Consistently performs below standard
Work Quality: Assignments are completed thoroughly, accurately, and in a timely manner.				
Work Quantity: Performs expected amount of work.				
Job Comprehension: Demonstrates understanding of systems, procedures, and products/services.				
Organizational Skills: Plans and prioritizes tasks.				
Business Acumen: Gathers and analyzes data; makes well-founded decisions.				
Initiative: Takes responsibility to look for other work when assigned tasks are completed. Contributes ideas and suggestions when appropriate.				

	Performs above standard	Performs to standard	Performs below standard some of the time	Consistently performs below standard
Leadership: Is assertive, speaks up when necessary, commands attention.				
Supervises others as required.				
Demonstrates dependability, is reliable, and follows through.				
Shows flexibility to the demands of his/her assignments.				
Demonstrates professionalism in dealing with subordinates, coworkers, and superiors. Tolerates stress while performing job; does not lose temper or get flustered.				
Communication: Conveys information clearly and quickly both to individuals and to groups.				
Effectively conveys information in writing.				

Comments: _____

Attendance: _____
Punctuality: _____
Overall Performance: _____
Strengths: _____
Weaknesses: _____

If there were a future opening in this department, I would/would not wish to hire this person.

Additional Comments: _____

It is hard to imagine other work-related experiences that are as valuable, given the supervision and the evaluation that are required by the college offering the co-op program. Don't overlook this splendid opportunity.

Two-Year Colleges

Two-year colleges, also called junior colleges or community colleges, can be public or private institutions. They offer programs that prepare students for professional technical careers, as well as for transfer to senior or four-year colleges. You can locate hundreds of two-year colleges that offer excellent retailing and related programs. Refer to Appendixes A and B in this book, which contain a comprehensive list of such schools. Write directly to each school that is of interest to you to get specific information about the institution and its programs.

There are significant advantages to considering a two-year college: tuition is often lower than at senior colleges; you can live at home and commute to college; highly specialized programs are available; the student body is frequently smaller, which may allow the less mature student greater opportunity to develop; and there is often a closer relationship with faculty.

Two-year colleges are important features of today's educational system. Remember that the two-year college is not an extension of high school, nor is it a smaller version of a senior college. It has its own special identity and makes a significant contribution to American education.

Carefully examine programs that are of interest to you and make sure that the courses will be transferable to a senior college you might move to in the future.

College Guides

Use your school or local library for assistance in getting educational information. You can find current directories to get up-to-date college data. The *College Blue Book of Occupational Education*, published by Macmillan, lists colleges by state and indicates the occupational programs offered.

Peterson's Annual Guide to Undergraduate Study is available for both two- and four-year colleges. It is published by Peterson's Guides. Each edition gives detailed profiles of campuses that include data on admission, financial aid, the student body, athletics, college life, and tuition.

The *HEP Higher Education Directory*, published by Higher Education Publications, Inc., will supply you with important information in your research.

The Diverse Field of Retailing

You have had a chance to read about the wide variety of activities in retailing. Retailing needs men and women who can perform many diverse duties. And the need for new professionals in this field continues to grow. The future of retailing looks bright for college graduates who are eager to prove themselves in this challenging industry. Here are some features of the retailing profession for you to consider.

• We are all shoppers and consumers, so retail stores exist just about everywhere. Retailing is not confined to a specific geographic area. You can find jobs in retailing in any part of the country or start your own business wherever there are people. You might even have the chance to work abroad.

• Retailers are always looking for well-trained and dedicated men and women to nurture and help grow with the business. Unlike many other career paths, retailing adapts to new changes and trends. It is a wonderful field for those creative and imaginative people who can react to its continuous changes.

• Retailing is a field that has long offered equal opportunity employment to women and other minority groups. In many firms there are more female buyers than male buyers. However, there is still a need for minorities in upper management.

• As a people-oriented field, it is perfect for those who enjoy dealing with others.

The plain fact is that retailing is not only an exciting business to be in, it is still one of the nation's top growth industries. And it offers more openings and opportunities than many other fields.

For recent college graduates, entry-level jobs pay anywhere from $24,000 to $32,000 in department stores, with specialty stores, chains, and buying offices offering somewhat less.

9

THE JOB SEARCH

RETAILING ACCOUNTS FOR more than $3 trillion in annual sales, just in the United States. And there are more than one million retail firms operating today; so, once you have decided to pursue a career in retailing, it is important for you to learn as much as you can about the field. It is also essential for you to learn more about yourself. As a job seeker, you need to be clear about your own interests and abilities, in addition to specifics about various career areas. Armed with this information, you will be able to make wise career choices.

It is not easy to know where to begin to take stock of ourselves. Indeed, it takes some of us a lifetime to understand what motivates and inspires us. And as we grow and develop, our values and interests may change as well. Now is the time to start paying close attention to those job-related interests that you can identify. Think about yourself as a worker and about the range of job-related assignments you may find yourself doing in the next thirty or forty years. Believe it or not, forty years is roughly the amount of time a worker spends on the job during a lifetime. Does that sound like a long time to you? With research and planning, you can make those years challenging and exciting. Workers do their best when they are involved in tasks that they enjoy and from which they gain a sense of satisfaction. Gather as much information as you can about yourself and the retailing industry, and determine if your own abilities and interests fit in with the demands of a retailing career.

Identify Your Accomplishments, Skills, and Interests

You can begin to find out more about yourself by sorting out what you enjoy doing, what you believe you do well, and what you think you would like to do in the future. In short, identify your marketable characteristics. Matching your strengths to those required in retailing will allow you to mesh your best qualities with what retail employers are seeking. An inventory of your accomplishments, your skills, and your interests can help you eliminate areas that may not work well for you, as well as help you explore alternatives and related career areas before you make your final decisions.

Keep in mind some of the facts uncovered by national surveys. Many workers in the United States are not happy with their jobs and believe that real opportunities for advancement are not available to them. In addition, far too many workers feel unappreciated and believe they are poorly paid for the work they do. All the more reason to make sure that you carefully select a career that will offer what appeals to you and fits well with what you have to offer.

Make a Personal Inventory

Itemizing your personal accomplishments will allow you to identify your likes, dislikes, abilities, and the kind of activities that you value. It is very helpful to put this list down in writing rather than just thinking about it. Try to remember the occasions that have been special for you and provided you with good learning experiences. Also include situations where you have been successful in school, at work, or in social or leisure circles. Your inventory should be a tally of your good and weak points, your interests, and your values.

Use the following sample inventory as a model for your own inventory. It shows accomplishments and activities and the required skills and abilities demonstrated to achieve them.

Knowing what you have liked and disliked in the past can help you identify future career possibilities. For every item you list in your accomplishments and skills inventory, think critically about how you felt about the event. Did you like or dislike it? For what reasons? Be sure to jot this information down, too. Listing these three areas side by side can give you the beginnings of a composite picture of you as a working person.

Accomplishments and Activities

School
Planned fund-raising flea market sale for benefit of the
   high school library
Passed tough math course in summer school

Work
Taught myself to do minor repairs on office copying
   machine on part-time job

Held part-time jobs through high school to help pay for school supplies and for my own pocket money

Social

Was member of first all-girl basketball team to win a trophy in local competition

Demonstrated Skills and Abilities

Good organizational skills, accurate record keeping, and ability to work with large group of students, delegate tasks, and communicate clearly

Can work under pressure, work with figures, and problem-solve

Ability to learn without supervision or instruction; self-starter; good manual dexterity

Ability to work independently and organize and manage time well

Can work on a team to successfully compete for a common goal

Clarify Your Values

Your values are the ideas and concepts that you feel strongly about and believe in. They vary from person to person. People in the same family often have different sets of values. Values are personal beliefs that represent what gives you great satisfaction. Some job-related values include nine-to-five work hours, recognition and status, variety of assignments, and opportunity to travel, to name just a few.

Rank the job-related values in the order of your preference. It may be difficult for you to decide which items are truly the most important and which items should be ranked ahead of others. The values that end up as the first five or six on your list are those you must pay special attention to. You should consider a career that allows you to incorporate those job-related values in your work.

If indeed you wish to consider a career in retailing, review your skills, interests, and values and compare them with the information you already have about jobs in the field. Keep in mind that your list of accomplishments and activities will grow as you acquire experience. You should reassess your inventory as you collect more information about retailing careers. You may find that you change your ideas about what is important to you as a result of new career data and more life experiences. Be open to all career opportunities that seem to be in keeping with your educational goals, skills, interests, values, and preferred lifestyle.

Aside from helping you make wise career choices, having a good understanding of yourself will allow you to present your best side to a potential employer. Unless you can identify your own strengths, it is hard to tell someone about them. Once you know yourself, you can focus on what you have to offer. We all have limitations and weak areas. These weak points may change and improve over time, so you should not view them as permanent shortcomings. In fact, your ability to identify a weakness now may encourage you to work hard in overcoming it. For example, if you have a history of turning in school assignments late because you are bogged down with your part-time job, you may decide you want to learn how to organize and manage your time more effectively. With some time-management skills under your belt, you may be able to hold onto your part-time job and complete all your school projects on time. This weakness—and how you addressed it—may turn out to be a selling point you can talk about to an employer in the future.

After you have researched your specific area of career interest and have completed your personal inventory, consider the following questions:

- What occupations have the most appeal to me?
- What aspects of each job interest me most?
- What don't I like about the job?
- What skills and aptitudes are needed? Do I have those skills and aptitudes?
- What is the typical career path for a beginning worker?
- Which of my values and interests are satisfied in this area of work? What is a typical entry-level job like?

Researching the Job Market

Don't overlook any possible resources when starting to collect information about job leads. Explore all of the following resources.

School Placement Office

If you are still a student, or if you are a recent graduate, make use of the placement services offered by your school. Many placement offices have computerized listings and extensive vocational libraries where you can also research companies. Consult with your career counselor about what facilities you can use and for how long after your graduation they are available to you.

Local or School Library

Most libraries now have many current career books and pamphlets as well as résumé guides. Larger libraries will have a collection of videotapes that offer tips on preparing résumés and conducting job interviews. You will also find many helpful trade directories and business journals. *Sheldon's Retail* and *Phelon's Resident Buyers Directory* will provide you with a geographic list of department stores, women's specialty stores, chain stores, and resident buying offices. The *Occupational Outlook Handbook*, published by the United States Department of Labor, is revised every two years. It surveys the national employment outlook and gives specific job descriptions and details about educational requirements, career paths, and salary ranges for thousands of jobs. Or you can write to the National Retail Federation, 325 Seventh Street NW, Washington, D.C. 20004. This largest trade association in the world includes the large chain stores as well as smaller, independently operated stores. The NRF offers many professional services to its members in the United States and in fifty countries abroad. *Chain Store Age/Trends, Discount Store News,* and *Apparel Merchandising* are trade newspapers that can be found in any business library.

Newspapers

Look at the classified ads in the employment section of your local newspaper. Sunday issues generally have the most listings. If you plan on relocating, start to check ads in out-of-town or out-of-state newspapers to get an overview of what the job market is like and what type of help employers in those areas are seeking. Look to see what background is required and what salary ranges are offered.

Telephone Directory

An excellent source of potential employers can be found in the yellow pages of your telephone directory. Look under specific headings, such as "specialty stores," "retail stores," or "resident buying offices." You can also locate trade associations in the directory, and then call or write for further information about members.

State Employment Service

Every state in the nation maintains a free employment service for residents of that state. You may even qualify for career counseling at your local state employment service office. Many employers routinely list positions with this agency, which is often an excellent resource for beginning workers.

Chamber of Commerce

Each city's chamber of commerce has a membership list of local businesspeople that is available upon request. This can be very useful when planning a job hunt in a new locale. You can write in advance to request a list of member retailers. Then mail a cover letter and résumé to the firms that interest you, indicating when you will be available for an interview.

Employment Agencies

Employers with private employment agencies list many fine jobs. Make sure the agency you decide to work with does not charge you a fee for helping you find a job. Read carefully all the forms you are asked to sign. You can find listings of employment agencies in the telephone directory, trade journals, and newspapers. Specialized agencies, such as those concentrating on merchandising and retailing, may be particularly useful to you, as they often provide applicants with detailed information about the job listing, the company, and its policies.

Local Employers in the Community

Your entry-level job may be waiting right in your own community. Investigate the local merchants in your neighborhood and in the areas nearby. Contact them and inquire about job openings. If no positions are available at the time you inquire, let these employers know of your interest in working for them, so that they can call you as jobs open in their firms.

Friends, Family, Recently Employed Graduates, and Others

Tell everyone that you know that you are job hunting, as they may be able to help you with job leads. Keep in touch with classmates who have recently been employed. Most people enjoy talking about their jobs and career goals and are willing to share job-related information. In fact, you can approach almost any worker in a field that interests you and explain that you would appreciate some time to chat about his or her work. This is called informational interviewing, and it is an informal way of getting helpful employment details from people who are working in your chosen field. You can ask workers questions such as:

- How did you find your first job?
- What educational background did you need to start in your job?
- What skills are most needed in your work?
- What do you like best about your job?
- Can you tell me about a typical day?
- What advice would you give to a beginner who is considering this field?

- What related fields can you suggest I look into?
- Can you tell me what you did on your first job?
- Are there other people in this field you could introduce me to?

When talking with workers, make it clear that you are simply interested in gathering information and that you do not expect to be given a job lead. And remember that in some situations, busy workers may not be able to speak with you at great length. Ask if there would be a more convenient time for you to meet with them.

The Cover Letter

Your cover letter introduces you to the reader, who is generally an employer or an interviewer. It should convince the reader to review your attached résumé and consider you for a job interview. Always enclose a cover letter when you mail a résumé to a prospective employer. Try to find out who is responsible for the hiring in a particular firm, check for the correct title and spelling of that person's name, and address your cover letter directly to him or her. If you are not able to get this information, address your cover letter to the personnel or human resources director of the company.

Your cover letter should not be longer than three or four paragraphs and should never exceed one typewritten page. Keep the letter simple—it should be brief and to the point—and avoid repeating information that you have already stated in your résumé. The person reading your cover letter should be able to quickly learn of your interest in applying for a particular position. A well-written and interesting cover letter should persuade him or her to read your attached résumé for more details about you. The cover letter also must be neatly typed and grammatically correct. Never use photocopied or duplicated letters. Individually print your letter on good quality white paper, and make sure that you sign your name just above the line where it is typewritten.

Personalize your cover letter so that the reader feels you are writing specifically about that firm and that you have genuine interest in that organization. Slant your cover letter toward what you can offer the company.

Your cover letter should encourage a prospective employer to want to learn more about your background and your future goals. A thoughtfully designed cover letter will help you get what you want—a job interview.

Look at the following cover letter. Note that it clearly states the reason it is being sent in the first paragraph. That is your chance to identify the position you are applying for and mention how you learned about it. A brief statement about your background and why you believe you can fill the spot comes next. Close on a positive note, expressing your interest in setting up an interview. You can do all this in just a handful of sentences.

The Résumé

A résumé is a very important tool in your job hunt. It is a brief description of yourself and provides information about you, your school and work background, and several personal interests or hobbies. All of these details should work together to create a strong portrait of you. A résumé acquaints the reader with your goals, interests, qualifications, and experiences. It may be written in a traditional manner or in an individualized style. A well-written résumé

Sample Cover Letter

Matthew Philips
8 West Walk
Dunewood, New York 11734
June 3, 2003

Mr. Ira Alan
Human Resources Director
Alan's Clothing Store
Fair Harbor, New York 11734

Dear Mr. Alan:

I am interested in applying for the sales position in your store that you listed in the Dunewood School employment office.

My part-time and summer sales experience plus my course work as a merchandising major have given me an excellent background for the opening. I am looking forward to a career in retailing.

I will call your office next week to arrange for an interview at your convenience.

Yours truly,

Matthew Philips

is no guarantee of getting a job, but it may be very helpful in getting you that all-important interview.

Most prospective employers expect to receive a résumé from you in advance of the interview or at the time of the interview. There is no one perfect way of presenting information about yourself, but many people think of a résumé as a way of selling yourself on paper. By carefully describing what you have accomplished and by highlighting your best points, you are, in fact, creating an advertisement for yourself. This can be a very personal picture you paint for the reader. A poor résumé will merely report what you have done, leaving it up to the employer to decide if your background is right for the job. A thoughtfully written résumé will detail your background in a clear and well-organized manner, easily allowing the employer to see why you are qualified for the position.

Think of your résumé as a marketing document that will allow you to compete for the interview in a businesslike and professional manner. Be prepared to invest time and effort in the preparation of your résumé. It is an excellent investment. It can bring interest and attention to you as a candidate and persuade a prospective employer to grant you an interview. Here are résumé-writing guidelines that beginning job seekers should keep in mind:

• Revise your rough draft as many times as necessary until you are convinced that you have detailed all areas of importance.

• Point out what you have accomplished in school or on the job, if you have past work or volunteer experience. Describe abilities that you have that would be of interest to the firm. Be frank about your accomplishments without boasting or bragging.

- Include a goal or job objective to help the reader pinpoint your immediate or future interest.

- Avoid abbreviations, initials, and contractions on your résumé. Do not type the word *Résumé* at the top of the page. Never include your photograph.

- As a beginning job seeker, your résumé should not exceed one typewritten page.

- Sloppy résumés, or those with typing, spelling, or factual errors, are unprofessional and unacceptable.

- Allow enough space between categories of information so that your résumé is easy to read and creates a pleasing impression.

- There is no need to include names of references, but be ready to list them on an employment application form or discuss them at an interview.

- Complete sentences are not necessary. It is more important to be brief and concise in your statements.

- List the jobs you have had, beginning with the last one you held and ending the list with your first job. This reverse chronological order allows the reader to see what your most recent experience has been.

- Emphasize any changes in responsibility on the job. Employers will be impressed with your ability to assume more responsibility and move up on the job.

• For beginners without significant work history, any minor experience, including volunteer work or community service, is important. It shows an employer your ability to handle responsibility in a variety of settings.

• List your school course of study or major courses, particularly if they relate to the position you are applying for.

• Everyone has something to offer. Focus on your talents in your résumé and once again at the time of your interview. Remember, your résumé is your best advertisement.

Résumé Outline

Design your résumé so that the following areas are covered:

Heading

Your name, street address, city, state, zip code, telephone number, and/or E-mail address should appear at the top center of the page or in the upper corner of the page. It will identify the résumé and let the employer know how to contact you. This is the only personal information that should be included.

Objective

List your immediate employment goal by a specific job title or field. Make sure it is in keeping with the job for which you are applying. Not every résumé must include an objective, particularly if you wish to consider several unrelated areas of work. If you decide not to list an objective, be sure you can clearly describe the position you want at the interview.

Education

If you have a college degree, list it and omit high school data. Indicate the name of the school, dates of attendance, the kind of degree received, and any school honors or scholarships. If your educational background is directly related to your job objective, carefully itemize the relevant course work or other preparation that seems suitable, such as workshops or seminars. You can also include extracurricular activities in this section, such as student government, clubs, yearbook, or student newspaper experiences.

If you have no college background, list your high school training or any course work or other training, if it is related to the job you are seeking. Always list your most recent education first.

Work Experience

You may have accumulated some work experience from part-time or summer jobs. Describe your responsibilities and how you used your various skills, using as many action words as possible. List all industry-related exposure you have had, including attendance at professional meetings or trade association events.

As you gain professional experience in the industry, you will be able to delete the incidental jobs from your résumé. Until then, show the reader that you have had some work responsibility by listing any and all jobs, particularly if they were recent. You don't need to go into elaborate detail, but you should describe your accomplishments and the skills you used.

List your most recent job first and note the duties you performed and any promotions you may have received. Employers are often interested in learning that students have held part-time jobs and maintained good school grades as well.

Unpaid Experience

Do not be modest about describing unpaid activities. Volunteer work often impresses employers. This can include volunteer or internship experiences in your church, local hospitals, community agencies, or civic groups. Describe this area just as you would paid activities.

Special Skills and Activities

This part of the résumé is optional and may not serve every job hunter well. Use it only if you can present interesting or unusual aptitudes or talents to the employer. Do you speak more than one language? Have you a unique hobby? Are you a sports enthusiast, an amateur photographer, a skilled musician? A brief line or two about your special activities may be interesting to the reader and gives a personalized note to your résumé.

These are the major categories that are typically found on résumés. Place them in an order that suits you. For example, extensive work experience might be placed ahead of educational experience, as it may be more important for the employer to notice your work activities. Of course, other categories such as military service or extended travel should be added if they apply.

There is no need for beginners to list references. By highlighting your education and work experience, you show the reader that you are a qualified candidate. If the employer is interested in offering you a job, you should then be ready to give the names and addresses of several references.

Try to get the permission of two or three supervisors or past teachers who would be willing to have a potential employer contact them to discuss your work habits and your skills. Keep a list of the names, business addresses, and telephone numbers of your references. You will then be prepared for a reference check. Never use anyone's name without getting his or her approval in advance.

The simplest type of résumé for the beginning job hunter is a chronological résumé. You begin by listing your most recent experiences at school and work, and describe the rest in reverse order. This style of résumé is useful for recent graduates, as it focuses on the skills learned through their schooling, or for graduates with limited work experience. It is not recommended as a format for those with big gaps of unemployment or those who have been job-hopping in a variety of fields.

Describe your role on jobs and your accomplishments with action words. These verbs will help give your résumé a stronger and more assertive tone. Some examples of action verbs are "designed," "arranged," "established," "coordinated," and "sold."

Résumé Checklist

Rate your own résumé by comparing it against the following checklist:

- **Overall appearance.** Is it neat and professional looking? Easy to read? Neatly spaced? No typing, spelling, or grammatical errors?
- **Layout.** Is it well laid out on a single page with ample margins? Do your bestselling points stand out?
- **Relevance.** Is there unrelated or unimportant information that can be deleted?
- **Content.** Can the reader get a quick picture of your qualifications and abilities?

- **Action orientation.** Do sentences begin with action words?
- **Specificity.** Does your résumé avoid generalities and focus on specific information?
- **Accomplishments.** Are your skills and accomplishments emphasized?
- **Completeness.** Is all the important information about you included? Does your résumé do the job of convincing the reader to invite you to a job interview?

The following page shows a sample chronological résumé that you might find helpful.

Sample Résumé

Matthew Philips
8 West Walk
Dunewood, New York 11734
(555) 583-8058

Objective:
Assistant Store Manager

Education:
Fashion Institute of Technology, State University of New York
Major: Fashion Buying and Merchandising
Degree: Associate in Applied Science, May 2003

Major Courses: Fashion Marketing, Consumer Motivation, Buying and Merchandising, Marketing Principles
Related Courses: Apparel Construction, Textile Science, Fashion Art and Design

Honors and Activities:
Retailing Society Scholarship 2001–2003
Dean's List, Fall 2002
Member of the Merchandising Society

Work Experience:
9/02–12/02—Macy's Herald Square:
Work-study assignment in men's shoe department. Assisted customers, arranged displays, maintained stock, increased departmental sales by 22 percent.

Summers 2001 and 2002—Camp Northwood, Remsen, New York:
As a camp counselor, planned and supervised activities of ten- to twelve-year-old boys. Was in charge of wilderness trips.

Skills:
Fluent in Spanish.
Computer literate in Word, Excel, Powerpoint.

10

The Job Interview: Make It a Success

You have taken the necessary time to do your own personal inventory of interests and skills and have prepared a perfect résumé and cover letter. Now you are ready for the next step—preparing for the interview. The job interview is a critical step in the employment process. The purpose of the interview is to allow the employer to make a decision about your employment with the company. Skilled interviewers can learn a great deal of information about you from your cover letter and résumé, your appearance, and the manner in which you answer questions during the interview. The job interview is also your chance to find out if the position is right for you.

Preparing for the Interview

The job interview is a situation where advance preparation can really work for you. The candidates who are hired are not always the most qualified. However, they are probably the most qualified at selling themselves. Use the time you have with each interviewer to convey the best about yourself. It is your chance to convince the interviewer that *you* are the best-qualified person to fill the job.

Unfortunately, many job hunters do not do the proper homework necessary to present themselves in the best possible light. Remember, a beginning job, gained as a result of a successful interview, may pave the way for an exciting and challenging career. Once you have set a date for an employment interview, keep the following details in mind.

Time and Place

Be sure you know the exact date, time, and place of the interview. Try to get the complete name of the company and of the person who will be interviewing you. Find out how to pronounce the name of the interviewer if it looks difficult. All these details should be kept in a small notepad. Do not rely on your memory.

Researching Companies

Researching prospective employers is an enormously important part of your job search. If you don't know much about the organization and its products or services, you are at a distinct disadvantage. Find out all that you can about firms that are interesting to you. The larger organizations will have annual reports or other descriptive materials available to the public. You may want to work with your librarian to locate business news clippings in the library's vertical files for firms you are interested in researching.

Let everyone you meet know that you are eager to start your job hunt. Make a habit of going directly to the places where people are working in your area of interest. Ask questions. Find out about the background and education of the workers, what they like about their jobs, and what the negative aspects are. You can also find out about companies this way. Is it a pleasant place to work? Do promotions come from within? Does the company offer benefits, such as tuition reimbursement? If you can get the name of the person in charge of hiring, write it down for future use.

Take advantage of any materials your school placement office has about the various companies that recruit on your campus.

Talk to your placement counselor, teachers, and the people you know who work for the company. If the firm you are researching manufactures a product, telephone the sales office and ask what stores sell the product in your area. Then visit those stores to view the item and familiarize yourself with the price range and the manufacturer's line of goods.

Take notes on the information you discover about each firm and review them before each interview. This will make you feel—and appear—more knowledgeable. This information may provide you with material you might want to discuss during your interview. Try to find out the following information before you have your interview:

- What does the company do? Does it sell, service, manufacture, or distribute a product?
- Who are the company's customers? Are they consumers or other businesses?
- Is it a large or small operation? How many employees does it have?

For larger firms and corporations, try to find out:

- Names and titles of the key executives
- If it is a local, national, or international firm

- If it is a publicly or privately owned company
- What the company's growth pattern has been in the recent past

Do your research. It will pay off.

Travel

Allow for enough time to get to your interview so that you arrive about ten to fifteen minutes before your appointment. Remember, traffic jams and other delays are unpredictable, but showing up late for an interview is never acceptable. Getting there a bit early gives you the opportunity to relax and get ready to meet the interviewer in a more leisurely fashion. Nothing is more upsetting than dashing into an interview out of breath and out of sorts.

Application Forms

Many firms, especially the larger ones that have a personnel or human resources department, will ask you to complete an employment application form. Be sure you come prepared with a pen to the interview. Fill out the form neatly and completely. A messy or hard-to-read form can be a sign that you are a careless or sloppy worker. Bring along your notepad if you can't remember all the important dates you will need to provide, such as dates of graduation or dates of employment on past jobs. Be sure to answer all questions so that the form is complete when you turn it in.

Appearance

How you look is a major factor in your overall presentation. The clothes you choose to wear and the impression you make give an interviewer an immediate idea of how businesslike you are. Dress in a professional manner for the interview. A rule of thumb is to avoid extreme, trendy looks.

Don't arrive with your arms filled with packages or schoolbooks. Never bring friends or family members with you to the interview. The first impression you make is a lasting one. Interviewers are very skilled at making quick judgments. Use the interview opportunity to make an excellent impression on everyone you meet at your interview.

The Interview

You might be nervous during the interview. This is only natural. After you have had several interviews, you will have a better idea of what interviewers expect. Chances are you will be more at ease as you have more opportunities to practice your responses. Each interviewer's style will vary, and every interview you have will be different and unique. Some people will greet you with warmth and real interest in you and your background. Other interviewers will be more formal and impersonal. Some interviewers are talkative and chatty, while others expect you to take the lead in directing the flow of conversation. Be prepared for all possibilities by practicing and planning in advance of the interview. Think about the best answers you can give to commonly asked questions. Strengthen your answers by citing specific examples. Practice talking about your background, your interests, your school experience, and your plans for the future.

Go over this information with your placement counselor, a friend, or in the privacy of your room in front of a mirror. Be aware of both your verbal and nonverbal presentation. Your body language conveys a great deal about you. Good posture at all times is essential, even when you are seated. Avoid slouching or slumping in your chair. Don't fidget with your hair or your clothing. Do not chew gum or smoke. If you are able to find out the name of the person interviewing you, use it in an opening greeting. Try to maintain eye contact during the interview, even though it is often easier to avoid the glance of the person you are talking to.

Never discuss personal problems or criticize past employers. Describe your background and qualifications honestly. Employers who hire beginners know that they cannot expect an extensive work history. Above all, try to convey a friendly and positive attitude. This will help put both the interviewer and you at ease. Be pleasant and businesslike. Smile as often as you can—and nothing is as effective as an ice-breaker in a difficult situation.

You should attempt to get information about the firm while giving information about yourself. Listen carefully and express interest and enthusiasm when you respond to the interviewer. If you have a feeling that the interview is not going well, don't allow your disappointment to show. Instead, try to review what went wrong after it is over and perhaps learn how to avoid those mistakes on future interviews.

Try to answer all questions fully without wandering off the topic. If you feel stumped by a particularly tough question, let the interviewer know that you need more time to think about your answer. Try to prepare a better answer to the question for the next time it comes up in an interview.

You can generally break down the interview process into a few distinct parts. It might be helpful for you to understand what you may encounter.

The Warm-Up

Interviews usually begin with a friendly exchange of greetings to help relax the applicant. Expect casual conversation about the weather, any travel difficulty in getting to the interview location, and chatty items of this sort.

The Interviewer Asks Questions

If the interviewer is doing a good job, the applicant will be allowed to talk about himself or herself after the warm-up through a series of questions from the interviewer. This allows the interviewer to determine if the applicant has the qualifications for the job and if he or she will fit in the organization.

Practice responding to these commonly asked questions:

- Tell me about yourself.
- Why should I hire you?
- Describe your strong points.
- What are your weaknesses?
- Why do you want to work for this firm?
- What are your proudest accomplishments?
- How would you describe yourself?
- Why are you interested in the field of retailing?
- How did that interest begin?
- How well do you work under pressure?
- How did you learn about this company?
- What do you want to learn on your first job?
- What did you enjoy most in school? Why?
- What can you contribute to this organization?
- How much money do you think you are worth?
- What are your goals and career plans?

The Interviewer Gives Information

Now the job of the interviewer is to sell the position and the company by giving job details and information about the firm, working conditions, and plans for growth. This is usually the point where there is some mention of salary and benefits.

The Applicant Asks Questions

Here is your chance to show that you have done some research. Asking questions will also indicate your interest in the firm. Before you enter the interview, prepare several questions to ask the interviewer, such as:

- What specific tasks will I be doing? (Ask only if the interviewer has not yet discussed this.)
- To what department/supervisor will I report?
- How often will my performance be reviewed?
- Is the firm planning growth or expansion in the near future? If so, in what areas?
- What sort of training or supervision can I expect?

The Wrap-Up

This portion of the interview may give you some idea of whether or not you will be considered for the job. The interviewer may indicate when you could expect to hear some word about the hiring decision or when to return for a second interview. It is also the right time to thank the interviewer for spending time with you. Always try to end the interview on a courteous, positive note.

The Question of Salary

It is important that you become familiar with the general salary range of the entry-level jobs you are considering. Your placement counselors or teachers can be a good source for this information.

And just reading classified ads in newspapers will give you a sense of what employers are offering.

If there is no mention of salary by the end of your interview, and the job appeals to you, you can freely ask the interviewer what salary the position will pay. The interviewer is just as likely to answer by asking how much you think you are worth, so you must be prepared to know and state the going salary rate. You would not serve yourself well by asking for an unreasonably high wage or settling on a salary far below standard.

You should bring up a discussion of salary only if you think there is a real likelihood that you and the job are suited for each other. Never raise questions about vacations, sick days, other benefits, or salary until all other aspects of the job have been explained to you.

The starting salary should not always be the major factor in deciding which position to select. It is very important for you to know the company's policy on salary review. It is possible to accept an entry job at a higher wage than your schoolmates and then discover that you are locked into that salary for a whole year because the firm's policy limits you to an annual salary review. Other beginners may have a chance to be reviewed for a raise in three or six months and be earning more than you in a rather short time.

Job Offers

It may happen that an interviewer will offer you a job at your first interview. In such a situation, you must be prepared to either accept or reject the job offer. If you feel sure that it is the job for you and you do not want to have further interviews at other firms, accept it courteously with a definite "thank you." Then be sure that you find out from the interviewer the exact day and time that you should show up for work. Find out whom you will report to and where you should report on your first day. Also make sure that you are clear about the starting salary. You might be asked to fill out forms for the personnel and payroll units, although this may wait until your first day at work. If you have interviews scheduled with other companies, remember to call and let them know that you are no longer available.

If you would like more time to consider the job offer, if you wish to discuss it with your family, or even if you want to have more interviews, tell the interviewer that you appreciate the job offer. Let the interviewer know when you will call back with a decision. Be sure that you make a note of when you agreed to call back and do so, regardless of your decision.

If you are unsure whether the job is suitable for you and you decide not to accept the job offer, express your appreciation for the offer and the interviewer's interest in you. You might even want to mention the reason you are rejecting the offer so that the interviewer will understand. For example, "As you described the position, I realized that I would not have the opportunity to learn about your computerized systems, and I'm quite interested in that area. However, thank you for considering me for the job."

If the interviewer does not say whether or not you are a candidate for the position, you should make a point of asking at the end of the interview. "I'm quite interested in the job. Will you be considering me for it?"

Interviewers need to know that you are interested in the job they are trying to fill. Make every effort to convince the interviewer that you can do the job and that you want a chance to prove it. Relax, smile, and show enthusiasm at the prospect of joining the company's workforce.

What Interviewers Look For

Although interviewers are always looking for new employees with good skills in specific areas, they also seek beginners with good attitudes about work. The qualities many interviewers value in a candidate include:

- Being well prepared for the interview
- Showing enthusiasm and expressing a willingness to work and learn on the job
- Honest, genuine answers to questions during the interview, rather than overconfident or arrogant attitudes
- Knowledge of the firm and of the industry
- High energy level
- The ability to deal with other workers
- The ability to accept criticism and grow and learn from errors

Interview Checklist

No interview is ever perfect. But you will find that they do get smoother with practice. It will help you to review questions you could not answer easily and work on better ways to respond to them.

Spend a few minutes after each interview to take stock of how it went. Honestly answer these questions:

- Did you arrive on time or a few minutes early?
- Were you dressed appropriately?
- Did you smile and greet the interviewer by name?
- Were you able to mention your skills and strong points?

- Did you show interest in working for the company?
- Did you answer most questions thoughtfully and completely instead of with single "yes" or "no" responses?
- Did you stay on track and not ramble on about unrelated issues?
- Did you ask the interviewer all you need to know about the job?
- Did you come prepared with reasons why you want to work for the company, reasons why the employer should hire you, and questions that indicated a genuine interest in learning more about the firm?
- Do you know what the next step is?

Keep a record of which interviewers expect you to call them back. Note which interviewers will be contacting you and when.

Try not to feel discouraged by rejections or think that no one wants to hire you. You will learn a great deal from your early interviews and will be able to use those experiences to do better in future ones. The job for you may turn up when you least expect it. But don't wait for exciting opportunities to come to you. Be active and follow up on all leads that interest you. Go after what you want.

Discrimination

Laws exist to protect job hunters from discrimination in a job interview. Title VII of the 1964 Civil Rights Act makes it illegal to discriminate in hiring. The intent of the law is to allow all qualified candidates a chance to apply and compete for available jobs. It is illegal to discriminate against a candidate because of age, religion, race, sex, national origin, marital status, or certain physical disabilities (as long as they do not prevent the applicant from doing the job described in the interview). Most organizations make a genuine effort to uphold the law. But do keep in mind that the hiring decision is made by the employer, provided it is not based on discriminatory reasons.

If you are not hired after an interview, do not jump to the conclusion that you were a victim of illegal discrimination. Job seekers who really believe that they were rejected because of discriminatory practices must thoughtfully review the situation and be sure that they can back up their claim. Even a well-documented case against an employer will mean an investment of a great deal of time and effort, and there is no guarantee of success in opening up the job to the candidate in question.

If you wish to register a complaint, discuss fully the details of the situation with a lawyer representing the local office of the United States Equal Employment Opportunity Commission. You can write to it directly for material about laws and applicants' rights:

U.S. EEOC
1801 L Street NW
Washington, D.C. 20507

Your First Job

Your first position in retailing deserves a great deal of your attention and energy. The first job often sets the stage for a series of advancements up the career ladder. It is the best time for you to begin to develop professional skills and sort out career choices that the field can offer you. You can test out and improve your interpersonal and communications skills. You can also examine the areas that you believe are particularly weak in your background and make efforts to bolster them by signing up for courses or applying yourself to on-the-job learning experiences.

Your first job in retailing can be an exciting and challenging experience. Capitalize on it by keeping the following in mind:

Be Ready for Hard Work

You will be expected to pitch in and apply yourself from the moment you step into your job. Beginners are observed and evaluated more frequently than senior workers, so be ready for lots of people to be paying attention to the kind of job you are doing.

Be Flexible

Be cooperative and assist your coworkers whenever you are able to without interrupting your own work routines. You will surely need their assistance at some point, and then you can more freely ask for help. Become known as a worker who is always ready to pitch in.

Be a Doer

You can impress your coworkers and your supervisor as well with your energy and your enthusiasm for getting the job done. You will soon earn the reputation of a worker who can be relied upon. This will serve you well when employees' records are reviewed for promotion.

Observe Everything

Use your eyes and ears and learn as much as possible about every operation you have contact with. Don't limit yourself to just your particular responsibilities. You can pick up valuable tips and information about other jobs and how other departments function. Note how others handle their responsibilities. You will learn the ropes of the organization more quickly and employers will appreciate your interest in the larger picture of their business.

Find a Mentor

Try to seek out a senior worker or a supervisor who recognizes your talents and interest in the firm. Your mentor might be able to give you tasks that will help you learn and progress, as well as helpful information about the company that is often hard for beginners to learn about. Mentor relationships can be especially valuable in larger, more impersonal firms.

Respect Your Colleagues

Experienced workers can be a great source of guidance and advice for you. Go to your coworkers to ask simple questions about routines and procedures. You can respect their experience. Be sure that you check with your supervisor for concerns you have about guidelines for your specific duties.

Learn from Mistakes

Mistakes happen to all of us. Learn to acknowledge when you have made an error and try to profit from it by recognizing what not to do the next time. No one can demand perfection on the job all the time, especially from a beginner. Admitting your mistakes will help you gain respect among your coworkers.

It's Up to You

Now you have gathered some information about the field of retailing and the range of careers it may offer you. As well, you may be learning about yourself and the things that you do well and value. Give as much energy and thought as you can to your career. You don't want to place yourself in a work situation that will result in years of boredom and frustration. You can look forward to forty or more years on the job. Do not allow those thousands of working hours—a vital part of your life—to be anything but satisfying and rewarding.

Often the most gratifying careers do not follow a straight path. There are detours that occur for us all, some of which are completely unforeseen. Be flexible and make room for those detours as you move along. Always be open to those new areas of work that your lifestyle will allow—full-time jobs, weekend or evening positions, temporary assignments, new locations, or new skills.

Continue to think about how you can apply your skills and experience to innovative projects. Never turn down the chance to learn something new, whether in a formal school setting or on-the-job exposure. Those skills may serve you well at a later time. Additional education and training are always a plus.

And never forget how important you are. Leave time for your own personal growth and development. Family involvement, ongoing education, travel, relaxation, and a thoughtfully planned career can all add up to enrich and enhance your route to success. You can make it happen.

CASE STUDIES IN RETAILING CAREERS

BECAUSE RETAILING OFFERS a wide variety of opportunities, the field attracts many different people, all with unique personalities and abilities. The following case histories trace the career paths of men and women who are currently working in different areas of retailing. By working hard to develop their skills, they have all achieved success in retailing.

Strive to Be the Best

Joanne had always been fascinated with "color and clothing and putting things together." She held part-time sales jobs in retail stores throughout high school and after graduation enrolled in a four-year college to study fashion buying and merchandising. Originally, she was set on becoming a buyer. But by the time she graduated with a Bachelor of Science degree, her goal had changed.

She was eager to consider the broad area of manufacturing rather than focus on her earlier buying goal.

After a brief stint as an administrative assistant for a textile manufacturer, Joanne was not sure what direction to go in. It seemed as though a year abroad might have been just right at that time, but those plans fell through. Joanne realized that it was essential for her to spend her time and energy concentrating on planning her career.

She began by reading as much as possible about industries that interested her. There seemed to be excellent opportunities available in the cosmetics field. She spoke to the sales analyst from whom she was purchasing her cosmetics, and learned more about the exciting possibilities of that industry. In fact, the sales analyst was so informative that she convinced Joanne to seriously consider a job with her cosmetics firm and even arranged for her interview appointment. Joanne was hired immediately as a part-time salesperson, and after four months, a full-time sales spot became available. Just six short weeks later a position as counter manager opened, and Joanne made a smooth transition into that position, even though she was a very new worker for the company. She stayed in that role for two years, supervising one other sales analyst and building up a loyal following of customers.

Joanne was then transferred to a counter manager position at Bergdorf Goodman in Manhattan. This assignment lasted for one and a half years. Joanne supervised two other employees and continued to build up a solid business. With an excellent work record behind her, it was only natural that she was promoted to field development manager. At present, Joanne is happy in this job. She is responsible for recruiting in the northeast region of the country. She concentrates on the busy areas of New York, New Jersey, Connecticut, Philadelphia, and Washington, D.C. Her job is to scout for other enthusiastic people who will be trained as sales analysts for both full- and part-time positions in the major retail stores.

She now sees herself as "selling cosmetics through other people." She knows that friendly and dedicated salespeople are the key to the company's loyal base of customers, and it is Joanne's job to recruit those people. Joanne never dreamed she would end up in this aspect of retailing, but she is very pleased with her career. She loves the freedom of movement her job offers her, being able to set her own work schedule, and being in a different store every day. In fact, it is hard for her to think about a feature of her assignment that she does not enjoy.

Joanne believes that her future will involve moving up the career ladder to training manager or account executive. But right now she is having a great time working hard and striving to be the best that she can be, and she is well rewarded for her efforts.

Color, Fabrics, and Clothing

Debbie says she was always fascinated by colors, fabrics, and clothing. It was not until she was a merchandising student at the Fashion Institute of Technology that she had her first taste of retail sales, both as a work-study assignment and as a part-time job. At that point she was convinced that she wanted to become a buyer.

After completing a four-year degree, Debbie entered the labor market and landed a job as a production assistant for a lingerie manufacturer in New York City's garment district. She tested those waters for just three months before it was clear to her that the work was far too technical for her. The FIT placement office helped her find her next spot in a major buying office as an assistant to the product manager for home furnishings items. Debbie felt comfortable in that job, and learned to report on trends in home fashions, handle the paperwork involved in importing items, and send telex messages overseas. Debbie was the buying office's liaison to member stores and to vendors. She remembers feeling that she wore many hats and always found it very interesting. She learned a great deal about life in a buying office, and after one and a half years felt ready to move on to a position of greater responsibility.

At present Debbie is an assistant buyer for a chain of more than one hundred clothing stores for men, women, and children. Her specific area of responsibility is menswear, and she believes she has been given a chance to learn a lot about the market and gain a great deal of hands-on experience. She writes orders for purchases her buyer makes, deals directly with vendors, and enjoys the opportunity of becoming very familiar with the menswear market. She spends at least two days a week visiting resources and has had great exposure to the many manufacturers and wholesalers in her field. She spends time using her retail math skills, figuring markups and markdowns, and planning the distribution of goods to the chain's stores. She also analyzes and evaluates the different sales figures of each store to help determine future purchases. Debbie works with a computer for order entries and to get printouts on various styles and information about how well items are selling.

She is convinced that the buying office segment of retailing is for her and is confident that she will soon progress to a buyer's spot.

The Myth Was True

Danya remembers always wanting to be a buyer, even though her part-time work experience as a high school student was in the nonrelated areas of waitressing and baby-sitting. Because she did not believe she had a strong enough academic bent, she decided to research more practical college programs that would prepare her for immediate employment upon her graduation. She discovered a buying and merchandising major that was highly regarded by those in the field and decided to enroll in that two-year program. She thoroughly enjoyed her college experience and discovered the broad scope of careers open to her. Her class in small store operations was a particular eye-opener for her, as she now seemed to lean toward management positions rather than jobs that would lead to a buying career.

With this in mind, she applied for an entry-level position as an assistant store manager in training for the Gap. It was then that Danya realized that what she thought was a myth actually was true. While she was researching the field, she frequently heard that employers are delighted to hire graduates of her program. And this was truly the case with Danya. She was offered a job on her very first interview. Her comprehensive background and solid skills in the merchandising area would indeed open many career doors for her.

After four months in training, she moved on to the assistant manager position in the store. Because that particular retail unit had no store manager at that time, it was an excellent opportunity for Danya, along with several other assistant managers, to handle a variety of responsibilities. She learned all store operations and was pleased to pitch in and perform tasks that a store manager might have handled, including dealing with the payroll and supervising and managing the staff.

She loved what she was learning about all aspects of managing a store and after a year was transferred to another location, where she was quickly promoted to store manager. She remembers with great pride that she was just twenty years old and the Gap's youngest store manager, handling a two-level retail operation that had a $750,000 sales volume.

She thoroughly enjoyed that spot but felt ready to move on and consider the world of wholesale. As a sales manager for a manufacturer of imported sportswear, she was now in a position to sell to buyers. Although she still enjoyed the sales aspect of the position, she did not really care for the traditional Monday through Friday work schedule and began to miss the retail life. She allowed herself a full year to learn more about this aspect of the industry before she was drawn back to retailing. At this point, she decided to work for a major department store.

Danya chose Lord and Taylor's executive training program. Because of her varied work history, she was able to bypass some of the entry-level assignments and moved into a slot as a branch assistant buyer for dresses in the New York City store. The position gave Danya responsibility for overseeing the dress department of forty-two branch stores. She loved the job and was fortunate to have a very seasoned buyer as her boss. She found a great mentor in her supervisor, who allowed Danya to accompany her to the market frequently and shared her knowledge with her. After four months, Danya was promoted to a department manager of dresses in a branch store, where she stayed on for a year and a half, supervising an assistant and ten salespeople.

To her great surprise, Danya was approached by a representative of her current employer, the Talbots chain of women's clothing stores. Talbots sought a top-notch store manager for a store that was about to open. Danya was hired as the store manager and had full control of the merchandising of goods, staffing, and customer relations for the new operation. Because she was able to do such a fine job of running that store and handling a $1.5 million volume annually, Danya was selected by Talbots to open its New York City flagship store, which does more than $4 million in business yearly.

Her talents at successfully assuming that huge responsibility brought her to her next and current position with Talbots—district manager. Danya is responsible for seven stores in the chain in New York and New Jersey and for a total sales volume of $15 million annually! This takes her on the road daily within the New York/ New Jersey area, visiting the stores and working very closely with store managers. Danya's greatest sense of satisfaction derives from the opportunity to help in the professional development of the store managers. In fact, she received a Talbots award for "The Best Developer of People."

Although Danya has great responsibilities and a very busy schedule, she enjoys every minute of her day. She is generally at one of the stores by 9:00 A.M. and stays on until 7:00 P.M., Monday through Friday. And Danya's goal seems very much within her reach—to become a regional manager for Talbots and eventually share her retail expertise with young men and women by teaching in college. Judging from the way Danya's career has taken off, it is bound to happen.

Launching a Dream

Paul was raised in rural Louisiana with little or no exposure to the world of fashion, except for the magazines he read. He gravitated toward studying fashion buying in a local college, and after one year of that program decided to make other plans. While still a college student, Paul held a part-time job at JCPenney. His supervisor there suggested that he consider other programs of study that might satisfy his creative spirit. After a bit of research about various college programs, Paul discovered a menswear design and marketing major at a New York school and transferred to New York City to complete his education.

This change seemed to work just right for Paul, as he became more interested than ever in men's fashions at a time when the menswear industry was experiencing a major shift. Menswear was beginning to move from a rather traditional, predictable apparel area to one moving ahead in excitement and fashion.

Paul's concentration in fashion marketing introduced him to fashion forecasting and fashion direction. It was then that he was able to clearly identify his dream. He realized that although the design world was not the right spot for him, the fashion director's role had enormous appeal. His feelings have not changed since his graduation more than ten years ago.

Interestingly enough, Paul's first work experience was not in retailing but in the wholesale area. He was hired as a designer of men's hosiery for a major manufacturer and gained excellent experience, learning a great deal about color and yarns during the nine months he was in the manufacturing aspect of the fashion industry. He was contacted by Macy's, who had his résumé on file from his initial job-hunting campaign, and was quickly hired as its menswear fashion coordinator. That began a long and solid working relationship with the firm. Paul worked at the Herald Square store for one and a half years, reporting to the menswear fashion director and immersing himself in every aspect of Macy's large and fashionable menswear department.

When an opening occurred in Macy's Paris fashion office, Paul was delighted to be its candidate. He began as a freelance consultant for the store, covering the European markets and trade shows, and quickly began full-time work for Macy's. In that capacity he dealt with the menswear buyers for all of Macy's stores and traveled through Europe with them—introducing the buyers to the new resources he had uncovered and getting heavily involved in product development.

Paul's work was so important to the growth of Macy's menswear areas that he was asked to return to the New York City corporate office, but he was not ready to leave Paris just yet. He worked as a freelance consultant for other clients, as well as continuing to work closely with Macy's.

As Paul's reputation and experience in the menswear area grew, he received a wonderful offer from Saks Fifth Avenue. He was finally lured back to New York City from Paris to start work as the associate fashion director for menswear for Saks. Since then Paul has been fortunate enough to work closely with that firm's fashion director and continue to build his reputation and exposure in the menswear area.

Paul knows his position is very desirable and very sought after, and his future plans include getting to learn about the markets in the Far East, as well as assuming greater responsibilities and authority. For Paul, much of his dream has already become a reality. His next goal is to become the fashion director of a major retail operation.

From Schoolteacher to Personnel Manager

Ako's interest in retailing began in college. She had no part-time work experience at all while attending high school, and it wasn't until her senior year that she did what so many teens in Hawaii do—work in a pineapple cannery for the summer. At the University of Hawaii, Ako began her studies in courses that would lead to a degree as an elementary schoolteacher. However, a part-time job as a sales floater in a retail store dramatically changed Ako's career path. Her interest in retailing was sparked when she was assigned to one department and then to the next, allowing her to become a "mini-expert" in many product areas.

While Ako was still a student, she enrolled in a fashion seminar run by the local Sears store. Grooming, poise, and fashion were discussed at those sessions. Ako must have been a memorable pupil, as she was contacted by Sears and asked to become an instructor for the fashion seminars while still a student at the university. Ako was trained by Sears and worked with other more experienced instructors. She then dealt with various groups of people, ranging from senior citizens to toddlers.

Ako's exposure to student teaching as part of her course work at the university, coupled with her experience with retailing, enabled her to make the decision to return to the university after completing her education degree for a design and merchandising program. She now recognized that her interest was in that area, and Ako never did get to apply for a teaching position. She claims that part of her retail interest must be credited to her mother, who always owned her own business and was an entrepreneur.

While enrolled in the University of Hawaii's design and merchandising program, she heard about a relevant college program in New York and quickly decided that it made sense for her to learn about the world of fashion and design where much of it was going on—in New York City. And so she went as a visiting one-year student without friends or relatives in New York City—and she loved it. One of Ako's courses in running a small business required her to interview a retail store owner. After researching her project and identifying a shoe store that interested her, she interviewed the owner and ended up getting a sales job in the shop as well. With as much enthusiasm for her work today as she had five years ago as a trainee, Ako still praises the retail industry: "The diversity of the field is part of the excitement. One day is just never the same as the next, and the constant change and challenge are so exciting."

Ako points out that retailing is an area for those who enjoy making decisions and who have the self-confidence to deal effectively with others. She has learned to be a very good negotiator in her daily dealings. When hiring new trainees, Ako tries to select those with good analytical skills and some facility with numbers. And she is always looking for people who are able to think of new ways the organization can make money. As personnel director for a major chain of retail stores, Ako is convinced she has found the right career and enjoys reflecting that it all came about because of a part-time sales job.

From Direct Marketing to Retailing

Leslie was born in upstate New York and had many experiences in retailing as a high school student. He held several part-time sales jobs, and by the time he graduated, he was determined to select a buying and merchandising program in college. After doing the appropriate research, he decided that the Fashion Institute of Technology (FIT) was his only choice. Although his family had concerns about his going to school in New York City, he immediately settled into the dorm life and the program and loved both.

Convinced he really wanted a four-year baccalaureate degree, Leslie completed the two-year program and then went for a marketing major for the remaining two years. He graduated with a Bachelor of Science degree in 1987.

One of the many exciting courses Leslie enrolled in was direct marketing. He was eager to take that class because he was very aware of the prominence of direct marketing and the mail-order field. "The course was just fascinating and really stirred up my interest in that industry even further."

As no job seemed to be available in the direct marketing area at the time Leslie graduated from college, he took an entry-level position with a well-known apparel manufacturer, helping to coordinate samples and acting as an administrative assistant. After several months on the job, his boss was fired. Leslie then paid a visit to the placement office at FIT. While researching job leads there, Leslie was drawn to the position he currently holds—a buyer's assistant for Avon. This major corporation puts out several catalogs each season, and Leslie is pleased to be working very closely with the buyer for sportswear. Together they attempt to estimate sales projections for each item of merchandise that appears on the catalog page. He is also learning to work with a computer.

Leslie is convinced that the course in direct marketing helped him land this terrific job. He was able to talk knowledgeably about the field at the interview, and he is truly excited about his beginnings in this most fascinating, growing industry.

12

Retailing in Canada

Over the last century, Canada has grown from a heavily agrarian economy to one of the world's leading trading nations. The retail field in Canada has enjoyed impressive economic gains in the recent past. The Canadian retailing industry now employs more than one million workers, and retailing is a major source of Canadian employment. Most retail trade takes place in planned shopping centers, similar to the shopping malls of the United States. Not all shopping centers are in suburban locations. In fact, most Canadian cities have one or more major shopping centers, often a mix of both office and retail space, in their downtown areas.

An Important Retail Market

Canada has as long a retailing history as the United States. Indeed, with a history of more than three hundred years of trading, Hudson's Bay Company is one of Canada's leading retailers and North America's oldest corporation. HBC opened the Canadian Arctic in the late 1800s, establishing remote trading posts in the Hudson's Bay territory. The company continued to dominate the world fur trade through the 1970s. HBC is now in the midst of major store renovations and merchandise upgrades and is seeking to expand into new regions, such as China.

In 1989 Canada and the United States officially formed the world's largest free trade area, which extends from the Arctic Circle to the Rio Grande. This allows both countries to exchange goods and services totaling more than $200 billion each year. The basis of this free trade area was the elimination of all tariff and nontariff trade barriers on goods and services.

Trends

In 1996 about four million Canadians fell into the fifty-to-sixty-four-year-old age group, a group that has disposable income to spend. These folks are hardly "old" in their outlook, and they look forward to retail markets for everything from books on tape to nutritional gourmet foods. Canada's senior citizens are a relatively prosperous market segment, receiving two-thirds of their nation's bond and bank interest. Many in the over-sixty-five group have diverse sources of income and few financial obligations. They are living longer and spending more, characteristics that make them an increasingly attractive target for smart retailers. In fact, America's most popular malls have become major tourist destinations for Canadians. By car and on bus tours, eager shoppers cross the border from miles away to take part in this retail shopping experience that both Americans and Canadians have grown to love.

New trends will see retailers eager to please value-conscious Canadian consumers. The newest retail developments have been freestanding, warehouse-style "mega-stores," which offer discount prices and a wide selection of enticing goods. Canadian retailers will have to work harder to compete with some of the American superstars that are discovering Canada's lucrative retail market. They have already learned that Toronto is Canada's largest retail market— larger than retail sales in Montreal and double the retail sales of Vancouver. With more than ten million square feet of retail space, Toronto's downtown area is the third largest in North America, after New York City and Chicago.

Some of America's most prestigious retailers have already crossed the border to capture sales and market share of the Canadian customer. In 1994 Wal-Mart Stores, Inc., the world's largest retailer, purchased 122 Woolco Stores in Canada. Wal-Mart executives have been busily redesigning each of these stores. The plan is to have all store traffic pass through soft-goods areas, such as apparel and accessories, and then move through hard-goods departments, such as housewares and appliances. The reasoning behind this layout is that profit margins of soft-goods items are higher, and Wal-Mart is determined to capture the spending power of the Canadian customer. With wide aisles, bright lighting, and attractive signage, the impact has already been felt. Wal-Mart has actually changed the way Canadians are being served by other retailers, breaking the established notions of high prices and mediocre service. Canadian retailers have quickly moved to meet the challenge by offering classroom training sessions to employees, as well as one-on-one coaching to ensure that a shopper's retail experience is a positive one.

Local Canadian shoppers will benefit enormously from the competition generated by the entry of U.S. mega-retailers into Canada. Canadian retailers, of course, may dread the increased competition posed by the large warehouse-type chain stores. However, with active pricing and high-quality customer service, small retailers are managing to stay afloat. This is now the time to win back the loyalty of the many Canadians living near the border, who have routinely shopped in the United States, where they believed they got more service and more for their money. Canadians have long enjoyed the experience of shopping in off-price and outlet stores, and now the new American entries are expected to add a challenge to the Canadian retail scene. Sportmart, Computer City, the Gap International, Kmart, Toys 'R' Us, and Home Depot have joined the group of American retailers who have advanced into Canada.

America's favorite shopping activity has been discovered by Canada with the construction of huge malls in Toronto, Montreal, Vancouver, and Alberta markets.

Canadian Mills Mall, opened in 2001, is the first new major shopping complex built in Canada in the past decade, and it has brought a wonderful mix of American retailers to Canada. Shopping aside, these malls offer fun and entertainment for the family and have become social centers while offering a huge variety of quality merchandise at attractive prices.

The retailing industry in the twenty-first century faces new challenges and changes. The loss of many well-known department stores, as well as the mergers and takeovers common in the 1980s, will make this century an unusual and exciting time for the Canadian retail world!

The *Annual Directory of Retail Chains in Canada*, published by Monday Reports on Retailers in Toronto, is an excellent retail resource. It contains an alphabetical list of retail companies and product categories as well as other essential information, including the year the firm was established, price categories, buying policy, locations, new outlets planned, total sales, and the names of buyers.

The *Canadian Almanac and Directory*, published by Copp Clark, provides information about specific areas of retailing in addition to apparel, such as sporting goods, tableware, giftware, and accessories. It also includes addresses of associations, publications, government agencies, and universities.

Appendix A

Retailing Programs in the United States

Following are U.S. colleges and universities offering degrees in retailing, retail management, retail merchandising, retail marketing, retail sales, and fashion/apparel merchandising.

Alabama
Auburn University
Bessemer State Technical College
John C. Calhoun State Community College
Gadsden State Community College
Jefferson State Community College
University of Alabama
University of Montevallo
Wallace State Community College at Hanceville

Arizona
Northern Arizona University
Pima Community College
University of Arizona

Arkansas
Harding University
Southern Arkansas University

California
American River College
Chabot College
Chaffey Community College
College of the Desert
Columbia College
Diablo Valley College
Fashion Institute of Design and Merchandising
Golden West College
Las Positas College
Long Beach City College
Marin Community College
Orange Coast College
Pasadena City College
Saddleback College
San Francisco State University
Santa Clara University
Shasta College
Sierra College

Colorado
Arapahoe Community College
Colorado State University
Community College of Aurora

Connecticut
Cultural Connecticut State University
Gateway Community College
Middlesex Community Technical College
University of New Haven

Delaware
Wesley College
University of Delaware

Florida
Florida State University
Indian River Community College
International Fine Arts College
Palm Beach Community College
Webber College

Georgia
Athens Area Technical Institute
Savannah Technical Institute

Hawaii
Kapiolani Community College
University of Hawaii

Idaho
College of Southern Idaho
Lewis-Clark State College

Illinois
Belleville Area College
Black Hawk College, Quad Cities Campus
Chicago State
City Colleges of Chicago, Wright College
College of DuPage
Elgin Community College
Illinois Eastern Community Colleges,
    Wabash Valley College
John A. Logan College
Joliet Junior College
Kaskaskia College
Kishwaukee College
Lincoln Land Community College
McHenry County College
Oakton Community College
Parkland College
Richland Community College
Rock Valley College
Southwestern Illinois College
University of St. Francis
Wabash Valley College
Waubonsee Community College
William Rainey Harper College

Indiana
Ball State University
Indiana State University
International Business College
Purdue University
Vincennes University

Iowa

Des Moines Area Community College
Hawkeye Institute of Technology
Iowa Central Community College
Iowa State University
Iowa Western Community College
Kirkwood Community College
Muscatine Community College
North Iowa Area Community College
Western Iowa Tech Community College

Kansas

Allen County Community College
Barton County Community College
Hutchinson Community College
Johnson County Community College

Kentucky

Eastern Kentucky
Henderson Community College
Maysville Community College
University of Kentucky
Western Kentucky University

Louisiana

Louisiana State University
Louisiana Tech University

Maine

Husson College
Thomas College

Maryland

Allegheny Community College
Charles County Community College
Harford Community College
Howard Community College
Montgomery College, Germantown and
    Rockville Campuses

Massachusetts

Acquinas College at Milton
Babson College
Bay State College
Bristol Community College
Cape Cod Community College
Dean Junior College
Endicott College
Framingham State College
Holyoke Community College
Lasell Community College
Middlesex Community College
Mount Ida College
Newbury College
Roxbury Community College
Simmons College

Michigan

Bay de Noc Community College
Cleary College
Davenport College of Business
Delta College

Eastern Michigan University
Ferris State University
Lansing Community College
Michigan State University
Northwood Institute
Western Michigan University

Minnesota
Alexandria Technical College
Dakota County Technical College
Lake Superior College
Minnesota State College—Southeast Technical
North Hennepin Community College
Ridgewater College
St. Cloud Technical College
St. Paul Technical College
University of Minnesota Twin Cities

Mississippi
Hinas Community College
University of Mississippi

Missouri
Fontbonne College
Jefferson College
Longview Community College
Maple Woods Community College
Northwest Missouri State
Penn Valley Community College
Southeast Missouri State University

State Fair Community College
Stephens College

Nebraska
University of Nebraska, Lincoln Campus

Nevada
Community College of Southern Nevada

New Hampshire
Hanser College
New Hampshire College

New Jersey
Atlantic Cape Community College
Bergen Community College
Berkley College of Business
Camden County College
County College of Morris
Gloucester County College
Jersey City State College
Ocean County College
Passaic County Community College
Raritan Valley Community College
Thomas Edison State College (a correspondence school)

New Mexico
Albuquerque Technical Vocational School
Clovis Community College

New York
Bryant and Stratton Business Institute
Cazenovia College
City University of New York, Baruch College
City University of New York, Bronx Community College
City University of New York, Westchester
   Community College
State University of New York
   Cayuga County Community College
   Community College of the Finger Lakes
   Dutchess Community College
   Erie Community College
   Fashion Institute of Technology
   Genesee Community College
   Jamestown Community College
   Jefferson Community College
   Mohawk Valley Community College
   Monroe Community College
   Nassau Community College
   Niagara County Community College
   North Country Community College
   Onondaga Community College
   Orange County Community College
   Suffolk County Community College
   Sullivan Community College
   Tompkins/Cortland Community College
   Ulster County Community College
Syracuse University

North Carolina
Alamance Community College
Asheville Buncombe Technical Community College
Blue Ridge Community College
Craven Community College
East Carolina University
Lenoir Community College
Pitt Community College
Surry Community College
University of North Carolina
Wayne Community College
Western Piedmont Community College

North Dakota
Bismarck State College
Lake Region State College
North Dakota State University
University of North Dakota

Ohio
Belmont Technical Center
Bluffton College
Bowling Green State University, Firelands College
Columbus State Community College
Dyke College
Edison State Community College
Hocking Technical College
Jefferson Technical College
Kent State University
Miami-Jacobs Junior College

Miami University, Oxford Campus
Muskingum Area Technical College
Northwest Technical College
Ohio University
Sinclair Community College
Stark Technical College
University of Akron
University of Rio Grande
University of Toledo
Wilmington College
Youngstown State University

Oklahoma
Connors State College
East Central University
Oklahoma State University
Southeastern Oklahoma State
University of Central Oklahoma

Oregon
Bassit College
Clackamas Community College
Lane Community College

Pennsylvania
Bucks County Community College
Butler Community College
Cedar Crest College
Central Pennsylvania College

Community College of Allegheny—Allegheny, Boyce,
  North and South Campuses
Community College of Beaver County
Community College of Philadelphia
Delaware County Community College
Drexel University
Harcum Junior College
Harrisburg Area Community College
Marywood College
Montgomery County Community College
Pennsylvania College of Technology
Philadelphia College of Textiles and Science
Philadelphia University
Pierce Junior College
Pittsburgh Technical Institute
Sawyer School
Seton Hill College
Westmoreland County Community College
York College of Pennsylvania

Puerto Rico
University of Puerto Rico, Mayaguez Campus

Rhode Island
Community College of Rhode Island, Knight/
  Flanagan Campus
Johnson & Wales University

South Carolina
Aiken Technical College
Florence-Darlington Technical College

Midlands Technical College
University of South Carolina

South Dakota
South Dakota State University

Tennessee
Belmont College
Trevecca Nazarene University
University of Tennessee

Texas
Alvin Community College
Baylor University
Collin County Community College
Lamar University
Sam Houston State University
Tarleton State University
Tarrant County College
Texas A & M University
Texas Woman's University
University of North Texas

Utah
Brigham Young University
Dixie State College of Utah
Latter-Day Saints Business College
Utah State University
Weber State College

Vermont
Champlain College

Virginia
James Madison University
Marymount University
National Business College
Norfolk State University
Tidewater Community College
Virginia Commonwealth University
Virginia Tech University
Virginia Union University

Washington
Central Washington University
Centralia College
Columbia Basin College
Highline Community College
Lake Washington Technical College
Pierce College
Shoreline Community College
Spokane Falls Community College
Walla Walla Community College

West Virginia
Marshall University

Wisconsin
Gateway Technical College
Milwaukee Area Technical College

Moraine Park Technical College
Northeast Wisconsin Technical College
University of Wisconsin, Stout
Western Wisconsin Technical College
Wisconsin Indianhead Technical College

Appendix B

Retailing Programs in Canada

Following are Canadian schools that offer programs in marketing, marketing management, fashion merchandising, and retail management.

Marketing Programs

Ontario
École des Hautes Études Commerciales
Fanshawe College
Georgian College of Applied Arts and Technology
Niagara College of Applied Arts and Technology
Ryerson Polytechnic University
St. Clair College of Applied Arts and Technology
Sheridan College
University of Guelph
University of Ottawa

New Brunswick
University College of Cape Breton

Quebec
Bishop's University
Université du Quebec à Montreal
University of Saskatchewan

Marketing Management

British Columbia
Capilano College

Alberta
Northern Alberta Institute of Technology

Ontario
Niagara College of Applied Arts & Technology

Fashion Merchandising

Alberta
Olds College

Ontario
Centennial College of Applied Arts & Technology

Retail Management

Ontario
Niagara College of Applied Arts & Technology
Saint Clair College of Applied Arts & Technology
Sheridan College

Appendix C

Trade Publications for Retailers

Chain Store Age. Focuses on news of interest to managers and executives of chain stores.

Discount Merchandiser. Reports on discount merchandising including manufacturing, retailing, and advertising.

Discount Store News. Concentrates on news related to discount stores: new products, industry trends, visual merchandising.

Marketing News. Covers information for marketing professionals about trends, market research, and retailing concepts.

Retail Control. A bimonthly magazine focusing on retail trade and accounting issues in the retail field.

Retailing Today. A monthly newsletter for retail managers focusing on issues in the retail industry.

Stores. A monthly trade magazine that offers news of general interest to retailers.

VM & SD. A monthly magazine presenting information on merchandise presentation and store planning.

About the Author

Roslyn Dolber has been an enthusiastic proponent of the fashion industry for more than thirty years and the director of career counseling and placement at New York City's Fashion Institute of Technology (FIT). Thoroughly familiar with the wide range of career opportunities in fashion and its many allied areas, she has counseled and placed hundreds of students and graduates. Her professional affiliations include the Metropolitan New York College Placement Officers Association (director), the Eastern College Placement Officers and the State University of New York Career Development organizations, and the Northeast Association of Student Employment Administrators.

In addition to her role at FIT, Ms. Dolber speaks on fashion-related careers in the New York metropolitan area. She has contributed articles on this subject to several industry publications and has written and helped produce a filmstrip on surviving the job interview. She is the author of *Opportunities in Fashion Careers* as well as a college guide for high school students with learning disabilities, *College and Career Success for Students with Learning Disabilities*.